SIX MUST DIE

SIX MUST DIE

VICTORIA WLOSOK

LB 100 YEARS

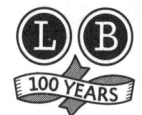

LITTLE, BROWN AND COMPANY
New York Boston

This book is a work of fiction. Names, characters, places, and incidents are the product of the author's imagination or are used fictitiously. Any resemblance to actual events, locales, or persons, living or dead, is coincidental.

Copyright © 2026 by Victoria Wlosok
3D wire copyright © iStock.com/SpicyTruffel; burned paper © Nils Z/Shutterstock.com
Cover art copyright © 2026 by Sammy Yeun. Cover design by Gabrielle Chang.
Cover copyright © 2026 by Hachette Book Group, Inc.
Glass pattern, blood splatter, and dripping blood copyright © various contributors at Shutterstock.com; 3D wire copyright © iStock.com/SpicyTruffel
Interior design by Michelle Gengaro.

Hachette Book Group supports the right to free expression and the value of copyright. The purpose of copyright is to encourage writers and artists to produce the creative works that enrich our culture.

The scanning, uploading, and distribution of this book without permission is a theft of the author's intellectual property. If you would like permission to use material from the book (other than for review purposes), please contact permissions@hbgusa.com. Thank you for your support of the author's rights.

Little, Brown and Company
Hachette Book Group
1290 Avenue of the Americas, New York, NY 10104
LBYR.com

Simultaneously published in 2026 by Hachette Children's UK
in the United Kingdom.
First Edition: March 2026

Little, Brown and Company is a division of Hachette Book Group, Inc. The Little, Brown name and logo are registered trademarks of Hachette Book Group, Inc.

The publisher is not responsible for websites (or their content) that are not owned by the publisher.

Little, Brown and Company books may be purchased in bulk for business, educational, or promotional use. For information, please contact your local bookseller or the Hachette Book Group Special Markets Department at special.markets@hbgusa.com.

Library of Congress Cataloging-in-Publication Data
Names: Wlosok, Victoria, author.
Title: Six must die / Victoria Wlosok.
Description: First edition. | New York : Little, Brown and Company, 2026. | Audience term: Teenagers | Audience: Ages 14 and Up | Summary: "A fractured group of friends fight to survive a killer escape room in rural Tennessee." —Provided by publisher.
Identifiers: LCCN 2025023693 | ISBN 9780316510370 hardcover | ISBN 9780316511384 ebook
Subjects: CYAC: Escape room games—Fiction | Survival—Fiction | Mystery and detective stories | LCGFT: Thrillers (Fiction) | Novels
Classification: LCC PZ7.1.W617 Si 2026 | DDC [Fic]—dc23/eng/20250320
LC record available at https://lccn.loc.gov/2025023693

ISBNs: 978-0-316-51037-0 (hardcover), 978-0-316-51138-4 (ebook)

Printed in Indiana, USA

LSC-C

Printing 1, 2025

To those grieving living people:
You are not alone.

And to all my ex-friends:
You're lucky none of this actually happened to you.

"So it's caught up with us."
–Lois Duncan, *I Know What You Did Last Summer*

"I want to play a game."
–Jigsaw, the *Saw* franchise

UNITED STATES DISTRICT COURT

EASTERN DISTRICT OF TENNESSEE
GREENEVILLE DIVISION

CATELYN ADLER; ILLARIA CESARI;
and EDWARD MITCHELL-MOORE,
    Plaintiffs,
    v.
RANDALL JAMES and TALIYAH MAY,
    Defendants.

Case No. 2:25-CR-00123-JRG-DCP

EXHIBIT A
Pre-Recorded Witness Testimony

Excerpt from Transcript of Witness Testimony

1. **SHERIFF STALLARD:** Okay, we're recording. We have your consent
2. to record, correct?
3. *[MULTIPLE VOICES OVERLAPPING IN UNISON]*
4. **Q.** Hang on, slow down. I need the mic to pick you six up separately.
5. One more time—do we have your permission to record? Individual
6. answers with legal names, please. You, with the bright red hair. Do
7. you consent?
8. **A. STEPHANIE ZAMEKOVA:** Yes, I do. And I'm Stephanie
9. Zamekova, Sheriff. That's Z-A-M-E-K-O-V-A.
10. **SHERIFF STALLARD:** Great, thank you. Let's go down the line.
11. **GUINEVERE MITCHELL-MOORE:** Yeah. Guinevere Mitchell-Moore.
12. **TOBIAS MATTHEWS:** Tobias Matthews. And yes, but—
13. **SANTO CESARI:** Of course. Santo Cesari. Anything to help.
14. *[SHORT PAUSE; SIRENS BLARING]*
15. **SHERIFF STALLARD:** The mic doesn't know you're nodding,
16. sweetheart. I need verbal confirmation.
17. **CHARITY ADLER:** I'm… Charity. Charity Adler. And I consent, t-too.

18. **MALACHI JAMES-MAY:** Uh. I guess I'm last, so…Malachi James-
19. May. I also agree to be recorded, especially since…God, my
20. parents. Are they on their way?
21. **SHERIFF STALLARD:** One second, son, hold that thought…Today
22. is Wednesday, May 21, 2025. I'm Sheriff Travis Stallard, recording
23. outside a burned-down shopping center in downtown Cedar Creek,
24. Tennessee. The time is 12:23 AM. Now, listen…none of you are
25. being held here. You can leave at any time. And you don't have to
26. answer a single one of my questions if you don't want to. Correct,
27. Mr. Lewis?
28. **MR. LEWIS:** Correct.
29. **SHERIFF STALLARD:** This is an informal interview. We're gathering
30. information—talking to emergency personnel, owners, primary
31. witnesses. The six of you fall into the last category, which is
32. why Mr. Lewis here is present as an independent supporter in
33. your interest while we wait for your parents to arrive on-scene. I
34. understand you all might be shaken, but we're here to help.
35. **TOBIAS MATTHEWS:** Help? Please. You suspect we're involved, so
36. just split us up already. Interrogate us. Make up evidence. Lie. Do
37. everything you're allowed to do.
38. **SHERIFF STALLARD:** Well, we are going to split you up, son, but
39. as I've said, we're simply collecting eyewitness testimony. I'm
40. going to get a sense of your whereabouts, see if I can get a handle
41. on tonight's timeline, but this is a collaborative process. There's no
42. need to stress over your responses—just be honest. Miss Zamekova?
43. **STEPHANIE ZAMEKOVA:** Yes?
44. **SHERIFF STALLARD:** I'd like to start with you.

45. *[LONG PAUSE]*
46. **SHERIFF STALLARD:** Okay. We're at 12:27 AM, so why don't we
47. take it from where we normally do?
48. **Q. STEPHANIE ZAMEKOVA:** And where would that be, Sheriff?
49. **A. SHERIFF STALLARD:** The beginning.

CHAPTER ONE

Wednesday, May 20, 2026, 10:51 PM

I'm kind of a pathetic person.

In front of me, the five cars of my estranged friends loom like silent giants, their metal bodies aglow in the mercurial vapor emanating from BREAKOUT Escape Rooms Inc.'s LED-lined storefront. I mentally check them off as I roll past: Guinevere's glittering Mercedes. Tobias's hatchback. A banged-up Chrysler that must be Santo's sitting a little too close to Malachi's smiling black-and-pink company minivan. I pull my rusted Jeep into the moon-silvered space next to Charity's brand-new BMW and kill the engine.

Jesus. I can't believe I came.

Midnight is just over an hour away. By now, every self-respecting business run by managers with a modicum of work-life balance in Friendship Springs, Tennessee—population 2,834—should be closed. Except BREAKOUT hasn't been a self-respecting business for a while. And judging from the empty vehicles parked around me, we're all here.

Wordlessly, I reach for the crisp invitation sitting atop my armrest console. It's been there since I fished it out of my mailbox a week ago, piled in among IT'S NOT TOO LATE TO APPLY! college brochures, an overdue EMDR therapy bill notice from Call-Me-Diana, and a couple of graduation gift checks. I bite my bottom lip as I assess the cardstock for what feels like the hundredth time. There's an xed-out smiley face on one side—BREAKOUT's company logo—and bright pink words on the other.

READY TO PLAY AGAIN?
NEW LOCATION, SAME OLD RULES.
Wednesday, May 20 @ 11 PM.
Sevier County Plaza, Suite 263.
An escape room in honor of Matteo Luca Cesari.
Arrive 15 minutes early.
Because secrets won't keep themselves.

"It's a threat, right?" I ask Dr. Quack, the founding member of the rubber duck army currently wedged between my Jeep's windshield and the dash. Talking to an inanimate bathtime object isn't ideal, but as far as my hypnotherapist is concerned, there are worse mechanisms for coping with what I've been through—the divorce and everything that happened with Dad in the aftermath, my traumatic brain injury, the fallout of the horrible accident last spring—than asking a rubber duck doctor for a second opinion.

Besides, I know who sent this invitation. At the very least, I know who I *want* to have sent it. And with him here tonight... Well, that changes everything.

Dr. Quack side-eyes me from underneath his molded head mirror. He always looks like that, though, so instead of taking his MD skepticism to heart, I reassess the view ahead. Most of the storefronts in the strip mall are peppered with COMMERCIAL SPACE FOR LEASE signs; the businesses that are still operational include an obscure big-box retailer, a Chinese restaurant with faded menu photos plastered against its darkened windows, and an arcade that reminds me of the bowling alley I used to work at back in my hometown.

My fingers twitch with suppressed memory: *Liberally applying FunkAway to disgusting synthetic foam insoles for $10.50 an hour. Holding my breath as Guinevere won a glow-in-the-dark rubber duck for me from the claw machine. Booing Charity for rolling every one of her strikes using the EZ-Bowler ramp. Listening to Malachi complain about incorporation paperwork over slices of too-greasy pizza. Watching Tobias realize he's allergic to Red 40 after his first bite of said too-greasy pizza made him break out in hives. Soaking in Santo's easy laughter every time Matt botched a spare. Editing blog posts on bathroom breaks.*

After what happened last May, though, I stopped showing up to Perfect Strike until my manager stopped calling me in.

Quiet-firing, my best friend would have called it. But that doesn't matter now, because tonight I'm in Friendship Springs, and Friendship Springs is nothing like Cedar Creek.

Despite being only twenty-eight miles away, Friendship Springs is one of the exurban Sevier County offshoots whose businesses were left behind in the mad scramble to turn other parts of East Tennessee into glitzy tourist traps—*Come climb North America's longest tree-based skybridge at Anakeesta! Snap photos with shrunken human heads at Ripley's Believe It or Not! Ride the Lightning Rod at a theme park dedicated to country music icon and local legend Dolly Parton!*—which means the death throes of the American shopping center are visible in every razor-scraped, paint-peeling inch of this place. It looks defunct. Dismal. Depressing.

Except Suite 263, that is. It seems that not even the slow, steady creep of small-town deindustrialization can diminish the allure of BREAKOUT; from here, an enticing kaleidoscope of colors staccato through the franchise's frosted glass windows: purple, yellow, red, blue.

I glance back at the card in my hands. *Because secrets won't keep themselves.*

"It looks open," I hedge, aware that I'm walking on eggshells. That I'm suggesting something dangerous. Dr. Quack stares at me silently in the neon-lit escape room's glow. In response, I tuck a strand of bright red hair behind my industrial-pierced ear and stare at the sign pasted just below the company's smiley-face window decal: THIS AREA IS SUBJECT TO CCTV SURVEILLANCE MONITORING.

God. Twelve months ago, this would all be routine: getting out of my car, walking toward the building, meeting up with the others in the air-conditioned lobby. Except we haven't spoken to one another in a year, and our high school graduation is tomorrow, and there's a not-insignificant part of me that wants to tear up the ominous cardstock invitation, hit play on Dad's old *Sawdust* CD, and gun the engine until I'm back at home. This isn't a good idea. The accident is still so raw for the six of us... and even without the gaps in my memory, my dreams are haunted enough by woodsmoke, burning flesh, and crackling bone for me to recognize a waking nightmare when I see one.

But I came here for answers, and the people who know me better than I know myself are already inside. So instead of hitting the gas and reversing out of the parking lot, the flapping soles of my broken Converse sneakers stay rooted to the Jeep's footwell. I am here, in this moment, and I know what I need to do.

Don't get stuck. Make a decision. Choose.

"Okay. Okay, okay, okay." I press the backs of my palms into the skin under my brow bone and inhale, counting every second of the four it takes my lungs to expand. *You're already here.* I hold it for seven. *You already made the choice.* I exhale for eight. *You have nothing to lose.* I lift my hands from my face and blink at the judgmental rubber duck militia. "I'm going."

I slip the invitation into my leather trench coat, twist my keys out of the ignition, and hop onto the concrete of the parking lot. The arid air smells like gasoline, urine, and mid-May heat. I tip my chin to the starless sky; we're overdue for a storm. In front of me, BREAKOUT strobes like a siren song. OPEN. OPEN. OPEN.

"Wish me luck," I tell Dr. Quack as I lock the car. His unimpressed stare bores into my back as I shake out my hands to stave off the pre-room jitters, but I don't let it faze me. I did it. I'm here.

And now, it's finally time.

• • •

As soon as I step into the escape room lobby, a cold blast carrying the warring scents of nacho cheese, over-sprayed cologne, and shea butter lotion erupts goose bumps over my skin. I shiver, then pull my coat tightly over Dad's worn the Killers T-shirt and count my inhalations in my head. It's probably not a great sign that I'm already on edge, but it's not like I have a choice. My point of no return was approximately a quarter gallon of gas ago.

To keep from spinning out, I turn my focus to the interior of Suite 263. The BREAKOUT Escape Rooms Inc. franchise of Friendship Springs, Tennessee, has the same lobby components as any other escape room business: a counter adorned with laminated QR codes linking to an online waiver; a row of shelves displaying an array of photo-ready props with slogans like WE (ALMOST) ESCAPED, TRUE DETECTIVE, and MY MOM SAID I WAS SMART; and a kiosk with the kind of branded garbage (logo-stamped shot glasses, hoodies, ugly vinyl stickers) that would immediately knock off a half star from the "Merchandise Offerings" rating on my blog. But I don't run *There's No Escape* anymore. And despite the tacky wares the company is peddling, the rest of BREAKOUT is effortlessly elegant: walls illuminated with color-changing LED strips. Dark black-and-pink-swirled epoxy floors complementing the midnight-black crushed-velvet couches pushed up against the tinted panels of an area labeled the *Briefing Room*. Neon signs depicting locks, keys, and chains in magenta, cyan, and indigo.

It's slick. Cool. And nothing like the mom-and-pop vibe of the storefront I remember.

"We've rebranded," the polo-clad teenager lounging behind the lobby counter offers over the ambient white noise of the ceiling HVAC unit. He takes a sip from his BREAKOUT-branded thermos before he nonchalantly looks up from his computer monitor, appraising me, and my entire body stiffens.

Malachi James-May looks the same way he always does—thick locs tied into a high ponytail, wireless earbuds sticking out of his ears, dorky black-rimmed glasses perched above his million-dollar grin—and even though it hurts to see him, his unchanged appearance is comforting. At least something here is still familiar.

"I can see that." I don't want to linger in the threshold, so I settle for shoving my hands in my pockets as I take a small step toward the counter. "I mean, this is a huge change, right? It looks nothing like the old one."

The old one. It's a quaint euphemism, especially when you consider the Cedar Creek BREAKOUT is now a smoothie and juice bar built on top of scorched earth, but I give it to him. Our Game Master can have it.

Malachi sets down his thermos. "That's kind of the point, Z." He spreads his dark-skinned arms. "Welcome to our flagship location. This is our prototype for investors and franchisees. Hopefully, there'll be a BREAKOUT Escape Rooms Inc. in every state in the South before too long. As you may have noticed, we've made a lot of improvements: We have a new air filtration system, a redesigned website, and an up-and-coming social media presence, thanks to yours truly. You should drop us a follow—we're @BreakoutEscapeRoomsTN on almost every platform." Malachi nods to a custom-made sign hanging behind him. "Oh, and we're also a PokéStop."

"Cool," I tell him, even though I'd rather gouge out my eyes than have anything BREAKOUT-related on my feeds. "And impressive. A few coats of fresh paint can truly cover up anything, huh?"

A shadow passes over Malachi's face, but it's gone as soon as I register it. Maybe I imagined it—a trick of the LED lights. "It's good to see you, Z," he says. His tone is warm enough, but his dark eyes remain guarded. "I know it's been a hard year."

"For both of us, I thought." My gaze drifts to the merchandise kiosk. "Seems like your parents are doing fine, though."

"We've been lucky," the Game Master says. "Got a deal on the lease in exchange for improvements to the property."

"Improvements?" I scoff, but there's a lump forming in the middle of my throat. "I didn't know Sevier County Plaza sponsored a negligent homicide discount."

Malachi doesn't take the bait. "Well, it's about time you showed. You cut it to the wire, actually—a few more minutes of waiting, and we'd have to start tonight's game without you."

"You knew I was coming?" This time, my words are raspy. Wrong. *Jesus, Steffi, get a grip.* I'm glad my hands are in my pockets so Malachi can't see them shake.

He shrugs. "It's tradition, isn't it?" he asks, clearly relishing my disarmament. He picks up a nacho from the dregs of the checkered carton in front of him—mass-produced arcade food from next door, no doubt—and swirls it around in what's left of the radioactive-orange cheese. "Y'all booked a room. *Arsonist's Revenge*, 11:00 PM."

My stomach lurches. *Blaring alarms. Sweat pooling at the base of my spine. Choked screams, acrid bile, and stinging eyes.* I blink to clear the fragments of memory, unable to tell if they're real or imagined, and refocus on Malachi. "Let me get this straight. Your family is in the middle of a high-profile lawsuit for a fire that started at one of their locations, and now BREAKOUT is offering an escape room named *Arsonist's Revenge*?"

Malachi's smile widens. "What can I say? People are curious, and curiosity is good for business." He crunches the nacho between his too-white teeth. "You of all people should understand that."

I want to ask so many follow-up questions. But even though Malachi is part of my former friend group, he's not who I need to talk to tonight. "The others," I say instead. "Are they here?"

"Malachi. If she's not coming, then let's get this over with," a scathing voice demands before the James-Mays' only child can answer, and my throat tightens as the paneled door of the *Briefing Room* slides aside and Guinevere Mitchell-Moore stalks into view.

She's taller. Tanner. Her long half-up caramel-brown hair is adorned with tiny star-shaped claw clips, and she's wearing a cream linen crop top, a Madagascan sunset moth forewing necklace, and the low-cut neutral-toned patchwork pants she thrifted with me at the Underground after we both bombed our APES exam sophomore year. Her storm-gray eyes cut to mine, and her full lips curl into a sneer. "Oh, good," she says, the word slicing straight across my sternum. "You made it."

"Didn't know the party started without me." I give my invitation a little wave, and Guinevere rolls her eyes. In the glow of the lobby, with the colored lights glinting off her bare olive-skinned shoulders, she looks indestructible. Divine. But since the accident, she's been through it, too: a slew of psychiatric evals, a top-rated equine therapy rehabilitation program all the way in Lenoir City, too many prescribed and then discarded mood stabilizers to count. I know, because I've devoted myself to it—to piecing together her postfire life, bit by incandescent bit, from her hotshot federal judge father's Facebook photos and Cherokee Affinity Club Google Alerts and newspaper clippings from the *Tennessee Star*.

Guinevere crosses her arms, her track-star muscles tensing, but the bottled rage swirling in her gaze isn't my problem. She's been pissed at everyone—and everything—since Matt died. As if dating him for four out of the nine months that he and his brother lived in Cedar Creek gives her the right to grieve more than the rest of us. As if she can blame me for the fact her boyfriend was my best friend. As if it's my fault she kissed me after his funeral.

"Before we get started, Z, I'll need you to fill out the liability release form," Malachi says, tapping the laminated QR code taped to the lobby counter, and I blink to clear the phantom taste of Guinevere's warm lips from my mind. Back in professional

Game Master mode, I see. "Bathrooms are down the hall. Everything else is already set up, so once you submit your waiver, we'll be ready to—"

"ZAMEKOVA?!" an incredulous voice bellows, and before I can blink, I'm being crushed in a bear hug clouded by sandalwood and aromatic aftershave. Guinevere's hurricane glower dials up to Category 5, but it doesn't matter.

Because Santo Xavier Cesari, the person I came here to see, is suddenly beaming at me.

"Hey," I say, voice breathless, lungs recovering as I take a step back to soak in Matt's brother. Unlike Malachi, Santo looks so different now compared to the last time I saw him—stringy bleach-fried curls flopping into his thick eyebrows, a smattering of new moles around his glittering eyes, a fresh piercing punctuating the edges of his healing purplish-orange skin—but he's still my dead best friend's identical twin, which means the only way to fend off the grief that rolls through me at the sight of his burn-scarred face is to bite down on my own tongue so hard that it almost bleeds. "You're back in town."

"Hey yourself," Santo says, casually adjusting the collar of his crewneck—tour merch from the Hu, his favorite band—like everything is fine. Like it couldn't be better. The ghost of a smile tugs at his mouth, and my chest constricts with the familiarity of the gesture. Trying to get through this next hour might just kill me.

After his brother's funeral, Santo wiped his socials and vanished from Cedar Creek, opting instead to finish his senior-year GED requirements as an exchange student in Perugia, Italy. As a result, he mostly managed to escape the death threats, hallway rumors, and scathing op-eds that plagued the rest of us in the months after Matt's death. But Santo didn't just succeed at avoiding the local hate mail; over the course of the past year, my increasingly desperate attempts to reach him went unopened, unanswered, and unread. When I brought up the fact that he went no contact to Call-Me-Diana, my hypnotherapist, she said Santo likely needed space to process what happened to us. But I don't understand how he felt okay with disappearing after everything we went through. And I definitely don't understand how he can stomach being back in BREAKOUT so easily, standing here in the wash of the now-purple LEDs as if we're not all stained with the exact same tragedy.

"I like the hair," I tell him, praying he doesn't notice the tremor in my voice. "It's..."

Less like Matt's, I almost say. But then I don't.

Santo grins. "Yeah. Different, right? Figured I needed to cover up these fucking burns somehow." He flicks an untoned yellow-blond strand out of his face, revealing a single charm—a silver cross—dangling from his right earlobe. "I wanted it to be more platinum, though, so I'm not sure how long I'll keep it now that I'm back in town. I've already gotten strange looks from basically a million baby boomers while pumping gas at Pal's." Behind the counter, our Game Master clears his throat. "And Mal thinks it's weird," Santo adds, rolling his eyes with equal parts exasperation and endearment, "but he's wearing outdated Jordans, so his fashion opinion is henceforth null and void."

I blink to buy myself a few seconds to register everything Santo just told me. His voice, like his updated aesthetic, is more difficult to understand now that his larynx is lined with vocal scars. Then again, none of us escaped the fire unscathed: Tobias's asthma—and, strangely enough, laundry list of allergies—worsened from the smoke inhalation. Guinevere developed COPD symptoms. Charity has keloid scarring straight across her upper chest. Malachi managed to avoid physical injury, but his online fanbase across his influencer accounts, @Mal.The.Reel.King, plummeted as a result of his affiliation with BREAKOUT's scandal. And thanks to a charred beam that knocked me unconscious around the time the flames first erupted, I don't remember anything from the night of the accident besides the kind-faced paramedic who held my hand in the flashing ambulance. How I managed to give eyewitness testimony to Sheriff Stallard for fifteen minutes without him realizing I had a severe head injury is beyond me, but that's the kind of expertise I've come to expect from the Sevier County Sheriff's Department.

For the past year, though, I've had to live with the fact that not only do I not know how I managed to stumble out of the flames ravaging Cedar Creek's BREAKOUT *Wanderland* escape room last May, but I can't remember why my best friend—why Matteo Luca Cesari—didn't.

Malachi sighs, grounding me back in the BREAKOUT lobby of Friendship Springs. "I'm telling you, it's not your look."

"When did you?" I ask Santo. "Get back, I mean."

He furrows his bleached brows. The left one has a shaved slit in it; the other sports a studded curved barbell. "A week ago? I flew in for graduation. Though I should say"—Santo slips a ring-adorned hand into his baggy pants and pulls out a rectangle of black-and-pink cardstock that's identical to mine—"this is one hell of a welcome."

Guinevere snorts just as the door of the *Briefing Room* slides open to reveal a short, pale, skinny girl with her hair in two ash-blond Dutch braids. "You came!" Charity Noelle Adler squeals with a level of enthusiasm only a well-seasoned student body president can pull off. Her face is sharper than I remember. There's something clutched in her skeletal hand—her own invitation, maybe?—but before I can get a good look, she's squeezing my midriff and adding a note of nauseatingly sweet perfume to Santo's lingering aftershave and our Game Master's cologne.

"It's wonderful you're here," she sings as she pulls away. "We missed you!" In the glow of the lobby, it's easy to notice the level of understated coordination between Charity's Tennessee-River-pearl-studded earlobes, smart black slacks, and houndstooth-patterned blazer. She's dressed like she's about to take charge of a board meeting or artfully cuss out a PTA member instead of play an escape room, but there's nothing subtle in the way her overplucked eyebrows lift in surprise when she notices what I'm wearing.

"I'm not late, am I?" I ask, attempting to distract her by emulating her fake-ass sincerity. "I know the invitation said to arrive fifteen minutes early, but..."

Her gaze lingers on my leather trench coat for a half-second too long before her attention darts to her watch. "No, you're fine! You're just the last to arrive, so Gee said you weren't going to make it. But"—Charity's doe-brown eyes flit back up to my face—"here you are!"

"Here I am," I repeat.

She pouts sympathetically. "How are you?"

"I've been better," I tell her. I've definitely looked it, if the LED-lined mirror behind Malachi is anything to go by. There are fragments of my junior-year self visible in the graduating senior who stares back—the split ends of my blunt curtain bangs as fire-engine red as the Swiss Army knife attached to my car keys, the barely visible U-shaped shackle of the shitty stick-and-poke padlock tattoo my friends helped ink below my collarbone at the start of last summer when the seven of us felt invincible, the pockmarks by my chapped lips where my old snakebites used to sit—but that's all they are. Individual pieces. Not me.

"Good," Charity says distractedly, throwing a quick look over her shoulder at the hallway door. "I'm doing better, too." She smiles, and I'm instantly reminded that after the accident, my childhood best friend didn't see a trauma specialist or double up on melatonin gummies or resign from even one of her pre-law extracurriculars. Instead, she spent the summer after Matt's death canvassing for proposed amendments to the Tennessee Fire Code, and her fall reaping the benefits of fundraising for the Cesaris' legal funds through writing self-aggrandizing college essays.

Now that she isn't trying to suffocate me, I realize she isn't clutching her own BREAKOUT invitation but a folded-up square of paper. Charity's smile tightens. "My graduation speech," she says by way of explanation, tucking the page into the front pocket of her blazer. "Don't tell my mom, but it's not finalized yet."

Huh. It's funny: Even though Charity and I met in first grade during a heated game of four sqaure that culminated in us both being sent to the principal's office—leading to my mom and Congresswoman Adler deciding that scheduled playdates may help their children resolve their creative differences, and the two of us subsequently spending a year beheading Barbies in the playroom of Charity's pristine McMansion—I still can't tell when she's lying.

"Where's Tobias?" I ask her instead of probing further because there's no point in attempting to get a high school politician to tell you the truth.

Charity rolls her eyes. "Bathroom."

"Where else would he be?" Malachi adds, which makes Santo and Charity laugh. A smile tugs at the corners of my lips, but then Guinevere scoffs, and I immediately feel a twinge of guilt for wanting to join in on a joke at the expense of someone who isn't here. It's not Tobias's fault that he has IBS and spends a lot of our group gatherings running from toilet to toilet. Then again, he showed up completely shit-faced to the last escape room we did, so it's fifty-fifty on what's actually holding him up tonight.

"Just so you know, Mal," Santo says as the hallway door behind Charity opens, "I'm not liable for drop-kicking you if you jump-scare us during our game." He pauses. "Hold on. You're not planning to do that, are you?"

Malachi shrugs. "I like to be behind the security camera, not in front of it. But Game Masters never reveal their secrets."

"Not unless they're legally required to." From the hallway, Tobias Quinton Matthews pushes his tortoiseshell glasses up the bridge of his crooked nose until the lenses flash against the cold

LED lights. The air thickens as he strides forward, wiping his freckled hands on his maroon CEDAR CREEK HIGH SCHOOL CHESS CLUB sweatshirt, but Malachi—to his credit—manages a smile. "Hi, Steffi," Tobias adds. "We didn't think you'd show."

Charity wrinkles her own nose. "You're, like, one to talk, seeing as you've been in the bathroom for the past"—she checks her watch—"seventeen minutes?"

"Keeping tabs on me, Adler?" There's a calculating hardness behind Tobias's hazel eyes as he stares at Charity, dropping his over-the-shoulder duffel bag to the epoxied floor, and danger prickles the back of my neck for the first time since I stepped into BREAKOUT. None of my friends have ever made me feel unsafe, but that was before the fire. Before the invitation showed up in my mailbox. Before I got this chance to recover my memories. Though if Call-Me-Diana knew I was attempting to restore my amnesia through immersing myself in the escape room franchise where I first got my TBI, I'm pretty sure she'd drop me as a client forever. Then again, she's an unlicensed hypnotherapist, so who's to say?

Whatever off-putting vibe Tobias is curating, though, Charity must sense it, because her gaze falls. He nods, effectively ending the conversation, and pulls out his phone. Within a minute, he's completely tuned out from the world. There. That's the Tobias Matthews I remember, too.

Without realizing it, I let out a soft sigh, which makes Tobias glance up at me. Seconds later, my own phone buzzes with a notification: *Keep your eyes to yourself.*

I send a quick message back: *cool thanks, i probably won't. btw nice sweatshirt. ironic, huh?*

Tobias instantly scowls, and a little thrill goes through me. Two can play at this game.

"Great!" Santo says, clapping his hands together. His fingernails are painted with cracking black nail polish. "Now we've gathered all six of us."

"Right," Guinevere says. "So..."

Santo blinks. "So what?"

When she doesn't answer, I pocket my phone and meet Santo's gaze. "So," I continue for her, trying to ignore the apprehension swirling in my stomach, "when are you going to cut the theatrics and reveal why you invited us here?"

The accusation is a no-brainer; the cardstock is completely Santo's style. One last spontaneous getting-the-gang-back-together hurrah for our broken friend group: part grad party, part Cesari twin birthday celebration, and one hundred percent opportunity.

Santo laughs. "Hang on," he says, his eyes dancing between us. "I'm confused. This isn't, like, something y'all planned to surprise me?" His smile strains as he turns to Malachi. "I thought you sent the invites."

"No," our Game Master says. There's a glob of cheese dotting his embroidered company polo. Santo's shoulders slump, but before I can dwell too much on the current state of his situationship, Guinevere's accusatory glare cuts to me.

"Malachi didn't send the invitations; Stephanie did."

A strangled, surprised bark bursts from my lips. "Me? Are you serious?"

I found my invitation in an unmarked envelope last Wednesday afternoon. No return address. And even though I almost let my social anxiety get the best of me, I drove to Friendship Springs tonight because I was hoping for some goddamn closure. Because I need to know what happened. Because I can't remember the night of the accident, and no amount of bilateral tapping or nature hikes or literal hypnotherapy sessions can tell me what the people standing in the franchise that killed my best friend can.

Because even if we haven't truly spoken since the night that he asphyxiated a year ago, everyone currently inside BREAKOUT was there when Matt drew his final breath. Which means that playing tonight's escape room is my last chance to learn the truth from the only people who know it.

"Honestly," I tell Guinevere, ignoring the dark voice in the back of my mind that whispers my post-accident memory isn't quite what it used to be, "I wish I'd been smart enough to come up with something like this." *Pathetic. Monster. Fraud.* "But I didn't plan tonight."

"Didn't you send them?" Tobias asks Charity before Guinevere can respond, pausing with his thumbs hovering over his phone screen. "As our student body president, you're our answer to problems faced by the modern teenager: generative AI plagiarism, club treasurer embezzlement, surreptitious bathroom vaping..." He tilts his head, and the LEDs catch on his russet curls. "And you're always organizing little bake sales and 5Ks and blood donation drives. This kind of event planning seems right up your alley."

Charity shakes her head, but the motion is more like a sharp snap; a clipped *right-left* that leaves no room for discussion. "I thought it was you."

"And Santo thought it was Malachi, and Guinevere thought it was Steffi, and Steffi thought it was Santo." Tobias blinks, and I frown. His eyes look unfocused. "The point is, none of us are taking credit for organizing this. So why are we here?"

It's a good fucking question, especially when the invitation showing up in my mailbox means there's someone out there who refuses to let sleeping dogs lie. Who knows that secrets won't keep themselves.

Slowly, we turn to look at Malachi, who freezes with another nacho halfway to his mouth. Guinevere points at him. "You're in charge of reservations. You don't like any of us anymore, especially with the ongoing lawsuit—"

"Nah, that's between our families," Malachi says. "We're chill. Besides, I'm not trying to create more work for myself. The only reason I'm here tonight is because *Arsonist's Revenge* got booked."

"But you don't know by *whom*?" Charity presses. She's always been great at getting answers out of people—why isn't the Stomp Out Cancer bake sale garnering more publicity, why didn't we put up as many posters for her student body president reelection campaign as we promised, why didn't all of BREAKOUT's sprinklers go off on the night of the fire—and even Malachi isn't immune to the beguiling capabilities of her inquisitive head tilt.

He shrugs. "Prepaid gift card."

"Oh," Santo says, suddenly staring at his cardstock invitation like it might burn him. "Weird."

A silence descends over the escape room lobby. Save for the buzzing OPEN sign plastered against the smiley-face-decaled window—and our collective breathing—everything is quiet. And I can picture the end of this moment so perfectly: Malachi shrugging. Charity worrying the strands of her freshwater pearl necklace. Guinevere stalking out through the EXIT doors. Tobias tucking his phone back into his pocket and nodding goodbye. Santo turning his back on me.

It could be over so easily, this freak misunderstanding, this flame-eaten photograph, this already-unforming memory. I could watch everyone walk away; I could leave Friendship Springs without learning how the fire stared; I could be forced to stop clinging to the past I can't remember. But then I catch another glimpse of myself in the mirror behind our Game Master, where the same anxious, stomach-sick, worn-down version of myself that I've become in the past year stares back, and it hits me, here in this lobby with its glowing lights and its corny merchandise and its promise of the brainteasers I fell in love with because of Dad: If I allow myself to turn away from BREAKOUT now, nothing will change. I'll get back in my duck-filled Jeep and I'll choke down my burning questions about the fire and tomorrow I will walk across an elevated stage at the LeConte Center at 7:00 PM in Pigeon Forge knowing I robbed myself of the once-in-a-lifetime opportunity to get real answers.

And I can't let that happen, because I'm wearing Matteo Cesari's leather trench coat, and the seven of us used to play monthly escape rooms together back when he was still alive, and I'm so tired of feeling lost without him.

Before I can overthink it, I take out my phone again and scan the first QR code my camera latches on to. "What are you doing, Stephanie?" Guinevere hisses, eyeing my device as the waiver loads on my screen. But I fill out the first text box. Then the second. And the third, because I need to hold on to this feeling. I want to get closure. I've been baptized with tears and ash and plastered blood, and even if the details of the night that tore our friend group apart keep slipping through my fingers like smoke—even if *secrets won't keep themselves* is a threat—I need to stay, because tonight is the night I'm going to find out how my best friend died.

So I shrug, turn to face Guinevere, and say the words, knowing this is the first time we've all been back together since the fire killed Matt exactly a year ago: "I want to play the game."

• • •

yelp.com | Recommended Reviews: BREAKOUT Escape Rooms Inc.

Located in Friendship Springs, TN | Have you been here?
Write a review!

STAY AWAY! ★☆☆☆☆
Posted by Rob Whitefeather at 5:46 PM
If I could give 0 stars I would. Distracted, unhelpful Game Master...extremely disorganized room... repetitive and malfunctioning puzzles...unsanitary bathroom...all in all, a terrible experience. AVOID THIS PLACE AT ALL COSTS!

CHAPTER TWO

Wednesday, May 20, 2026 10:56 PM

I can feel everyone looking at me. Their heated stares burn into my dead best friend's coat, spiking my heart rate, but I force myself to keep my hands still as I scan the unfamiliar verbiage of the waiver. I've already filled out all the boxes at the bottom, mainly out of spite, but it seems like a good idea to read through the black-and-pink legal jargon before I hit SUBMIT. At any rate, this wording seems a lot more airtight than the document's past versions.

BREAKOUT ESCAPE ROOMS INCORPORATED
Sevier County Plaza, Suite 263
Friendship Springs, TN 37876

PARTICIPANT AGREEMENT, WAIVER, AND RELEASE OF LIABILITY

I hereby release and agree to hold **BREAKOUT ESCAPE ROOMS INCORPORATED** harmless from and waive on behalf of myself, my heirs, and any personal representatives any causes of action, claims, demands, damages, costs, expenses, and compensation for damage or loss to myself and/or property which may be caused by any connection with any services received from **BREAKOUT ESCAPE ROOMS INCORPORATED.** I understand this release discharges **BREAKOUT ESCAPE ROOMS INCORPORATED** from any liability or claim I, my heirs, or any personal representatives may have against the escape room with respect to any bodily injury, illness, medical treatment, property damage, or death which may arise from any services received from **BREAKOUT ESCAPE ROOMS INCORPORATED.**

I CERTIFY I HAVE READ THIS DOCUMENT IN ITS ENTIRETY AND FULLY UNDERSTAND ITS CONTENT. I ACKNOWLEDGE THIS IS A RELEASE OF LIABILITY AND A CONTRACT AND I SIGN IT OF MY OWN FREE WILL.

I glance up at Malachi. "Or death?" I question.

He nods before taking another sip from his thermos; I catch a whiff of black coffee. "Covering our bases. You know how it is."

Do I? I read over the legalese a second time, my throat bobbing, and try not to let my nerves show. This boilerplate is new, probably because of the legal battle the James-Mays are still embroiled in with Illaria Cesari (and a few of our parents) over Matt's alleged wrongful death, but its underlying meaning is clear: If anything happens while I'm locked inside the escape room, I can't sue BREAKOUT. And neither can anyone else.

God. Even though I'm furious that a four-by-six-inch piece of foil-stamped cardstock is all it took to bring us back together after twelve long months, there's no turning back now. I need to be decisive, because after the ashes of last year's fire settled and the six of us emerged from the ensuing media feeding frenzy with only our already-failing interpersonal relationships as casualties, the rest of my friend group was able to just...move on. Santo fled the country. Guinevere weaponized her identity as the grieving girlfriend to guilt her federal-judge father into sending her to bond with ponies and practice horseback, archery, and ax-throwing at a place called Wild Hearts Equine Therapy & Outdoor Sports. Charity incorporated the tragedy into her personal brand and won over $250,000 in scholarships from places like the Rotary Club, the CCHS financial aid office, and our local bank. Tobias channeled his energy into getting reinstated on the CCHS chess team before they promptly kicked him off again. Malachi churned out a series of @Mal.The.Reel.King videos inspired by the accident and skyrocketed his notoriety as a result.

But my estranged friends remember what happened on the night of the fire. They *know* what went down in *Wanderland* on the night Matt died; I don't. Despite my bimonthly hypnotherapy sessions with Call-Me-Diana, my traumatic brain injury can only surface warped, psychedelic, amnesia-fueled flashes: flickering Cheshire Cat smiles. Melting flamingo-shaped croquet mallets. Ticking oversize clocks that run backward until my dreams flood with flames and I wake up sweat-slicked, gasping for air, and convinced I smell smoke. So if I'm going to be in Friendship Springs tonight, then I'm going to re-create the circumstances of last year's accident in the hopes of regaining my memories. I'm going to check a box agreeing that the system's carefully generated cursive counts as my signature. And I'm going to hit SUBMIT on the waiver.

Yes, I want to do the escape room. Again.

"Stephanie, we shouldn't play!" Guinevere snaps. On my phone screen, BREAKOUT's hot-pink smiley face logo pops up with the words *Thanks for helping us keep you safe! We look forward to welcoming you to your one-of-a-kind immersive escape experience.* "If none of us are claiming responsibility for sending the invitations, then we have no idea who lured us here."

"Yeah. I'm, like, with Gee on this one?" Charity says, glancing at the laminated QR codes with her glossy lips puckered in slight distaste. "Going through with the game now seems...weird."

"Does it?" Tobias takes a step forward, coming into the pink-and-blue neon-sign light, and my breath catches at the dark bluish-purple bruise blooming around his left eye. Despite the fact that his early-life farm exposure should've led him to develop a robust immune system, Tobias has always had the constitution of a sickly Victorian child. As a result, his battered duffel contains more first aid supplies than the school nurse's office, including (but not limited to!) an EpiPen, a bottle of Flonase, Band-Aids, medical gauze, and enough Tylenol to knock out a Clydesdale. But he's not one for fistfights. So what the hell happened to him?

"We're already here," Tobias continues before I can ask about his injury. "Clearly, we arrived intending to play the room whether or not we knew who sent the cards, so our uncertainty surrounding the organizer shouldn't change our intentions now."

"It's up to y'all." Malachi takes another sip from his thermos, his gaze flicking between us. "I've set up *Arsonist's Revenge* already, and I'm fine with running your game. But if you guys wanna call tonight off 'cause you're freaked, then I'll just need your deposit back."

I turn off my phone and pocket it, vindicated by the undercurrents of panic, frustration, and rage that've been pinballing through my veins since last May. I'm not certain voluntarily locking myself inside a room with a mélange of people who hate me will un-repress my memories, but at this point I'm out of options. To date, my knowledge of Matt's death is encapsulated entirely by its corresponding Crime column in the *Tennessee Star*: Seven teenagers walked into an escape room a year ago. Only six walked out.

Despite my many grievances with BREAKOUT, surrendering myself to tonight's escape room is the only way to glean the truth. It's why I forked over the necessary cash to the employee at the run-down twenty-four-hour gas station near my house with gritted teeth and drove twenty-eight miles to this ironically named town, despite the fact that my stash of saved tips from late-night Perfect Strike shifts is rapidly dwindling. It's why I signed the waiver. It's why I'm here, pathetically stumbling through talking to my ex-friends instead of my rubber duck collection. I'm so desperate to do this. I can't move on until I understand.

And besides, there's nowhere else for me to go tonight, anyway.

"It's supposed to be for him," I whisper. "That's what the invitation said, right? *An escape room in honor of Matteo Luca Cesari. He died a year ago today.*" I swallow, looking at everyone scattered around the LED-lit lobby. "He's been on my mind a lot lately. The accident and the fire and…" I blink back the tears threatening to well up in the back of my throat and start again. "The way I see it, we've been given a chance to honor his memory. His life. The kind of person—the kind of friend—he was, for the first time since he passed. So if we're putting it to a vote, then I choose to stay. It's what Matt would have wanted. And regardless of who sent us the cards, that's why we're here. Because it feels right to do this. For him."

I dig my nails into my palms to stave off the awkward silence gathering in BREAKOUT's lobby. At the same time, though, I can't help glancing at Santo. I hope that he, at least, understands why I want to go through with the game. It's been a year of obfuscated facts, of wrongful death claims and sleazy lawyers, and regardless of how unsettled I personally am by the invitations, I can't help but feel like they're proof that there's more to Matt's death than most of Cedar Creek has been led to believe. They're a *sign*.

"Zamekova's right," Santo says after a beat, and my jaw unclenches at his vocal support. "Today's been...awful. This whole week's been awful, actually. I haven't been eating. Or sleeping. My hair is falling out in clumps. Momma's been so stressed with the job and her lawsuit"—here he throws an apologetic glance toward Malachi, who dips his head in acknowledgment—"that she's barely at home, and even she's noticed that I'm fucking falling apart." He sighs. "You know, what the six of us went through last year...that kind of trauma doesn't exactly make for a good study abroad icebreaker, regardless of how many depressed teenagers you meet in your Italian gothic architecture class. But when I got the invitation, I realized I didn't go through the fire by myself. And even if we don't talk anymore—even if we haven't talked since my brother died—I'm glad I don't have to spend the anniversary of the night I lost Matt alone."

In the glowing lights of the lobby, a heavier silence punctuates his words. But this time, I notice tears free-falling down Charity's sharp cheeks. Malachi's lips are trembling. Guinevere's balled her manicured hands into fists, and even Tobias looks touched.

Santo nods at me across the room, and a rush of gratitude floods me. *There*, his dark gaze seems to say. *Sixty minutes to figure out what the rest of our friends are hiding about my twin brother's death.*

Ha. Now I *know* I'm imagining things. Thank you, TBI-induced hallucinations.

"Wow," Charity breathes, wiping her mascara trails with fluttering fingers. "Santo, that speech was, like, beautiful? Maybe you should be on stage at our graduation tomorrow."

Next to her, Tobias hums in careful agreement. "You're right," he tells Santo. "The anniversary effect exacerbates the emotions associated with grief. For me, the invitation came at the right time. I'd like to do this for Matt, too."

"Fine," Guinevere snarls, not to be outdone. "Then I guess we're playing."

"Excellent," Malachi says, coming out from behind the counter. In addition to the cheese glob, nacho crumbs litter the collar of his embroidered pink-and-black company polo. "*Briefing Room* time."

We follow him into the enclosed space one by one, where our collective body heat immediately mixes into another nauseating combination of smells. It's dark in here, too. Apart from a row of LED-strip-lined lockers sitting against the wall, the *Briefing Room* has no real light source. Eerie.

Charity wastes no time in claiming the crushed velvet love seat. Tobias slides onto the other, back to fervently typing, and Santo and Guinevere settle on opposite ends of the three-person couch. Malachi remains standing. The steel HVAC above us rattles as I squeeze into the only spot left, which is between my dead best friend's twin brother and my dead best friend's girlfriend. Fan-fucking-tastic.

"All right," Malachi says brightly. "To begin, welcome to BREAKOUT Escape Rooms Incorporated. My name is Malachi James-May, obviously, and I'll be running your game tonight."

"Also obviously." Santo smiles.

I press my thighs together and attempt one of my four-six-eight breathing exercises from hypnotherapy, flooding my nostrils with bougainvillea and white sage and charring meat.

Growing up, Randall James and Taliyah May were pillars of our community. Their Black-owned business sponsored everything from elementary school musicals to junior prom car wash fundraisers; their hot-pink smiley face logo is plastered across the backs of 95 percent of the CCHS-affiliated T-shirts I own. Once their business in Cedar Creek burned down, though, they stopped being able to donate to events as often. The PTA iced them out, their local fanbase dwindled, and Mal picked up more shifts to make up for the Game Masters who quit their jobs in solidarity—or protest—after the lawsuit was filed.

But even though Malachi's parents own BREAKOUT, he's not supposed to be running a game this late by himself. And something about this feels wrong even now—us, back at BREAKOUT for the first time since the accident. Him, standing in front of us with his signature toothy grin. The weight of the ongoing lawsuit settling around the *Briefing Room*'s empty spaces.

"Here at BREAKOUT," Malachi continues, "we strive for an immersive escape game experience. That being said, too much immersion can be costly—so please do not jump, pull on, or climb objects within the room. Remember: If it takes more than two fingers of force, you probably shouldn't be doing it." He glances at Tobias. "You also won't need any outside equipment while you're in the escape room. No pocket screwdrivers, no bolt cutters, and especially no Google. In fact, I'm going to ask y'all for your phones before we enter, so that BREAKOUT can keep things fair for our future players." At this, Malachi opens the leftmost locker and slides out the plastic bin within expectantly. "Come on," he coaxes when none of us move. "You know the rules. We can't have you taking photos or recording audio inside."

There's an edge to his easygoing voice, though. An underlying agitation. Briefly, I wonder if it's because of *Cedar Creek Confessions*, but I hand over my device before I can think too much about it either way.

A scowl settles over Tobias's face as his thumbs pause over his screen. "It's a liability to prohibit players from taking personal electronics into the escape room. What if I need to call for help? Or respond to a text?"

"All player groups will be provided with a walkie-talkie for pertinent communication," Malachi says. "I'll also be in contact with you for the duration of the game, and BREAKOUT's implemented a variety of additional safeguards in our most recent renovation for increased peace of mind. Y'all will see them as we head inside." He pauses. "Plus, you already signed the waiver."

Tobias's scowl deepens. I know I'm probably just being paranoid and whatever he's doing on his phone—I keep getting glimpses of his screen—is none of my business. But still, I'm relieved to see him hand Malachi his device to place inside BREAKOUT's smiley-faced bin.

After the rest of my ex-friends follow suit, Malachi smiles. "Wonderful. Now, inside *Arsonist's Revenge*"—he reaches beside him—"you can use this walkie-talkie to ask me for up to three hints. I've got an identical walkie-talkie, as well as live camera feeds inside the room, so I'll be able to guide your game from the control room." His smile widens. "Unless I'm not paying attention, of course." When none of us laugh, Malachi does. "Kidding!"

He asks who wants to be in charge of the walkie-talkie. Santo volunteers, the handoff is made, and then our Game Master finishes by pulling out a series of different locks—wordlock, numbered padlock, direction lock—and providing a refresher on how to manipulate each one. As a former escape room enthusiast, it's the same rundown I've heard hundreds of times before, but something about tonight feels... different. There's an unease bubbling in my stomach that refuses to settle; part of me wonders if I'm actually ready to be back. Right now, though, it doesn't matter, because BREAKOUT's Game Master is already heading out of the *Briefing Room*, and we're all following him.

"After we rebranded," Malachi says as he opens a door to a midnight-black hallway outfitted with yet more LED lights, "my parents changed a lot of our internal and external processes. You'll be glad to know that our new security measures are top-notch... And if any of you need reassurance at any point during the game, please let me know. Your safety is my top priority."

We pass a pair of entwined lime-green swans, a blinking eye, and a sign reading FIND YOUR OWN PATH as we follow Malachi, but the hallway isn't long. It seems the Friendship Springs BREAKOUT only has three operational rooms, each labeled with their name and best escape time in a scrawl of UV-reactive chalk: *Haunted Mansion* (17:42). *Alien Abduction* (31:29). *Arsonist's Revenge* (—:—).

Do it for Matt, Steffi. Don't turn around.

Next to the door of *Arsonist's Revenge* sits a built-in fire extinguisher, and my mouth goes dry as Malachi flips through his key ring. I wonder if this is part of the *additional safeguards* our

Game Master alluded to. I wonder if the James-Mays made sure to update their sprinkler heads and fire control panels alongside their new epoxy flooring, too.

Santo nods to the huge blackboard sitting against the opposite wall. "A lot of cool ones, huh? Looks like a decent list."

I follow his gaze. The blackboard includes every room, past and present, across all three BREAKOUT locations in Cedar Creek, Pigeon Forge, and Friendship Springs. A few are unfamiliar to me—*Ghost Pirate's Curse, Chemistry Class*—but others I recognize from our past games: *Moonshine Cabin, Serial Killer's Hideout, Egyptian Tomb, Deranged Clown Circus, Raiders of the Lost Temple,* and *Hijacked.*

"Here she is," Malachi says, swinging the door open and stepping inside. My breath hitches as I cross the threshold, and then it completely stalls in my throat as my eyes adjust to the gloom of the actual escape room. For a second, despite the fact that we're twenty-eight miles from Cedar Creek, I'm almost convinced we're standing exactly where Matt died last year.

"Oh, I forgot to mention," Malachi says, his white teeth unsettling in the escape room's crimson floodlights, "we renovated this suite using the same schematics as the BREAKOUT in Cedar Creek, so this layout may look familiar to y'all."

Familiar? *Arsonist's Revenge* is built exactly like *Wanderland*. A shiver crawls up my spine. If franchise sister rooms exist, then Friendship Springs is Cedar Creek's identical twin.

"Huh," Santo says, scratching the back of his neck. "This is… uh… definitely something."

It's not decorated like *Wanderland*, though. Instead, it looks like your average mountain cabin. There's a kitchenette, a dining area, and an entertainment center. A stationary night scene peeks out through gingham-curtained fake windows; an ambient hum of cicadas, crickets, and owls filters in from speakers hidden among fake-log wall panels. The fridge has an amalgamation of postcards, photographs, and newspaper clippings haphazardly stuck to it with ABC magnets; the hardwood table is piled with laminated maps. A coatrack sits in the corner of the room opposite a large locked trunk. On top of the trunk lies a blank chalkboard, a piece of white chalk, and a small lantern.

Man, there are clues in here. Puzzles to solve. Memories to recover.

"All right. Welcome to *Arsonist's Revenge*, our newest room," Malachi says. "You'll notice we've got a couple of locks around here with self-explanatory stickers marked GAME MASTER ONLY. You won't be able to open those, so don't waste your time. Also, if you need to leave the room for any reason at any point in the game, feel free to use this emergency mechanism to disengage the magnetized door."

Malachi flips up a translucent case by the entryway, revealing a red RELEASE button, and I inhale. Did we use something like this to escape *Wanderland*? Why can't I remember? What actually happened to Matt?

Breathe in for four seconds. Hold for six seconds. Breathe out for eight seconds.

"Just make sure you hold it down for a bit—it can be a little finicky. But remember, using the button won't count as escaping." Malachi flashes a smile. "To win the game, you'll need to punch the correct four-digit code into this keypad. The clues in the room will lead you to the numbers, so pay careful attention. There's a chalkboard in case you want to take notes; if you run out of chalk or lose it, let me know so I can bring you more. Also, there are hooks on the back of the door for jackets or bags."

At this, Tobias immediately takes Mal up on the offer, hanging his duffel bag on the leftmost hook; Charity, smiling, tugs at her blazer but doesn't remove it. I tuck my hands into the pockets of Matt's trench coat. It's staying on.

"Now," Malachi says once we're all situated, "are y'all ready to hear how you've found yourselves in this arsonist's cabin?" Before we can answer, he's already launching into a rehearsed monologue about how we'll all burn alive in an hour unless we find a way to put a stop to a crazed inferno-setter who decided to take the name of the Great Smoky Mountains literally. The fictional BREAKOUT narrative is based on a real arsonist, I think—a disgraced fire chief in a neighboring county whose rampage led to Code Purple air quality alerts around Appalachia for weeks before they caught him—but it feels doubly ominous with the shroud of my best friend's fire-related death lingering around us.

In front of me, Malachi wraps up his speech by asking, "Will you be able to break out?" And honestly, I'm not sure. Before I stepped away from the sponsorships and the newsletters and the SEO tracking, I'd completed 267 rooms and blogged about my spoiler-free experiences inside almost all of them on *There's No Escape* to an audience of over thirteen thousand fellow escape room aficionados. But within my own friend group? Despite us playing monthly rooms, the seven of us always goofed around too much to piece together any substantial clues. I never blogged about the games we played, either. With Matt, Charity, Guinevere, Santo, Tobias, and Malachi, I was off the clock. I got to just...enjoy the games. Find the love in playing for the sake of it instead of hitting a brand deliverable or snapping a compelling thumbnail photo or crafting the perfect language surrounding the release of a new room I accessed early with discounted media tickets. Inside the safe bubble of my friend group, I didn't need to be an expert in Caesar ciphers or puzzle flow or the Baader-Meinhof phenomenon. I just got to be a normal teenager hanging out with her friends. Looking back now, that time of my life reminds me of the easy years before my parents' divorce, when Dad and I first started playing rooms together and I fell in love with escaping.

Then the fire happened, and I lost everything. My friends. My blog. My memories. Matt.

My life.

"Okay," Malachi says. "Any last-minute questions?" When none of us say anything, he nods to the LCD monitor mounted in the corner of the room. "Your time starts as soon as this door closes. Good luck!"

"We're going to need it," Tobias mutters, scrubbing with his shoe at a slick trail of varnish made to look like gasoline near the room's threshold.

"What the hell is your problem?" Guinevere snarls, rounding on Tobias as the door shuts behind Malachi. Charity's doe eyes ping-pong between the two of them. A burn-scarred grin tugs at the corner of Santo's mouth; he's clearly entertained by the show. I shake my head and return my attention to the screen. Despite what Malachi said, our time is still frozen at 60:00.

For a second, the screen flickers. The timer disappears, replaced with a flash of hot pink burning brightly against my eyelids: YOU'LL PAY FOR THE FIRE.

When I blink again, though, the words are gone. Jesus. If Malachi's trying to terrify us, it's working.

The ambient cabin noises swell. The screen brightens, and our Game Master's newly disembodied voice wishes us good luck again over Santo's walkie-talkie. Our time reappears on the monitor: 60:00.

And then it starts counting down.

● ● ●

CEDAR CREEK CONFESSIONS

posted one month ago

Did you miss me, Cedar Creek? I've certainly missed you.

We have a lot to talk about.

I can't wait to dive in.

UNITED STATES DISTRICT COURT

EASTERN DISTRICT OF TENNESSEE
GREENEVILLE DIVISION

CATELYN ADLER; ILLARIA CESARI; and EDWARD MITCHELL-MOORE, Plaintiffs, v. RANDALL JAMES and TALIYAH MAY, Defendants.	Case No. 2:25-CR-00123-JRG-DCP

EXHIBIT C
Instagram Direct Messages from Stephanie Zamekova

Instagram Direct Messages from Stephanie Zamekova

#deadchat

11:25 PM

> hey, we're still on for tonight, right?
>
> i just wanted to check. i'm here parked outside of golden dragon and mal is wondering what the holdup is

11:37 PM

> hello?

11:46 PM

> guys, we really can't do a whole escape room with only one person

11:50 PM

> okay, if y'all don't show up in literally the next two minutes
>
> i swear i'm venmo-requesting the deposit back from each of you

guinevere.m.moore:

will you chill the fuck out, stephanie

like christ

i'm on my way. should be there in five

tobias_is_never_quinton:

i will, unfortunately, also be there soon <3

charity.adler:

Same!

Tell Malachi we love him and sorry for making him wait Xx

santo.77

matt and i are pulling up now, see everyone in a bit :)

11:52 PM

you're still good with what we're doing, right?

you don't think it's wrong?

guinevere.m.moore:

christ. relax, steffi. everything is going to be fine

besides, you know the consequences if you back out now

yeah. i know.

guinevere.m.moore:

great. glad to hear you're done pussyfooting. 3 mins away

see you soon

guinevere.m.moore:

you will.

just remember

after this, it all ends. for good.

CHAPTER THREE

Wednesday, May 20, 2026, 11:00 PM

"So...are we going to divide and conquer this shit?" Tobias asks, giving each of us a skeptical once-over from his position by the magnetized door. "Assign roles? Agree to check in with one another after set time increments?"

He's deliberately ignoring Guinevere's comment, which is smart. Tobias navigates social interactions like a game of chess; between his prescriptions and his obsessive tendencies, he believes it's possible to prepare for anything. But clearly someone caught him lacking lately. I frown at his black eye, trying to get a closer look without him noticing I'm staring again. *Keep your eyes to yourself.* Who was he texting so frantically earlier? What does he know? Why did he even show up at BREAKOUT tonight? To find out, I'll need to play the long game. Except I've only bought myself an hour to find out what my ex-friends are hiding. And the clock—now at 59:53—is already ticking away.

"Thinking back to our earlier experiences," Tobias continues, "I'd attribute our past failures to a general unawareness of our surroundings, an inevitable communication breakdown, and an underinvolved Game Master." Here, Tobias pointedly glances at the blinking security camera mounted next to the LCD monitor. "To obtain a better outcome, we should attempt to mitigate at least one of these variables moving forward."

"I heard that," Malachi's voice garbles over Santo's walkie-talkie at the same time Guinevere snaps, "We're playing an escape room, Tobias, not conducting an experiment using the scientific method or whatever the fuck. Stop psychoanalyzing us and start *looking around the room.*"

She's right. If this were a normal game, I'd already be trawling through the couch cushions, popping open the entertainment center's DVDs, and scrutinizing the assortment of fake fruit arranged in the center of the dining table. I'd send the HOME, SWEET HOME doormat skittering across the concrete floor with a well-placed kick. I'd scan the cabin scenery in every fake window after diligently rattling the gingham-patterned curtains. I'd try lifting the framed cabin photographs by the clothing rack to see if they're concealing a hidden safe. And after my initial curiosity was satiated, I'd snatch up the chalkboard and take inventory of every single lock within this eight-by-sixteen-foot area. My fingers twitch with the suppressed urge to begin cataloging: the wordlock on the trunk, the two numbered padlocks on the fridge handle, the combination lock on the kitchen cabinet. *There's No Escape Rule #4: Always pay attention to your surroundings.*

Jesus. I'm already slipping into escape-room blogger mode, and I've only been back inside BREAKOUT for twenty-two seconds. Maybe I've missed this more than I thought.

Tonight, though, I can't play the game how I would under normal circumstances. Instead, I grit my teeth and stay by the magnetized door with my hands tucked in Matt's leather coat. I willingly stepped inside *Arsonist's Revenge* tonight. So did my former friends. And we all have our own agendas—our own reasons for being here—even if I don't know those reasons yet. As for me, I intend to draw out our sixty minutes for as long as possible. After this, we're each going to go back to pretending the other members of our ex-friend group don't exist—which means if I want closure, I'll need to suppress my ability to puzzle out clues quickly in favor of making this cobbled-together form of extreme exposure therapy work.

Santo grins; his canines glint in the red LED light. "I mean, we *should* strategize. After all, we've never beaten one of BREAKOUT's rooms before." He wiggles his paint-chipped fingernails in my direction. "Good thing we have an expert with us."

"I'm not much of an expert anymore," I warn, glancing up at the countdown: 59:37. Every second counts.

"Well, it's not like you helped us win any room we've done in the past," Charity says, dropping into a dining table chair with a light sigh. "So, like, maybe you never were?" She rubs her eyes before she takes out her graduation speech and unfolds it. Lovely. "At worst, though, we're locked in here for the next hour. We may as well make the most of our time."

"Easy for you to say when you're once again prioritizing politics over your friends," Guinevere spits before stalking off toward the entertainment center. Santo shrugs and heads toward the kitchenette with an apologetic look at Charity. I glance sideways at Tobias.

"And everyone is spreading out to do their own thing again," Tobias says, striding forward to snatch the lantern sitting on the end table. "Wonderful."

Now that everyone's claimed a different part of the room for our initial search, I head for the coatrack, where I'll be able to strategize in peace. *Arsonist's Revenge* isn't a huge escape room. The players are always in plain sight of one another, so there's nowhere I'll be able to go throughout the course of the game to catch a moment alone, to escape the already-building tension, to truly *think*. Unease gnaws at me as I assess the clothes draped across the coatrack: a worn lumberjack flannel, a faux-raccoon-tail-adorned hat, and an old CCHS hoodie. My brows crease at the last item—CCHS merch here, all the way in Friendship Springs?—before I dig my fingers into its lint-speckled kangaroo pouch. Were things always this tense between the six of us? I don't think so, but maybe my Swiss cheese brain has not only blocked out my memories of Matt's death but rounded out the hard edges of all my ex-friends' personalities, too.

I shake my head to dislodge the thought. Whether they're bad people or not, the other players are also my primary witnesses. I need to start digging for information from them, although I'll need to be careful with how I do it. I still suspect that Santo arranged this get-together, but the truth is, any of us could have dropped off those invitations. We still know one another's addresses from birthday parties and post-homecoming sleepovers and drunken game nights; it would be easy for each one of us to slip a piece of cardstock into everyone else's mailbox. I can still picture our houses in my mind: the Mitchell-Moores' carpeted basement where Guinevere and I snuck shots from the expensive tequila in her parents' oakwood alcohol cabinets, the sprawling outdoor pool in Charity's backyard where we played Truth or Dare in our swimsuits under the open night sky, the fenced-in pens on the Matthews family farm where Tobias and I would take turns bottle-feeding baby goats, the laughter-filled PowerPoint nights at the Cesari twins' duplex, the large flat-screen TV of Malachi's parents' home theater.

Inside the CCHS hoodie, my fingers hit something cold and cylindrical. A clue.

Ha. Maybe I've still got it.

I don't want to be too hasty, though. Every new clue discovery means less time for *Arsonist's Revenge* to jog my memory of *Wanderland*. Which means that tonight, I'm not following *There's No Escape Rule #7: When you find a clue, shout it out loudly*. Tonight, I'm sabotaging our game.

Malachi's voice comes in over the walkie-talkie: "Remember, if you get stuck, y'all have three hints—but if you use all three, your time won't count for the leaderboard."

"Malachi," Guinevere says, "no one likes an overinvolved Game Master." Her eyes meet mine for the briefest second, still swirling, still hurricane, and I'm suddenly reminded of how the two of us used to spend hours teaching each other elementary

Czech and Cherokee on the floor of her childhood bedroom, back when things between the two of us were so much easier: *DSoDS. Agasga. Prší. It is raining. GSoDE. Tsagasgv. Pršelo. It has rained. DSoDS VᏜ ZC). Agasga doyi nogwu. Venku právě prší. It is raining outside right now.* But then her judgmental glare flicks back to the dials of the TV, and the moment passes. The thunderstorm of her volatile emotions—anger, frustration, and residual longing—temporarily subsides.

I exhale. I'm not delusional—I know I'm not Sheriff Stallard, or Call-Me-Diana, or a reporter from the *Tennessee Star*. I can't be too direct with my line of questioning. But I can't be too hesitant, either. Which means I need a good target. Someone who won't be too difficult to press about the circumstances surrounding the fire; someone who can help me get warmed up.

My eyes fall on Charity. She spent her senior year shepherding our class through tragedy as a paragon of grief. Right now, though, her lips are moving silently as she reads over her graduation speech. She's not even pretending to help us look for items to escape *Arsonist's Revenge*.

I slide into the dining chair next to hers and nod at the paper in her hands. "Did you manage to find a clue already?"

"What, this? No." Charity laughs, her breathy voice high and soft. "I'm rehearsing my speech, remember?" Her glossy mouth pinches with concern. "Oh, wait. You probably don't. You know, since you, like, forget a lot of things now? Because of your…" She points to her temple, blinking at me with her fake-innocent doe eyes.

"My brain injury?" I say flatly. "Yeah. Memory is kind of a problem for me."

Charity sets her speech down and sighs. "Well, that's what I'm doing. It's, like, stressful, though? After the public scrutiny my mom faced after first expressing support for BREAKOUT and then joining the lawsuit against it, I feel like I owe it to her to say something meaningful tomorrow. But I've rewritten this stupid speech a million times by now, and the wording still isn't right."

"Maybe you can practice with me," I suggest. "I wrote a lot of blog posts for *There's No Escape*—I know a thing or two about appealing to your audience. Ethos, pathos, logos, kairos, et cetera."

I reach for her speech, hoping to find a line in it that I can cherry-pick to pivot into interrogating her about the fire, but her hand snaps across the paper before I can read a word. "Thanks, but I, um, also took AP Lang? And I'd rather fix it myself. It's just, like, you know, your standard cookie-cutter SBP address: *We've worked so hard and reached this goal after years of hard work; we'll change the world; our future starts now.* Obligatory Dolly Parton quote. Go, Warriors! Et cetera." She abruptly stands, a tight smile plastered on her sharp face, and my stomach curls inward at the way she just mocked me. "Either way, you're right—I agreed to be here, so I should probably be playing with everyone else. Catch you later, though!"

Before I can react, Charity adjusts her watch and hurries to assist Santo in searching through drawers in the kitchenette. Jesus, I already miss my plastic ducks. Worse, I only have one goal and I'm already failing. I suppress the urge to bang my forehead against the dining table. While our conversation amounted to nothing, it's still early-game. The clock's only at 58:43—I'm making good time, so I can't be too dejected. I need to be more careful, though; there's no way I'm finding out what happened to Matt like this. If I want to succeed, I'll need to change my strategy. If I can't learn about the fire through talking to my ex-friends, maybe I should focus on actually playing the game and praying the truth reveals itself as I'm going through the motions.

Chrrrk. The walkie-talkie in Santo's hands hums to life, and Malachi's baritone filters through the room. "The arsonist who kidnapped you returns at midnight, so be thorough," he says. "Especially regarding objects above and below your natural eye level, like those framed black-and-white cabin photos."

Damn. If Malachi keeps dropping hints we didn't ask for, we're going to escape with fifteen minutes to spare. Unsolicited GM advice is my biggest pet peeve; back when I ran *There's No Escape*, I used to score franchises on Puzzle Autonomy in addition to Atmosphere, Merchandise Offerings, Prop Utilization, and a slew of other factors. Any company whose PA score was lower than three out of five always received an embedded GIF of a giant rubber duck with laser eyes and the text *NO ONE LIKES AN OVERINVOLVED GAME MASTER* burning into the screen. Malachi knows this, which is why he's always been great at letting our friend group solve puzzles at our own pace. That's one of the main reasons we've never escaped a BREAKOUT room before—opt out of the spoon-fed hints designed to make people escape faster, and you may never end up escaping at all.

So why is Mal urging us along tonight?

A flicker of uncertainty dances across my face as Tobias moves toward the black-and-white cabin prints and raises his lantern to assess them. I need to understand how Matt died—who planned the outing, where the fire started, why he didn't escape the room in time—but I also can't shake the weirdness of this entire night. There's something off about *Arsonist's Revenge*. And either our Game Master is in on it...or he feels it, too, and he's trying to usher us out of the situation faster by spoiling the game.

I'm not sure which option I prefer.

"Again," Tobias says as he cranes his neck upward, "I don't understand what I'm supposed to be looking at. Remember the communication breakdown I mentioned earlier? This is it."

While he's assessing the photographs, Guinevere grabs the walkie-talkie from Santo. "Malachi. Do not give us hints unless we explicitly ask for one. Got it?" she snaps, shoving the device back at Matt's twin before Mal can respond.

I glance at the countdown before my gaze returns to her: 56:22. Time to try again.

"This is kind of disturbing, isn't it?" I start. "Combing through a BREAKOUT room without your boyfriend?"

Guinevere scoffs. "Of course it's fucking disturbing. In case you haven't noticed, Stephanie, we were blackmailed into coming here. The little speech you gave in the lobby? Totally impressive and everything, but we would have done the room without it."

I inhale, not knowing how to properly navigate a conversation with someone I haven't spoken to since Matt's burial; someone I've only seen in glimpses for the past year, through congested hallways and late-night news clips and a *Warrior Minutes* profile about reconnecting with her distant Cherokee heritage by studying the language. But then I pause. *Blackmailed?*

The gears in my head turn. "Wait," I tell Guinevere, "can I

see your invitation?" At her dark expression, I hold out my hand. "Seriously. Please?"

She snorts. "Knock yourself out," she says, reaching into her patchwork pants and handing me her embossed card. I scan it and immediately blanch.

"Shit," I whisper, my head pounding as I stare at the hot-pink wording. "Hey, um, guys, what do each of your invites say?"

Tobias turns away from the cabin photographs. "Why? Planning another blog post?"

"No, because I'm developing a theory that they were personalized to us." I shove a random assortment of items cluttering the dining table aside—place mats, flameless LED tea lights, the fake fruit bowl that definitely seems like it's going to be important later—to make room for the unique invitations in my hands. "See? These aren't the same."

In the kitchenette, Charity pulls out her own invitation. Santo does, too, but he and Charity swap each other's and then throw them on the dining room table. I glance at Tobias. He sighs before he hands his card to Guinevere, who reads it and then places it next to mine.

The hairs on my arms stand on end as I stare at the variations of the black-and-pink cards. All five start the same—*Ready to Play Again?*—and continue with the venue information, but the final lines are different. Where mine reads *Because secrets won't keep themselves*, Guinevere's finishes with *Or everyone will know what you did*. Santo's ends with *This time, you'll make it right*. Charity's reads *For another opportunity to be a leader*, and Tobias's says *Since you're no stranger to friendly competition*.

"Huh," Guinevere says. "Look at that."

Jesus, none of this feels real. Seeing my friends in the flesh, being back inside BREAKOUT, interacting with puzzles like I'm running *There's No Escape* again…It's hard to reconcile. Only a few hours ago, I was staring at the ceiling in my bedroom, listening to one of Dad's King Crimson vinyls, avoiding Mom, and dreading the pomp and circumstance of tomorrow. But now…

"I can't believe we didn't notice this earlier," Santo says. "This is weird, right?"

Charity frowns. "What's interesting is that we weren't all explicitly blackmailed. When you look at the rhetoric on these cards, in fact, a few of them present tonight like…"

"Like a second chance," Santo finishes for her. His dark eyes meet mine across the dining room table, and I struggle to keep my expression neutral as I glance back at the message on his own invitation: *This time, you'll make it right.*

Heat against bubbling skin. A neon green EXIT *sign. Carcinogenic smoke. Blaring alarms. Screams.*

I blink, and the vision disappears. Holy shit. That was a memory. A real one.

They're starting to come back.

The walkie-talkie buzzes again. "Hey, y'all," Malachi says, a note of uncertainty in his voice. "This feels strange to me. Are you sure you want to continue playing?"

Tobias nods. "One hundred percent."

"Yes," Santo says.

Guinevere's lips twist with disdain. "I mean, we all want to get something out of this, right?" she says. "So we're staying."

"Besides," Charity chirps, "this is, like, probably nothing."

Or it could be a clue, the voice in the back of my head rasps, but I'm too rattled by the fact that my plan is actually working to care. I can't afford to think about clues right now—not when I need to pull it together if I'm going to have any hope of making it to the end of the hour. Tonight's objective isn't escaping; it's about staying here for long enough to force my brain to spontaneously recover my memories of *Wanderland*.

Santo claps his hands together. "Well, since we've already wasted"—he looks up at the monitor—"three minutes of our allotted escape time, and we're all in agreement on staying, we may as well go back to playing. None of us have found anything important yet, right?"

I shake my head, thinking guiltily about the unknown cylinder hidden in the CCHS sweatshirt, when Santo grins. "Except for this." He opens his burn-scarred palm, revealing a glinting key, and adrenaline zips up my spine.

"Where did you get that?"

"I found a magnetic chain inside one of the kitchen drawers, and Charity and I used it to fish the key out of the sink drain. All we need to do now is figure out what it unlocks."

"Well, did you try that?" Guinevere asks, pointing to the padlocked trunk pushed up against the couch by the entertainment center. Santo moves toward it and the rest of us follow him, pulled in by the promise of a large prop being opened. Strategically, it's not a good decision for all of us to be here—*There's No Escape Rule #11: Always work on a different puzzle than your teammates*—but we crowd in around the trunk anyway, our breath collectively held as Santo fits the key into the metal and twists. The lock snaps open.

"Ready?" my best friend's brother asks, sliding the shackle out of the lock plate. A wolfish smile plays at the corners of his mouth as he lifts the latch, his painted fingernails catching the light of Tobias's lantern, but it disappears from his face almost instantly.

Inside the trunk is a body.

• • •

CEDAR CREEK CONFESSIONS

posted 15 months ago

I know you missed me, Cedar Creek, so let's dive right in: We need to talk about Malachi James-May. That's right—on today's docket, I'm shouting the hallway whispers that have plagued our local Game Master since last Tuesday, when his parents announced the grand opening of yet another BREAKOUT location. Have you already been?

What unsuspecting patrons of BREAKOUT Escape Rooms Inc. may NOT know, however, is that they're not only signing up to be recorded by the escape room's security cameras with every game they play, but that the footage of their team stumbling around inside a dark room may also be used by CCHS's very own amateur filmmaker—or that the audio may be lifted for one of his scripts. So if you were thinking about getting hot and heavy in Moonshine Cabin this weekend...think again.

Place your bets on how long it'll take the James-Mays to put out an official statement...or go to their website and book a room to find out the truth for yourself. Of course, I encourage all of you to draw your own conclusions. I'm not here to make definitive judgments—I'm simply here to share relevant information with you, the good people of Cedar Creek High.

Go forth and play fair, y'all. Just remember...you may end up in more than BREAKOUT's archival footage if Malachi James-May is your Game Master.

MATTEO

293 Days Before the Accident

While being the new kid is never easy, it gets significantly harder when your identical twin is behind the wheel. To be honest, I don't know how Santo managed to obtain his license. But as we crest over the hill leading to our latest high school and a slew of kids flinch as my brother clips the sidewalk, I realize I might get attached to this view: lush blue-green mountains, a bright and cloudless sky, a marquee reading WELCOME BACK, CEDAR CREEK WARRIORS!—

Santo floors it over a speed bump. The cheap gas station black coffee I'm currently guzzling, too hot and weirdly sticky, sloshes all over my lap. "Shit!" I hiss. "Are you serious? We're in a school zone, asshole. Stop going forty in a twenty-five—I look like I just pissed myself."

"Not my problem!" Santo sings, jerking the steering wheel with a manic flourish. Our car skids into the upperclassmen parking lot and narrowly misses smashing the side mirror of a silver BMW. "I don't want to be late."

My hair is falling into my face again, but I make no effort to push it away. Instead, I open the glove compartment and stuff a million napkins into my pants. It's currently 7:17 AM, which means classes won't start for another forty-three minutes. This simple fact doesn't stop Santo from dragging us inside the building, though, where we retrieve our matching class schedules from an annoyed-looking receptionist with an extremely heavy Southern accent and lipstick on her teeth.

"Thank you!" Santo tells her, waving, and then the two of us duck into the cafeteria, where the early arrivals are shunted until classrooms open. Every conceivable booth is filled, and my brother frowns. "What the hell? This is a rural school. Shouldn't there be somewhere to sit?"

"I know," a voice chimes behind us. "Unfortunately, it's always like this. Totally insane, right?"

I turn around, spotting a girl with bright red curtain bangs sitting at her own booth with a group of her friends: a tall curly-haired ginger with a case of bad acne, a beautiful brunette, a dude with a locs ponytail and an anime T-shirt jamming out to whatever's playing in his hot pink earbuds, and a short blonde.

"Uh, yes," my brother says. "By the way, your hair is sick."

The girl with dyed hair smiles. "Thanks. I'm Steffi, by the way. Do y'all want to sit with us? We have the room."

"Do we?" the brunette says, raising a skeptical eyebrow at the napkin-induced bulge in my jeans. Fuck. But after the redhead gives her a look, the other girl sighs and slides over. There's a general shuffling as the others move down the padded booth. Santo, of course, doesn't waste a second before dropping down with a loud, appreciative sigh and an expectant look in my direction. Great.

I take the open seat next to the girl with dyed hair and try to stop my irritation from showing. At a few of our past high schools, we've run into the overly eager first-day types, but their enthusiasm never lasts. Once they figure out my brother and I are a package deal—and that we're not interested in joining their D&D group or their lacrosse team or their HOSA – Future Health Professionals chapter—the bright-eyed student recruiters typically disappear into the throng with their flyers, their friends, and their hollow promises of free food, never to be seen again.

This group has clearly squished together to make room for us, though, and the seating situation isn't as uncomfortable as I thought it'd be. Whatever. Baby steps.

"We always fight with the band kids to try and sit at our usual table," the *One Piece* T-shirt Guy says without taking out an earbud. "You'd think they'd respect the social contract by now, but it's a lawless land."

"Not what I expected for the middle of nowhere," Santo says with a grin, and the two are immediately sucked into their own conversation comparing band programs and complaining about people who play the tuba—which, fair.

"You know, if you're interested in broadcasting," the girl who invited us to sit here says, noticing my TALCOTT KELL BROADCASTING CLUB T-shirt, "you should join *Warrior Minutes*. We deliver the weekly news, but it's super low commitment. You go into the studio, film for about an hour a week, and basically goof off for the rest of the time."

"Or you could avoid that mistake and join the chess team instead," the tall ginger adds, glancing up from his phone screen to assess me. "Do you play?"

I blink, amused. Is this Southern hospitality, or are these people just neurotic as hell?

"Yeah, I dabble. Anyway, thanks for the recommendation," I tell the redhead. "Next time there's an opening, you should text me. Maybe I'll show up."

"You won't," she says. But she gives me her phone, anyway, and her eyes don't drop from my face until I finish typing in my contact info and hand the device back to her. "Whoa," she says, scanning the screen. "Weird area code. What brings you to Tennessee?"

I motion to Santo. "Our mom's job relocated her. She's in the restaurant industry, and she got an opportunity to manage this place called Pizza Plus."

"For real?" *One Piece* T-shirt Guy asks. "We love Pizza Plus. Can y'all get us free slices?"

Santo nods. "We'll hook you up," he says. But then his eyes cut to mine for a second, and I know he's thinking the same thing I am: We might not even stay long enough to learn most of these well-meaning people's names. Navigating the restaurant industry with a determined single mom means seven relocations in three years, which also means we're not staying in Cedar Creek for long enough to put down roots. All we can do is keep our heads down, do our work, and hope the school district doesn't fuck us over too hard when it's time to transfer in a month or two.

It also means that nothing we say while we're here matters. Although out of the two of us, Santo's always been worse at understanding that.

"There," the artificial redhead says, turning her phone screen to me. "I just sent you a text."

I squint at the screen, which reads: *hey! this is steff :)*

"Hang on, before you answer that," the blonde says, speaking for the first time since Santo and I sat down, "are either of you juniors? If so, I could really use your vote for student council!" She leans forward and unzips a battered backpack covered in various buttons: I catch a few, reading THOUGHTS AND PRAYERS ARE NOT ENOUGH, BISEXUAL AND STILL NOT INTO YOU, and HOT GIRLS VOTE! before the flap folds in on itself. "I should still have... some lollipops... in here somewhere..."

"Leave the lollipops alone, Charity," the brunette tells her exasperatedly. She's gorgeous, even though she's currently staring at me with the face of someone who just found gum stuck to the bottom of her Free People sandals. "He doesn't look like the voting type."

"Hey," Santo says, bringing a hand to his heart in mock offense. "He has my face, thank you very much. And I'm definitely the voting type. How else am I going to fight for my right to kiss men with tongue unless it's at the polls?"

He winks at *One Piece* T-shirt Guy. Holy shit, we've been inside this cafeteria for a total of six minutes and my brother is already building his roster.

"You don't, like, know that? So shut up, Guinevere," the blonde—Charity—tells Guinevere. She pulls out a mystery-flavored Dum-Dum in triumph and turns toward me. "If I give you this, will you vote for me?"

Steff grins. "Just so you know, if you say yes, that definitely counts as taking bribes."

"I'll do it!" Santo says, snatching the lollipop and unwrapping it. "Don't worry, though. You had my vote the second your friend let us sit with you, so this is a win-win-win."

Guinevere smiles at my brother. "Maybe we misjudged you," she offers. Her attention turns to me. "What about you, though? What's your deal?"

"Well, Matt loves chess," Santo says around his lollipop before I can open my mouth. "He played on the team at a few of our old schools. I'm terrible, though. He beat me in four moves once, and I haven't touched a piece since." My brother cracks the hard candy in half and swallows it whole before he sticks out his hand; today, his fingernails are bright blue. "I'm Santo, by the way."

The tall ginger takes it. "Tobias," he says, his eyes flicking back to me. He's wearing a T-shirt that reads OCCAM'S RAZOR: THE OBVIOUS CHOICE. "So, Matt. You play? Scholar's mate works on your brother, clearly—but if you're up for a challenge, you should attend our upcoming interest meeting."

Leave it to Santo to expose me as club fodder on our first day here.

"Maybe," I tell Tobias. Though if the chess team is actively recruiting, it may not be my scene. At our last school in North Carolina, we used to set up a table during Club Week and promise students $100 if they could beat a player on the team. Most people never did; if a student played well, though, then we'd invite them to actually try out. Our members were vetted. Anything else just comes off as too desperate to be professional.

I spend the rest of the time talking about random shit with Tobias, Guinevere, Charity, and Steff until the bell rings and people start dispersing. As we slide out of the booth, though, we walk to class in a group. Steff invites us to sit with them again at lunch, Charity reminds us to vote in the upcoming election, and Tobias texts me the details for a chess club interest meeting and sends me a friend request on Chess.com.

"This is all great," Santo says as we linger in the hallway, "but what my brother actually needs is a part-time job so he can buy his own car."

Steff lights up. "Seriously?" she says, and two seconds later, I have the email of the regional manager at a local bowling alley called Perfect Strike that she tells me is currently hiring for $10.50 an hour. "It's not great money," Steff warns, right before my expression falls at the pay, "but the staff are super chill, and we get one free meal every shift." She grins. "Besides, I've gotten decent at bowling. We hang out there most of the time after school anyway; send me your résumé, and I'll drop it off with Joanna after my shift next Tuesday."

So, who knows? Maybe this school won't be so bad after all.

CHAPTER FOUR

Wednesday, May 20, 2026, 11:04 PM

My pulse skips. Under the crimson glare of the escape room's precision floodlights, I can't immediately reconcile the trunk corpse as human. Jagged flesh protrudes around its ears; its closed eyelids are unnaturally smooth. But as soon as my tongue unglues itself from the roof of my mouth, I realize the body elicits knee-jerk disgust because it's a dummy. A fake—albeit an expensive, uncannily realistic one—made of Flex Foam and Perma-Blood.

My stomach turns. *Prop Utilization: 4.6/5.*

"Damn," Santo mutters, crouching to examine the prop body face-to-fake-face. The constellation of fresh Italian sun–induced moles around his eyes shift as his forehead creases. "Is it just me, or is anyone else starting to get seriously creeped out by this room?"

"It's not just you," Guinevere replies, her tone clipped as her ivory fingernails gravitate to the resin moth-wing sitting at the base of her throat. Briefly, I wonder how long it took her to get ready tonight; if she dressed up specifically because she knew she would see me; if she suspected I'd come, even though she told everyone that I wasn't going to make it. "Christ. I thought we were playing *Arsonist's Revenge*, not *Lair of the Psycho Killer*." She drops the necklace before a sneer settles across her Cupid's-bow lips. "Are you still glad we're here, Stephanie?"

I want to respond. I want to say something back, to defend myself, to break through to the girl who dated my best friend before he died. We're both grieving Matt's loss so deeply—I know that being here has to be hurting her, too. But the anxious knot growing in my throat with every second I stare at the dummy's paint-cracked face keeps my jaw locked tight. I don't owe Guinevere anything. And right now, I don't think I could speak even if I tried.

Call-Me-Diana's voice echoes in my head: *This is a PTSD response. Your negative emotions surrounding escape rooms are resurfacing, and that's okay. Focus on your breathing. Find a space to self-soothe. Ask your friends if they have time to talk.*

"This isn't Steffi's fault," Charity says as my fingers connect with the cool metal of the Swiss Army knife in my pocket. "Like, we all agreed to play the game? We all signed waivers. We all showed up tonight." But her eyes stay fixed on the Flex Foam body, and her mouth presses itself into a thin line.

I run my thumb back and forth over the knife's silver cross, fighting back the panic metastasizing through my bloodstream. *Don't freak out. It's fine. You're used to seeing props like this, remember?* But the grotesque not-exactly-flesh feels different with the context of Matt's death weighing on us. It's more sinister. Real.

Santo activates the walkie-talkie. "Dude, what's up with this mannequin?"

There's a second of stretched-out silence, and then Malachi's laugh crackles through the device. "Got you good, didn't it? Man, y'all's reactions were priceless. I wish you could see your faces!"

Santo flips off the camera's blinking red dot. Malachi chuckles again, saying something about how he *couldn't help himself* and that his *followers are going to get a kick out of this,* and then the static of the walkie-talkie disappears, leaving only the ambient hum of crickets and the looping, mournful hoot of a prerecorded barn owl.

Charity lets out a breathy laugh. "See? It's just a stupid joke."

I nod, switching out the grounding cold metal of the Swiss Army knife for the familiar sensation of threading the ratty leather belt loops of Matt's trench coat through my fingers instead. *Inhale through your nose.* Everything is fine. *Exhale through your mouth.* It's not a real body. *Notice how your nostrils sear with the phantom scent of cedarwood and gasoline, and then let it go.* Nothing bad is going to happen to us tonight.

Wait. Gasoline?

I tilt my head, waiting to see if the memory will unfurl itself, but nothing happens. "Okay," I whisper instead, hoping I've successfully staved off the fight-flight-freeze response of my nervous system. "Let's just...keep going. No more jump scares."

"No more jump scares," Charity agrees, and Guinevere and Santo nod. Tobias, however, picks up his lantern and slinks off toward the cabin prints without another word. A pang shoots through my chest as I watch him; he's not even pretending to enjoy this. If I had to guess, he's still brooding over Malachi taking his phone. He has no reason to be so pissed, though. There hasn't been a new *Cedar Creek Confessions* post since this morning, and that had nothing to do with Tobias or any of his friends on the chess team—and everything to do with tonight's invitation.

I redirect my attention to helping Santo, Charity, and Guinevere move the bloodied dummy in order to keep the pepper-inside-my-nose feeling from turning into full-blown tears. Once the Flex Foam body is sprawled out on the surrounding area rug, it looks a lot less intimidating, allowing the three of us to focus on riffling through the trunk's contents. Right now, I'm too dysregulated to fight against the game. I need to discover a valuable clue. Gain back control. Fend off the uncertainty coursing its way through my veins.

"So, what have the rest of you been up to?" Santo asks as we toss a pile of nylon rope, a yellow plastic lemon, and a couple of flannel jackets onto the floor. I know he's trying to mitigate the awkward tension, but it's not exactly working. "You know...since we last saw each other?"

God. I wish Matt were here.

"Oh, the usual," Charity says as we finish our overhaul. There's one last object hidden inside the trunk—an iridescent DVD with hand-drawn flames licking out from the center—and I frown as she sets it aside. "Trying to stop myself from murdering my entire student council cabinet in cold blood. Working on public service projects. Pretending I'm a perfect daughter to boost Mom's House reelection campaign. She pulled a ton of strings to get me this summer internship on Capitol Hill, but I've been fighting with her nonstop about actually going. The older I get, the more I doubt I want to pursue politics, especially with everything that's going on in the US right now. But since that's what my family knows, that's what's expected of me, so it's been...interesting." A private smile flashes across her face. "I did get a full ride to George Washington, though. I'm going in with a political science and public policy double major, but I might, like, switch to philosophy and business once I'm there?" Her doe eyes flick to Santo. "What about you?"

"Rehab," Santo offers, and Charity's smile disappears.

"Oh," she says. "Do they, like, have AA meetings in Italy?"

There's a sinking feeling in the pit of my stomach as I pick up the discarded DVD. I've never found one inside an escape room before. Fake numbers used for landline phone puzzles? Sure. TV dials that need to be rotated a certain way? Definitely. Laser harps controlled by RFID sensors? 100%. But a DVD? No. Never. They're just too easy to fuck up, and the headache from a player group scratching or breaking the disc isn't worth the trouble for most Game Masters—or franchises as a whole, that is.

Prop Wear & Tear: 2.8/5.

That being said, the win objective of every escape room is different. And if our invitations were personalized, and Malachi included the Flex Foam body inside *Arsonist's Revenge* as a practical joke, it's not a stretch to believe that he might be messing with us more than he's letting on. There's only one way to find out, though.

I stand up and move toward the entertainment center, tuning out Santo, Charity, and Guinevere's conversation behind me. There's only so much catch-up about pulling trig and brushing manes that I can stomach before I need to extricate myself from the collective small talk.

Santo doesn't let me escape so easily, though. "What about you, Zamekova?" he asks as I crouch in front of the entertainment center. "How have you spent the past year?"

My fingers tighten around the DVD. *"You'd know if you read my texts, checked your WhatsApp, or opened any of my letters,"* I imagine telling Santo as I scan the knobs and dials attached to the console below the television. But instead of confronting him, I only shrug. "Not doing much. Trying to keep my head above water, mostly."

Charity tilts her head. "And after graduation?"

"Yeah, I'm taking a gap year," I answer, hoping she can't hear the edge in my voice. "My grades weren't so stellar near the end, so it'll be good to figure out what I want to study."

That last part is a blatant lie. I know I want to major in game development at the Savannah College of Art and Design, but I've been too nervous to actually submit my application. SCAD offers rolling admissions year-round, so it's technically not too late for me to go if I get in, but getting publicly caught up in the scandal surrounding BREAKOUT last year—plus the fact that I haven't created a new blog post on *There's No Escape* since the fire—means I doubt they'd accept me even if I managed to get my shit together for long enough to apply. That's a tall order, though; my debilitating grief means that I've only managed to keep down chive-and-cream-cheese bagels for the past three months, and that my dyed hair only looks passable when I dry-shampoo it because I can't expend the energy to wash it anywhere but my sink, and that my family abroad almost never hears from me because most days the thought of sending a simple WhatsApp message to the Czech Republic feels more difficult than breathing. I doubt SCAD would want me. But Decision Day has also already passed, which means that if they don't accept me for their winter quarter in January, I'm not attending college *anywhere* this cycle.

Every time I stare at the online application portal, though, I feel like throwing up. I don't have anything to put in a time-based media portfolio apart from my old escape room reviews, and those don't show anything besides how good I've gotten at criticizing other people's art. And just how passionate can I claim to be about game development, anyway? It's not like I've designed any escape rooms of my own; over the course of my four years at CCHS, I've just gotten paid to attempt them. I might not be talented enough to do what I love, and I definitely can't handle my dream school telling me that. So for now, it's easier to succumb to the fallacy of Schrödinger's college application: If I don't send my portfolio in, they can't accept *or* reject me.

Tobias nods from where he's still scrutinizing the cabin photographs. "That makes sense. I guess most universities don't exactly offer degrees in breaking out of escape rooms, right?"

I force myself to blow out an even breath as Tobias visibly gives up on assessing the photographs, moving to check the HOME, SWEET HOME mat instead. There's nothing under it. "Right."

"You should join me at UT," Santo offers. I glance up from the television console, surprised, and he shoots me a grin from where he's still huddled with Charity and Guinevere. "Get away from Cedar Creek for a while."

I tuck a strand of hair behind my ear, attempting to convey aloofness even as my cheeks warm. "It's still Tennessee."

"Not far enough away, huh? I get it." Santo winks before standing up and moving to the end table to glance over the laminated maps. "In that case, going abroad may clear your head. I've had enough of Italy, though, so I'll take my chances with public health here."

Public health? That's not what Santo wanted to major in last year, but I guess the pivot makes sense after everything he went through with his brother. "Cool. I'm happy for you."

"Yeah, thanks." He shrugs. "I figured it's better than doing nothing."

I inhale, but I'm not sure if it's Santo's comment or the cold air from the HVAC that stings.

"Did you figure out where that goes?" Tobias asks, crouching next to me and peering at the entertainment center.

I jump before curling my fingers around the DVD. "Um, no. Not yet," I say, but Tobias is already pulling the disc from my hands. He feeds it into a hidden slot—*crrrrrk*—and shoots me a condescending look that seems to say, *Are all women this stupid, or is it just you?* Briefly, I consider leaning into the violent streak most journalists in Cedar Creek are convinced I possess and gifting him a second black eye. But then the TV flickers to life, and all the monstrous thoughts swirling through my mind dissipate.

It's a video of the six of us. Grainy, black-and-white, time stamped. Me, Guinevere, Santo, Tobias, Charity, and Matt. Drooping clocks with wavering hands on the floral wallpaper. Tea party chairs adorned with silky bows. Sparkling cork-stoppered vials labeled DRINK ME and miniature plastic fruit tarts labeled EAT ME and in the center of a table, a teapot labeled OPEN ME. Malachi in the control room, like always, watching us over the blinking surveillance cameras.

Blood thrums in my ears. This is in-game footage of the night Matt died in Cedar Creek's BREAKOUT: *Wanderland* escape room. Footage the James-Mays' lawyers claimed didn't exist when the lawsuit went to court. Footage that *shouldn't* exist.

I don't realize I'm shaking until Tobias puts his freckled hand on my arm and asks, "You okay, Steffi?"

"Are you?" I retort. "Look at the goddamn screen!"

I'm watching an echo of myself—a much happier, much healthier, much livelier echo—beam as Matt laughs at whatever joke I just told him. Behind him, Guinevere sneers as she jostles past us. In the background, Santo works with Charity and Tobias to read a laminated limerick about where to place six magnetic teacups in order to open the not-quite-ceramic set piece sitting in the center of the decadent fake food.

In the video, our *Wanderland* countdown passes 59:18. Inside *Arsonist's Revenge*, the LCD screen is at 56:31.

Tobias turns toward the TV. "Santo," he says, and the name is a command. "Gee. Charity. You need to come see this."

I reach toward the TV, my trembling fingers meeting ice-cold glass. Behind me, there's a muttered obscenity, and then movement in my periphery as Santo mumbles words I don't understand into the walkie-talkie. Is he talking to Malachi or to himself? Does it matter? Why the fuck are we here?

The TV shuts off. My heart is pounding so fast, it feels like it's going to explode. "Why did the video stop?" I whisper, my gaze flickering across the dark screen. My mirrored self stares back, wild-eyed, and I struggle to keep my lower lip from wobbling. If the girl in the lobby looked nervous but determined, the version of me reflected in the entertainment center looks terrified now.

"I don't know if your cams caught that, Malachi," Santo says, "but can you explain why the hell there's a DVD from our *Wanderland* game inside *Arsonist's Revenge*?"

Malachi's response is immediate. "What? *Shit*, man. Listen. That's not supposed to be in there." There's a rustling sound on the other end of the walkie, as if Malachi is flipping through a bunch of papers, but I'm not sure if I'm buying the act he's selling. "The mannequin, sure, but otherwise...No, none of this is in my Game Bible. I don't..."

Santo lifts the walkie closer to his burn-scarred mouth. "How is this here, Mal?" he asks. Despite his damaged vocal cords, every hoarse word is carefully enunciated. Practiced. Pointed. Pained.

"Better question: What did we just watch?" Guinevere shrieks. "Your parents claimed they lost everything in the fire!"

"I don't know," Malachi replies, the panicked edge in his voice unmistakable despite the walkie-talkie's sputtering audio. "This isn't...I didn't set that up. It doesn't—*brrrt*—make any *sense*."

"If BREAKOUT uses a cloud-based software to back up its cameras, then I'd say it makes perfect sense," Tobias responds coolly. "Your parents lied about losing the surveillance clips in the lawsuit. And you accessed the archival security data from our game to mess with us tonight, just like *Cedar Creek Confessions* accused you of doing with your videos on @Mal.The.Reel.King."

I can't stop shaking. First the Flex Foam body, and now this.

Charity's eyes widen with shock; now, she looks more like a deer about to be pulverized by oncoming traffic. "Is that true, Malachi?" she asks. "Did you invite us here because of what happened to your family business...Because of what we did last year?"

Guinevere glares at Charity and flicks her wrist smoothly across her neck—the universal symbol for *cut it out*. But it's too late. I snap my head up from the TV screen, my eyes narrowing on Charity's flushed face. "Why? What *did* we do?"

"Nothing," Charity says too quickly, her gaze darting first to Guinevere, then Santo, and finally Tobias before it settles on me. "We were cleared by Sheriff Stallard, Steffi. Remember?"

There's a tense beat where we all stare at one another, and I realize my ex-friends are lying. They're afraid of the footage because its existence proves whatever secrets they buried in the ashes of Cedar Creek's BREAKOUT last spring didn't burn along with Matt's body—instead, they're still out there. And if those secrets were caught on tape, then they might compose a case—an incriminating, damning, concrete case which could change the outcome of an ongoing lawsuit.

I suddenly feel lightheaded. Guinevere's dad is a federal circuit judge. Charity's mother is a member of the House of Representatives. Tobias's parents own Matthews Farms, which supplies produce to several of our local grocery stores, and the Cesari twins' mom manages Pizza Plus, a chain that has a lot of influence in the tri-county area. My parents are immigrants, and they don't hold any local positions of power—except when I think about the trust Dad created to safely store my revenue from *There's No Escape* until I graduate from high school, I realize they may wield more power than I think.

Jesus, my instincts were right—everyone in this room *is* hiding something. And even if this escape room is a setup—even if we're being punished for what happened on the night my best friend died—playing the game means revealing the truth.

Which means my own win objective just changed.

"Malachi?" Santo asks. "Did your parents lie about the footage? Did you lure us here to make us pay?"

"I don't—" Malachi's voice cuts out before fading back in. "....this—*chrrkk*—all. I'm going—*skkkrzzz*—come inside and reset your—okay? If it's—*chrk*—I may need—*chrrkkk*—get help. Before I—*brrrrrt*—let me—back at my...at my...Game Bible..."

"Is he going to let us out of here?" Guinevere demands, grabbing for the walkie-talkie. This time, Santo smacks the hard shell of the device flush against his chest; Gee's outstretched nails close around open air. "Is that what he just said?" Her hurricane eyes are wild. "Tell him not to go anywhere. Tell him to unlock the fucking door!"

Santo holds down the button. "Hey, Mal? Just come get us out of here, okay? Please. Come unlock the door." A pause. "Can you hear me? Over."

But there's no response from the owner's son.

Panic flares in my chest. Right now, I still have time to figure out the truth—the LCD screen is only at 53:43. But if Malachi lets us out of *Arsonist's Revenge* early, then I'm never going to get answers. And I *need* answers. Not just because Matteo Luca Cesari was my best friend, but because *Cedar Creek Confessions* is back.

Because I need to know if one of us killed him.

"Tell him he's, like, cutting in and out?" Charity tells Santo, the overhead floodlights glinting off her expensive pearl earrings. Santo hands her the walkie with a warning glance directed at Guinevere, and Charity raises it to her glossy lips. "Try speaking again, Malachi." There's another crackling sound, and her frown deepens. "We're losing you."

"I can't do this," Guinevere cries, retreating to the open space of the kitchenette. She whirls around, takes two steps forward on the dingy retro red-and-white diamond-shaped kitchen tile, and then falls back. My heart rate spikes just from watching her. "Why is he cutting out? What if he's not coming?"

"He's coming," Santo says, but he doesn't sound completely certain. Through the overhead speakers, prerecorded cicadas hiss and snap at each other. Guinevere is pacing restlessly now, her stiletto fingernails weaving in and out of her scalp.

She's going to mess up her claw clips.

The thought is so absurd, I almost laugh, but the sound gets caught halfway up my throat. None of this is funny.

"We should give Malachi the benefit of the doubt," Charity proposes. "Maybe he's, like, having technical difficulties?"

"Oh yeah? And what about the fucking video we just saw, huh?" Guinevere snaps, stopping in front of the fridge. "Was that a technical difficulty, too?" She pauses, and my attention snags on her beautiful face as her nails unhook themselves from her hair. "What the hell," she murmurs in a completely different voice, and for one dizzying second, I can't place the emotion running through her voice. It's so out of character for Guinevere, so unnatural, that a chill runs down my spine as soon as I identify it:

Fear.

"What?" I ask, trepidation coating the syllable. Guinevere doesn't respond, though, so Santo straightens and strides over to her. So does Charity. And Tobias. And me.

She's staring at a photograph stuck to the fridge with one of the ABC magnets. In it, Matt stands against Cedar Creek's BREAKOUT photo wall with the six of us, his head thrown back in raucous laughter, his sharp face silhouetted against the free-handed lock-and-chain mural that decorated the local franchise of yesteryear. He's wearing the trench coat. One of his arms is effortlessly slung atop my shoulders; the other is curled around Guinevere's waist. Next to her, Santo grins with endearingly crooked teeth. Beside him, Tobias smiles awkwardly while Charity and Malachi throw up matching peace signs, completing a haphazard selfie with our typically behind-the-scenes Game Master at the forefront of the camera.

This is from the first escape room we ever did as a complete group. The one which kick-started our monthly tradition: *Moonshine Cabin*.

Guinevere tears the photograph off the fridge. "What the fuck is this?" she whispers. But next to her, Santo pales. "Flip it over," he instructs. "There's something written on the back."

She does. Pauses. Glances up at me. Looks back down at the premium Kodak paper.

"Well?" Charity prompts.

"Six friends," Guinevere reads, her voice trembling. "Six secrets. One hour to spill them…" She swallows. "Or everyone dies."

• • •

yelp.com | Recommended Reviews: BREAKOUT Escape Rooms Inc.

Located in Cedar Creek, TN | Have you been here?
<u>Write a review!</u>

PLAY THIS ESCAPE ROOM! ★★★★★
Posted by Lillie Snyder at 2:11 AM

My friends and I came here on a whim for a birthday party because Perfect Strike was closed, and we were so glad we did! None of us had ever done an escape room before, but our Game Master was super helpful and his hints let us break out of *Ghost Pirate's Curse* with four minutes left on the clock. Give Malachi a raise, and THANK YOU SO MUCH BREAKOUT!

Response from BREAKOUT Escape Rooms Inc. at 8:22 PM

Thank YOU for coming, Lillie! We're so glad you and your friends enjoyed *Ghost Pirate's Curse*. We hope to see you again! **—The James-Mays**

CHAPTER FIVE

Wednesday, May 20, 2026, 11:08 PM

I can't believe it. Even as I stare at the threat on the back of the photograph, it doesn't feel real. Except it is. It has to be, because so many other impossible things have happened recently. Because *Cedar Creek Confessions* is back online after an eleven-month-long hiatus. Because the allegedly lost footage of our *Wanderland* game exists, at least partially, inside *Arsonist's Revenge*. Because, as Guinevere flips the photograph back over and I fight the anxiety-induced blockage growing in my throat, it's clear there's only one other person in the world who looks like Matt: dark eyes, warm sun-kissed skin, crooked half-smile.

And his pre-burn-scarred face is scratched out in the photo, along with all of ours.

"This," Santo whispers. No mischievous light gleams in his dark brown eyes now; no sly grin curves his waxy mouth. There's just his sharp-edged, ashen face. "This is…"

"Us." Tobias grabs the other side of the photograph to steady Guinevere's shaking hand while Charity's fingers flutter to her open O mouth.

"Are you serious, Malachi?" Guinevere whirls around to bare her teeth at the security camera directly overhead. "This crossed a fucking line!"

The walkie-talkie remains silent, and nausea crawls its way up my clogged throat. Maybe Malachi is too embarrassed to speak on this part of our game. But maybe…

"It's fine," I say, surprised at how level my voice sounds. "It's a prank. A mean-spirited one, sure, but it's like the props we've encountered throughout past BREAKOUT games: The principal's mug shot in *Friday Night Lights* that opened the safe containing our alleged criminal record. The ominous plaque in *Museum Art Heist* that told us which question to ask our live actor security guard in order to receive a skeleton key. The severed foam head hidden inside *Moonshine Cabin* that was only meant to distract us."

For a second, I almost believe the lie.

"Is it?" Charity asks. She bites her lower lip. "Last year, we showed up to the Cedar Creek BREAKOUT to play *Wanderland*. An hour later, Malachi's family business burned to the ground." She fiddles with the end of one of her ash-blond braids. "And the threat on the back of this photograph? It's personal. It's here for a reason. It's..."

"A warning," Santo finishes. I dig my nails into my palms. *Six friends. Six secrets. One hour to spill them, or everyone dies.*

"Where is Malachi?" Guinevere demands. "He's in the control room, right?"

A dark cloud passes over Tobias's bruised face. "Didn't he say he was coming to reset our game?" There's a beat during which Charity audibly whimpers. "Wonder where he is."

"Maybe he's not coming at all," I offer, my gaze locking back onto the fridge. My gut twists as I register the rest of the items stuck to its rusting surface. I *recognize* these.

THE TENNESSEE OBSERVER

Subscribe Today for 15% Off Your Annual Subscription! | Donate | Contact Us

New details released in wake of local business fire: Caused by wiring issues, experts claim

<u>Teenager dead after tragic escape room accident in Cedar Creek, Tennessee</u>

Sevier County Daily: Single mother files lawsuit against BREAKOUT Escape Rooms Inc. for wrongful death of 17-year-old son; "I just want justice."

Guinevere follows my gaze. "These are all about Matt," she says. "These are all clippings of articles that came out in the weeks after he died."

And suddenly, I can't breathe. I'm suffocating, choking on emergency sirens and smoke and the smell of crackling flames, and there are too many eyes on me and the wood-paneled, gingham-curtained walls are closing in. Every story about Matt—the reports on the fire, the updates on the lawsuit, the obit his mom asked us all to contribute to before the funeral—is here, inside BREAKOUT. Names jump out without me looking: *Stephanie Zamekova. Charity Adler. Tobias Matthews. Santo Cesari. Guinevere Mitchell-Moore. Malachi James-May. Matteo Cesari. Matteo Cesari. Matteo Cesari.*

"Zamekova, you good?" Santo asks. His fingers alight on my shoulder, sending pins and needles through the leather of his brother's trench coat, and I'm suddenly reminded of Tobias touching my arm earlier with a nearly identical question. Everyone keeps treating me like I'm about to break, and maybe I am, because all the newspaper headlines about my best friend are in here tonight: Matt dead at seventeen, because of the alleged criminal negligence of BREAKOUT Escape Rooms Inc. His mother, Illaria, suing the James-Mays in the months afterward. Congresswoman Adler publicly standing behind the family-owned business and then switching sides to join the lawsuit. Sheriff Stallard and his too-blue eyes and his lengthy investigation. The GoFundMe for the James-Mays' legal counsel that raised over $50,000, thanks to Charity creating it and Malachi promoting it on his socials with a series of increasingly desperate videos. The badly cleaned windows at CCHS on the day we returned to school, where we could still read the spray-painted words: HE DESERVED IT. The drawn-out court battle and Santo's disappearance and the reemergence of our school's gossip account, *Cedar Creek Confessions*, exactly a month ago.

Don't be pathetic. Don't get stuck. Breathe.

"Yeah," I rasp. The wood-paneled walls zoom out. *Arsonist's Revenge* sharpens. I register the heavy car keys in my pocket, and the soft baby hairs on the nape of my neck, and the slightly damp I LOVE PRAGUE socks that I chose to rewear today instead of doing my laundry because pouring detergent is just one of the many tasks that is now monumentally difficult in the wake of Matt's death. "Yeah, I'm good."

I don't know if it's true. Santo doesn't seem convinced, either, but he nods, his stringy yellow-blond hair flopping into his face, and steps away to give me space. When I refocus, though—when I can actually feel my body again—I realize that nestled among the recognizable clippings which used to swim against the backs of my eyelids on nights I'd wake up screaming, stuck to the bottom of the locked fridge with a NO PLACE LIKE HOME magnet, is one I've written. The final post from my blog.

• • •

THERE'S NO ESCAPE
REVIEWS | WINNING TIPS + TRICKS |
FIND YOUR NEAREST GAME |
CONTACT STEFFI

I almost died in an escape room fire. Now, authorities believe my friends and I set it.

Typing out the words to this post is surreal, but I don't know what else to do. Over the past three years, I've turned my obsession for escape rooms into my life's passion and chronicled the journey for the incredible community I've managed to build here. From compiling beginner-level game hacks through <u>my list of rules for escaping</u> to <u>establishing partnerships with seventeen TERPECA-ranked rooms</u>, this blog has allowed me to form lifelong friendships, build my self-confidence, and live out my dream of sharing my love for escape rooms with others.

But now my best friend is dead.

I don't know what to do except write about it, I guess. So here I am. Writing about it. Because the sheriff of Sevier County is looking into the fire at BREAKOUT Escape Rooms Inc. and blaming my friends—the teammates I played *Wanderland* with—for it, which isn't fair. We did nothing wrong. And they're not considering other options. In fact, they won't even *begin* to consider them without public pressure. So my only power lies in mobilizing my thirteen-thousand-strong audience to fight alongside me for the truth amid this tragedy. The real truth.

With me? Call the sheriff's office at 865-555-0327 or visit seviercountysheriff.com to leave an anonymous message urging the Sevier County Sheriff's Department to investigate alternate causes of the fire at BREAKOUT Escape Rooms Inc. Or tell the owners of BREAKOUT how you feel; the phone numbers of Taliyah May and Randall James are linked below, along with their personal emails.

Thank you for listening, #TheresNoEscapeNation. I hope y'all understand if I take a step back from posting for a while. And please: Tell your friends you love them, while you still can.

Tears well up in the back of my throat. I could quote that blog post in my sleep. I agonized over the wording for hours, trying to figure out how best to suggest that my best friend's death wasn't an accident; but in the end, the police didn't find anything amiss when they interrogated us, so Sheriff Stallard attributed the fire to faulty wiring and hit BREAKOUT with a monetary fine. The department publicly apologized, and the six of us were supposed to just…move on. But I lost Matt along with my memories on that warm spring night, and no one in this room has ever told me why.

A nervous laugh bubbles through my chapped lips. "One of my blog posts is in here, too."

Charity's throat bobs. "So is the most recent *Cedar Creek Confessions* post," she says, tapping a printout of the Instagram caption I just looked at this morning. "This is intentional. Just like the invitations and the fake body and the security footage." She sniffs. "It's here for us. *Arsonist's Revenge.*"

Guinevere's storm-gray gaze cuts to me for the second time in the past minute, and my throat tightens. We should have never come here. I should have never persuaded everyone to play.

"Let's stay calm," Tobias advises, adjusting the bottom of his chess team sweatshirt. His fingers twitch, and I think about the way his unfocused gaze slid over Santo's scars earlier. His black eye. How he's shown up wasted to 11:00 PM escape rooms before. Is he slurring his words, or am I just imagining things? "This may just be a prank, like Steffi said. Malachi—or someone else *Cedar Creek Confessions* targeted—messing with us."

I chew the inside of my cheek as I glance at Santo. He's been devastatingly in love with Malachi ever since Mal agreed to partner with Santo and the rest of our GSA to promote a queer-friendly Spring Fling dance unaffiliated with CCHS last year—and judging from their brief interaction in the lobby earlier, Santo's feelings haven't changed. His inner conflict is clearly visible on his face: We're trapped in BREAKOUT. Malachi is our Game Master. What the hell is happening?

Santo pulls the walkie-talkie up to his mouth and presses the button. "Mal, come in. Are you on your way? Over."

"Sometimes it takes a second," Charity offers when the walkie-talkie stays silent. But the device doesn't crackle to life. Whatever the reason, Malachi's dropped out of contact. Not good.

I look back at the newspaper clippings. "People thought we set that fire," I say, drawing out the words like they might make more sense the longer I turn them over in my mouth.

Tobias scoffs. "Yeah, all the townies thought we did it."

"We're townies, too," Guinevere snarls, "and we didn't." She raises her chin in defiance, but Tobias is right. It was the most prominent theory: We started the fire. We wanted to kill Matt. Except there were a million different rumors that circulated about the six of us after Matteo Luca Cesari died inside BREAK-OUT. And when the general public wasn't blaming us as a collective, they were pinning Matt's death on us as individuals: His twin brother. His girlfriend. His chess rival. His student body president. His Game Master. His best friend.

Santo. Guinevere. Tobias. Charity. Malachi. Me.

"Arguing isn't, like, going to help?" Charity says. "What's done is done." Her voice is too bright. Too soft. Too high. "The sooner we find the keypad code, the faster we forget about this." She glances at me, her gaze measured, and guilt tugs at my parchment-paper throat.

"Do you think Malachi is still here?" Tobias asks. "He could be gone by now."

"*Gone?*" Guinevere repeats. "This is an escape room, and he's our Game Master. His parents own the business. You think he would leave us here alone when he's liable?" Her nails are digging into her neon-soaked upper arms. "I'm sure that would go over well in court. Again."

"Well, not with the new waiver." My voice is hoarser than I hoped it would be, and I immediately wish I hadn't said anything. But we need to talk this out. "I mean, all of us signed it, right? And I'm no lawyer, but it seems to cover the James-Mays' asses well."

Tobias's gaze lowers to the concrete floor. Jesus. I'm going to be sick.

"After the lawsuit started…" Santo starts quietly. "Malachi iced us out, right?"

"I mean, the six of us stopped speaking long beforehand," Guinevere snaps. "The pact—"

"I'm not talking about that," Santo says smoothly, his gaze cutting to the security camera, and Guinevere presses her full lips together. I keep my expression neutral, but mentally I file the information away: *the pact*. "I'm talking about how Malachi stuck his neck out for us last year. He snuck his parents' copied keys, let us into a functional room right before midnight, and monitored our game." A muscle jumps in Santo's jaw, and I tuck my shaking hands back into my pockets. "The entire time he does this, he's being sweet, because"—Santo's breath hitches—"I persuaded him to help us out. But then things go wrong, and there's a fire, and Mal is implicated, so he drops out of contact with us." Santo's dark eyes cut between our faces, his eyebrow piercing catching on the LED lights. "Right?"

"What if Malachi sent us the invitations?" Charity says. "Think about it: He controls our puzzles, the decorations, the monitor, the speakers, the camera, and he has access to the feeds from the control room." She pauses, letting the words sink in. "It's been, what, like a few minutes since he told us he's coming?" She glances up at the countdown, which is now at 53:11. "And he still hasn't let us out. In fact, he hasn't, like, said *anything* in a while."

Charity has a point. Malachi said he didn't send the cards, but he could be lying. While we're all close—the foundation of my friendship with our Game Master, in particular, is built on shared Lunchables, swapped Quizlet links, and long FaceTime discussions about the harsh realities of influencer culture—are we close enough for Mal to let the fire go? For him to forget we razed his livelihood? For him to forgive me for doxing his parents and dragging him into a goddamn *murder investigation*?

Santo nods. "I mean, on the anniversary of the fire, we all arrive at Friendship Springs' BREAKOUT for a room named *Arsonist's Revenge*. And now we're stuck here, and the clues are about us. About the accident. About my brother's death."

"But we chose to play," I add quietly.

I think about *Cedar Creek Confessions*. I think about my best friend's secrets and his lies, and the reaction from the CCHS student body when the truth came out. The accusations that spread like wildfire after the *Star* broke the news of Matt's death: that the six of us were murderers, that the six of us were victims of an extensive cyberbullying plot, that the six of us wanted to enact revenge. That we wanted Matteo Luca Cesari gone.

Are those rumors the reason that Santo is playing the game tonight, despite the fact that BREAKOUT killed his brother? Is he also trying to claw at the shreds of his life before the accident ripped it all apart? Was he hoping that if he entered *Arsonist's Revenge*, Malachi James-May would give him answers? He defended me in the lobby earlier; we'd shared a look. Brain injury–induced hallucinations aside, he has to be here to figure out the truth, too.

"Charity's right." I glance at the photo sitting on the kitchenette. "I don't know if it's a prank or a sick joke, but Malachi's the one who lured us here. He has to be—nothing else makes sense."

I can't believe anything else, either. Over the past year, I've become an expert in grief. The dark, ugly, twisted kind that people don't talk about: overeating, undereating, being unable to bring myself to shower or brush my teeth or change my bedsheets for weeks at a time. Falling asleep in every class period because I spend my nights doomscrolling to avoid my own thoughts or picking at my cuticles until my fingers bleed. There are so many moments, still, where I catch myself about to text Matt before I realize he's gone. I search for his face each time I pass someone in the stairwell at CCHS. I listen for him in the old vinyl records we used to play together. Tomorrow, I know I'll be waiting for his name at graduation.

And it won't come. Apart from the obligatory passing mention (*In Memoriam*) in the printed pamphlet, there will only be staggering silence. All those people sitting in the stands of the LeConte Center. The empty weight folded around where he used to be.

"It could be Malachi. It could be someone else. Until we have more data, we shouldn't jump to conclusions." Tobias frowns. "I mean, the James-Mays are franchising, right? They're trying to expand their business to Nashville, and even beyond Tennessee. I don't see why their son would risk their business opportunities by violating BREAKOUT's protocol." His expression darkens. "Besides, Matt made a lot of enemies before he died."

All the people featured on *Cedar Creek Confessions* come back to me: Alyssa Hayes. Jacob Webber. Student Resource Officer Debbie Clinton. Catherine Oxendine. Mr. Foxfield. The leveled accusations and the amateur exposés and the blowout consequences. Alyssa's acceptance to Stanford was rescinded after the *Cedar Creek Confessions* post about her B&E went live. Webber lost his scholarship to play lacrosse at Calvin University once *Cedar Creek Confessions* targeted him. SRO Clinton got fired for tackling a student without probable cause—a charge that

Principal Buchanan would've been all too happy to sweep under the lumpy rug hiding the rest of our high school's secrets if the superintendent hadn't been made aware of the viral video *Cedar Creek Confessions* managed to obtain from the hallway security cameras. Catherine's family-owned sandwich shop went under after the account exposed her for forgetting to wear gloves to HOSA competitions—*because if she's not practicing proper handwashing on her patients, why should we trust her to make our subs?* Foxfield was put on administrative leave for his involvement in last year's senior prank. And at least a half dozen other faces I can't recall right now. All the people whose lives were forever altered because Matt determined they needed to pay for the crimes he'd decided they'd committed.

God. If this isn't our Game Master's doing—at the very least, if Malachi isn't working alone—then our list of suspects just got ten times longer. Not to mention that outside of the notorious gossip Instagram account Matt ran, there are a slew of other locals I'm sure wouldn't mind seeing the six of us suffer: Laurel Harkness, the hounding reporter from the *Tennessee Star* who refused to take no for an answer after last year's fire. All the men that Santo left heartbroken on his quest to make Malachi jealous. Every opponent Tobias crushed during his three-year stint on the chess team. The constituents Charity stepped on during her meteoric rise to head CCHS as our senior class president. Every unsuspecting BREAKOUT player who ended up clipped and posted on @Mal.The.Reel.King. The jaded subscribers who sent me hate mail after I shuttered *There's No Escape.*

"I know Mal," Santo says, interrupting my spiraling thoughts.

"And the timing is definitely suspicious, and his feelings about us might have changed in the past year. But honestly, this whole setup...the invitations and the security footage and the photograph? This isn't him." He tips his chin to the Flex Foam body. "Cheap practical effects? Sure. That has Malachi written all over it. But blackmail? That's too far."

"Be reasonable," Guinevere hisses. "Who else could be behind this? No one except Malachi has the authority and the resources to mess with a game room on this scale."

"Unless there's something going on?" I ask, finding the courage to be bold. "If someone has a confession to make...If someone has something they'd like to say...now's the time."

"Steffi, what are you talking about?" Charity purses her glossy lips. "If this is about that Instagram account coming back online, we've already talked about it."

"What? We have?"

"Yeah," Charity says. "Well, the rest of us did, before you came tonight." The words hit me like a one-two punch. *They discussed it without me.* "We're not running *Cedar Creek Confessions*. Our only motive related to the fire is wanting to move on from it. But there are people in this county who won't let us—I mean, just look at those articles!" Her throat bobs. "And you know who they are."

I turn my focus back to the battered fridge. The articles decorating it are clearly handpicked for our personalized murder board, but apart from the fact that they each have to do with our friend group and the death that tore us apart, there's nothing obviously off about them. They're just mundane printouts. Unless...

"Actually, I don't think the newspapers are only here to

freak us out," I tell Charity, scrutinizing the details of the faded articles—the dates, the captions, the photos. A lot of the time, being good at escape rooms hinges on paying attention, noticing patterns, and forming connections. It's not just about luck and timing, although that can definitely be part of it. Instead, it's about seeing the world differently. And maybe it's because I'm a little weird, but I've always had a knack for that.

"What do you mean, Steff?" Santo asks.

"Well, there's a wordlock on the lockbox by the coatrack and the woven wastebasket, right?" I point to the opposite corner of the room. "So maybe these articles are part of *Arsonist's Revenge*, and we can get closer to escaping just by playing the game with our new and, uh, more...personalized clues."

"Maybe," Santo acknowledges. "Or maybe they're just here to mess with us."

But I see it. "No," I insist, scanning the articles before I turn toward the group. "Where's the chalkboard?"

Charity hands it to me, along with a piece of white chalk, her fingertips touching mine for the briefest of moments, and I offer her a nod. There's a crowd watching me now, I realize as I turn back to the newspapers. My ex-friend group may be rooting for me to solve this puzzle; they may be secretly hoping I fail. Either way, I can't let it faze me.

Because some of the headlines are printed in a slightly smaller font size.

I scribble letters without even referencing the chalkboard, my eyes darting between headlines: The *s*, the *t*, and the *a* in "Main Line Sprinklers Failed to Activate, Chief Fire Marshall Reports."

Two *c*'s, two *a*'s, and an *i* in "Emergency Medical Services Arrived on Scene 13 Minutes After Fire Began." The *e* and *d* in "Foul Play Suspected." Two *n*'s, another *i*, another *t*, and the *w* in "Community Craves Answers in Wake of Teen's Tragic Death."

"How many letters are on the wordlock again?" I ask, already starting to whisper-count. I erase a ballooning *d* that looks too much like an *o* with my pointer finger and start over. My chalk penmanship isn't stellar on a good day, but it's especially poor with a ticking clock over my head: 49:34.

Across the room, Tobias calls, "Eight."

My vision swims, but my mind remains maddeningly blank. Usually, I'm a pro at word games. When our group chat was still active, no one would play Anagrams with me after Tobias traded in his Android for an iPhone and we could finally send Game-Pigeon requests back and forth, because I'd always win. But standing here, with my ex-friends' gazes boring into me, I can't seem to think of a single word in the English language containing the fifteen letters printed on the blackboard-painted cardboard in front of me. *INCIDENTS*? No, that's nine letters. *ANTIDESSICATED* is only fourteen. Jesus. Why isn't my brain functioning properly?

Charity's warm breath hits the shell of my ear. "What about *IT WAS AN ACCIDENT*?"

A chill goes through my body. "Try *ACCIDENT*," I direct, turning, and six seconds later Tobias pops the iron shackle and starts removing a conglomeration of items from the lockbox: a metal square, a glittering bunch of plastic grapes, and a small brass key.

"Well, it worked," he says, laying out the objects one by one. "I don't love that the word to unlock it was related to us, though."

Even though I can't believe I didn't recognize the trick earlier—the content of the newspapers rattled me more than I'd like to admit—I'm glad we're finally getting somewhere. If every targeted clue within *Arsonist's Revenge* is still a puzzle solution, then we can find the keypad code and make it out of here before midnight.

My excitement is short-lived once I realize the rest of the players aren't celebrating; instead, they all look vaguely sick. None of us are able to deny the inevitable any longer: the printouts, the photograph, the name of the escape room itself. Malachi being so unfazed about us waltzing through the front door of his family business a year after the first location burned down with us in it. The security camera footage on the DVD. Him letting us back into BREAKOUT despite the lawsuit.

God, I can't believe this is happening. As if it hasn't been bad enough, dreading this day, this horrible anniversary. As if my phone didn't immediately show me the emergency lights and laughing selfies labeled ONE YEAR AGO as soon as I turned off my alarm this morning. As if Matt's face isn't emblazoned on the backs of my eyelids every time I close my eyes.

As if I didn't stand outside the Cedar Creek strip mall for twenty-six minutes, waiting for everyone to show up, assuring Malachi between staring at my reply-barren messages that *They'll be here, just give them another minute, please, they said they'd come.*

My heartbeat staccatos at this new snippet of memory, but the more I try to focus on expanding the image, the more unpleasant ones from my court appearance bubble to the surface of my mind. I testified against the James-Mays. We all did, because Matt's death was an accident. *IT WAS AN ACCIDENT.*

My throat goes dry. But if it wasn't...
What else could it be?

• • •

The Tennessee Star

MENU | NEWS | WEATHER | SPORTS | LOG IN | SEARCH

Teenager dead after tragic escape room accident in Cedar Creek, Tennessee

By Laurel Harkness | Thursday, May 22, 2025, 1:42 PM UTC−5

A birthday party turned deadly last Wednesday after a local escape room went up in flames.

CEDAR CREEK, TN (KSIB)—Tragedy struck this week in Cedar Creek after a fire broke out within BREAKOUT Escape Rooms Inc., killing 17-year-old Matteo Cesari. Four other teenagers were injured during the blaze. One additional teen was hospitalized.

The teenagers originally gathered inside the franchise to celebrate the birthdays of Matteo and Santo Cesari, two teenagers from Cedar Creek. According to BREAKOUT Escape Rooms Inc.'s website, its escape rooms are available to book for "private events, corporate team-bonding exercises, and parties." The location first opened in 2016. It is headed by longtime Cedar Creek residents Randall James and Taliyah May. A second branch in Pigeon Forge is also operated by James and May.

The fire is believed to have started within the escape room itself, although its cause is not currently known.

First introduced to the public in 2007 by Takao Kato of SCRAP Entertainment Inc., escape rooms are interactive puzzles in which players are typically locked inside a room voluntarily for one hour, during which the players must search for clues hidden within the room in order to escape. In recent years, these experiences have only grown in popularity. In the United States alone, there are an estimated 2,000 active escape room locations.

Construction on a tertiary franchise location in Friendship Springs, Tennessee, is currently underway, although there is no news yet on how the Cedar Creek fire will impact BREAKOUT's future plans. BREAKOUT did not respond to a request to comment by email or phone prior to the publication of this story.

The cause of Matteo Cesari's death is believed to be smoke inhalation. An investigation is currently ongoing.

This story will be updated as we learn more.

CHAPTER SIX

Wednesday, May 20, 2026, 11:13 PM

Santo shakes his yellow-blond head. "I know I advocated for playing the game earlier, but we need to forfeit. This is getting too personal; we should leave."

Tobias dips his chin. "Agreed."

"It's, like, for the best?" Charity says. "Especially since Malachi isn't here to reassure us. I doubt he'll be upset that we left. But I'll see y'all tomorrow at graduation!"

I open my mouth, ready to protest, but Guinevere smirks at me before I can lay out an argument for why, exactly, I believe we should all stay in the disturbing room. "Looks like it's four to one," she says before she walks over to the emergency RELEASE mechanism, flips up the translucent plastic cover, and slams her manicured hand down on the button. She waits a second. Four. Six. Eight.

The door doesn't open.

"What the hell?" Guinevere mutters. She hits the button again. The magnetized door stays locked.

Again.

Nothing happens.

Again.

On the LCD screen above us, the countdown continues ticking: 46:53. 46:52. 46:51.

My stomach does a nauseated backflip. If the RELEASE button isn't working, then we're actually trapped in here. Me, with my faulty memories. My estranged friends, with the secrets they've been keeping.

"Try it gently," Charity suggests. "Remember the two-finger rule?"

"Fuck your two-finger rule," Guinevere growls, her voice rising in agitation. *SLAM. SLAM. SLAM.* "Why the *shit* isn't this working?"

"Hang on, let me see." Shadows from the lantern dance across the walls as Tobias joins Guinevere, but Santo beats him to the mechanism itself. His chipped fingernails pry off the red casing of the RELEASE button, revealing a jumble of exposed copper filaments dangling from a protruding tangle of black, red, and yellow cords underneath. I inhale. That doesn't look good.

"Holy shit," Santo breathes. "It's the wires. They're cut."

"Move," Guinevere demands, pushing him aside. "What do you mean, cut?"

"It's a clean break on every single one," Santo continues, his hoarse voice pitching higher in panic, "which means they didn't fray—they were tampered with." His cross earring glints in the light. "On purpose."

"Jesus," I whisper. "Wait. Do any of you remember if the wires were like this when Malachi let us into the room?"

"It's not like any of us were messing with the RELEASE mechanism then," Charity says, "so why does it matter?"

Santo frowns. "Because if the wires were cut before, then it means Mal set us up," he says, meeting my gaze across the room. "But if they were cut after... it means one of us would be at fault."

Even in the swimming glow of the LED lights above us, I can see everyone's face pale. I draw in a ragged breath. The entire value proposition behind paying to lock myself in an escape room for an hour lies in knowing what I signed up for, which is typically spaceships or haunted houses or jail cells. Anatomy classrooms and serial killer lairs and ancient Egyptian tombs. But all of those take place in a safe, controlled, supervised environment. The room should never actually be *locked*, especially when most franchises are increasingly leaning toward a "no real locks" policy to legally cover their asses.

Goddamnit.

Charity glances at Tobias suspiciously; Guinevere's thunderstorm glare darts first to her dead boyfriend's brother, and then to me. I stare at the silent walkie-talkie clutched between Santo's fingers and swallow my own rising hysteria. The clock is only at 46:35 and we're already turning on one another. At the same time, the emergency exit isn't working—and we know it was deliberately tampered with—which means tonight is escalating. Building and building and building. And there has to be a responsible culprit.

"Steffi," Charity breathes, her voice as high and soft as ever, "do you still have that Swiss Army knife attached to your keys?"

"Yeah, why?" I ask, sliding a protective hand inside Matt's leather trench coat. I know what she's implying and I don't appreciate it. "I didn't cut the wires. And if someone borrowed my knife, I would know."

Except when I pull out my car keys to prove my innocence, they're lighter than usual. And as I look at the familiar attachments on my carabiner—the small rubber duck keychain I won in eighth grade through Jump Rope for Heart, my student ID card holder with my baby-faced freshman year photo, my Jeep Wrangler's fob—I realize the Swiss Army knife isn't among them.

"What the hell? I just had it." I lick my lips. "Okay, very funny, Charity. You got me. Can I...uh...have my knife back now?"

But Charity's gaunt face is already blanching. "It was you," she whispers. "It was *you*."

"What? No! I've had my keys in my coat this whole time. I didn't..." Except everyone is staring at me, and my skin is prickling with unwanted attention. "Y'all, come on. This is ridiculous."

"You just said if someone borrowed your knife, you would know!" Charity juts out her chin, exposing the keloid scars that flash across her upper chest like lightning.

"Yeah, because I didn't think it was *gone!*" I close my eyes and force myself to inhale. Nice deep, slow breaths. Everything is going to be fine. It will be fine. It *has to* be fine.

"Look," Santo says, holding up his ring-adorned hands, "we could all use a minute to chill out. Let's take a breather to spread around the room, search for clues we missed, and work toward opening these locks. There's nothing—"

"No," Charity says coldly. "Things don't just, like, disappear?" She crosses her arms. "We're in an enclosed space, which means someone has the knife." Her delicate throat bobs. "Everyone turn out your pockets."

Tobias blinks. "What?"

"You heard me," Charity says, her usual baby-voice upspeak newly soft and serious. "Turn. Out. Your. Pockets."

"We're in an escape room," Tobias says with a sniffle, and I wonder if his chronic sinus problems are acting up again, if he's secretly huffing Flonase, or if he's just being a dramatic asshole. "There's so many places to hide a Swiss Army knife in here, Charity. And besides, do you think that if any of us actually cut the wires, we'd be stupid enough to keep the knife on us?"

Charity cocks her head. "I don't know," she says, her words taking on a dangerous edge as she reaches into her houndstooth-patterned blazer and withdraws a tampon, a grapefruit-flavored ChapStick, and the keys to her BMW. "But I'm willing to find out."

I close my eyes. Our infighting was bad enough when we were friends, with all the drama from *Cedar Creek Confessions* and the squabbles over Perfect Strike games and the routine bullshit of our day-to-day disagreements. Once, Matt blew up our *Minecraft* server after Tobias gloated too much over the outcome of one of their Chess.com matches, and I had to play mediator for a week between the two of them, even though I was the one who paid out of pocket to host the realm. When Guinevere first started up her Etsy shop to sell her resin moth-wing jewelry, Charity asked so many questions about her target market that Gee left our group chat and refused to rejoin it until Charity apologized to her face—and bought a set of black swallowtail earrings to show that she meant it. Malachi and I have had long arguments over the ethics of paid promos up at the town water tower; Charity threw a fit targeted at all of us when we didn't help her hang up SBP campaign posters nonstop during the election junior year; Santo's had issues with Tobias's general know-it-all energy. That's what a friend group does, though. People rub each other the wrong way sometimes, but you stick it out, because being temporarily uncomfortable is the price you pay for community.

Now, though, the six of us haven't properly interacted since Matt's death, which means we also have 365 days of built-up baggage between us. And I have no idea how to manage that much lingering resentment anymore.

Guinevere breathes out a nervous laugh. I half-expect her to take Charity's side, accuse me of slicing up the RELEASE mechanism, and demand that I strip in front of everyone to prove I don't still have the knife on my person, but she doesn't move. "Are you serious?" she asks, and this time, her ire is directed at our student body president. "We don't have time for you to lead a little search party, Charity. What we *need* to be doing is asking Malachi why he cut the wires in the first place." She raises her glare to the security camera. "Do you hear us, Mal? I know you did this. And if you try anything funny, my dad's attorney is going to eviscerate this shithole."

Our Game Master doesn't answer, and I swallow. I'm not sure about his intentions, but I know we need to stay calm. Just because *Arsonist's Revenge* has become more...tailored over the course of the past fourteen minutes doesn't mean we should automatically assume the worst. I know escape rooms, and this is still an escape room. We can still escape.

"Malachi," Guinevere demands again, the anger laced through her voice as familiar to me as the holes spiderwebbing through my pilling band T-shirt, "you can't ignore us forever." She aims a kick at the magnetized door, but her boot doesn't even dent it. It's industrial-grade, just like everything else the James-Mays upgraded during the reno. And if we can't get the door open, we're not going to be able to leave.

Tobias crouches until he's eye level with the destroyed wires. "The way I see it, we have three options. We can try repairing the internal wiring mechanism, we can keep playing the game in order to find the keypad code—assuming there still *is* a keypad code, which is risky, knowing the room's already been altered in several ways—or we can force the door." His right eye twitches. "With the way this looks, fixing the wires is a long shot. Continuing to play is questionable, too, because it's not a stretch to assume that *Arsonist's Revenge* has been modified to prevent the possibility of escaping. But breaking down the door is impossible, because it's magnetized."

"And without a working emergency exit," I add, "the only way to override the door lock is through the Game Master's master key or the control room console."

"What about guessing the keypad code?" Santo suggests. "Can we try inputting numbers at random?"

"Even if we only need four numbers to unlock the door, that's ten thousand possible permutations. With five, it's one hundred thousand." Tobias glances upward, his hazel-brown eyes actively calculating. "Assuming there are no repeated numbers increases our odds a little—one out of five thousand forty for four digits, and one out of twenty-seven thousand two hundred sixteen for five digits. But even at an input rate of one combination for every three seconds—which is generous—we'd need about five times the seconds we currently have to cycle through each one."

Guinevere punches four numbers into the keypad sensor: 6-9-6-9. The mechanism flashes red; the door remains locked. She tries another combination: 0-0-0-0. Red again. Her fingers gravitate toward 1-1-1-1 next, but Tobias stops her before she can input it.

"Don't try any more," he warns. "We might only have three attempts."

I lick my lips. "So our only option is the second one, then: keep playing the game to find the keypad code."

"What a great deduction from the girl with permanent brain damage," Guinevere retorts. "Our Game Master is threatening to kill us if we don't reveal our secrets, but oh sure, let's breeze through *Arsonist's Revenge!*"

I grimace. I've always known that friendship breakups can hurt more than romantic ones, but with Guinevere, I feel like I experienced both at the same time. If anything was ever slowly brewing between us, though—our late-night gaming sessions, the jokes we both made about how she should just leave Matt for me, all the times she reacted to a text I sent in the group chat when everyone else let my quips go ignored—the TOD on our toxic, vaguely sapphic more-than-friendship is the night her boyfriend died. Maybe it's because she felt guilty for leading me on while she was dating someone else, and that guilt couldn't withstand Matt's death. Maybe it's because she never actually liked me in the way I wanted her to. Maybe it's because I'm a little delusional and completely imagined our entire not-exactly-a-relationship in my head. Whatever the reason, I'll be okay with not knowing. But I won't be okay with leaving Friendship Springs—with leaving BREAKOUT—without understanding the specifics of my exact involvement in the devastating fire last year.

Guinevere's gaze moves back to the photograph, and I know she's also remembering the flames that destroyed everything: alleged video recordings, six figures' worth of audiovisual equipment, her love life. "This is a vendetta," she continues. "We're at Malachi's mercy. And if he's already succeeded in trapping us in here…" She narrows her eyes. "There's no telling what he can carry out next."

"Fine," Charity bites out. "Then what if we tried…I don't know, just talking to Mal? We still have the walkie-talkie. We might be able to convince him that we're innocent." She blinks. "We were all there on the night Matt died, but that isn't a crime. We were cleared by the sheriff. So if this is some weird penance thing, why not make sure our Game Master, like, knows that?"

Attempting to reason with Malachi is definitely an option. I take a deep breath, attempting to ignore the danger prickling the nape of my neck. There's just over forty-five minutes left for me to recover my *Wanderland* memories and gain the closure I desperately need. No matter what my ex-friends want to do, I need to stay here until I pry the full truth about Matt's death out of them. One way or another. One morsel of crucial information at a time.

"Just, like, think about it?" Charity says, her voice light as she picks up the weird square object from the eight-letter lockbox. Her watch instantly sticks to it—it must be a magnet. Charity seems to realize this, too, because her forehead creases as she walks over to the garbage disposal switch by the kitchenette. "If Malachi is trying to turn on us, then it might be time to tell this town the whole story. Get ahead of the blackmail. Because, like, guys? I don't want to lie anymore." She tucks a stray strand of ash-blond hair behind her ear, and the LED lights catch on her Tennessee River pearl earrings as she lifts the magnetic square against the disposal switch.

CHRKKKKKK!

Blood explodes over my face. Someone screams, and maybe it's me, but I only register short-burst images: pulp, bone, ooze.

Splattered walls. Breathless silence. And on the tiled floor of the *Arsonist's Revenge* kitchenette, the slumping, mangled body of my childhood best friend.

Charity Noelle Adler is dead.

● ● ●

yelp.com | Recommended Reviews: BREAKOUT Escape Rooms Inc.

Located in Friendship Springs, TN | Have you been here?
Write a review!

Family-friendly fun! ★★★★★
Posted by Diana Weider at 1:12 PM

The room we did was well-polished and immersive. My kids and I would absolutely book another, and I'll also be recommending it to my clients as a fun de-stress activity!

CHARITY

184 Days Before the Accident

I'm only here because of Steffi.

Growing up, after we got over the four-square incident, the two of us were close. We went to the same church potlucks, liked the same jankily animated Barbie movies, and played the same co-op video games: *Guitar Hero*, *Mortal Kombat*, *The Sims*. We had our birthdays at the same venues: bowling alley; Dollywood; our houses, swapping giggle-whispered secrets in the dark. But now, all we share are the memories of a childhood where we hadn't yet outgrown each other. That, and a lunch period where Steffi is clearly more interested in discussing the latest *Cedar Creek Confessions* post—this one about Jacob Webber and his disgusting nudes-swapping lacrosse team group chat—than the logistics of hosting a student body presidential candidate debate on *Warrior Minutes*.

"Jesus." Steffi bows her head as if in prayer. "May that fucking homophobe never touch a lacrosse stick—or any girl in a fifty-mile radius—ever again."

"He's a senior," Malachi adds, crunching a baby carrot between his teeth. "I just checked his LinkedIn—he's already signed to a D3 school in Michigan, according to this grammatically egregious post, so this may not even mess things up for him. Though maybe it's time to add a child porn–distributing blond athlete to one of my videos."

"Remember what happened with Alyssa Hayes?" Tobias looks up from Game Review on Chess.com, apparently deciding this conversation is interesting enough for him to engage in. "There's no evidence that the group chat was leaked internally. Which means that unless *Cedar Creek Confessions* legally obtained the screenshots—which I doubt—the accusations against Webber won't hold up in court."

Guinevere makes a face. "You'd be surprised," she says, probably because her dad—whom we all, including Gee, call Your Honor—had her at fifty and has presided over more federal circuit cases than he knows what to do with. That doesn't matter too much to my mom, though, who's convinced that Judge Mitchell-Moore is currently at the height of his career, as a result, whenever our parents get together, every hangout becomes an impromptu photo op. I can't say I blame my mom too much for that, though. After all, the older I get, the more I realize just how much I've inherited her insatiable taste for both power and prestige.

Next to Guinevere, Matt's lips curl upward. "Well, I guess we'll just have to wait and see."

I tug at the fraying friendship bracelet cutting into the skin of my bony wrist to avoid staring down my uneaten CCHS-provided lunch: a tray of gut-churning nachos slathered with gelatinous fake cheese, a whole wheat peanut butter sandwich (which, ew, carbs), and a nauseating fruit cup that looks like it's 50 percent formaldehyde.

I don't like that Matt is here. Along with joining us for lunch at our usual table, he and his brother now walk us to class, carpool with us to Pal's Sudden Service after school for Dr. Enuf and frenchie fries drowning in an off-brand version of Lawry's Seasoned Salt (both of which I refuse to touch), and join us at Perfect Strike on Tuesday nights for bowling. Despite the fact that I've witnessed Santo nearly total my car multiple times in the upperclassmen parking lot, I don't mind him—he's sharp-witted, can name at least twelve US presidents, and plays off Malachi and Tobias well—but Matt isn't doing me any favors when it comes to winning the popular vote. Right now, I need to be zeroed in on focus-grouping slogans and figuring out which issues I want to frame my candidate platform around as a bisexual white girl who needs Young Life, the Gay-Straight Alliance, *and* Future Farmers of America on her side, not associating with the trench coat–wearing, greasy-haired new kid that the girls in my AP Comparative Government and Politics class refer to as "school shooter" under their breaths.

"And besides," Matt continues, directing his attention to Tobias as he stabs a spork into the communal apple sitting in the center of our lunch table, "it doesn't matter if the police take the account's word for it. The court of public opinion rules every time."

I clear my throat. "But isn't *Cedar Creek Confessions* basically promoting hearsay? I mean, like, I know it's just a gossip account," I say, collecting myself. My mom's advice echoes through my head: *If you pretend to be dumber than you actually are, then you'll force people to underestimate you, and that's how you can catch them off guard for long enough to get what you want.* "But it's also a little unconstitutional, right? Like, where are the safeguards? The fact-checkers? The students daring to stand up to these...unfounded claims?"

"That's the thing, though." Steffi's eyes are bright as they lock on mine. "The claims aren't unfounded, Charity."

"True," Santo says. "Whoever *Cedar Creek Confessions* is, you know they always bring receipts."

Matt smirks. "It's almost like they know what they're doing," he adds, and my eyes narrow at him across the table. He stares back at me, his gaze measured, and then he stabs another spork into the apple right in front of me. Amazing.

I know enough about high school politics to recognize when my opinion is unwanted, so I admit defeat and pull out my phone. It's stupid; I shouldn't have time for rumors. Unfortunately, if I want to stay at the top of the Cedar Creek student government pecking order and keep my résumé in shape for college application season, I need to be prepared to act on everything our locally notorious gossip columnist dishes out. Because gossip *is* political. Anyone who claims otherwise is lying to themselves.

"You're both right," Steffi says as I swipe up to unlock the screen. "At first, I thought the account was just a fad. But it's actually impacting the student body in a lot of ways." She frowns. "Yeah, wow. Maybe we should run a piece on it for *Warrior Minutes*."

"Right after you finalize a date for the debate, right?" I ask with a saccharine smile.

"Sure," Steffi says distractedly. "I still don't have one, by the way, but I'll let you know as soon as I hear back from Ms. Henson."

My smile stretches. "Great."

I glance over at the double doors leading to the courtyard, where Mr. Foxfield is on lunch duty, and meet his gaze for a second before my eyes flick back to my phone screen. The Wi-Fi in the cafeteria is always spotty, which means I'm forced to assess the hotspot options and pick the lesser of three evils: *getyourownshit* (Matt's), *what's your password* (Steffi's), and *iPhone* (Tobias's). At least his network isn't private.

I connect my phone and check my messages. No new ones since this morning's *Cedar Creek Confessions* update.

"Charity, are you going to eat that?" Malachi asks, pointing to my untouched nachos. I shake my head and push the checkered carton toward him with a sigh.

"All yours."

God. I understand that the high school political machine runs on this shit, and a group chat made exclusively for student athletes to swap photos that technically count as child pornography is a huge fucking deal, but Steffi agreed to iron out debate details with me during lunch and instead all she's done for the past fifteen minutes is flirt with Guinevere and encourage Matt's stupid analysis of the Instagram account that cropped up a few weeks ago and that everyone is now obsessed with.

I pick up my whole wheat sandwich as a last resort and nibble at the crust with my teeth. The thing is, *Cedar Creek Confessions* isn't even that original. We've had anonymous gossip accounts at CCHS before—we're a high school with about nine hundred students nestled deep in the mountains of East Tennessee and are locally renowned for shit-smeared bathroom stalls, girls who get White-Claw drunk and roll their Jeeps off twisting mountain roads, and abortions that happen in secret across state lines. There's a lot to talk about all the time, and because most of us have gone through K–12 together, everyone knows everyone. Which means everyone's business is open to public scrutiny.

As a student body presidential candidate, part of my job description is keeping tabs on the whispered threats, bitchy rumors, and targeted half-truths that run like sewage through the hallways of this school. Knowledge is power, after all, and in this case, knowledge also helps me tailor my campaign pitches. It's easier to gain a vote after I approach Brandon Reid with promises to stock two-ply toilet paper in every school bathroom (contingent on my election) when I know he's the one relying on it to wipe feces off his hands after defacing school property. Despite my targeted advertising, though, most of my information comes from the network of whispers I personally collect from band kids, theater geeks, good Southern-boy Christian jocks, goth girls, future dropouts, and eavesdropping art teachers. That takes real effort.

Occasionally, though, some *Gossip Girl* wannabe will start circulating an anonymous form within the halls, and a corresponding account that posts screenshots from it will surge in popularity. But then the form owner will burn out, or get exposed and abandon the account, or start posting pictures of people's pets for money, so it never reaches critical mass.

Except this time is different. Because instead of simply posting other people's nasty takes, *Cedar Creek Confessions* collects multiple submissions on the same topic before making their own post, with their own commentary, detailing the most egregious incidents. I know, because I submitted my own form—just to try it, just to see—and nothing happened. It's been three weeks since my celebrity blind about *There's No Escape* got sent in, and there hasn't been even a murmur of the blog's scandal—or Steffi—in any of my classes.

I guess it wasn't wild enough to warrant a takedown. As a result of the thoroughness of whoever is behind the account, though, the followers of *Cedar Creek Confessions* are rabid. People are whipped into a frenzied mob whenever there's a new update, which means influence. Power. Like, everything I want.

Which also means that if I can find out who runs the account and use their format against my competition for SBP, I'm guaranteed to win the election. And becoming student body president will give my Common App essays the boost they need to help me get into a college as far away from Cedar Creek—and the disordered eating habits borne out of my image-obsessed mom's constant politicking—as physically possible.

Steffi has just put in her earbuds when Guinevere snatches one. "What are we listening to?"

"The Killers. *Sawdust*. Same as always."

"Still?" Guinevere's lips quirk. "Haven't you had their album on repeat since, like, homecoming?"

"Stalker," Steffi says. She tilts her device to engage the privacy screen. "Nosy, too."

Matt scowls, stabbing a third spork into the apple, but Guinevere doesn't seem to notice—or if she does, she doesn't seem to care. Instead, she leans her head toward Steffi's free ear. "I'll have you know your Spotify listening history is public information," she murmurs, and Steffi bites back a smile.

Santo's eyebrows rise slightly; as for me, I don't even hide my eye roll. Do they think we're stupid? Anyone can see there's something going on between the two of them, but maybe I shouldn't be so worked up. Guinevere and Matt only went on one date—he asked her out a couple weeks ago, but I've had no time to debrief with Gee because the Cult of Student Council runs my life. I should probably tell her to break up with him and keep her dignity intact. But it's not Matt I'm mad about.

I'm about to put my phone face down on the table and attempt to at least lick off some of the peanut butter from my glorified Uncrustable when a text from my mom comes through: *Don't forget about dinner on Saturday with the Buchanans after Habitat for Humanity. Do you still fit into that white dress from freshman year? Bring it for afterward. There will be photographers!*

My stomach clenches, and I can physically feel myself losing the little appetite I had as I set down my uneaten sandwich. I'm still not at my goal weight; I still look terrible in all of my mom's campaign photos. Instead of dwelling on it, though, I just quietly pack up my lunch. Matt glances at me. "You okay, Charity?"

"Yeah," I say. "Just not hungry."

"Oh my God," Santo whispers, drawing Matt's attention away from my uneaten food. "Don't look now, but Alyssa just stood up from her table. I think the other cheerleaders are finally kicking her out because of the *Cedar Creek Confessions* post. You know, the one about the crickets."

Malachi nods. "I heard they're not even letting her walk at graduation. Tragic, right?"

"Poor girl," Guinevere says, watching her go, but there's a hint of mirth in her voice as her eyes trail Alyssa's sobbing form out of the cafeteria.

"Well, good thing that's not us." Malachi grins.

I suppress a shudder. Not yet, at least.

"Listen," Malachi continues, crunching one of my uneaten nachos between his teeth. "If y'all are sick of bowling, we can head over to BREAKOUT after school and see if I can slot us in for a room. Y'all haven't played *Moonshine Cabin* yet, right?"

Steffi lights up at the suggestion. Ever since her dad took her to her first escape room, she's been addicted. The only reason she's even working at the bowling alley is to save up money for *more*—just last month, she took a weekend trip to Georgia to try a new interactive heist-themed room and review it for her blog. It would be endearing if she weren't so insufferable about it. Or if she wasn't so focused on building up her own ventures that she stopped having time to help out with mine.

"Great idea," she says approvingly. "We haven't done an escape room in a while, and it might be good to get our minds off of *Cedar Creek Confessions*." She smiles. "Besides, Santo and Matt haven't played one with us yet. We need to initiate them, you know? It's long overdue."

Matt blinks. "What?"

"Don't worry about it," Steffi says, still all smiles. Guinevere snorts.

Malachi dusts his hands. "Well, BREAKOUT is certainly the go-to place for stress relief," he says. "You wouldn't believe how many corporate types we get at our Pigeon Forge location. All the Patagonia-vest-clad finance interns basically shoulder one another out the door in the spirit of team building."

"Way to sell it," Santo says, smirking at Malachi. "Matt and I are definitely down."

The bell rings, signaling the end of lunch, and Steffi shoots Matt a smile as he picks up their latest lunch creation: a Red Delicious with a water-bottle-cap hat, a Sharpied smiley face, and three spork legs stabbed into it at awkward angles. Matt lobs the Frankensteined apple at the trash can, the rest of us cheer as it falls inside, and for a moment, the latest controversy surrounding the most recent *Cedar Creek Confessions* post is almost forgotten.

Almost, but not quite. Because despite whatever happens next, everything at Cedar Creek High is already changing.

CHAPTER SEVEN

Wednesday, May 20, 2026, 11:15 PM

I don't have time to think—I only react. Hands clutching my knees. Saliva waterfalling down Matt's leather trench coat. An acrid burn in the back of my throat, and warm blood seeping into my broken canvas sneakers. Real blood. Because Charity Noelle Adler—our student body president, Congresswoman Adler's daughter, and the girl whose Barbies we beheaded on the steps of her Dreamhouse when we were kids—just fucking died in front of us.

"Charity?" Guinevere asks, her voice unnaturally high. "Charity, can you hear me?"

But she can't, because her ash-blond head is caved in. Chin slumped. Thin limbs rag dolled. And beneath her, a terrible dark pool. Spreading closer. Inching toward us across the concrete BREAKOUT floor.

"Holy shit," Tobias says, stepping backward. There's a fine crimson mist sprayed on the lenses of his tortoiseshell glasses. His sweatshirt. His freckled neck. "That fractured her cranium." He blinks, staring at the metal lattice of the ceiling above us, but I can't tear my eyes away from Charity's body for long enough to follow his gaze. "The pound-force that must have taken... Can't be more than twelve feet... And depending on the weight..."

Tobias keeps mumbling under his breath, something about newtons and constant area and inverse proportions, but his words are jumbled in my mind. This can't be real. Charity is supposed to be standing here, agonizing about delivering her SBP speech to a class of 267 people tomorrow, with her Tennessee River pearls and her stretched smile and her brain. She's not supposed to have cerebrospinal fluid gushing down her mangled neck. I'm not supposed to see her shattered skull.

Santo gags, running to vomit into the cabin's woven wastebasket, just as Guinevere steps forward. "Charity?" she repeats. But there's no use. A person is dead inside BREAKOUT. Again. And this time, I'm always going to remember. This time, I'm never going to be able to forget.

The rest of my senses flicker on one by one like faulty light bulbs: smell, taste, touch. The escape room is a mélange of glistening bone and flickering fluorescents, and there's a gargantuan cinder block embedded in Charity's perfect ash-blond head.

"She's gone." My words are matter-of-fact. Wooden. Out-of-body. "There's probably an electromagnet in the ceiling that released the cinder block once she activated the garbage disposal; it's just like the Heart of the Ocean necklace that dropped in *Escape the Titanic*." I swallow as a fresh wave of guilt engulfs my major organs. I encouraged us to enter *Arsonist's Revenge*. I signed the waiver. I wanted to find out who's behind the return of *Cedar Creek Confessions*. I persuaded everyone to play.

And now Charity is dead, because of me.

Hot tears spill down my bloodstained cheeks and seep into the heather-gray fabric of my dad's old T-shirt, and I suddenly remember jamming out to "When You Were Young" on *Guitar Hero III: Legends of Rock* with Charity during late-night slumber parties—my dad singing along from the kitchen to cover up our discordant notes, the two of us increasingly out of breath but still managing to headbang to the chorus like true rock stars, the indescribable high that surged through my veins when the music crescendoed and we both activated our Star Power—right before more memories crash into me like a tidal wave: Charity with her hair in pigtails, her hands on her hips as she lectured two boys on the playground for chasing us with sticks; Charity in the middle school cafeteria, sharing her poblano soup with me because I forgot my lunch; Charity with a smattering of summer freckles dusting her skin, freshly sixteen, watching from the silt-sludge bank of Watauga Lake as Tobias, Guinevere, and I trawled the muddied water for her missing sunglasses. Her response when we finally found them: *Like, thank you guys so much?*

Nausea sweeps through me, and I wrap my arms around my

stomach like I can physically stop myself from retching. Except I can't. Charity was just talking to us a minute ago, calm and collected and in control. How did this happen? What in the ever-loving fuck is going on?

"Steffi's correct," Tobias says, his gaze still fixated on the steel ceiling beams. "I didn't see it happen—it happened so fast—but the cinder block must have released from right there"—he points above the kitchenette—"when she activated the sensor. Crushed her head in, from the looks of it." His brows furrow. "Assuming the ceiling is ten feet above us, and using a weighted average of six hundred fifty newtons of pound-force as the standard median a human cranium can withstand before breaking, the total mass of the block can range anywhere from one hundred thirty-two to two hundred eighty pounds."

"Which is relevant how?" Guinevere rasps over the sound of Santo throwing up. She sinks into a dining chair and pulls out a cinnamon Altoids tin with shaking hands. She can't even open it.

Tobias shrugs. "Maybe it's a clue. What do you think, Steffi?"

I try to say something. Anything. But my nostrils are searing with hemoglobin and the acerbic tang of bile, and my vocal cords refuse to do anything except vibrate with the aftershocks of my own dry heaving. God. I'm trapped inside BREAKOUT with a bona fide dead body, a limited air supply, and four people—*now three*, the dark voice in my head whispers—who hate me. So maybe I don't know anything anymore.

For the first time all night, I feel a pang of longing for home. I miss my bedroom with its sun-faded band posters and its downy comforter and the trinkets I've collected over years of concerts and school trips and family vacations. I miss the sound of Mom's disgusting kale protein shakes whirring away in the blender. I miss the smell of the rhododendrons flowering in our backyard—anything that isn't copper blood or aromatic aftershave or candy-scented perfume.

The back of my throat fills with tears.

"Did any of you tell your parents that you were coming here tonight?" I whisper, hating the rawness of my voice, the hopeful lilt to my tone. "Or do any of you have, like, Life360 on your phones?"

Guinevere finally succeeds in prying open the Altoids tin she uses to hide her cigarettes from her parents, and I briefly wonder if setting off the BREAKOUT fire alarm might disengage the magnetized door. Still, the last thing I want to do while we're inside *Arsonist's Revenge* is start a real fire.

"Mine used to, but I disabled it," she says, her voice shaking. "And no, I didn't tell them I'd be here. Are you kidding? With the lawsuit, my dad would have me on lockdown for the whole summer if he found out I willingly set foot inside another BREAKOUT escape room."

I watch her for a second, wondering if she's going to light up, and blink in surprise when she withdraws a nicotine patch instead of a Marlboro and slaps it on her blood-splattered arm. She glares at me, her eyes red-rimmed, so I turn to Tobias.

He hiccups. "I'm technically breaking curfew by being here, but neither of my parents understand how location-sharing works. They're not big on technology, you know?"

From the woven wastebasket next to the coatrack, Santo wipes his mouth with the back of his hand and grimaces. "Momma was already asleep when I took the car; Pizza Plus has been wearing her out lately. But even if she were awake, I don't think I would have told her. I mean, I thought it was a surprise party, remember?"

Another bolt of panic cracks through my chest. I didn't tell anyone where I was going, either, much for the same reasons my ex-friends kept our not-quite-midnight rendezvous a secret: I didn't want my mom to worry. After all, my best friend died inside BREAKOUT. Even if she's not technically my legal guardian now that I'm eighteen, I doubt she would have appreciated knowing I was being lured back here a year later via an anonymous invitation with no return address.

Jesus. I'm so stupid.

I try to inhale, but I can't breathe. Because we don't have our phones, none of us can text Malachi and demand answers. We can't call 911. We can't ask for help from our families or the Friendship Springs Police Department or even Sheriff Stallard. Instead, we're genuinely stuck inside *Arsonist's Revenge* with my childhood best friend's dead body. And nobody knows where we are.

Just as the familiar symptoms of an imminent anxiety attack start flooding my veins, the LCD monitor flickers in my periphery and dread pools at the base of my spine. Because instead of displaying our countdown, there are now words on the screen.

SIX FRIENDS. SIX SECRETS. ONE HOUR TO SPILL THEM, OR EVERYONE DIES. The LCD monitor changes to the hot-pink smiley face of BREAKOUT's company logo. Blinks back to black. Shudders. *DO YOU BELIEVE ME NOW?*

Involuntarily, my gaze drifts back to Charity's mangled body crumpled by the sink in the kitchenette. I've seen blood and guts and gore before—on my Explore page, in video games, via death-compilation YouTube videos the edgy eighth-grade boys who rode my bus in middle school raucously laughed at while my stomach churned for reasons that had nothing to do with motion sickness—but this is different. This is someone I knew. A girl with real aspirations and a go-to coffee order who braided dandelion crowns with me during Field Day and always picked Casey Lynch over Judy Nails and wanted to improve CCHS for all of us.

Another flash from the screen: *MAYBE YOU NEED ME TO SHOW YOU.*

My heart pounds in my temples; the roof of my mouth is as dry as the cement in the Sevier County Plaza parking lot. *Breathe, Steffi. Inhale for four seconds. Hold for six. Exhale for eight.*

But none of my grounding techniques can prepare me for what happens after the hot-pink smiley face of BREAKOUT vanishes from the screen. Because the ambient white noise of the speakers switches out for a voice. An incredibly familiar voice.

"Hey," my dead best friend says calmly. *"My name is Matt Cesari. I died last year."*

Across from me, Guinevere's olive-skinned face drains of all color just as the queasiness in my stomach explodes. Matt is here, inside BREAKOUT. Or, at least, his voice is: dark and rich and thick, surrounding us entirely.

"Is he in the control room?" I whisper. "Is he alive?" Anger, fear, and hope surge through me in equal measure, but then rational thought kicks in: My best friend died last May. Even if I can't remember it, I know he inhaled too much carbon monoxide in *Wanderland* while the fire raged around us. I went to his funeral. There was an investigation and an obituary and an official death certificate.

So how is this possible?

"*Over the course of the next forty-five minutes,*" the voice of Matteo Luca Cesari continues, "*you'll need to prove you have what it takes to survive a BREAKOUT escape room. After all, there's still time for you, even if there wasn't time for me.*"

A photograph appears on the screen, replacing the hot-pink BREAKOUT logo. It's the same selfie Guinevere found on the fridge, complete with our scratched-out faces. The lump in my throat grows bigger. I try to focus on breathing; I'm worried I might pass out if I don't.

"*But tonight, players, in order to walk out of* Arsonist's Revenge *guilt-free, you'll need to break out properly. And in order to do that, you will need to face everything that terrifies you about yourself.*"

The LCD monitor changes again, flicking to the grainy camera feeds from *Wanderland*. Guinevere chokes back a sob at the sight of Charity, alive and well, in the black-and-white CCTV footage. Next to me, Santo's dark eyes glisten with unshed tears. But across the room, Tobias remains completely expressionless. How is he not losing his shit right now?

"*Charity. Because you have failed to escape in time,*" Not-Matt continues, "*you have been eliminated, and your secret will now be revealed for you.*" A beat of silence. "*Ironic, right?*"

On-screen, the footage skips forward. At first, the frames are as blurry as my memories; indistinct one moment, sharp the next. But then the video stabilizes, and I understand. If the DVD I found contained the beginning of the allegedly lost *Wanderland* footage, then this is the next part of our gameplay: Charity on the screen, twirling a braid around her finger, lightly pushing Matt inside the Queen of Hearts's Rose Garden with a sweet smile. Swinging the hedge door shut. Wedging a flamingo-shaped croquet mallet through the door handle to prevent him from being able to open it from the other side.

What the fuck.

"Is this deepfaked?" I ask, my voice pitching upward. "You know, AI or something?"

"The voice has to be," Tobias replies, his LED-bathed face grim. "But the footage? That's real."

On-screen, the *Wanderland* video pauses. The hot-pink smiley face reappears, and then, through the speakers, Not-Matt's voice: "*Don't say I didn't warn you. Because that's the thing about secrets... they burn you up inside.*"

The smiley face disappears. Our countdown timer reappears on the LCD screen: 44:22. We're over a quarter of the way through *Arsonist's Revenge*, and I just heard the voice of my dead best friend for the first time in a year. I slide against the nearest wood-paneled wall and gag until my throat burns.

None of this is random. This isn't just a game anymore, or a sick prank, or a botched inside joke.

It's revenge.

• • •

"Damn," Tobias murmurs, staring at the monitor with unfocused eyes. Is he drunk or high or just in shock? "This is all so fucked up, right?"

"Maybe it was an accident," Santo says quietly. "A...malfunction of some kind."

"An accident?" Guinevere shrieks, whirling around to face Santo, the multicolored star-shaped claw clips snaggled in her caramel-brown hair vibrating with fury. "A cinder block doesn't just *accidentally* bash a girl's head in."

Santo ducks his head in shame, exposing a dribble of vomit on the collar of his crewneck. I know he's just trying to protect Malachi, but his reasoning is starting to get ridiculous.

"Guys?" I whisper. "What are we going to do about Charity?"

There's a migraine mounting at the edges of my temples. Usually, escape rooms are always reset after a player group finishes their game. Flex Foam limbs are locked back into their respective trunks, polyurethane millipedes are tossed into ceramic vases in specific combinations, and paintings are rehung on walls to hide four-digit safes. But if someone wanted, a Game Master—or a Game Master's accomplice—could manipulate the reset, purposely fuck with the win conditions of any given room, and manipulate the various puzzles to cause fatal injury. It wouldn't be too difficult to swap out one prop for another, to tweak the clue sequence outlined in Malachi's Game Bible, to turn BREAKOUT into a Rube Goldberg machine designed to kill. And with Charity gone, it's entirely possible that continuing to progress through tonight's game will mean certain death for every single person in our player group.

Not-Matt's earlier words swirl through my mind: *There's still time for you, even if there wasn't time for me.*

A chill runs down my spine. Before Matt died, his mom was always uprooting him and Santo—a new boyfriend, a new state, a new start—and his social skills suffered for it. He talked about it once, on a night where we all snuck moonshine up to the water tower and watched the lights of Cedar Creek sprawl out to the fuzzy outer edges of Sevierville—how he and Santo never stayed anywhere long enough for him to feel comfortable; how the twins had learned early on that they could rely on only each other; how hard it was to take their friendships seriously when Matt knew that nowhere was permanent, that each town was just another pit stop, and that every single one of their seven high schools in the past three years was exactly the same: boring people, boring classes, boring unspoken social rules.

That was the night I'd decided that I wanted Cedar Creek to be different for both of them. I wanted to *make* it different. I wanted to be Matt's best friend. But I didn't know he was obsessed with vigilante cyber justice, with cleansing Cedar Creek from the filth clinging to its rural American underbelly, with holding others accountable. And as a result, there were a lot of people who wanted

Matt dead when the truth came out. And now there are a lot of people who may want us dead by association.

Santo is the first to answer my question. "We should probably... move her."

I close my eyes. Jesus.

"Or," Tobias counters, "we should leave her where she is. If there's someone masterminding this, then this counts as evidence. We don't want our fingerprints on her body." He pushes up his bloodstained glasses with a nonchalant index finger and my stomach flips. "Although we should probably decide which one of us is going to retrieve the note on that cinder block."

Without meaning to, my eyes travel to the concrete brick embedded in Charity's skull. A strangled half-scream, half-laugh escapes me. Tobias is right—there's a note on top of it. God. Is this part of the fucking *game*?

When no one moves, Tobias shrugs before he takes off his glasses and starts to clean the lenses with the edge of his chess team hoodie. "We can draw straws for it, if that's easier. Rock paper scissors, maybe?"

Santo's dark gaze drops to the area rug. Guinevere is still vibrating. Tobias is still cleaning.

I clench my hands into fists. "I'll do it."

The words surprise me. They must surprise the other players, too, because Santo's yellow-blond eyebrows draw together in confusion, his curved barbell piercing glinting in the LED light. "Steff... are you sure?"

Am I? My shirt is damp with sweat, my tongue is pressed firmly against the roof of my mouth, and my shoulders are tight.

But then I stand up, and I realize I'm serious about this. Matt may have pissed off a lot of people before he died, but we clearly pissed off someone, too. Someone who wanted Charity dead. Someone who might want us all dead. So right now, I need to focus on staying sharp, mobile, and alive. I am here. I am getting answers. I am not backing down.

"Yeah," I rasp as I make my way toward the kitchenette. The flapping, broken soles of my Converse sneakers squelch as I step into the oily black pool of Charity's blood. For the second time tonight, I feel everyone's eyes on me: Guinevere's glassy fear, Tobias's inscrutable stare, Santo's concerned gaze. *Don't slip. Don't fall. One step at a time.* "I'm sure."

Closer, closer, closer still until my vision short-circuits halfway to the cinder block and I freeze. I expected another post-failed-escape-attempt photograph from BREAKOUT, but this is evidence from the trial. Specifically, a printed sheet of paper from EXHIBIT B showing our group text messages from the night of the fire.

"Hurry," Guinevere urges. I close the distance to the taped sheet—*don't look, don't look, don't look*—and rip the page away with a quick jerk. There. Got it.

"Nice," Santo says as I return, tracking blood all over the tiled floor. I can't believe that we only stepped inside *Arsonist's Revenge* seventeen minutes ago; it feels like a lifetime has passed since then. Another one of my friends is dead. I'm not sure who I can trust. And here the rest of us are: survivors of a second senseless escape-room-related tragedy.

This time, I know the drill; I flip the paper over. "*It's been a year. Here's your second chance,*" I read. "That's all it says."

"Great," Guinevere spits. "That's definitely not cryptic."

Except we've already found a slew of items. And this makes sense to me.

"What are you doing?" Tobias asks, but I'm already gravitating to the two numbered padlocks bolting the fridge door shut.

"How many seconds are in a year?" I ask him.

He doesn't miss a beat. "Thirty-one million five hundred thirty-six thousand."

3-1-5-3-6-0-0-0. Split between two padlocks, that's 3-1-5-3 and 6-0-0-0, which seems like a long shot. But as I line up the last digit on the first padlock and pull down on the U-bar, there's a satisfying click as the lock pops open. And after the second combination works on the second four-digit padlock, I swing the handle of the rusting fridge outward and I forget how to breathe.

What's inside isn't the interior of a fridge, but a hollow frame just large enough for me to squeeze through. It's not very accessible, and it doesn't seem like it was designed with anyone but ten-year-olds in mind, but BREAKOUT's always sacrificed ADA compliance for smoke and mirrors. Still, though. As I stare into the carved-out blue-LED-lit space beyond the threshold, for a single second, the ghost of the escape room aficionado inside me—the one who isn't haunted by the image of Charity's bloodied body—appreciates the artistry.

We're moving forward. We're still progressing in the game.

And I've just unlocked a second room.

• • •

THE TERMS OF THE PACT:

- **WE NEVER SPEAK OF THIS NIGHT TO EACH OTHER.**
- We never speak of this night to the press.
- We never sell one another out to Sheriff Stallard.
- We never play another escape room at BREAKOUT.
- We never tell Stephanie the truth.
- **IN OTHER WORDS... TELL NO ONE.**

CHAPTER EIGHT

Wednesday, May 20, 2026, 11:17 PM

My pulse quickens as I duck under the jamb of the fridge door and emerge in the second set within *Arsonist's Revenge*. This area is smaller than the living room, but its main features are the same: speakers playing white noise water sounds, another LCD monitor showing our remaining time (42:39), and vibrant floodlights that cast elongated shadows under a blinking security camera.

As my eyes adjust to the semidarkness, more props emerge: bags of fake ice. A walk-in shower with a built-in mirror and a ragged plastic liner that's been artfully bloodied, *Psycho*-style. Four cheap-looking Rorschach inkblot prints hanging above a corner toilet. A mop, bucket, and rubber gloves arranged beside a bathtub with a folding shutter cover. To my right, there's a large electrical box held shut by a direction lock; a puzzle of PVC pipes composes the wall to my left. A single exposed light bulb flickers above me, reflecting off of the body of a rubber rat tucked away behind an industrial sink, and when I glance at the sink's accompanying mirror, I catch a glimpse of my blood-splattered face and recoil.

It's a bathroom.

"Move, Stephanie," Guinevere hisses, and the feeling of her hot breath against my neck is enough to startle me into clambering the rest of the way in. The remaining players slowly fill in the rest of the space, and my eyes snag on each of their blue-LED-bathed expressions as they enter: Guinevere's rage, Tobias's confusion, and Santo's disbelief. Because scrawled on the white-tiled wall beside the industrial sink, in bleeding bloodred paint, are the words ONE BY ONE.

"Shit," Santo whispers. "This officially isn't funny anymore."

Tobias nods. In the eerie glow of the lantern he's holding, he looks paler than usual. Sicklier. "Amen."

An unnerving clank echoes from somewhere above us, and I jump before craning my neck to the scaffolding overhead. Just like in the lobby, an HVAC duct bisects the ceiling. Huh. Looks like the renovations Malachi mentioned were extensive after all.

Tobias steps forward, nearing the scrawled threat, but Santo stops him before he can reach it. "Hold on," he says, his hoarse voice tight with unspoken warning. "Let's be careful, all right?"

It's a valid comment. Charity is dead, and the rest of us are back to exploring like nothing's wrong. We're going through the motions of an escape room even though we just watched the LCD monitor play out her secret, and we're doing it while covered in her blood, while running into new threats, while she's splayed out in the kitchenette with her brains dribbling out of her. I choke down a scream and force myself to focus on my breathing. Four. Six. Eight. I can't succumb to this flashbang of fear. I need to recover my memories before we escape *Arsonist's Revenge* and call Sevier County Emergency Medical Services to extract Charity's mangled body—Jesus, because that's what she is now, a body—and shut down BREAKOUT for good.

Otherwise, her death will be for nothing.

"We can't let fear slow us down," Tobias counters, his gore-splattered russet curls catching the light as he rounds on Santo, and as much as I hate how callous the words are, he has a point. "Even if the clues are fucking with us, we need to assume *Arsonist's Revenge* is still a game we can win."

"Are you brain-dead?" Guinevere retorts. perching on the edge of the bathtub. She closes her eyes. "Charity died, and we're just going to *keep playing*? Can you even hear yourselves right now?"

"No, we're not," Santo says. His dark gaze locks on mine, and I fight the urge to inhale. "All we need to do is let the clock run out. As long as we make it to morning, another Game Master will show up with their master keys and then we're home free."

A smirk curves Tobias's lips. "The code for the fridge door worked, though, didn't it? If we wait too long, we forfeit our chance to unmask whoever brought us here. Continuing to collect clues is risky, sure, but doing so may let us piece together who's doing this to us, why, and how to take them down."

"THIS ISN'T ONE OF YOUR CHESS MATCHES!" Guinevere screams, blood-tinged spittle flying from her canine teeth. "You can't *dance your king* out of this one, Tobias! It's not pawn for pawn, or rook for rook, or even queen for queen. It's us. It's REAL PEOPLE. Not pieces to force trades and win material with!" Her chest heaves, her collarbone glistening with equal parts sweat and viscera, and I redirect my attention to the industrial-sink-and-rubber-rat combo to keep myself from emptying the contents of my own stomach. The countdown is at 41:52.

Tobias's voice is uncharacteristically quiet. "I know that."

"Do you?" Guinevere snarls, still shaking as she adds more nicotine patches to her arms. "Then you probably also realize we're going to die in here, right? We're basically being murdered because of what we did to Matt last year, and this entire game in Friendship Springs is just one huge fuck-you from BREAKOUT!"

Tobias doesn't answer her; he doesn't need to. But at the same time, I file away another piece of information: *because of what we did to Matt last year.*

We, as a collective.

"Is it me, or is it getting hot in here?" Santo asks, pulling at the collar of his Mongolian throat-singing folk-metal band crewneck. At first, I think he's saying it just to distract us from the awkwardness of the moment. But then I realize that his bleached hairline is damp with sweat, and then I'm suddenly attuned to the oppressive heat on my own blood-warmed skin. The amped-up temperature reminds me of the time I convinced my parents to sign up for an outdoor escape room while we were on vacation in Central Florida, and we ended up nearly getting sunstroke in eighty-degree weather. Back then, Dad made us sit in the shade while he went to let the owner know that we were tapping out early and bought us ice-cold gas station waters to guzzle during the car ride afterward. Here, though, there's nothing we can do to adjust the air-conditioning, despite the rattling cooling system clamped to the ceiling. We can only suffer.

Guinevere scowls. "Malachi must have turned up the heat."

"Again, we don't know if he's behind this." This time, Santo wipes his face with the bottom of his crewneck, exposing a sweat-slicked stomach covered in bruises. He catches me staring and frowns.

BANG!

My attention snaps back to the bathtub; the sound was the plastic tub cover folding in on itself. "Hold on. Is that...blood?"

Guinevere immediately jumps to her feet. "Christ," she mutters. "Once we get our phones back, remind me to write an incredibly scathing Yelp review for this entire goddamn franchise."

"Uh, so," Santo starts, glancing at the pair of gloves across the bathroom. They're the kind that go up to your elbows, which is downright threatening in light of the tub's freshly discovered contents. "Maybe there's something inside."

Guinevere pulls a face. "You can't be serious. You think we should reach *in*—" She cuts herself off. "You'd have to be deep in blood to even have a shot at brushing the bottom, and that's assuming there isn't a bear trap lurking in the bathtub's depths."

I bite my lip. Tobias is sporting a black eye; Santo has bruises on his stomach. Were they threatened before coming to BREAK-OUT? Is that why they're both here?

I turn my attention toward Tobias, who's staring at the blood-filled bathtub with a look of sick familiarity on his freckled face. For a second, his family history sparks in my mind—the hundred-acre farm in the Tennessee backwoods passed down from his great-grandparents, the Concentrated Animal Feeding Operation sprung from it that still supplies work to dozens of laborers in the American South—and my gut twists. Did he do this?

Did he fill the bathtub with CAFO-sourced blood from Matthews Farms?

"Come on," Santo tells Guinevere, forcing my attention away from Tobias's nauseated face. "We can do this. This is part of the escape room, hypothetical bear traps aside." He picks up the long gloves and dangles them in front of me. "How about you, Zamekova? Are you game?"

Before I can respond—or even better, start questioning

Santo—Tobias steps forward. "I got it," he says, taking the gloves. He slides them on, and then he plunges an arm into the glistening black liquid before pulling out a piece of slick, dripping plastic. "Hand me a rag?"

Guinevere throws him a towel, and Tobias swipes it over the film as the rest of us crowd him. With the blood wiped away, I recognize the photograph as *Serial Killer's Hideout*, the second escape room we ever played with the Cesaris. But I also know what the image is supposed to look like—Charity and Guinevere cheesing as they ironically sorority-hug Santo; Tobias mid-eye-roll with his arms crossed as I stand on my tiptoes to give him bunny ears; Matt, with shaggy dark hair curling just underneath his angular chin, holding a sign reading CRUSHED IT! while a beaming Malachi points at a whiteboard with our total time (73:59, because he gave us an extra fifteen minutes to escape the room out of pity)—and instead, it's entirely blood-soaked. Someone has painstakingly removed the glossy overlay of most of the photo, leaving only Matt's silhouette protected from the blood; the sign in his hands now reads, YOU'VE BEEN CRUSHED!

Tobias turns over the photograph. If there were ever any words on the back, though, they're now unreadable. In other words, this clue is completely useless.

"Amazing," Guinevere says dryly. "Another fucked-up picture of us at BREAKOUT."

My throat thickens. Mentally, I add this new photo to my running list of Things Gone Wrong: the cut wires, the first photograph, the articles, Charity dying, the *Wanderland* video,

Not-Matt's voice coming in through the speakers, ONE BY ONE, and now this. My lower lip wobbles against my will.

Santo must notice that I'm about to start sobbing, because he jerks his head toward the fridge door. "Hey, Zamekova, can we talk about something in private for a second?"

When I nod, he slips into the other room, and I follow him.

"Santo, what happened to—" I start to ask, but he holds up a hand to stop me before I can finish. When I close my mouth, he throws a glance over his shoulder and lowers his voice.

"Listen, Steff," he says. "You're the only person here who fully understands how escape rooms work, which means you're my best bet in one that's been messed with."

A bead of sweat slips down my back, though I'm not sure if it's from the increased temperature or my own trepidation. "I doubt you want my help right now. I'm the one who persuaded everyone to play, remember? Charity is dead because I couldn't let your brother's death go. Because I thought I had this...unshakable reason for playing *Arsonist's Revenge*."

"Yeah, and because we all showed up tonight." Santo's dark eyes spark with conviction, and I'm suddenly reminded of the charred remains of the Cedar Creek BREAKOUT lot twelve months prior. "We're all responsible. You may think you persuaded everyone to play, but they made their choice as soon as they stepped into BREAKOUT. We all did."

A lump forms in my throat. "Why are *you* here?" I ask Santo, dropping my own voice. "I saw your bruises. Are you in danger? Did someone hurt you?"

When I blink, my invitation is emblazoned against my

eyelids: *Because secrets won't keep themsleves.* Behind Santo, the LCD countdown is at 40:00. Each second slithers like the sweat snaking down my spine. If he won't answer me, then I need to open up to him.

"Look. I came tonight because I need answers," I say, hating myself for how my voice cracks in the middle of the last word. "About your brother." Santo's gaze doesn't move from my face, so I force myself to keep going, over the sounds of hooting owls, chirping crickets, and cicadas hissing like fire sprinklers. "I mean, all of you can *remember* what happened during *Wanderland* last spring. I only have these...fragmented pieces of memory. So if you want my help, I want yours, too. And I want you to be honest with me."

Santo swallows. "I can't tell you what happened on the night my brother died, but I can tell you that I knew Malachi didn't plan a fun birthday surprise for me." He laughs, and a shadow falls over his red-LED-lit face. "I've been getting weird messages since we buried Matt. Did you know that? Texts from his old number, eerie emails, voicemails where someone just breathes into the mic before hanging up. I thought coming to BREAK-OUT tonight might help me figure out who's behind it, but I'm still in the dark. And now Charity is dead." Santo sucks in a sharp breath. "So. You're not the only one with questions."

Huh. I know we all have our own reasons for showing up tonight; there's too much at risk otherwise. If I know myself and my former friends, though—and with each passing second within *Arsonist's Revenge*, I'm beginning to suspect I don't know them as well as I thought—we all believe we can outsmart this situation.

Maybe we've overestimated our abilities, though. Maybe we're not clever enough to get out of here alive. What did I think I could do—storm the sister location of the franchise that slaughtered my best friend and demand an explanation from the people who have been consistently ignoring me for exactly a year?

Ice creeps through my veins even as my skin burns. I know my own motive, and now Santo's told me his...but what about Guinevere? Tobias? Malachi? Charity?

"And the bruises?" I ask.

"Courtesy of an asshole who picked a fight on my way from the airport." A smile plays at the corners of Santo's lips, but there's no humor in it. There hasn't been any in his expressions since Matt died; though if he acted differently in Italy, I have no way of knowing. "So, Zamekova, what do you say? Do you want to break out of BREAKOUT together?"

He says it so easily, like it's a given, but the truth is, there's no way to promise our survival. Not with Charity's crushed body lying less than six feet away. The older I get, in fact, the more I realize that nothing in life is guaranteed—not friendships, not relationships, and definitely not life itself. Even Santo Xavier Cesari, with his perpetual laughter and his crinkling dimples and his endless patience, ghosted every single one of us after Matt's burial. He did it thoroughly, too: deleted social media, stopped responding to texts, and left me to flounder alone for the entirety of my senior year. I had to friend his nonna on Facebook just so

I knew he wasn't dead. For months, all the news I got about him came from the internet, overheard snippets of hallway gossip, and our local newspaper: *Lawsuit! GoFundMe update! Six-month anniversary Tennessee Fire Code think piece!*

"Yeah," I tell him. "Okay. There's a clue in the CCHS hoodie by the coatrack; you can start there."

"Perfect," Santo says, flashing a smile as he saunters away. "By the way, Zamekova... if you want answers? Start by figuring out why everyone's here."

I exhale slowly, watching him go, and my nose stings on the up breath—*don't cry, don't cry, don't cry*. Matt's twin brother is avoiding me. He doesn't trust me, despite his carefree exterior, and now that he's back in Tennessee—and within BREAKOUT, where he literally can't leave—he's only using me to help him, because he knows he can't win the game alone.

From the kitchenette, Tobias glances at me, and I flinch. For once, his hazel-brown eyes aren't unfocused—they're locked right on mine. How long has he been standing there? Did he follow Santo? Just how much of our conversation did he overhear?

"Be careful," Tobias says quietly, stepping around Charity's slumped body. "You can't trust him." He glances at the blood around her corpse before his intent gaze flicks back to me. "You know that, right? You're not stupid."

Heat—the rage-filled kind—rushes to my cheeks. "Excuse me?"

"Think about it," Tobias insists. "No one in this room has a better motive to pick us off one by one. Santo's getting revenge for his brother's death, and he's not going to stop until we're all dead." He combs a hand through his russet hair, his black eye sinister in the lantern light. "It's as good a motive as any."

"Not better than orchestrating another accident to get the insurance payout from BREAKOUT," I snap. "I saw you on your phone in the lobby—you never signed that waiver. And what about your face, huh? Did you get into a fight, or are you experiencing some kind of rare medical condition that made you fucking desperate?"

The words are out before I can take them back. Tobias blinks, pure surprise flickering over his face for less than a millisecond, but then he's back to cool and aloof and impossible to read. The mask he wears when he's about to decimate his chess opponent.

"Is that what you think?" he says softly. "That I'd kill Charity—and you and Santo and Guinevere and Malachi—for money?"

Is it? Tobias and I have always bonded over our shared identities; he's pansexual and demiromantic, I'm panromantic and demisexual, and we're the only people in a fifty-mile radius who actually get what that means to each other without all the requisite explaining. He kicks ass at playing the French horn, he's great at board games, and his favorite way to spend his remaining time is by watching YouTube video essays on abandoned theme parks, obscure SEGA games, and the extensive lore behind low-budget animated films. He's hilarious and genuinely interesting, and I needed his company after Guinevere and Matt started dating and the first hairline fracture in our friend group appeared. But after Matt died, Tobias stopped being someone I could rely on, and all the things I used to love about him—his dedication, his analytical mind, his memory—turned into things I resented. He became obsessed with fire trivia. He got hooked on a slew of new medications that made him even more erratic than he already was. He showed up crossed to a state competition and threw a tantrum so vulgar that he got kicked off the chess team *after* they'd reinstated him post-cheating scandal. And even though we're here together now, I don't think I can trust *him*, either.

I glance down at my marred hands. The bloody upwellings, the ripped nail beds, the uneven keratin. How many times do I need to explain this? How much more of this can I take?

"No," I tell Tobias, my voice measured as I prepare to parrot the lies I've heard all night. "I think that Charity's death was an accident and none of you made a pact to keep whatever the fuck happened last year a secret and that everything inside *Arsonist's Revenge* is a practical joke and my Swiss Army knife will *definitely* turn up again. I think that none of us were responsible for the fire last year or the outcome of the lawsuit or the invitations tonight, and I honestly just *love* playing games and I cannot wait to get home safe and sound!"

Tobias smiles. "So you *have* been paying attention," he says, as if I'm a toddler who just grasped the concept of a bishop only being able to move along diagonals, and I'm so fucking insulted that I almost scream. But then his freckled face turns solemn. "Except you're not the only one."

Before I can dwell on what that means, exactly, he takes a step toward me. "I know why you're here, Steffi," Tobias says. "I know you're worried about what you did last year." He tilts his head; the LED lights catch on his filmy lenses. "At this point, though, my suspicions regarding who set up this room for us lie with everyone equally: Malachi. The James-Mays. Sheriff Stallard. A deranged sociologist. Jacob Webber. Alyssa Hayes. Mr. Foxfield. Any other poor soul targeted by *Cedar Creek Confessions*. Jigsaw." He appraises me carefully. "You."

I balk. "Me?" I ask, although I guess it makes sense. Tobias has clearly mulled over his options, and I kind of suspect him, too. At the same time, though, I can't stop hot guilt from pooling in my lungs. Even if my friends and I haven't been on the best of terms—or any terms, really—since Matt's death, I still credit the people in this room for helping me make it through high school alive. Am I the kind of person to accuse them of murder with no proof? Is this escape room *making* me that kind of person?

Jesus. If Charity were here, she'd point out the flaws in Tobias's reasoning. She practically lived and breathed *innocent until proven guilty*, and right now I need to channel her mantra. I can't let fearmongering get to me; I'm an objective voice of reason, and just like with my blog, I'm not going to make any definitive judgments about anything—or anyone—until I've collected the evidence necessary to come to a conclusion.

Atmosphere: Suspicious. Alibi Offerings: Minimal. Fallacy Utilization: Straw Man.

"Well," I tell Tobias, "good luck with that." And then I push past him and duck through the fridge door, finding myself once again in the bathroom set of *Arsonist's Revenge*.

"Find something?" Guinevere asks. The fraying cuffs of her patchwork pants are stained with black-and-orange splotches I'd rather not think about the origins of. She's staring at herself in the mirror of the walk-in shower; there are noticeably more nicotine patches on her arms. I blink at her, and she raises a brow in response. "What?"

"I thought you quit after Matt died."

Guinevere shrugs. "Having COPD means you risk exacerbating your symptoms if you smoke, so this is what I'm doing now," she says as I move to examine the electrical box. The lock holding it shut still isn't open. Guinevere sniffs. "But don't act like you care either way."

Even though she's not actively lighting up, I can still remember the smell of her thick smoke. The memory turns my stomach, singes my nostril hairs, forces me back to the empty place in my mind where the night Matt died should be. *Repressed memories*, Call-Me-Diana always calls them. *We're going to try and unlock your repressed memories. Don't be so hard on yourself—repressed memories are difficult to deal with for everyone. Your repressed memories exist, trapped inside you, and you need to let them escape.*

"You're right," I tell Guinevere. "I don't care."

She scoffs. Like this, with translucent scales plastered all over her skin, she reminds me of a venomous snake: beautiful, muscled, and impossible to handle when threatened. "Well, maybe you should, because Charity's death is basically your fault."

Jesus, I hate her. I hate all of them. But I need them, and I don't know who I am without them, and I can't stand the fact that my ex-friends mean so much to me even now.

"What, no response?" Guinevere goads, turning away from the shower mirror. "You playing sheriff with Charity earlier is the only reason she even started searching for clues in the first place. If you didn't need to know everything, none of this would've happened."

"Yeah, well you don't need to be such a raging bitch," I snarl, whirling around to fully face her. "I know your boyfriend is dead and you're grieving and it hurts. Believe me, I get it. I'm fucking furious. I *still* cry myself to sleep; some nights, I can't even cry at all. There are so many moments where I just want to pick up my phone and text him, or call you, or eat lunch in our regular booth in the cafeteria, watching Malachi inhale Charity's uneaten food while Santo laughs at something stupid Tobias said. Feeling all these emotions? It's *infuriating*. But I didn't do anything to you. When Matt died, I lost just as much as you did. So don't take your anger out on me."

"Why?" Guinevere spits, taking a step toward me. "Have you ever stopped to wonder why you're grieving your supposed *best friend* as much as the person who *loved* him?"

Now it's my turn to scoff. "You never loved Matt."

Guinevere's nostrils flare. "If you want to make an enemy tonight," she replies, reaching out to jab a single stiletto into my sternum, "be prepared to watch your back."

With that, she jostles my shoulder with her bare one before slipping through the fridge door. I watch her go, my stomach churning, until I realize I'm the only person left in the bathroom.

Overhead, the LCD screen is at 38:05.

For the first time all night, my heart twinges with protectiveness for Malachi. Maybe it's the fact I'm being accused with no proof, but I suddenly feel that even though there's a real chance Mal could be doing this to us—after all, he holds the power to modify our in-game experience as our Game Master, and he also has a strong motive as the son of the owners: exact revenge on the people who ruined his family business one year ago—the way he suspiciously dropped out of contact (and the undeniable fact that he, at least partially, set up tonight's escape room) doesn't necessarily mean he's involved in Charity's death.

Because the truth is, all of us are prime suspects:

Guinevere Jade Mitchell-Moore, the sharp-edged grieving girlfriend with a nasty nicotine addiction.

Tobias Quinton Matthews, the black-eye-addled chess rival who refused to sign the escape room waiver.

Santo Xavier Cesari, the charismatic twin brother with bruises of unknown origin who definitely has skeletons in his closet.

Or even Stephanie Marie Zamekova, the loner best friend with a traumatic brain injury and a long-dead blog about this exact hobby.

Because I don't trust myself anymore. Not since Matt died. Not since I've been waking up in the mornings with large swaths of the day just...missing from my mind. And ever since I found the cardstock invitation in my mailbox—ever since we all showed up at BREAKOUT and I've been hearing the dark voice in the back of my head that keeps calling me a monster—I've been wondering...

What if I'm the one who orchestrated all of this?

CHAPTER NINE

Wednesday, May 20, 2026, 11:22 PM

The countdown is at 37:59, and the four of us—because there are only four of us now, with Charity dead and Malachi missing in action—are finally following *There's No Escape Rule #17: Split up as much as possible.* Except we're all in different areas not because of strategy, but because we don't want to interact with each other. The latest photograph being too blood-logged to serve as a viable clue means low team morale. Our game is no longer about honoring Matt, or mourning his death, or even coming together in search of answers.

Instead, it's turning into a twisted psychological experiment.

I shake my head to dispel the thought and opt instead to refocus on my surroundings, even if my hopes for uncovering something fruitful aren't exactly high. Within escape rooms, I've always prided myself on my spatial intelligence—growing up bilingual in a small town where most people can't point out the country your parents are from on a map basically primes you for a superiority complex—but I'm not a team player. I can pull my weight, but I don't work well with others.

I know it; the people trapped with me know it, too. They're aware of my flaws.

All too aware.

After I poke around the bathroom set for a bit—the pristine toilet lid, the thankfully empty toilet bowl, the toilet tank that's filled with an unsettling ream of papers that I flip through for only a few seconds before self-preservation kicks in and I decide to put them back until I know what to do with them—my attention returns to the electrical box beside the fridge door. There's a standard warning decal plastered atop its otherwise unassuming exterior—the whole classic yellow triangle, exclamation mark, DANGER: HIGH VOLTAGE deal—but there's also a purple direction lock keeping the latch shut, so the breaker panel within should be part of the room. Apart from the warning decal, the puzzle reminds me of one in a TERPECA-ranked room I worked to crack over the summer in Boston my sophomore year. Unlike that room's pristine direction lock, however, this one is rusted around the edges of its lock bar. I picture Matt alive, frowning, flicking the joystick-like contraption in cardinal directions: *left, left, left*. Left-handed. Where we left off. Left for dead.

We'll need to get this open, I imagine him saying in his real voice, one dripping with sarcasm instead of a robotic, computer-generated facsimile devoid of life. He crosses his arms, smirks, leans against the doorjamb as a fuzzy-edged apparition frozen at seventeen. *Any ideas?*

"A few," I murmur, turning around to glance up at the Rorschach prints.

I'm not screwing around anymore—we need to call for help, and the sooner we get back to the lobby, the sooner we can get our phones to report Charity's death. If BREAKOUT is rigged against us, another "accident" could occur at any second... which means I'm no longer sabotaging our game to buy us time. Right now, I need to focus on what I do best: escaping.

"The canvases look like they're depicting classic inkblots, but the negative space in each one forms an arrow. From left to right, you'll want to put the code in as up-left-down-down."

A small smile slides across Matt's face. *You've been holding out on me, Steff.*

Despite the grim circumstances, I almost smile back. "I don't know what you're talking about." I walk over to the electrical box; Matt vanishes as soon as I pop the direction lock open. Adrenaline rushes through me at the sound. God, I've missed this.

I lift the latch and swing the casing open to reveal the breaker panel, where an orange banner reads WARNING: ELECTRICAL HAZARD. AUTHORIZED PERSONNEL ONLY. Inside the box, though, there's no faint hum of power, no whirring energy, no sparking wires. Just one empty cylindrical slot molded in plastic casing. A slot for the clue I told Santo about earlier. It must be a fuse.

Conventional puzzler wisdom says to thread used locks back

through their latches, so I poke my head through the fridge door after complying. "Hey, I opened the electrical box!"

There's No Escape Rule #7: When you find a clue, shout it out loudly.

Tobias doesn't react to the words—he's preoccupied by aimlessly picking up pieces of plastic fruit from the dining table—and Guinevere is sitting on the worn couch, near-catatonic, with her trembling arms wrapped around herself. But Santo perks up, and then he's standing exactly where I just pictured his brother.

"What unlocked it?" he asks, nudging the direction lock. When I tell him about the Rorschach print code, he nods. "Ah, of course. Want to do the honors?" He offers me the fuse, the amused expression on his burn-scarred face now expectant, and something about the assumption in his glittering eyes makes me shake my head.

"Wouldn't want to steal your moment," I say softly.

Santo's ring-adorned hand loosens around the cylinder. "Hmm," he says, disappointed, and then he slots the fuse in himself before I can warn him.

The bathroom set floodlights switch from their original color to a brilliant magenta, and Santo dusts his hands before raising a bleached eyebrow at me. *See? What did you think would happen?*

I exhale, unable to help but feel like I just failed some kind of test. Jesus, maybe *Arsonist's Revenge* is making me more paranoid than I thought.

Directly in front of us, the wall that spelled out *ONE BY ONE* when the lights were dark blue now reads *WE ALL FALL DOWN.*

"Great. Now that that's out of the way, we need to figure out how to get out of here," Guinevere snaps, coming through the fridge door, and I settle into the cadence of her anger that feels as familiar as breathing. "How to *seriously* get out of here," she adds. "If we're encountering puzzles like this after what happened to Charity"—she gestures to the WARNING sticker on the electrical panel—"we need to come up with an actionable plan other than *play the game and hope it doesn't kill us.*"

"I agree," Santo says. "If we're going to stand any kind of chance, we need to work together as a team. Deal?"

Unease itches its way through my bloodstream as I recall my initial trepidation toward Tobias. My grievances with Guinevere. My still-swirling suspicions about Santo. I frown and tamp down the raw emotions. Reemergence of *Cedar Creek Confessions* a month ago aside, stolen Swiss Army knife aside, cut wires and creepy photographs and handpicked newspaper articles and rigged wordlock solutions and eerie bathtub blood aside, we're all trapped within *Arsonist's Revenge* together. Getting answers about Matt will have to wait. Right now, staying alive is the only thing that matters.

Guinevere nods, so I nod, too. *There's No Escape Rule #3: Trust your team.*

Santo smiles. "Good."

"The only question is, what else can we do?" Tobias asks as he ducks through the fridge door to join us. I guess he got tired of fruit. "There are no windows. No emergency exits, no manual overdrives, and no way to set off the fire alarms without lighter fluid—and Guinevere quit smoking, so she doesn't even have her Zippo anymore." He rubs the bridge of his nose in frustration. "Since the wires to the emergency mechanism are cut, we're trapped in here. All we can do is scramble for clues and hope it leads us to the keypad code."

I tilt my head. "Tobias has a point," I hedge. "Even though there may be deadly consequences, working through the remaining puzzles is the only surefire way to escape *Arsonist's Revenge*." I look down at my blood-soaked sneakers, and for the first time tonight, I'm hyperaware of the fact that we're all being watched: by one another, by our Game Master, by whoever else is possibly monitoring the blinking security cameras mounted next to the LCD screens in both rooms. "But Santo's theory from earlier makes sense, too: If we do nothing, we'll probably be let out by a BREAKOUT employee when this place opens at ten AM tomorrow."

"Get to the point," Guinevere snaps.

I lick my lips as I drift toward the industrial sink. When I flip the tap, no water comes out.

"Do any of you remember *There's No Escape* Rule Number Nine: Always check every alcove?" I ask, moving on to the toilet. "On my blog, I used that tip for rooms with bathroom sets, like PanIQ Escape Room Atlanta's *Jailbreak*." I lift the tank lid and set it on the tiled floor. There, curled around the pristine flush valve, is a ream of familiar papers—the ones I found only a few minutes earlier. "But it applies here, too." I glance at each remaining player: Guinevere, Tobias, Santo. "These are building schematics for Suite 263."

"Incredible," Guinevere says, throwing up her manicured hands. "I'm so glad you've bestowed us with your absolutely useless input on this situation."

"What are you suggesting, Steffi?" Tobias asks, ignoring her, even though I'm sure he already knows.

I focus on laying out the mechanical plans on the tiled set floor before responding. *Four. Six. Eight.* If my mind is on my dead friends or our infighting or Gee's rude comments, then I'm not bringing my A game. And that's dangerous for all of us.

When I finally look up at him, though, I'm certain this plan can work.

"Air," I tell Tobias, a real smile tugging at the corners of my lips for the first time since we stepped into *Arsonist's Revenge* as I point directly above me. "We can use the HVAC to escape."

• • •

CEDAR CREEK CONFESSIONS

posted 15 months ago

So, Cedar Creek. Let's talk about Alyssa Hayes and last week's notorious senior prank.

Here's the sitch: Mr. Foxfield left the window of his office unlocked for the senior class to get into the high school after hours for the purposes of a harmless senior prank. Head cheerleader Alyssa Hayes orchestrated the prank and came to an agreement with Mr. Foxfield. Sources say the seniors told Mr. Foxfield they wanted to move a few desks to the lobby, TP the cafeteria, and put streamers in every bathroom on the third floor. But what actually happened is the senior class released five thousand live crickets into the building around 5:30 PM on Thursday. And now Alyssa and thirteen other students—Grant Richards, Tyler Duvall, Mary Coffee, Yadriel Peña, Natalie Eu, Bryce Woodward, and Gina Homesley among them—are all facing criminal breaking and entering charges that will impact their permanent record. As the ringleader, Alyssa has the most severe charges. Stanford has rescinded her acceptance, and none of the students involved will be able to walk at graduation.

Scandalous, right? I know. Word on the street is that these criminal charges are impacting the postgrad plans of not only our dear Alyssa Hayes, but also the other student athletes involved. Here at Cedar Creek Confessions, we're not exactly sure how this will play out moving forward, but be sure to watch your step in the hallways for the next few weeks—we're told the exterminators did not, in fact, catch them all. (Here, of course, I'm referring to the live crickets. Many are still at large in the second-floor boys' bathroom.)

Either way, seems like that bitch got what she deserved.

Until next time, Cedar Creek!

UNITED STATES DISTRICT COURT

EASTERN DISTRICT OF TENNESSEE
GREENEVILLE DIVISION

CATELYN ADLER; ILLARIA CESARI;
and EDWARD MITCHELL-MOORE,
  Plaintiffs,
  v.
RANDALL JAMES and TALIYAH MAY,
  Defendants.

Case No. 2:25-CR-00123-JRG-DCP

EXHIBIT D
Prerecorded Witness Testimony

Excerpt from Transcript of Witness Testimony

1. **SHERIFF STALLARD:** Can you state your name for the record,
2. please?
3. **MALACHI JAMES-MAY:** Can you tell me why I'm here first, Sheriff?
4. **SHERIFF STALLARD:**
5. Q. You work as a Game Master for BREAKOUT, correct?
6. A. You know, I don't understand why you're interrogating me. I am
7. a BREAKOUT Game Master, but—
8. Q. And you were the Game Master during the session that resulted
9. in an uncontrolled fire, the blocking of multiple paths of egress, and
10. the asphyxiation of seventeen-year-old Matteo Cesari. Correct? So,
11. once again… Your name, for the record. Please.
12. A. Malachi James-May.
13. Q. James-May, as in the owners of BREAKOUT Escape Rooms Inc.?
14. A. Look, everyone in Cedar Creek is aware that I'm the son of the
15. owners. Respectfully, Sheriff, you're not fooling anyone with this
16. know-nothing act. And I understand the whole county is breathing

17. down your neck for you to figure out why Matt ended up dead, but
18. believe me—you don't want to pin this on the Black kid.
19. **SHERIFF STALLARD:** And what about the kid who illegally let his
20. friends into a business after hours? A kid untrained in basic fire
21. safety measures, who didn't follow a building's outlined fire code,
22. and indirectly caused the death of a seventeen-year-old? Would
23. you blame that kid? Would you have questions for that kid? Would
24. you want answers from that kid?
25. **MR. LEWIS:** Stallard.
26. **MALACHI JAMES-MAY:** I didn't cause anyone's death, Sheriff.
27. Indirectly or not.
28. **SHERIFF STALLARD:** Don't be smart with me, son. Now, let's get
29. back on track. How—
30. **MR. LEWIS:** Hang on, Sheriff. I think we should take five. Mr.
31. James-May, let's get you a glass of water, huh?
32. **MALACHI JAMES-MAY:** I'm fine.
33. *[BRIEF INTERMISSION.]*
34. **SHERIFF STALLARD:**
35. Q. Once again, this is Sheriff Travis Stallard, resuming witness
36. interview with Malachi James-May at 2:05 PM. Malachi, can you
37. confirm you're resuming this voluntary interview of your own free
38. will? Just lean into your mic for me.
39. A. Yes, I am.
40. Q. Wonderful. And how long have you been working as a Game
41. Master for BREAKOUT?
42. A. Since the age of twelve. My parents own the business, so the laws
43. are different.
44. Q. What does your role entail?

45. A. Officially, I'm in charge of presiding over the games themselves.
46. I provide groups—both booked players and walk-ins—with
47. information about how BREAKOUT works and what our ground
48. rules are. I ensure that every participating player has signed our
49. nonnegotiable waiver, and then I also lead them to their game room.
50. Once a group starts their game, I monitor the cameras in the control
51. room while they play.
52. Q. Based on that description, I'm assuming you were in the control
53. room when the fire started, correct?
54. A. Correct.
55. Q. And how many cameras do you have access to in the control
56. room? How many unique feeds?
57. A. It depends on the room itself—*Chemistry Class*, our easiest room,
58. only had one. But *Wanderland* was rated at a five-star difficulty. It
59. had four cameras.
60. Q. Tell me, son: Did you see how the fire started?
61. A. No. It happened too quickly to tell, so I didn't notice the fire until
62. it was too late. But I left the control room as soon as I realized there
63. was an emergency. There was so much smoke in the hallway—
64. thankfully, it cleared long enough for me to see that the players used
65. the emergency escape to leave. I figured everyone had made it out, so I
66. ran outside to regroup with the others. I didn't fight the fire myself—at
67. that point, the flames were hot enough to melt my skin. But our rooms
68. are extremely safe. They're not fireproof, but we've passed inspection.
69. We're up to code.
70. Q. What about Matteo Cesari? Can you describe
71. your relationship with him?
72. A. Matt was a friend. I was closer to his brother, but we got along.

73. He liked the rooms at BREAKOUT. He liked talking to me about
74. the job.
75. Q. Your job?
76. A. Yeah. He was having problems with one of his managers at the
77. bowling alley, so he wanted to know if my parents were hiring for a
78. Game Master. He liked picking my brain about the role. He thought
79. he'd be good at it.
80. Q. Do you know which manager Matt was having problems with?
81. A. No. But honestly, Matt didn't get along with most people. He
82. was kind of a loner. Quiet and reserved. And he always wore this
83. trench coat that kids at school made fun of. They called him a school
84. shooter in the making, things like that.
85. Q. Great, Malachi. Just one more question: Were you aware
86. that Matteo Cesari operated *Cedar Creek Confessions*? After he
87. died, Matt's assets were seized by my department as part of the
88. larger investigation into his death. Files on his computer led us
89. to confirm that Matteo Cesari owned and operated the Instagram
90. account beginning on the twentieth of August last year. While
91. attending Cedar Creek High School, he created over seventeen
92. exposés, anonymously, through the account, about various
93. classmates.
94. MR. LEWIS: [*CLEARS THROAT*]
95. SHERIFF STALLARD: And you—and the rest of the kids inside
96. BREAKOUT when the fire started—were all people he targeted.
97. MALACHI JAMES-MAY: Is that part of the question, Sheriff? Because
98. it sounds more like an accusation to me.
99. SHERIFF STALLARD: Now, son—
100. MALACHI JAMES-MAY: I'd like you to keep in mind that holding

101. me against my will is a violation of my Fifth Amendment rights,
102. Sheriff, and—
103. **MR. LEWIS:** You are free to leave at any time.
104. **SHERIFF STALLARD:** Thank you for your time today, Malachi.
105. We'll make sure to follow up with you if our department has any
106. additional questions.
107. **MALACHI JAMES-MAY:** I'm sure you'd like to. But the next time
108. y'all wanna speak to me, you're gonna have to go through my
109. lawyer first.
110. [END OF INDIVIDUAL INTERVIEW WITH MALACHI
111. JAMES-MAY.]

CHAPTER TEN

Wednesday, May 20, 2026, 11:27 PM

"Okay, Steffi," Tobias says, cinching the nylon rope from the first room's padlocked trunk around one of the dining chairs to secure it to the dining table, "keep in mind that you're going to clang the shit out of these vents on your way to the control room. You won't have the element of surprise—if Malachi is behind this, he'll probably hear you coming."

I nod, but I'm only half listening, because my mind keeps flashing back to Charity's caved-in skull. I close my eyes and draw in a deep breath, attempting to snap out of it. *Be normal. Become the kind of girl who can work her way through an HVAC. Escape.*

But the truth is, I'm not equipped for this. *Arsonist's Revenge* already took the Cedar Creek High School student body president.

My childhood BFF. The girl who juggled a million extracurriculars and still had time for her friends. What's to stop this escape room from claiming me, too? Compared to Charity's golden girl track record, I'm a stain on my hometown, on the reputation of Sheriff Stallard, and on the history of this entire fucking franchise. Why do I deserve to survive if Charity Noelle Adler isn't coming out of BREAKOUT with us?

Standing in the hot, humid air of a Tennessee spring night. Charity across from me, idly leaning against the frosted glass of the BREAKOUT storefront as she snaps selfies for her own amusement. Tobias next to her, rubbing his hands up and down his freckled arms, leveling another glare at me. "Are you sure they're coming?" Guinevere's head on my shoulder as she takes a drag of her Marlboro Red. The hind wings of her resin luna moth earrings fluttering against her hair when she blows out the smoke.

"Steffi," Tobias snaps, jolting me back to the present. Jesus. That was real. Again, which means playing an escape room inside BREAKOUT with all my ex-friends is actually reversing my amnesia in a way that a full year of Call-Me-Diana's hypnotherapy never did. His impatient expression locks on mine, and I swallow the acid on my tongue. Damn. He's been talking this entire time.

"Sorry," I whisper, and I am. I wish I could pay attention, stay in the present, and stop losing myself in fragments of strange memories. "I hear you, though. Noise, control room, no element of surprise." I blink. "But we mapped out the layout together, right? So I'll be able to find my way back." I look back at the building schematics. "I remember the way, Tobias. Malachi told me the system is new, and the ducts are big—big enough to fit a person. It'll be fine."

"We're supposed to trust her?" Guinevere asks, cutting her eyes to Tobias in disbelief. This whole plan has come together rather quickly, but Gee is clearly still reeling from the fact I'm actually being trusted with this task. "She's the one who can't remember anything, and you're basing our entire plan on having her memorize a route?" Her nails dig into her arms. "Santo looked at the blueprints, too."

Matt's brother shakes his head. "I'm not going up there." When I glance at him, he frowns. "I mean, Zamekova's the best bet we have! Let's take a chance on her."

"Nice save," I mutter, stomach twisting as Tobias does one final tug on the rope. The dining chair wobbles a bit, but it holds steady. Steady enough for me to scale it, hopefully.

"Okay. If we're actually going to do this, you need to be one hundred percent confident you can pull this off." Tobias cocks his head. "Are you ready for this, Steffi?"

"Yeah," I tell him, tearing my gaze away from Santo's waxen face. Back to the metal shaft above me, to Matt's flickering silhouette dancing at the edges of the magenta-lit bathroom set, to the imagined ashes dripping from my fingertips and onto the white tiles below my sneakers. "Yeah, I am."

But what if I'm not? What if we've overestimated the capabilities of the HVAC itself? What if I can't find the control room? What if I plummet to my death? What if—

"Good," Tobias says, cutting off my thought spiral, and there it is again, that sense of brewing danger. "We're counting on it."

God, I hope I can pull this off. BREAKOUT's interconnected air ducts are practically emblazoned on the backs of my eyelids, but Guinevere is right—there's always a chance my memory will fail me. I can't show weakness, though. If I do, the other players will take this opportunity from me. And I can't stay inside *Arsonist's Revenge* any longer. It's part of *There's No Escape Rule #24: If your player group is annoying the fuck out of you, take a breather.*

Which means I need to brave the hodgepodge of precariously stacked furniture the others have assembled to aid me in reaching the HVAC. I stretch as I remember Malachi's house rules: *Please do not jump, pull on, or climb objects within the room. Remember: If it takes more than two fingers of force, you probably shouldn't be doing it.*

Luckily, the mouth of the vent isn't too high above us—we found enough prop items to significantly bridge the gap—but it'll still be difficult for me to clamber up the makeshift ladder, reach the metal lip, and find my way through the ducts and into the control room.

My dad's voice echoes in my head: *One thing at a time, Peanut.*

"Ready?" Santo asks. I nod, and he and Tobias boost me onto the dining table. Guinevere sucks her teeth as I outstretch my fingers, balancing my way to a dining chair with my hand against the tiled wall for stability as the legs teeter to one side—but there it is: the familiar determination that's fueled me through over two hundred escape rooms just like this one.

I crouch, waiting for the chair to adjust to my lower center of gravity, and then I—slowly, slowly, slowly—raise my body until I'm standing again. The HVAC is straight ahead, but I'll have to jump to reach it.

I glance at the LCD monitor, mumble a haphazard prayer, and launch myself forward, slamming into the HVAC's hot siding. My fingers immediately scrabble for purchase against the slick metal, but there's nothing to hold onto except stray nails and washers. Pain shoots up my forearms as my sweat-slicked left hand starts to slide off the metal lip.

"Come on, Zamekova," Santo calls. "You got this, Steff."

Somewhere below me, I dimly register the tower of furniture crashing to the ground, Guinevere cursing, and the continued sound of Santo's murmured encouragement. I fight against the urge to look down. I don't need to assess how high I'm dangling off the ground to know that if I let go now, I'll definitely break a bone.

My arms tremble. I don't have a choice. Jaw set, I strain my muscles until I catch the cuff of Matt's trench coat on one of the protruding spikes emerging from farther inside the HVAC. The leather snags, giving me enough leverage to wedge my right shoulder inside the vent, and then I twist, scrambling, until the material rips. Shit. The one memento I have to remember Matt by, and I just fucking ruined it.

The white flash of exposed nerve endings. Stars. Smoke. A falling beam. A guttural sound bursting from my mouth.

Rattling reverberates through my skull. I'm inside the vent. Matt's jacket is fucked, but the world didn't drop out from under me.

Cheers erupt from *Arsonist's Revenge*. "You good?" Santo shouts.

I press my forehead against the sweating metal and try to stop my rabbiting heartbeat. It feels like I'm within reach of a memory. A real one. One from the night Matt died. But I need to respond.

"Yeah," I say, surprised at how steady my voice is. "I'm good." I take another four-six-eight breath. "This may actually work." A beat. "What if I fall, though?"

"You're not going to fall." This from Guinevere, her tone clipped. "Just go. We all want to get out of here as soon as we can."

I try to concentrate, to expand the burning edges of the memory, but the scene slips through my fingers. I'm in the HVAC now. And the only way out is through.

Feeling suddenly grateful that I got a Tdap booster when I was fifteen, I unhook what's left of my mangled sleeve from the HVAC nail and start crawling through the air shaft. Despite my love for escape rooms, I don't love cramped spaces. But if this is a viable escape route—if the HVAC leads to any other room within BREAKOUT—then the four of us might actually escape *Arsonist's Revenge* without facing any more accidents. So I fend off the impending death-march swirling through my head; and I ignore the searing pain in my upper thigh as my skin scrapes against a protruding screw; and I breathe in mildew and dust mites as I clear the stationary blades of a giant axial fan, my knees shuffling forward, pretending I'm inhaling Dad's familiar sawdust-and-shaving-cream scent instead.

Him, I remember. No fire can take those memories away from me.

Dad got me into escape rooms. He was only a casual enthusiast, but he loved brainteasers: Einstein's Puzzles, Scrabble, Rummikub, Bananagrams. Our Saturdays were always reserved for family game nights: Mom laughing so hard at his wisecracks that she'd need to run to the bathroom in the middle of Go Fish; arguing over how many hotels you could place on Monopoly's Atlantic Avenue before the other players were legally allowed to beat you to death with their silver pieces; competing over who could solve the most clues in the *New York Times* crossword. For my twelfth birthday, he took me to Atlanta to play *Jailbreak* at PanIQ, and I've been hooked ever since. When Malachi's parents announced BREAKOUT's grand opening, the two of us were so excited to go together. Except we never got to.

My throat tightens. "Move on," I grunt, sliding through another curve in the HVAC system. The galvanized steel underneath me feels flimsier with every inch I gain while also simultaneously burning my skin, but all I can do is keep my head down, push forward, and hope I'll make it out.

I finish working my way through the curve, after which the ductwork branches off in three directions. Directly ahead, there's another huge fan. This one is also immobile, but I don't want to tempt fate more than absolutely necessary, so instead I turn my attention to the leftmost path. I'm about to go through it—thank you, mental map skills—when a rectangular piece of...something lying farther down the rightmost duct catches my eye. I furrow my brows and change course, wriggling toward the flat object until I can grasp it. I drag my hand backward and across another tetanus-inducing nail, and then I draw in an acetic breath as the page comes into focus in the low light.

It's another photograph.

"What the hell?" The words ripple off the air shaft, echoing through the metal—toward the control room, toward our Game Master, toward Malachi James-May—but right now, the only thing that matters is the tangible, sharp-edged memory in my hand.

Instead of depicting our scratched-out faces or our blood-steeped bodies, the third photograph, captured shortly after we completed *Egyptian Tomb* over winter break a year and a half ago, is completely normal at first glance. But the longer I stare at it in the baking HVAC's dim light, the more capital-W Wrong details I see, like I'm playing the world's most fucked-up version of I Spy: Charity's skin blurred to oblivion, Santo's smiling mouth pulled into a grotesque scowl, Tobias's missing eyes, Guinevere's rotated features, Malachi's distended jaw, my blackened pupils. Matt, standing directly in the middle, is the only one who looks normal. The sign he's holding has been edited, though. Instead of saying I WANT MY MUMMY like it did when Malachi took this selfie, it now reads NOT A FAN?

A drop of sweat slides down my spine. Whoever is keeping us within *Arsonist's Revenge* must have anticipated we'd try this. This is another fucking clue inside the goddamn HVAC.

We don't have the element of surprise at all.

Hands shaking, I flip the *Egyptian Tomb* photograph over. A sob breaks my lips as I read the message scrawled on the back. I have no idea what this sentence means, though I suspect I'll find out soon enough.

I tuck the photograph safely into my bra and double back through the vent, retracing my shimmied route until I'm back at the tri-fork. I take the leftmost path, like I originally intended, and follow it through its dips and curves until I emerge into the central area the schematics labeled as the plenum chamber. There's enough overhead space here for me to straighten slightly, but the crown of my head brushes the sheet metal above me even when I'm on my hands and knees. According to the blueprints, the various rectangular holes pocking the circular metal around me lead to other ducts. I've successfully made it to the beating heart of the entire system; now I just need to figure out which one of the connecting arteries will take me back to BREAKOUT's main complex and straight into the arterioles of Suite 263's control room.

I chew on my lower lip, trying to visualize the building schematics while also assessing my options when a draft of rancid, rotting air blows across my face. I blink tears out of my eyes, coughing, and attempt to duck under the collar of Matt's torn coat to shield myself, but that doesn't stop the stench from coating my tongue. Whatever is coming from the duct right in front of me, the smell is *foul*.

I cough again. "Jesus," I breathe, eyes still watering. Am I not alone? Is there a dead animal or something trapped up here with me? I know raccoons, mice, and even cats like to crawl into warm spaces during the winter, and that sometimes those animals curl up on a warm generator and get fried as a result, but it's the middle of May. We've had nothing but too-hot spring days for the past two months because East Tennessee's weather creeps into the high sixties as soon as we hit mid-March. And besides, Malachi said the HVAC was installed as part of this branch's recent renovations, which means the vents should be completely decomposing-carcass-free. There should be nothing here smelling like...like rotten eggs?

A distant warning sounds in my mind, but I ignore it in favor of crawling toward the putrid duct. I didn't build my blog empire on wussing out. Even if it's basically defunct now and I doubt it'll mean anything to SCAD, *There's No Escape* is the culmination of years of signing waivers for escape rooms wildly out of my comfort zone. My newsletter subscribers craved insights from thrilling, immersive, high-octane rooms, which meant I had to deliver, year after year, until I built enough of a following to monetize my hobby. Despite the terror I occasionally felt when interacting with live actors in different escape rooms across the county, forcing myself to be brave—if not for myself, then for my audience—made me stronger. Better. More resilient. I clench my teeth and square my aching shoulders. I may no longer be undergoing shit-your-pants levels of danger for the clamoring horde known as #TheresNoEscapeNation, but there's still a piece of me that knows how to push through fear. In a way, all the rooms I conquered for *There's No Escape* prepared me for this one.

BREAKOUT. *Arsonist's Revenge.*

I duck my head and clamber through the vent. The rotting smell gets stronger with every inch I gain. Desperate to find out what's causing the odor, my heart beats faster and faster until it's a reverberating buzz that propels me toward the looming grate ahead. I press a hand over my mouth to muffle my own breathing, but it's hopeless—the clanging of my knees against the HVAC's galvanized steel is pathetically loud as I peer through the metal grille. Instead of spotting an assortment of screens displaying BREAKOUT's live feed, however, I see a sprawling boiler room, complete with a working thermostat and a hissing emergency generator.

There's no one in it, but that doesn't matter, because the odor I've been following isn't coming from a putrefied animal. It's coming from here.

Across from me, the carbon monoxide alarm is blinking.

My heart stutters. Holy shit.

There's a gas leak inside BREAKOUT.

I close my eyes, newly hyperaware of every time I blink. I can't tell if it's my nerves exacerbating my physical reactions or the actual carbon monoxide gas messing with my breathing. If the alarm isn't blaring, the concentration can't be high enough for the gas leak to be life-threatening—at least, not yet. But it will be. I don't know when, exactly, but the leeching CO is probably already affecting our logic and reasoning skills.

Fuck. If we don't find a way to escape *Arsonist's Revenge* soon, the four of us are going to run out of air.

Even though watching the sputtering generator is kind of fascinating in a morbid way, this vent is a dead end, so I force myself to tear my gaze away from the boiler room and focus on the remaining paths of egress within the huge duct system. I should be close to the control room. I still need to find Malachi.

Moving through the rest of the HVAC is harder than I thought, though, especially now that I'm worried about every breath I take. I double back once again, terrified that I'm going to get lost up here like a twitchy-nosed rat scrabbling around in a maze, when a new metallic grate appears in the waiting dark like an answered prayer. I hold my breath as I creep toward it. Closer, closer, closer still, until I can press my face against the grille to reveal the room underneath me.

"Malachi?" I whisper against the metal slats, wriggling until the grate pushes into the skin of my jaw. I need to see the full picture. Our Game Master is here; I can sense it. He's just out of view, out of sight, out of reach. I reposition myself, tilting my right shoulder, craning my neck until every tangible thought in my head—memory or otherwise—evaporates.

Directly below me sits the array of HD monitors displaying three live feeds from BREAKOUT's rooms: *Alien Abduction*, *Haunted Mansion*, and *Arsonist's Revenge*. And slumped atop the control panel: Malachi Ashton James-May. Dorky glasses askew. Lanky limbs splayed. Arcade nachos abandoned, his knocked-over company thermos steadily dripping black coffee into a dark puddle on the epoxied floor.

I stare at him for a second, waiting for the telltale rise and fall of his chest, but nothing changes. There's just the steady *drip-drip* of the coffee, and the blur of my ex-friends inside *Arsonist's Revenge* on the monitors, and our Game Master below me, immobile, in a room I can't reach.

Panic claws its way up my throat. How long can a person go without breathing? I need to inhale for four seconds and keep the air trapped in my lungs for as long as humanly possible to figure out the answer, but my traitorous body starts hyperventilating instead. Why isn't he moving? Who's doing this to us, and why, and what do they want? My vision swims. Through it all, Mal doesn't move.

Which means that we were wrong. The person holding us in the escape room isn't our Game Master.

Our Game Master is dead.

• • •

yelp.com | Recommended Reviews: BREAKOUT Escape Rooms Inc.

Located in Cedar Creek, TN | Have you been here?
Write a review!

Did not like the food ★★☆☆☆
Posted by Kristen Saunders at 5:16 PM

The rental shoes and bowling lanes were okay but the food was not good. Greasy pizza and flat, warm soda...GROSS! Our son wants his next birthday here, but we will not be paying for anything from the food court.

Response from BREAKOUT Escape Rooms Inc. at 11:00 AM

> Hi, Kristen! We are an escape room business, not a bowling alley. Hope that helps!
> **—The James-Mays**

CHAPTER ELEVEN

Wednesday, May 20, 2026, 11:30 PM

I press a fist against my trembling lips to suppress my rising scream. Even if our Game Master isn't gushing blood from his neck, the sight of his lifeless body still sends hot nausea swooping through my stomach. Because if Mal isn't running our game, then who's puppeteering us?

Six friends, six secrets. One hour to spill them, or everyone dies.

Egg-scented bile rises in the back of my throat. I'm running out our countdown with every puzzle misstep, every bungled clue-solve, every mechanical error, and now my former friends are paying the price: Charity got her skull caved in. Malachi is face down in a carton of melted cheese. The emergency generator is gurgling poisonous gas into each of BREAKOUT's game rooms, we're all being blamed for what happened to Matt last year, and we're probably going to die in the same way he did.

My temple throbs, although I'm not sure if it's from the toxic fumes I'm definitely inhaling or the fear sledgehammering my pulse. There's a darker question at the heart of all this—the deadly revenge plot, our festering secrets, my desperate search for the truth—but because I don't feel ready to ask it yet, I force myself to push past the existential dread I feel about our imminent asphyxiation and refocus on the grille in front of me.

Unfortunately, one quick glance at the inch-thick steel sheet separating me from sweet freedom is enough to dash all my hopes of breaking into the control room to swipe Malachi's master keys. The vent cover is mounted from the outside, and there's no way my fingers can fit through the narrow slats of the grille in order to loosen a single screw.

In other words, I need to get out of here. I need to warn the others. I need to find my way back to *Arsonist's Revenge*.

As I retrace the path I army-crawled through the ductwork, though, I can't help registering the telltale signs of another anxiety attack tugging at my skin. Once I'm inside the escape room again, it'll be up to me to figure out who's picking us off. Which means that the goal of tonight is no longer using this hastily cobbled-together form of exposure therapy to recover the memories my TBI stripped from me, or piecing together the night that resulted in my best friend's death, or even fighting for closure from my ex-friends. It's about surviving. It's about catching a criminal. It's about breaking out.

I drag myself back through the vent branching off the boiler room to my left. Back through the plenum chamber dividing the control room from the main ductwork. Back through the tunnel leading to the immobile axial fan, the one I braved crawling through to get here. The whole time, though, I'm thinking about the generator and Malachi's too-still shoulder blades and the blinking light in the boiler room. If the four of us don't find a way out into the blissful open-air release of the Sevier County Plaza parking lot soon, we'll all die well before BREAKOUT opens at 10:00 AM tomorrow.

Jesus.

I'm almost done retracing my route through the HVAC—there's only the giant central fan left to drag myself through before turning right and emerging back at the mouth where I started—when Not-Matt's velvet voice bounces off the steel walls. *"Hello, players. Are you ready for more?"*

I freeze halfway through the axial fan's stationary blades. I can't help it—deepfaked or not, Matteo Cesari knows how to hold a captive audience. At the same time, every new syllable uttered by my dead best friend feels like getting hit by a train in slow motion, if that train also happened to know every salacious detail about the fire I've been unsuccessfully trying to piece together for the past year.

I shake my head to snap myself out of the trance and move to clear the rest of the fan, but then I realize that I can't move my right leg. Another piece of Matt's long leather trench coat is snagged on something behind me, preventing me from crawling forward.

I'm stuck.

Above me, a growing hum reverberates through the HVAC. Shit, shit, shit.

"*Malachi. Because you have failed to escape in time,*" Not-Matt continues as I ball the peeling fabric of the stupid fucking coat in my sweat-clammed hand, cursing, "*you have been eliminated, and your secret will now be revealed for you.*"

I can feel the hum in my ribcage, in my eardrums, in the soles of my feet. It's like the metal itself is singing. But I know the truth isn't nearly that beautiful.

It's the fans. They're turning on.

"*Now, this is a tough one. After all, he's everybody's favorite Game Master... but is he actually good at his job? Let's consult the footage, shall we?*"

"Please, please, please," I whisper, jerking the material of Matt's coat as hard as I can. Tears well up in my eyes. There's not enough room in the vent to wriggle out of it. If I can't free myself—

Blinding pain explodes through my calf.

Blood. A constellation of white stars. Light, and darkness, and pain. I'm going to pass out. I'm going to black out and inhale too much carbon monoxide and no one will ever find my fucking body.

I'm on the verge of succumbing to the blissful darkness when I hear Dad's voice in my head: *Stay awake, Peanut. There's always a way out.*

Is there? I don't know if I believe that anymore. But at the same time, I can't afford to fall unconscious when I still need answers about Matt's death. When I still need to interrogate my ex-friends about the pact, and the circumstances of the fire, and the part I played in *Wanderland* exactly a year ago. When I still need to hear the reasoning behind our group's subsequent friendship breakup. When I still need to find out if I'm actually the monster I'm terrified I am.

There's No Escape Rule #5: Embrace the burn.

New determination shoots through me, temporarily overpowering the agony, and I grit my teeth as time flashes and steadies for long enough for me to finish dragging myself through the last few feet of ductwork—forward, right, forward—before I'm almost at the open vent leading back into *Arsonist's Revenge*. White-hot fire surges through my muscles with every inch, but the screaming nerve endings in my leg are nothing compared to what we'll all suffer if I can't warn the others.

Right before I reach the metal lip of the exit, the HVAC judders threateningly. I yelp, startled, but the metal settles. "Okay," I whisper. False alarm.

A second later, the vent gives out from under me.

There's no way the ductwork was built for this, I realize, desperately attempting to avoid projectile-vomiting as I free-fall toward the tiled bathroom floor of *Arsonist's Revenge*. No one will be able to crawl through the HVAC after this. We've completely exhausted this escape route.

There's a shrill shriek, and for a second I'm terrified that the falling duct crushed someone on its descent, but when I crawl out from the dented, broken-off piece of the HVAC that cushioned my landing the first thing my blurred vision registers is Tobias, Guinevere, and Santo, all alive, staring at me open-mouthed.

"Hey," I tell them. "I'm back in the game."

And then I promptly pass the fuck out.

● ● ●

When I come to, the first thing I notice is that the bathroom set LCD monitor is at 28:21.

The second is that there's an expression I haven't seen before on Santo's unguarded countenance. His mouth is twisted, and his dark eyes glitter with calculated hate as he dabs at my bloodied calf with the sleeve of his crewneck. The migraine pulsing against my temples turns into a battering ram. Am I imagining things? I know that the swirling mix of adrenaline and pain in my bloodstream is probably making me dizzy, sick, and delusional. Santo doesn't hate me; Matt does. Or at least, he did. Right before he died.

"Feeling any better?" Santo whispers. "You're bleeding a lot."

When I blink, his bleached brows are furrowed in perfect concern. God, I must have imagined it. I start to nod—

Matt, exactly a year ago, baring his teeth in the dark UV glow of Wanderland. *There's a barrier between us—a door made to look like a plastic hedge—and I'm advancing, speaking words that are just out of reach, as my veins pulse with rage.*

I gasp as I'm pulled out of the murky shadows of memory and back into the second room of *Arsonist's Revenge*. The stars swell, threatening to whiteout my vision, but I don't let them. "Malachi," I rasp instead, about to share the awful news of what I found in the control room when a surge of nausea lodges itself in my throat. Wait. We're locked in here with a *murderer*. A killer. Someone who must have set up the cinder block electromagnetic sensor mechanism. Who must have messed with Malachi's coffee. Who must have slipped out through the doors of the control room the second they heard me clanging in the ceiling overhead.

Or maybe, the dark voice in the back of my mind whispers, *the mastermind behind all of this—the invitations, the photographs, the deaths—is you.*

Santo freezes. "What about him?"

I shudder. I went into the vents. I saw Malachi dead. I found a photograph from *Egyptian Tomb* with another chilling message. And I need to be careful with how and when I reveal those breadcrumbs to the others, because the next—I glance up at the LCD monitor—twenty-eight minutes and twelve seconds will change everything.

I lick my lips. If I can recall what happened in *Wanderland* last spring, I'll be able to deduce what's going on tonight. I just need to survive on enough borrowed time to figure it out—and especially now, because rooting out a psychopath depends on it.

"I...I didn't see him," I lie. "There's no way out through the HVAC. None of the vents are viable; I couldn't unscrew anything from the inside, especially without my Swiss Army knife. And part of the HVAC b-broke on my way back, obviously, so—"

Agonizing pain shoots through my nerve endings. The walls of the bathroom set stretch out in front of me, turning into sparkling tea party vials and spewing generators and the sight of Malachi's breathless body all at once.

"Steffi, what happened to you?" Tobias asks, his freckled face swimming into focus: wide hazel eyes, dark bruise bleeding black-and-blue around the edges, gore-sprayed glasses tangled in his russet hair. Guinevere stays back, her full mouth pinched, her crossed arms shaking.

"There was...a fan," I whisper. "But that doesn't m-matter." My hair is plastered to my face; my palms are soaked with blood. "I found...a generator. We're...we're being poisoned. With a gas leak. Here, within...inside BREAKOUT."

"Yeah?" Tobias says, his voice cracking as he swipes a hand across his sweating forehead.

"Yeah," I whisper. "It's just like last year. Except instead of a f-fire, we're dealing with carbon m-monoxide poisoning."

Which means the question is no longer a matter of *how*.

It's *when*.

• • •

CEDAR CREEK CONFESSIONS

posted 1 day ago

Are you ready? I know I am.

Let's play a game, Cedar Creek. Here are the rules:

1. There's always a price to pay for your past mistakes.

2. No one can win.

CHAPTER TWELVE

Wednesday, May 20, 2026, 11:33 PM

"So that's it?" Guinevere demands. "We're back to square one?"

"Not square one," Tobias counters as I run my tongue across my teeth, tasting metal and rotten-egg HVAC gas. "We can't discount our progress—we're solidly in the middle game now." He takes off his fogged-up tortoiseshell glasses and wipes them on his maroon chess sweatshirt with a scoff. "Not like it's getting any cooler in here, though. If I had to guess, the temperature's currently sitting at ninety-two degrees Fahrenheit."

"Why not give us the conversion to Celsius while you're at it?" Santo snaps. A muscle tics in Tobias's sweating forehead, but Santo's brief flash of rage disappears as another swell of stars overtakes my vision. "We need to stabilize Zamekova. Gee, go get the clothes from the coatrack in the first room. Tobias, bring your medical duffel." When neither of them move, Santo scowls. His silver rings glint in the LED light as he slides off his studded belt. "Now!"

"Tylenol." Tobias leaps to his feet. "You need Tylenol. And gauze."

Santo's eyes return to me, but I can only catch every fourth word he says: *Traumatic. Tie. Tourniquet.*

I don't have the energy to respond before Tobias coaxes a handful of pills between my cracking lips. Guinevere returns with an armful of clothes—the cotton lumberjack flannel, the hat with the raccoon tail, the pilling CCHS hoodie—and lays them out on the bathroom floor. Santo stares at the options, his gaze inscrutable. I blink, opting to stare at the hallucinatory patterns twisting in the sheet metal of the broken HVAC instead of at his heart-wrenchingly familiar face. Four of us left alive, and soon it might be three. *Ambience: 4.3/5. Difficulty: 5/5. Body Count: 2/6.*

"Steff, can you hear me? We're dealing with an unintentional...I'm going to...should staunch...bleeding until..." He blinks. "Okay?"

"Okay."

"Cool," Santo says. His cross earring glints as he leans forward to prop up my leg; his chipped black fingernails fumble with the fabric.

As he wraps the flannel around my knee, I resist the full-body shiver crawling up the nape of my neck. Instead, I focus on Santo Cesari's features: glittering eyes framed by innocent lashes, a constellation of birthmarks snaking up his slanting nose, the purplish-orange burn scars that glow like flames in the bathroom set's magenta floodlights. His stringy hair falls into his thick eyebrows while he works, and he makes no effort to push the strands away.

"Why didn't you tone it?"

"Hm?" Santo says, pulling the flannel taut against my skin.

"Your hair," I say, staring at his yellow-blond head. "You said you wanted it to be more platinum, but you bleached it and didn't tone it. Why?"

He shrugs. "I didn't know you were supposed to." When I don't answer, his gaze flicks up to my face. "Is that what you use? To get your red hair?"

I frown. "Yeah. I mean, I bleach it first, but toner helps to c-counteract the bleach's brassy yellow tones. Using toner before hair dye can also help your c-color go on more evenly, especially if you're working wi—"

"Are you sure you didn't find anything in the control room?" Santo asks, interrupting me. "Any sign of Mal? Any sign he's... you know... alive?"

I push down the regret on the tip of my tongue and steel my expression to meet his. I will not be the reason we lose focus. I know what's at stake. If I tell the truth about Malachi, the news will spread and the rest of us will waste our increasingly precious minutes pointing fingers instead of working together. "I'm disappointed, too," I murmur. "About the gas leak, about my stonewalled search for answers, about our friendship breakup. All of it. But I don't know any more than you do."

"Well, your plan may have failed," Santo says, looping the belt around my knee, "but I still trust you to get us out of here." A sad smile ghosts his face. "And the hair...I know it's ugly, but I changed it because I got tired of looking in the mirror and seeing my brother's face."

I squeeze my eyes shut and try not to hyperventilate. Images flash in my mind on rapid-fire: my childhood best friend's shattered forehead. The hot-pink smiley face on the cardstock invitation. Nails scrabbling against metal. My dead-end job at Perfect Strike. A whirring fan. The scratched-out photograph. The new post from *Cedar Creek Confessions*. My printed blog post on the fridge. The glistening letters in ONE BY ONE, WE ALL FALL DOWN. OPEN. OPEN. OPEN.

"You know the rest of the group thinks I'm faking it?" I tell Santo, emboldened by the fact that I have nothing to lose. "My amnesia." I swallow, the bitter aftertaste of Tobias's Tylenol on my tongue. "Actually, I bet you do, too."

His brows pull together. "What do you mean?"

I shake my head. "After Matt died, I reached out to you so many times. I sent texts. I left voicemails, and I mailed you letters with international fucking stamps, and I even redownloaded WhatsApp—which my grandmother in Přerov has been begging me to do for months, by the way—just to see if you'd reply to my Wi-Fi calls. And after the funeral...nothing."

Lightning cracks through my leg. I hiss a stream of expletives, but Santo doesn't meet my eyes. "I'm sorry," he says, but I can't tell which pain he's apologizing for.

Instead of thinking too much about it, I pull the *Egyptian Tomb* photograph from my sweat-soaked T-shirt. "Do you want to know something insane?" I ask Santo. "Whoever's watching our game knew we'd try to climb through the cooling system."

He stills at the sight of the photoshopped printout. "Did you find that in the HVAC?" he asks. "Do you think Mal planted it?"

"Someone had to, right? Though it might not be Malachi." I keep my focus fixed on Santo's face as I talk, prepared to back off the second anything seems off in his microexpressions.

But he remains impassive. His eyes cut to the fridge door, where Guinevere is going over the newspaper clippings in the kitchenette. "So you think…"

"Since we're being honest," I say, "let's just say I'm prepared to consider any possibility."

Right now, Santo is the only one I can trust. He would never hurt Malachi. He stares at me for a long time—longer than we can afford. But I let him.

"So you *do* want to team up," he says, his earring glinting in the light as he grins. When I nod, his expression turns serious. "In that case, let's keep this between us," Santo continues, glancing at the photograph. "At this point, we need to take any advantage we can get."

I take the hint and tuck the photograph back into my bra. "One condition: We trust each other until we get out of here. No more secrets. No more ghosting. No more excuses."

"Then it's settled," Santo says. He extends a single black-nail-polished, silver-ring-adorned hand to me, and I set my jaw as I take it. "We're officially partners in crime."

I shake his clammy hand. "Partners in crime," I repeat.

Santo pulls me to a standing position; I wobble, but my knees don't buckle. So far, so good. I don't know if it's the tourniquet or the painkillers or the possibility that my injury is less serious than we first thought, but I'm not in immediate danger of passing out. I'm lightheaded, but I'll be able to keep playing.

"So, Resident Escape Room Expert," Santo whispers, "what's next? The HVAC route may not have worked, but I'd love another chance at not dying in this room."

"Already working on it," I say, scanning the interior of *Arsonist's Revenge*. "We have the next photograph, which means we have the next clue: *Where you share your message matters*."

It feels good to be working out in the open again—even if we're inhaling CO and mercaptan while we do it—and it feels even better to have another person on my side. I'm no longer lone-wolfing it—I'm collaborating. Still, though, as Santo stares at me with newfound trust, I can't help the guilt that snakes up my throat. I'm keeping Malachi's death from him. From all the players.

"Great." Santo claps his hands together. "Oh! While you were gone, we found this. Maybe it'll help us." He gives me a handheld flashlight, and hope flutters its wings against my rib cage as I click it on and the beam shines faintly purple. It's a black light. A worldwide escape room staple, allowing you to see UV clues in places you've already checked. Oh, did you think you were done with the painting placards? Maybe look again. Go on, give that laminated diary one final sweep. The crisp fake bills in that envelope you found? Yeah, you might want to scan those, too.

"Have you found anything with it yet?" I ask.

"Nope. But you might." Another smile. "Come on, Zamekova. Let's go look around."

Holding the black light here makes everything around me feel too bright and too loud. "It may light up for more than just fake paint," I whisper as I sweep the beam across the bloodied bathroom tiles, trying not to think about how a few hours from now, forensics investigators may be doing the same with luminol and our blood. Our bodies. *Arsonist's Revenge* as a bona fide crime scene.

I readjust my grip around the black light. No, this is an opportunity. As long as we're finding pieces and connecting them, I'm getting closer to—

Above us, the LCD monitor flashes hot pink before it turns completely black.

"Did you see that?" I ask Santo. *There's No Escape Rule #1: Always keep an eye on the clock.* "What just happened to the screen?"

It's no longer running the countdown timer with its innocuous smiley face logo in the background. Instead, it looks dead.

Santo frowns. "Maybe the other one is working?"

I duck through the fridge door to check, still holding the black light, and Santo follows me. But the LCD monitor in the living room set isn't turned on, either.

My best friend's identical twin glances at me, shrugging, and helplessness surges through my body in response. We need to know how much time we have left on the countdown, which means we need to get past this new obstacle. But how?

Beside us, in the kitchenette, Guinevere impatiently riffles through drawers—oven mitt, wooden spatula, an assortment of plastic spoons—and the repetition of her nails scraping against the cheap wood burrows itself into my skull: *tick, tick, tock.* Tobias is back to scrutinizing the wall-mounted cabin prints. Charity is still slumped in front of the sink.

Oh my God. Charity.

Santo follows my gaze to her mangled body. "Please tell me you're not serious."

The comment stings, but I force my expression to stay neutral. "If you want to die in"—I glance up at the dark LCD monitor—"however many minutes, then be my guest. But we need to know the time."

Especially when we're running out of it.

I shoulder past Santo, stepping instead into the pool of Charity's oil-black blood, and Guinevere's storm-gray eyes snap to mine. "What the hell are you doing?" she asks, pausing with her hand curled around the wooden spatula, but I don't answer. Instead, I crouch to lift Charity's pale wrist—her skin still warm—and force myself to ignore how my own skin tingles with the weight of Guinevere's anger, Santo's guilt, and Tobias's judgment. I need Charity's watch.

But when I look at Charity's wrists, she's wearing only a pearl-studded bracelet.

You heard me, her soft voice goads in my mind. *Turn out your pockets.*

"Jesus," I murmur, drawing back from her body. "Her watch is gone."

"Oh my God," Guinevere snaps, retreating into the bathroom set, "you're fucking crazy, Stephanie." Santo shakes his head and follows her, and after a moment, Tobias stops looking at the wall prints and ducks through the fridge door, too.

My stomach clenches. I should have seen this coming: Everything inside *Arsonist's Revenge* is too well-timed to be running autonomously. The clues are too detailed. The videos are too targeted. The deaths are too…creative. Whoever's behind this has to know that. This is part of their master plan—the revenge setup, the twisted videos, the in-room puzzles based on last year's tragedy. And with Malachi out of commission, at this point in the game it's abundantly clear: Everything inside *Arsonist's Revenge*—the cut wires, the weird newspaper clippings, my stolen Swiss Army knife, the photographs, the rising heat, the carbon monoxide gas, Charity's missing timekeeper—is only here because of an insider.

Which means that the person doing this—the person keeping us trapped to play out their twisted revenge fantasy—is one of us.

To my left, the light in the bathroom flickers.

Two seconds later, both rooms in *Arsonist's Revenge* plunge into total darkness. No LCD monitors. No LEDs. No lantern.

There's a rustling. A thud. And then, worst of all: a bloodcurdling scream.

● ● ●

yelp.com | Recommended Reviews: BREAKOUT Escape Rooms Inc.

Located in Cedar Creek, TN | Have you been here?
Write a review!

The best experience I've ever had! ★★★★★
Posted by Leslie Zoebelien at 4:01 PM

My bridesmaids and I did *Deranged Clown Circus* together as part of my bridal shower after seeing the room reviewed on *There's No Escape*, and we had such a blast! A few of the puzzles weren't difficult to figure out, but some clues were a lot trickier than others. The game definitely gave us a run for our money HAHA! :) So happy it's close to home, too, though my girlfriends and I already made plans to check out the Pigeon Forge location next month. Five glowing stars!

98 Days Before the Accident

I'm not sure how to tell my boyfriend that I'm probably a lesbian. But even though letting Matt kiss me turns my stomach, it's less nauseating than the idea of confessing my sexuality.

Almost everyone in my friend group is queer, but I'm just not ready to be out in Cedar Creek, Tennessee. So instead, I suck it up. Endure his tongue against my tongue, his lips against my lips, his teeth against my teeth. Act fucking normal. Smile.

Matt pulls back, a strand of saliva stretching between us, and that disgusts me so much that I almost break up with him right then and there. But then I glance over at Steffi, who's watching us, and the words die in the back of my throat.

"You're good, babe," Matt says, his cold eyes assessing as he looks me over. Behind him, the lights from the arcade glitter as the overhead Sparefinder plays out my next ideal shot: PIN 3 SENDS THE 6 INTO THE 10 PIN. It's not a question. With his angular face so close to mine, all sharp jaw and strong nose and harsh Adam's apple, it's easy to see why he turned heads when he first arrived at CCHS. Add in his thick eyebrows, irritating smirk, and almost-black curls, and Matteo Luca Cesari becomes the perfect Build-A-Boyfriend.

When I look at him, though, my mouth only floods with the phantom taste of chili cheese fries and Nashville hot chicken.

"Get a room!" Malachi calls from our booth, and Tobias and Charity snicker. One of the Perfect Strike managers shoots us a look from behind the arcade bar, where she's monitoring both our group and a couple of nervous-looking sophomores on what looks like their first date, but then she goes back to reading her *Science Today* magazine without saying anything. When she's on the schedule, Steffi and Matt don't get shit for bowling with us. When their regional manager is here, though…

Well, they'd probably be resetting the broken LED-lit pinsetter of the sophomores in Lane Two instead of lounging around on the sleek maple benches with their bowling shoes on.

Instead of baring my teeth at Matt, I turn to the ball dispenser. "Yeah," I tell him, curling my fingers into the eight-pounder I've been using all night. "I am good." I glance toward my adoring fans. "Who's ready to watch me get another strike?"

Steffi boos loudly in response, and a smile curves my lips as I step toward Lane Six and line up my shot. We're in the tenth frame, which means I now have two additional chances to increase my points by a maximum of twenty. I'm already leading by thirty-four tonight, though, so anything extra at this point is just a bump to my ego.

I kiss the ball—a good excuse to get the taste of Matt's lips off my own—before I flick my wrist and release it. I hold my breath as I watch the marbled resin glint over and over, rolling toward the gutter before it curves at the last second. *BOOM.* All the pins go down, satisfyingly, and when I whirl back toward my friends, Steffi is grinning. My stomach flips.

"Damn, girl. Save some points for the rest of us!" Malachi calls, and I laugh to stave off the awkward feeling, unsure if Matt is going to kiss me in congratulations again. But my boyfriend isn't smiling this time. Instead, he's staring at the screen with our scores. A muscle ticks in his jaw. He didn't think I'd pull it off, I realize, and now he's definitely going to lose to me.

And Matt is a sore loser. It's his absolute worst quality.

Santo claps his hands together. "Well, that's game. Nice job, Gee." He nods to the scoreboard. "Want to play another? Mal's shift doesn't start for another hour."

Matt hums noncommittally. He's still staring at the scoreboard, and something about the way his teeth are clenched makes my heart drop. I know he's going to be an asshole before he even opens his mouth. "You have a lighter ball, though," my boyfriend says. "It's easier to knock down the pins when you don't have to use as much force to throw."

The comment doesn't gnaw at me, but the switch-up is insane. Besides, I'm sick from the cloying notes of Matt's aromatic aftershave. "Great. So, I'm going to take a smoke break," I announce to no one in particular, and then I shoulder through the employee exit while still in my bowling shoes, ignoring Steffi asking me if I'm okay, until I wind up in the dimly lit alley behind Perfect Strike with the cool air buffeting my too-hot face. Above me, the night sky is dark and starless. I pull out my lighter and realize I don't have my cigarettes on me—I left my pack in the car. Fuck.

The door opens, and I quickly move to wipe the glistening tears from my cheeks before I realize it's just Santo. He doesn't stare at me. Doesn't cock his head to ask what's wrong, or linger in the doorway, unsure of how to comfort me, or tell me that I need to suck up my rage and trot back inside. Instead, he just slides a pack of American Spirits out of his jeans and leans against the brick wall. I raise a pointed eyebrow at the plastic carton, and Santo sighs.

"I know. It's a racist-ass design—just like our school mascot, by the way—but unfortunately, I got hooked on these during the two-month-stint we spent in Portland and now I can't smoke anything else. What are we looking at?" he adds, offering me one, and typically that would get a laugh out of me, because the alley behind Perfect Strike is filled with nothing other than rusting dumpsters and, according to Steffi, tetanus-inducing shards of scrap metal. But tonight isn't a normal night.

"I'm just so fucking sick of your brother," I say, taking it. With my other hand, I snap my thumb against the flint wheel of my Zippo until the flame catches. I know it's a bad idea to shit-talk Matt to Santo like this—everything gets back to him eventually. But I'm tired of always pretending to be the perfect girlfriend.

And angry enough to smoke an American Spirit cigarette, apparently.

Santo nods and lights up with me. The flame dances over his face, illuminating his glinting canines, his mouth curling like its own wisp of smoke. "I know what you mean. He drives me crazy, too. But I'm the one who has to live with him, you know?" He exhales slowly before glancing at me. "You don't."

We stand and smoke in silence for a minute. The end of my filter burns sunset-orange; I find myself wishing that I had my Marlboro Reds instead. Eventually, Santo tips his chin back to exhale. "Gee. You know how you'll sometimes catch me staring at Malachi across the room?" he asks suddenly.

I relight my cigarette and take another drag. We've never talked about this out loud before, and even in the liminal space of the alley behind Perfect Strike, it feels a little dangerous. "Yeah," I tell him.

"That's how you look at Steffi. I don't know if Matt sees it yet. But I do."

I choke on the inhale, smoke stinging my lungs. Santo pats my back. Ash falls onto the cement and crumbles away between us.

"Don't worry—I'm not going to tell anyone," my boyfriend's brother says. "I don't think you're obvious about it, either. The only reason I even noticed is because Mal and I are doing the same thing. Or...at least, we might be. It's getting harder to tell, especially with how much traction that *Cedar Creek Confessions* post about him is getting. He's not out, either, so maybe he backed off because he's getting scared." He smiles sadly. "Or maybe he doesn't like me as much as I thought he did."

"Is it hard for you?" I ask before I can stop myself. "Keeping your feelings about him hidden like that?"

Santo sighs before taking another drag. When he blows out a plume of smoke, it catches on the floodlights bathing the dumpsters. Like this, he's almost like a wise, chain-smoking, gay angel.

"It's basically impossible," he finally says. "I'm comfortable being out, but it's caused problems for me at other schools. Matt's had to deal with that pushback, too, which is why we typically don't last anywhere for longer than a few months."

"Seriously?"

Santo glances over at me; his forehead is covered in a light sheen of sweat. "Let's just say *Cedar Creek Confessions* isn't the only gossip account I've dealt with in the past." He shakes his head. "You know, I don't want to make Mal's life miserable. I can't ask him to change for me, but I don't want to pretend for him, either. So, for now, we go to the water tower late at night, and we let our unspoken feelings linger between us." He flicks his cigarette butt toward the dumpster. "But sometimes, I do wish it was easier."

I turn toward him, my eyes bright from anger and nicotine and the thrill of speaking my mind. "So let's do something about it."

"About what?"

"Making things easier. This all started with *Cedar Creek Confessions*, right? So if we unmask who's behind the account and make them pay..." When Santo blinks, I shake my head. "Promise me," I insist. "I'm not taking no for an answer—promise me you'll help me unmask whoever runs the account. If not for me, then at least for you and Malachi. For Charity. For Tobias." I dig my nails into my palms. "For Steffi."

Santo stares at me for a long time. "Is this actually important to you?" he asks. I nod, and the action surprises me. It feels good to be honest about what I truly want for once. Finally, he sighs. "Fine. I promise."

"Pinky swear?" I ask, because this moment is the closest I've gotten to solidarity in all my years in Cedar Creek, and I can't tell him just how much it means to me.

He hooks his painted little finger around mine. "Yeah. Pinky swear."

CHAPTER THIRTEEN

Wednesday, May 20, 2026, 11:38 PM

"Guinevere," I whisper, shooting to my feet and racing through the fridge door just as the LEDs flood both rooms again. I stumble, caught off-guard by the unexpected burst of color—*Lighting Synchronization: 0.3/5*—and wince at the fresh pain sizzling up my calf as I land on the tiled floor of the bathroom. There's splattered blood in the grout, and I can't tell if it's mine or Charity's or Guinevere's. *No, no, no. Please, not Guinevere. I don't want it to end this way.*

I look up, and my heart flatlines. She's gripping the edge of the rusting sink, her olive-skinned arms trembling, but she's alive. Oh, praise Jesus. She isn't dead.

"Gee," I say softly. "What the fuck happened?"

Above her, the mounted LCD screen nestled in the corner between the bathtub and the curtained shower flickers back to life. *"Hey,"* Not-Matt's voice says casually, like this is just another escape room game night from junior year. But there are no videos this time. No photographs. No gimmicks. Just his voice and the gore-splattered walls closing in. *"Guinevere. Because you have failed to escape in time, you have been eliminated, and your secret will now be revealed for you."*

Except Guinevere hasn't been eliminated. She's breathing, the rise and fall of her resin-moth-wing-adorned chest steady in the dim light, and for now, I need that to be enough. She's safe. She was supposed to die, and she didn't.

"I...I ran into something, I think," she says, gesturing to her bloodied stomach with a red-streaked hand, and I'm suddenly reminded of sitting next to her on a middle school field trip to the Georgia Aquarium, watching raindrops race against the bus window, smelling the freshly washed scent of her caramel-brown hair. "Just...wasn't looking where I was going."

I slip off Matt's ripped-up trench coat instead of questioning her. "Here," I say. "Put this on. To stop the bleeding."

Guinevere eyes me. For a beat, I'm worried she's not going to take it. But then she accepts the fabric, pressing the worn leather of her boyfriend's trench coat against her wound, and for a moment it's almost like she's the girl who mailed me handwritten letters for every birthday. The girl who carefully scraped the bodies of moths from the light fixtures outside the CCHS science wing on warm March days to repurpose in her jewelry. The girl who used to love me, if only as her friend.

In front of me, Santo unfreezes. "Oh my God," he says, his smoke-scarred vocal cords rawer than usual. His rings catch on the magenta floodlights as he raises a hand to his heart. "I thought you were dead."

Guinevere laughs hollowly. "Disappointed?" she asks, but her manicured fingers tighten against the fabric. Now that she's covering the wound, I can't tell how serious her injury is. How much blood has she lost? Is the bleeding slowing? What's the depth and width of the cut?

"Making it in the art world requires connections," Not-Matt continues. *"But so does avoiding a lawsuit. Thank God your dad is a federal circuit judge, right?"*

I glance at Tobias. "Did any of you see what happened?"

He snorts. "In case you didn't notice, Steffi, all the lights went off before Guinevere impaled herself."

I open my mouth, ready to ask a thousand follow-up questions, but Santo raises a pierced eyebrow before I can. "Yeah, including your lantern. Odd time to turn it off, don't you think?"

Tobias narrows his hazel eyes. "Careful," he says softly. "Loss doesn't absolve you of blame."

"What the fuck is that supposed to mean?" Santo snarls, taking a step toward Tobias, just as the LCD monitor changes again. We're back to the hot-pink smiley face.

"You destroyed my mother's right to a fair trial after my death, because your father didn't want his network to know the truth: Your smoking habit started the BREAKOUT fire after you dropped a lit cigarette into a trash can filled with flammable paper."

Guinevere's face blanches as the next part of the black-and-white *Wanderland* footage fills the screen. Jesus. This is her secret—she started the fire.

"Hey," I say, turning back to Tobias and Santo. "Knock it off, both of you. You're teammates. Act like it."

My voice is confident—like I'm upselling a customer on a bowling package or hopping on a video call with an escape room business that's interested in comping my travel in exchange for a *There's No Escape* review—but I want to crumble into dust as soon as the words leave my chapped lips. Are we teammates? I'm not so sure. Did Tobias know the power would go out and that's why he turned off his lantern? How long has it been off? What happened to Guinevere? Did she run into something, like she said, or did someone stab her? Is Santo in on it? His argument with Tobias could be purely for show, or maybe Guinevere lured us here and hurt herself on purpose to divert suspicion away from her.

Or maybe you hurt Guinevere, my mind's dark voice suggests, *and your brain is so messed up that you don't even remember stabbing your knife into her muscled stomach over and over and over again.*

I inhale. Four. Six. Eight. *Calm the fuck down. Relax. Breathe.*

"Give me that." Santo snatches the lantern out of Tobias's limp grasp, rotating the base to turn it back on. "You can't be trusted anymore."

But can any of us? I press the flannel tourniquet against my bloodied calf and close my eyes against the rising tide of pain. The power dynamics within BREAKOUT are slowly shifting; Tobias is losing his competitive edge, and Guinevere's influence is ebbing with every drop of blood splattering on the tile below our feet.

The video on the monitor turns off. The countdown resumes: 21:47. "*Good luck, players,*" Not-Matt says, his tone gloating. "*Enjoy the rest of your game.*"

The speakers resume their white noise water sounds, and I shudder involuntarily. At least our timer is back.

Santo scoffs, heading out of the bathroom, and Tobias scowls before following him. My gaze drops to Guinevere. *There's No Escape Rule #16: When dealing with multiple rooms, try to keep at least one player in each one.* "Are you okay?" I ask her. "Do you know what happened?"

How are you alive?

She snorts, but the sound is tinged with pain. "You don't have to pretend to care about me, Stephanie. I wouldn't blame you if you left, too; I mean, I've been completely horrible to you all night." When I don't respond, Guinevere winces. "Come on. Now that you know I started the fire, you must hate me."

"To be honest," I tell her, "I'm just relieved you're not fucking dead."

Her hurricane eyes meet mine; in response, I force myself not to look away. I hope I'm not the one who stabbed her. Call-Me-Diana doesn't think my memory loss works like that, but I'm not so sure about anything anymore. I don't even remember how Matt asphyxiated in *Wanderland*, so how am I supposed to understand anything about *Arsonist's Revenge*?

Guinevere blinks. "Stephanie," she says quietly, "there's something I need to tell you."

My heart rate picks up. This is it; I'm finally going to get answers. The truth. Gee is going to tell me everything.

"Holy shit!" Santo exclaims from the other room. He materializes in the fridge doorway, holding an ax. "Do you guys remember the key from the locked trunk with the fake body? I just realized we never used it, so I tried it on the kitchen cabinet. Anyway, it worked, and this was inside." He twirls the ax around. "Maybe we can use it to tear down the walls. I mean, they can't be that thick, right? They're probably, like, ninety percent plywood and plaster. Insulation foam. We can hack into another room with this, get to the lobby, and leave BREAKOUT."

I shake my head. "The ax-head is rubber, and all these walls are covered in concrete. At best, we've discovered another useless prop. At worst, you've just found an effective bludgeoning tool." Jesus. I hope we're not expected to kill one another with this.

"Either way, the last two minutes change things," Gee says darkly. And she's right. Even though Guinevere is cradling her bleeding stomach, the fact that she's still standing proves an important (and critical) part of the new house rules in tonight's BREAKOUT game:

Avoiding death is possible.

● ● ●

Processing this new information feels like it'll take forever. Unfortunately, the LCD monitor is now at 20:42, so we don't have forever. We only have about twenty minutes left.

Every pore in my body is clogged with sweat and blood and mercaptan. There's a dead girl and potentially a murderer locked in here with us, a slew of unsolved puzzles ahead, and a sinister smiley-faced Game Master mocking us from every hidden inch of this place with Matt's voice. But there's still some buried, hidden part of me that loves escape rooms, that lives for the thrill of a good game, that isn't going to let my paranoia stop me. We have photographs from *Moonshine Cabin*, *Serial Killer's Hideout*, and *Egyptian Tomb*. Despite the dread seeping into my bone marrow, we're making progress. This is just an escape room. A BREAKOUT room. And goddamnit, we are going to find a way to break out.

I sweep the black-light beam around the bathroom, searching for a glimmer of fluorescence, when I catch a flash of movement in the shower mirror and startle. A stranger bares her teeth at my reflection, her shoulder-length red hair slick with sweat; her translucent skin shimmering with veins and splattered substances (smudged mascara, clotted blood, cerebrospinal fluid). I look like hell, but as long as my heart is beating, I can still escape.

"Hey," Santo says softly, materializing beside me in the mirror, and then, when I flinch: "Don't worry. It's just me."

But that's the problem, isn't it? It's never just him. Not when, even though he's burn-scarred, he still has my best friend's face.

Santo glances at Tobias, who is busy examining the bathtub now that his tantrum from earlier is over, and drops his hoarse voice to a lower register. "Listen, the latest clue from that HVAC photograph: *Where you share your message matters.* Do you think that could correspond with the PVC puzzle?"

I blink. "I'm not sure how you arrived at that conclusion, but I'm willing to hear you out."

"Okay, listen," Santo says. "When we initially stepped into this room, what was the first thing we noticed?"

I glance at the PVC pipe wall. "The scrawled letters that spelled out *ONE BY ONE*."

"Exactly. Clearly a threat, right?" He licks his lips. "Except... what if it's a *message*?" He looks back at the electrical box. "When I put the fuse in, the lights changed to show WE ALL FALL DOWN. But both of those threats were written on the PVC pipe wall. So, what if the messages are about the PVCs?" Santo says. "What if the pipes are meant to fall?"

I frown. "Even if they are, we risk ruining the setup every time we touch one—which, without a Game Master to reset the room, means we can't progress until we're absolutely sure we know what we're doing."

Santo raises an eyebrow when I say *without a Game Master*, and for a moment, I'm worried he's going to ask about Malachi again. But then he smiles. "We know what we're doing," he says, reaching for the top left PVC pipe. Sure enough, he unscrews it and sets it on the ground. "And look—the edges are even color coordinated. It's deliberate. A solution. Like the sieve markings we used to decode the master obelisk in *Egyptian Tomb*."

Excitement buzzes in my veins. "Santo, you're a genius."

He bows. "Thank you, thank you. I'll be here all night."

I bite back my despairing half-laugh and move to help him solve the rest of the puzzle. Not all of the PVCs come out of their structure, but a few are clearly supposed to and won't snap out, so I retrieve the rubber ax Santo found earlier and use it as leverage to clear a few of the pipes.

Before long, we're trading the ax back and forth, removing magenta- and cyan-ringed PVCs with almost surgical precision, until the remaining five pipes on the leftmost side of the puzzle form the number two.

I grin. Based on other escape rooms I've done, I mistakenly believed we had to connect pipes by their color, or follow the numbers in a certain direction, or add more to the structure. All this time, though, the solution lay in subtraction. Go figure.

The two of us work in tandem, falling into the familiar escape room loop of muttered *yeah*, *nice*, and *great job* platitudes. But soon, we're just double-checking our work: The remaining pipes do form numbers, but the code doesn't open the combination lock. We made a mistake somewhere.

"Hey," Guinevere says, appearing behind us. "I need the chalkboard."

"All yours," Santo says. She grabs it and nods in thanks before settling with her back against the edge of the walk-in shower, the chalk resting on top of the upturned bucket.

I reach over Santo to make sure the pipe in the middle of an eight shouldn't have been taken out to make a zero when he stops me. "You know, while you were in the HVAC, Malachi's secret video played on the screen. On all the screens, actually." His burn-scarred throat bobs. "That's why I thought something happened to him."

I pause with my hand around the base of the last PVC. It does need to be removed; the combination is 2-0-2-5, the year Matt died.

Get a grip, Steffi. Don't let him see you stumble through this. "Oh. What was Malachi's secret?"

Santo's dark eyes flash. "It doesn't matter. It wasn't true, anyway. Everyone always tried to pin Matt's death on Malachi, like my brother died because our Game Master was neglectful or bad at his job or just too exhausted to pay attention to the cameras. But we were the ones who fucked up last year, Steff. I've said it before, and I'll say it again: Tonight isn't Mal's fault."

Despite the fact that Santo won't look at me, it doesn't erase my memories of taking videos of him goofing off in AP Stats, or the way he used to grin while he doodled on my wrist with a ballpoint pen between periods, or the screaming laughter when he chased us through the cornfield maze at Kyker Farms. "Listen, Santo," I tell him, "it's been a hard year for us, but we'll get through this. We'll escape before the countdown ends. We'll call for help. Tomorrow, at graduation, we'll be able to...move on, you know? Officially." Tears well up in the back of my throat. "It seems impossible right now, but we have to believe the grief will lessen at some point. Everyone is always telling me that, and I used to think it was bullshit, but the alternative is giving up, and...we can't give up." I inhale. "It has to get better, right?"

Santo turns toward me, and I recoil at the palpable resentment swirling in his heated gaze. "Better? I'm getting my diploma without him when we spent our lives hitting milestones together. And you're telling me to *move on*?"

Behind us, garbled audio causes my heart to leap into my throat as Santo and I both turn toward the monitor, but it's only Guinevere messing with a tape deck. Where did she get that? *There's No Escape Rule #23: If you're stuck on a puzzle, get another player's eyes on it.* Her gaze meets Santo's from where she's sitting cross-legged on the white-tiled floor. She rewinds the tape, and it plays again.

"What are you—" Santo starts to ask, but Guinevere cuts him off with a finger to her lips. She scribbles something on the chalkboard, and then rewinds the tape. It's Morse code, I realize, which is always a pain to decode. She's not stuck after all.

I lower my voice. "I didn't know you felt that way," I tell Santo. "To be honest, I always thought your relationship with Matt was kind of...strained, especially with how he tried to control your love life. And after everything he did to you with *Cedar Creek Confessions*."

Santo's voice shakes. "He just wanted to protect me. Family is...complicated."

I furrow my brows. "Yeah, okay. Well, if you ever want to, you know, talk about Matt..."

Santo's lips twist with disdain. "I appreciate it, Zamekova. But we can talk later. For now, let's just see if these numbers work."

I follow Santo as he moves back into the other room. He starts lining up the dials on the lockbox's numbered padlock, and I pick at my remaining hangnails as I watch his silver rings dance. "Moment of truth," Santo says, pulling on the lock's U-bar. It pops, and something sticks in the back of my throat as he lifts the latch. We opened it.

Santo pulls out the fourth photograph and sweeps his purloined lantern over its gelatin emulsion surface. *Deranged Clown Circus*, the room we lost on Halloween night while in costume (Guinevere as Patrick Bateman from *American Psycho*, Charity as Barbie, Matt as J.D. from *Heathers*, Tobias as chess grandmaster Bobby Fischer, Santo as a BREAKOUT Game Master in a crisp pink-and-black embroidered polo borrowed from Malachi, Malachi as Jimi Hendrix, and me as a Raggedy Ann doll) comes into crisp focus.

But of course, it's never that simple.

My throat seizes. Instead of being scratched out or bloodied or eerily photoshopped, this time our faces are embellished with pen marks that are almost impossible to see head-on. As Santo tilts the photograph, though, the penmanship reveals itself: teeth outlined with careful precision, redrawn eyelids, stretching smiles. The effect is creepy as fuck; as I've come to expect, the only one of us left unaffected by the eerie enhancements is a stone-faced Matt, who holds up a sign reading READY TO FACE WHAT YOU DID? as he stares unblinkingly into the camera. I can't remember what it originally read.

"Weird," I breathe, trying to ignore the dull roar sounding in my ears. "This is a lot more…"

"Personal," Santo finishes grimly. He's right. There's an achingly deliberate hand at work here, one more artistic in its fury than the scratched-out *Moonshine Cabin* photo or the bloody *Serial Killer's Hideout* pic or the edited snapshot from *Egyptian Tomb*.

"I was going to say *psychopathic*," I tell him, staring at the glinting lines of our marked-up faces. Charity's arms, legs, and neck are all thickly outlined. Tobias's freckles are inky blots; Guinevere's pupils are too wide, blown out with blue pen. Malachi's lips and nose have both been traced over, and my brows have been altered to make me look shocked. Even Santo's curls have been messed with, swirling out from his face in freehand strokes.

"Yeah," Santo murmurs. He flips the photo over, still holding the lantern, and my breath hitches. Where the other photographs sported scrawled messages, this one has random, shaky lines etched into its backing.

God. The clues just keep getting more difficult to decipher.

Santo slips the photograph into his baggy jeans, the blood-splattered chains on his belt loops jingling, and paranoia instantly floods my nervous system. Why is he the one pocketing the photograph when we found it together? Why does the latest fucked-up clue feature pen embellishments when he's the one who used to draw on the back of my hand in the school cafeteria? The two of us may be working together, but I know Santo's still keeping secrets.

Tobias's words from earlier reverberate through my skull: *You can't trust him.*

"We need to split up," I tell Santo, instantly dry-mouthed. "Interrogate the others, see if we can figure out their motivations for showing up to BREAKOUT tonight while we figure out what the photograph's chicken scratch means."

"Good idea," Santo says, lowering his voice as Matt's girlfriend hisses in exasperation behind us. "Which player do you want to tackle?"

"I'll take Tobias. You take Guinevere." I glance up at the LCD monitor—our ticking clock's now at 19:16. "Let's regroup in five to share what we've learned, and then we'll switch off."

"Sounds like a plan," Santo says, already turning. "Hey, Gee! Can I help with that decoding?"

I take a step toward the fridge door and immediately hiss in pain as I stagger against the wood-paneled wall instead. When I'm standing still, it's easier to ignore the fire radiating from my wound. All this blood loss is making me woozy, and I know a tourniquet is only a temporary solution. Except I can't afford to think that way right now.

Blue smoke. Emergency lights. A headache throbbing at the edges of my sweat-slicked temples, and the dank smell of burning wood and grease pooling in my bronchial tissue. Mouths sliding off of plastic flowers. Fire-licked beams splintering in two. Tea trays melting into nothing. Slamming my aching palm on the emergency ESCAPE HATCH *button. Screaming as we pushed into the hallway. Baseline, animalistic instincts. Crawling through a silent hallway choked with ash and heat and dysfunctional sprinklers.*

A full-body shiver tingles from my neck to the base of my spine as I push myself off the wall and stumble through the pink and purple shadows swirling like flames around the kitchenette. Tobias is flicking through the DVDs by the entertainment center, his head bathed in red-light LEDs. Perfect.

"Hey," I tell him as I sink to my knees, gritting my teeth against the pain burning through my leg. I need to stay focused. Because I've seen Tobias play chess. He may look sickly, but against an opponent? He's ruthless. And for all his snark, I know he isn't willing to sacrifice his most important piece: himself. "Can I help you with something?"

"Why do you ask?" Tobias glances at me, irritation and suspicion clouding his expression in equal measure, and my Tylenol-chalked tongue gravitates to my upper palate in fear. This isn't going as well as I hoped, but I can't let a bad start dissuade me.

I attempt a nonchalant shrug. "Two heads are better than one, right?"

"Depends on the heads," Tobias says. His attention is focused on the plastic case in his hands. "Are you good with DVDs?"

When I nod—sure, why the hell not?—Tobias motions to the entertainment center in a *they're all yours* gesture before moving to stand. But I grab his freckled wrist before he can leave. "Let's work through them together. *There's No Escape* Rule Number Nineteen: In large player groups, work in pairs." I blink. "Maybe I'll catch something you missed."

"I seriously doubt that," Tobias mutters as I open the plastic casing of the first DVD. This one is labeled *Junior Year Friendsgiving*, but the inside is empty. "Besides, we're not exactly a large player group anymore, are we?"

The sentences nauseate me, but I can't lose focus. All that matters is playing the game. Getting closer to finding the keypad code. Escaping *Arsonist's Revenge*. Nothing more, and nothing less.

"It's admirable, you know. I've been watching you work through the clues tonight, and you've been doing a great job. You haven't let any of our complications rattle you." Tobias's unfocused eyes glaze over behind his gore-splattered tortoiseshell lenses as he stares at a spot above my shoulder, and I know without looking that he's staring at the oil spill of blood haloing Charity's once-perfect braids.

"Believe me, I'm rattled." I snap the DVD case shut—empty—and move to the next one. "But the only way out is through."

A smile finds its way onto Tobias's freckled face. "I remember that. From your blog. You always ended your posts with that line." His eyes flick from my childhood best friend's body back to me, and here it is: my opening.

"Tobias," I start, catching his gaze and holding it, "what happened during the fire last year?" My voice snags, but I move closer, tempted by the possibility of getting real answers. "Why is this happening to us?"

The two of us used to be so close. He set up my blog with malware protection and tinkered with the HTML formatting and advanced security settings until *There's No Escape* stopped popping up with the YOUR CONNECTION IS NOT PRIVATE window. He brought us farm-fresh eggs from his family's Rhode Island Reds once a month so Mom didn't have to pay for poultry products in the months we were struggling after everything that happened with Dad. He taught me when to force trades in chess, how to pick which side to castle on, how to leverage my material to get the other player to resign.

And I don't know what I expect Tobias to tell me, exactly. But when his hazel-brown eyes pierce mine, there's a startling clarity behind them.

"Because we killed Matt," he says.

● ● ●

CEDAR CREEK CONFESSIONS

posted 12 days ago

You know, you tried to silence me for telling you the truth. All of you wanted me tarred and feathered for daring to write what the rest of you only deign to whisper in private. Imagine: I freed you. I showed you the true faces of our classmates; I stepped in to create change when our administration cowered. For every scumbag that's gone unreported, unpunished, and unchallenged, this page has existed in antithesis. I created Cedar Creek Confessions to stand against tyranny; I created Cedar Creek Confessions to confront what society turns a blind eye to. But even though I knew I'd never be a fan favorite, particularly with those who had their careers or academic prospects ruined by my account, I'm not sorry. I'd do it all again in a heartbeat.

And soon enough, I will again.

CHAPTER FOURTEEN

Wednesday, May 20, 2026, 11:41 PM

A strangled laugh escapes my throat. "What?"

"We killed Matt," Tobias repeats, turning back to the DVDs nonchalantly, as though my field of vision isn't rapidly narrowing to a single pinprick of neon light. "You've figured it out by now, though, right? The invitations. The photographs. The clues and the puzzles and the escape room itself. *Arsonist's Revenge*." He shrugs. "The others don't want to tell you—they think you can't handle the truth—but the truth doesn't matter if the only way we're leaving BREAKOUT is in body bags." He pushes his glasses up the bridge of his sweat-slicked nose, and for the first time, I notice just how crooked it is.

It's broken.

"Don't get me wrong," Tobias continues, opening and discarding another empty DVD case, "it would be hard to set this up without Malachi's help. But the James-Mays own two different escape rooms, not just the BREAKOUT we burned down in Cedar Creek, and tonight has never been about the business. It's always been about Matt. And that has nothing to do with our Game Master, and everything to do with whoever wants revenge against us for killing a Cesari twin."

I'm going to fucking scream.

"I mean," Tobias says, "think about it, right? After the fire, with the press and the town and the sheriff, the *Tennessee Star* reported that the *Wanderland* fire was an accident caused by faulty wiring. Sheriff Stallard told the public Matt died from carbon monoxide poisoning, even though his body was too charred to identify him by his fucking fingerprints, and the townies blamed BREAKOUT for not being careful enough, for not complying with standard regulations, for not taking the proper precautions to ensure that a mistake like this wouldn't happen." He snorts. "But we left him there to die, Steffi." He sets aside another DVD. "All six of us left Matt in that escape room to fucking burn."

That's the thing about secrets... they burn you up inside.

"So, yeah," Tobias adds, "I'm impressed with your performance tonight. Your resilience. Your determination. Your unwavering resolve. But you still don't understand the game you're playing at, Steffi. And now, we're all paying the price."

"If I don't understand, then help me understand," I whisper. "Why did we want to kill Matt? Why did the fire spread so quickly—was it because of an accelerant in the escape room? Was it premeditated? Did we mess with the sprinklers?"

Instead of taking the bait, though, Tobias disarms me with a discovered attack. "What did you actually find in the HVAC, Steffi?"

I balk. "What?"

Tobias smirks. "See?" he says. "You're pressing me for details, but you don't trust any of us—not even me, and I'm the one who's come the closest to being honest with you all night." He hands me his unopened DVD and stands. "Let me know how that works out for you."

He weaves around the entertainment center, and I see it so plainly now, how the window of opportunity is slamming shut in front of me, so I blurt out the only words I know will make Tobias stop in his tracks: "Malachi is dead!"

"Malachi is dead?"

I turn. Santo stands in the fridge doorway. His expression is emotionless. Empty. Wrong.

He laughs. "Are you fucking with me?" he asks, glancing from me to Tobias, who's stock-still. Guinevere appears over his shoulder, her face cast in the shadows thrown by the LED lights, and I know she heard my outburst, too. "You're messing around, Zamekova. Right?"

"Cesari," I whisper instead of answering him, "did we fucking kill your brother last year?"

Santo glances at Tobias; Tobias glares at him and shoulder-checks him on his way into the bathroom just as Guinevere's storm-gray eyes flash with an undercurrent of violence. It all terrifies me. Who the hell are these people? What are they capable of? Why am I trapped in here with them, and why do I not know who any of them truly are?

Santo stares at me, his dark eyes hollow, and disappears back inside the bathroom. I scramble forward, not wanting to be left out, knowing I can't take it if my ex-friends abandon me again. I should have never lied to him. To anyone. But at the same time, my friend group's been keeping an even bigger secret from me, which means that I can't prioritize guilt, or pity, or even empathy tonight. There will be plenty of time for apologies once I figure out why we killed my best friend. Why Charity trapped him in the Queen of Hearts's Rose Garden. Why Malachi hid the footage. Why Guinevere started the fire. Why we left Matt in BREAKOUT to die.

"Malachi is gone," I whisper, my voice cracking. Tobias is standing by the shower; Guinevere is leaning against the solved pipe puzzle; Santo is gripping the industrial sink with one hand, white-knuckled. "I saw him in the control room while I was in the HVAC. I didn't tell you earlier. I... I wanted us to stay focused on escaping, but I messed up. I'm sorry."

Another shadowing memory taunts the edges of my vision—*the sweeping relief when my friends' cars began pulling up to BREAKOUT a year ago, the whispered barbs we exchanged while waiting for Malachi to unlock the exterior doors*—but it doesn't resolve itself into anything tangible before Santo drops the lantern.

"You didn't *mess up*, Zamekova. You... you *lied*."

Santo takes a step back, shaking his yellow-blond head—"I

can't believe I ever trusted you"—and déjà vu swells behind my skull: Charity's slow-motion death. Finding Malachi's body. Watching Matt's brother back into the exposed fuse box.

A high-pitched whining builds in my ears as Santo hits the electrical panel and is flung across the threshold, landing in the kitchenette just as the HVAC shudders and the fridge door slams shut. It refuses to budge when I rattle the handle, when I throw my entire body against it, when I call out Santo's name.

But my jaw unhinges, and the saliva in my mouth pools against my bloodied canines, and then I start screaming, and I don't ever stop.

SANTO

28 Days Before the Accident

Even though I love my brother, there are nights when I want to strangle him with the cord of his CPAP machine.

It's late. I need to be up for class in approximately four hours, which doesn't bode well for my performance on my upcoming US history exam, but I can't sleep. Instead, I'm sitting in bed, scrolling mindlessly through Instagram Reels with my earbuds in and my brightness on its lowest setting, cursing my brother's air-horn snores with every minute that adds itself to the top of my phone screen: 3:13 AM... 3:14 AM... 3:15 AM.

I sigh, swipe out of the *Survivor: Pearl Islands* compilation I've been watching—Sandra Diaz-Twine will always be my hero—and navigate to Malachi's account instead. If I'm going to succumb to the whims of my algorithm tonight, I may as well check on his feed first.

As soon as I double-tap his newest video, though, a notification pops up on the top of my screen.

Mal.The.Reel.King:
Hey. What are you doing up?

A smile finds its way onto my face before I can help myself.

oh, you know me. can't sleep.
i swear matt's new CPAP is louder than a fucking jet engine
it's not like i was going to set the curve for mr. hurst anyway,
though, so i guess it's fine?

Mal.The.Reel.King:
Lmfao. Are y'all still sharing that single bedroom?

yeah. it's absolute torture

I bite my lip, deliberating, and then exhale. Fuck it.

come get me out of here?

Typing bubbles from Malachi start up, pause, disappear, start up again.

Mal.The.Reel.King:
Depends. How knocked out is Matt?

I glance over at him.

> oh, he's definitely deep in REM.
> and not to be dramatic or anything, but my mom's out for the night

Mal.The.Reel.King:
Not you telling me your parents aren't home.
Didn't you just see me at the water tower?

> you know how it is. never enough time with you

Mal.The.Reel.King:
Corny.

> what a scathing indictment of my sincere and heartfelt message
> when will you ever return my sentiment, famous influencer
> Mal the Reel King

It's a joke, but it's also not a joke. There's a careful line to walk here; one I've become a little less adept at toeing lately, judging from these blatantly flirtatious texts. I'm not sure if being reckless is a good thing, but it's past 3 AM, so I'm thinking a little less with my brain and a little more with my...

Mal.The.Reel.King:
Careful. We wouldn't want Cedar Creek Confessions to get ahold of these messages, would we?

In the other bed, Matt snort-gasps. I frown as I reread Malachi's message. Maybe I'm sleep-deprived, but he's definitely flirting back. At the same time, though, he's also shutting me down.

I sigh and drop my phone on my chest without responding. I don't want to play these games. Even here, when I'm trying so desperately to get away from everything in the comfort of my own gray-shuttered duplex, the weight of *Cedar Creek Confessions* hangs over me like a cockblocking thundercloud. I've always found Mal attractive—always had a thing for the way he dresses, his easy smile, the way he carries himself and how his personality shines through his effortlessly viral videos—but the jury's hung on whether he likes me back, especially now that he's already been targeted once by our locally notorious gossip Instagram.

In the past, before *Cedar Creek Confessions* accused Mal of mining BREAKOUT's games for social media content, I'd noticed small things, like us texting when we didn't need to, or our prolonged eye contact when someone said something embarrassing at lunch, or how we'd stretch out small conversations at the end of the day just for an excuse to keep talking. There were other moments, too. Malachi's not a super physical guy, but there were enough fist bumps and high fives and shoulder-pats for me to notice.

It felt double-edged, the contact. It was never enough to mean anything, and definitely always enough to brush off in group settings, but he didn't do it with anyone else. And whether we were stepping out to meet the Pizza Plus delivery guy together or laughing over shitty whiskey we snuck into Perfect Strike, I always had fun with him.

But after the Instagram post, our relationship changed. Now it's a constant dance, an ebb and flow. BREAKOUT is doing well, but Malachi's reputation isn't.

Which is exactly why he wants us to be careful.

Without thinking, I pick my phone back up and navigate to *Cedar Creek Confessions*. I need to stop keeping up with the account. I need to break this fixation. But when I locate the hefty accusation again—Malachi misusing his master key privileges to pull escape room security footage for his mega-popular *Imagine You're Trapped in This Crazy Location and Your Partner Says THIS* series—guilt pools in my stomach. Mal confessed that he lifted game conversations for his video scripts during one of our late-night talks up at the water tower. After the *Cedar Creek Confessions* post went live, he told me that I was the only one who knew, that I had to have sold him out somehow.

Another message comes through my screen.

Mal.The.Reel.King:
You know, that actually reminds me. I wasn't going to say anything, but while I have you here.

During our last Warrior Minutes sound check, Z said she thinks there's something weird going on with your brother. Don't get mad, okay? But TBH I agree. Is he okay?

I know that's kind of a loaded question, but the vibes are off.

He's been snapping at everyone a lot more lately.

And he's become super...withdrawn.

I pause. Earlier today, Matt texted me after Malachi and I had covered all our usual conversation topics at the water tower: the positive press with Laurel Harkness touring the Pigeon Forge BREAKOUT location for a *Star* article, and the upcoming escape-room-sponsored show choir fundraiser endearing the business to Sheriff Stallard, who basically rules our town; which shows we've been bingeing lately; how much we both hate our AP Environmental Science teacher.

Be home for dinner at seven, my brother's text read. But he may as well have said, *Don't do anything embarrassing in public with Malachi. I don't want it getting back to the school.*

I reread Malachi's DMs, and then I glance over at Matt again. His phone is charging on the edge of his nightstand.

Don't do it, Santo. Turn off your own phone, close your eyes, and go to bed.

My socked feet hit the carpeted floor. Since the duplex is new to me, I don't have every creaking floorboard mapped in my mind. I don't want to risk waking my brother, but at the same time, this feels long overdue.

I'm just going to look. I'll look, and I won't find anything, and

I'll know Mal was wrong. I'll be able to tell him that, and everything between the two of us will be better for it.

I creep across the room. Moonlight filters in through the window blinds as I cross the invisible line separating my half of the room from my brother's. We're temporarily sharing because Momma couldn't find a three-bedroom on the market that didn't extend her commute by an extra forty-five minutes, which isn't ideal. But if we move soon, it won't matter. Nothing will.

Matt stirs, and I freeze with my fingers inches from his shattered phone screen. But then his breath evens out again and he turns back toward the wall. All right. So far, so good.

I pick up Matt's phone, unplug it, and retreat back to safety. For a second, I'm worried that attempting to unlock his device with my own face won't work, but I shouldn't be. People are always telling us that we're the most identical set of identical twins they've ever met. Case in point: Matt and I have been in Cedar Creek for almost eight months now, and our new friend group still gets us mixed up. But even if our outward appearances are basically carbon copies, the physical is where it stops—especially when lately, the chasm between us has been widening as if the secrets that once brought us together are now only tearing us apart.

I blink blearily, my eyelids heavier than they were just a second ago, as I assess my brother's home screen. His wallpaper is a photo of the two of us, which takes me by surprise—him and me as laughing babies, wearing the same shirt, chubby arms slung around each other, though even I'm not entirely sure which of us is which—and his app configuration is almost identical to mine.

I navigate to the Notes app first, because if I were hiding something important, that's where I would keep it, but it's empty apart from an old grocery list: *Milk, eggs, bowtie pasta, butter.*

I smile. Matt's never been the journaling type.

I move to the Camera Roll next and all my earlier fondness dissipates—doesn't my brother know how to use the Hidden folder on his phone?—but by then I'm already swiping past idle games we used to play together in seventh grade, various subscription-based streaming services, two calculator apps, and a fitness widget he uses to count his total steps per day. I frown and go back to the previous screen. Who in the world needs two phone calculators?

As soon as I click on the application, though, I understand why. This calculator is password protected.

Damn. It looks like Malachi was right—Matt has something to hide after all.

By the time I crack his password, it's 4:34 A.M. Inside, there's a list of...our old schools?

> Sandhill Prep: WzuNt#4rF231s0i2
>
> Hillwood High: XB3nP89kjr!W45
>
> Talcott Kell: 7yHdXc883$pLt5
>
> Bridgewater Academy: PL67u%nBv*992e
>
> Blue Ridge Technical Institute: !K#3rTfgjxCKlm5
>
> Western Community College: 3R4@Ty?QeW52489%
>
> Cedar Creek: 43E!rFt78016#vBsL!69

My gut churns. No, these are log-ins. Passwords. All for

schools that had their own versions of *Cedar Creek Confessions*: *Sandhill Secrets*. *Talcott Kell Whispers*. *BRTI News*.

Beside me, my own phone buzzes.

Mal.The.Reel.King:
Santo, you good? I think I'm going to turn in for the night.

I'll see you tomorrow, okay? Try to get some rest if you can, and good luck on Mr. Hurst's test. I'm sure you'll do great.

I don't answer. Instead, I go back to the *Cedar Creek Confessions* Instagram on Matt's phone, the room now muted whirls of color as I stare at the glow of his shattered phone screen. A sinking realization settles deep into my bone marrow as I scroll through the posts, each one whipping by faster and faster, carousels blurring into oblivion with each quick stroke of my thumb. The account. The messages, the style of the captions, the pointed exposés. The targets: the Bible-thumping cheerleader he hates, the homophobic lacrosse team captain who called me a slur in Spanish class on our first day, the sweet but social media–focused guy he wishes I spent less time hanging out with. It's him. It's Matt.

My brother runs *Cedar Creek Confessions*.

And now I know the password to his account.

CHAPTER FIFTEEN

Wednesday, May 20, 2026, 11:44 PM

I only stop screaming when bright pain cuts through my nerve endings like a slap. Because it was a slap. Guinevere Mitchell-Moore just slapped me.

"Snap out of it, Stephanie," she snarls, her breath hot against my ear, "or I swear I'll backhand you next. You can't do anything for him. Santo's dead, but we're still here. Surviving. That's what matters now."

My cheek smarts, but the pain does diminish my hysteria—mainly because now I'm fucking *pissed*. I want to scream again, to unravel the blood-logged tourniquet my best friend's brother tied around my calf, to do anything except hiccup a series of breaths that feel like not breathing at all. Except when I unstick my useless tongue from the roof of my mouth, Santo is still gone.

It feels like losing Matt all over again.

"Guess the warnings on the breaker panel were there for a reason," Tobias deadpans from where he's sitting with his back against the far wall.

The bathroom set LCD monitor flickers to life. *"Hey,"* Not-Matt says, and my frigid heart door-slams straight into my curling toes. *"Santo. Because you have failed to escape in time, you have been eliminated, and your secret will now be revealed for you,"* Not-Matt's voice continues over the speakers. *"Unfortunately, betrayers must pay in the end…and my brother was no exception."*

Beside me, Guinevere's gaze flicks upward, the rectangular light of the LCD screen reflected in her newly red-rimmed eyes, and her fingers grab my arm in shock just as the back of my throat tightens. Because this time, it's not just Not-Matt's disembodied voice being pumped through the speakers while we stare at that stupid hot-pink smiley face.

No. This time, BREAKOUT's logo fades out until Matteo Luca Cesari's haunted expression fills the screen.

My best friend stares right into the camera. *"My brother had a lot to hide,"* he says, and I choke back another scream. Despite every session I've spent in Call-Me-Diana's office, fighting tooth and nail for a second chance with my ex-friends, being inside BREAKOUT tonight is making me realize I should have let go of the past while I had the chance. I've been desperately clinging to scraps of memory, delusionally building up relationships in my head with people who no longer care about me, and it's culminated in this: the knowing curve of Matt's smirk, the deadly flames reflected in his lifeless eyes, the glitches curling at the edges of his hair like a blurred postcard sent straight from uncanny valley. Because there is no camera. Matt is dead; the six of us went to his funeral. Guinevere kissed me after I drove her back from it in the rain. Charity brought those stupid white roses, and Tobias tossed a wooden king onto his casket along with all that soil, and Malachi spent the whole service sitting next to Santo, his hand quietly resting on the other's knee.

This is just a cruel way to further rattle us.

I grimace, briefly wondering if our real Game Master—the mastermind who methodically plotted this out—pulled a photo from Matt's personal Instagram or the news or even one of the BREAKOUT lobby photographs taunting us tonight and used it as the underlying tissue for this deepfaked video of Matt's not-real face. Because here he is now, blinking, breathing, brought back to life through digital software and lines of carefully crafted code and whatever the fuck else, buried but alive. Gone but not gone.

Frustration wells up in the back of my throat. We're still being targeted. It never ends.

And yet, I can't look away.

"*Santo wanted to kill me, too*," Not-Matt declares, and my stomach curdles. Forget my fucked-up calf or the gore matted in my hair or the carbon monoxide permeating my T-shirt, because *this* is what's going to send me over the edge: the idea that whatever happened to Matt a year ago, Santo was in on it. All these piled-up questions, no answers, and only fifteen minutes left to glean any fucking closure from tonight's escape room.

"*We had a fight,*" Not-Matt continues, a too-wide smile gracing his lips. "*And it came to a head inside BREAKOUT. He wanted to prove a point about* Cedar Creek Confessions. *He didn't agree with what I was doing to the student body, even though I was doing it to keep him safe.*"

I exhale. Even if the specifics of the night I found out Matt ran CCHS's most notorious gossip Instagram account now elude me like wisps of smoke, I remember the emotions: the sharp sting of the freshly waxed floor. The way my Converse sneakers seemed to sink right through it. The spinning denial, the slotting pieces, the resolved clues. *Cedar Creek Confessions.* It was him.

Until now.

"Do you have any idea who could have brought the account back?" I whisper. Guinevere is still clutching my arm. "The newest posts. They're different. Written in a...copycat style. But they're even more threatening."

From the other side of the bathroom, Tobias shakes his head. "The account password got changed. I spent hours trying to get back into it—including in the lobby earlier—but we've been logged out. I don't have access anymore."

Is he being sincere? How should I know? I only saw him pretend to sign the waiver.

Guinevere's hand drops to mine. "It's wrapping up," she

breathes, her eyes still locked on the LCD monitor, and my heart rate spikes at her trembling voice and her mussed hair and her fake fingernails. Her mixed signals, her jealousy, her pain. It's probably fine—Guinevere isn't tech-savvy enough to revive the *Cedar Creek Confessions* Instagram. But what if Tobias is lying, and the two of them are in on this together, and Gee is only curling her warm fingers against my skin to distract me?

"The seconds are ticking away, players." Not-Matt smirks. *"You don't have much time, so try to escape fast. And while you do… take note of what it feels like to be trapped inside BREAKOUT."* He doesn't blink. *"Take note of what it feels like to be waiting to die."*

The video ends, and I stifle a sob. None of our plans have worked. The HVAC failed. Trying to get Tobias to open up only resulted in Santo's death. Charity and Malachi are gone. Guinevere is losing it. And yet, what else can I do except work with the others? For my own sanity, I need to assume I'm safe until we're down to the final two. Which means that as long as I'm not the next dead body inside *Arsonist's Revenge*, I might be alive at midnight.

Right now, though, I need all the help I can get.

With blood-slicked fingers, I reach into my sweat-soaked bra and pull out the photograph from *Deranged Clown Circus*.

Guinevere's nails grip my skin, and I hiss. "Watch it," I warn. But she doesn't seem to hear me. Instead, her pupils dilate as she takes in the image.

"Where the hell did you get another picture?" she asks.

Tobias edges closer, intrigued, as my throat bobs. No more

secrets, no more lies, no more deaths. "Santo and I found it in a lockbox," I say, and then I flip over the photograph. "Not that it's anything but a bunch of scribbles."

Guinevere swallows. "No," she says, "that's shorthand." At my confused stare, she licks her lips. "You know, like in stenography?" She shakes her head, pulling her hand away from mine, and I'm suddenly reminded of her federal judge father and also, inexplicably, all the long-lashed and beautiful horses she got to spend her summer with in Lenoir City. "They use it in court."

Tobias sits up straighter. "Do you know how to read it?"

"I don't," Guinevere admits. "But I bet we can decode it."

She's right. If our captor didn't want to give us a chance, they would've blown us all up the second we stepped foot inside *Arsonist's Revenge*. As long as the three of us are still alive—even without a Game Master, even without my memories, even without a functioning puzzle room—we can still win. Despite the title of my long-abandoned blog, there's always a way out.

Oh my God.

"Where's the black light?" I ask, and immediately we're all searching: under the rubber rat, in the grooves of the blood-filled bathtub's folding shutter cover, on the shelving of the walk-in shower. Finally, Tobias finds it propped up on one of the bags of fake ice and turns it on, and I inhale as he trains the beam over the industrial sink's corresponding mirror.

The filmy surface lights up UV-blue.

Hope swells in my chest, but then it deflates just as quickly as I compare the blacklight mirror code to the writing on the back of the *Deranged Clown Circus* photograph. "It doesn't match."

"But it's a mirror, though," Tobias says, staring at me. When I blink at him, he sighs. "Mirrors flip objects, right? So maybe we need to flip the photograph, too." He takes the *Deranged Clown Circus* selfie and holds up the Kodak photo paper to the sink mirror, where the loops and dashes rearrange themselves until the two correspond.

"Of course," I breathe.

As we begin transcribing the letters—*S*, *E*, *C*—I fill out words for the sake of time. "That's *SECRETS*," I say, so we skip the next four letters in the sequence. We hit *A-L-W*, and Tobias fills in *ALWAYS*.

"Last word," Guinevere says, and then we have the whole phrase: *SECRETS ALWAYS LEAK*. There are exactly five bloodied tiles separating my shoes from hers. "Christ. It's another fucking joke," she says, near tears, and the too-hot air crackles with the tension of another impending rupture in our delicately reconstructed friend group.

Power. Emergency generator. A gas leak here, inside BREAKOUT.

"What do you think, Steffi?" Tobias asks carefully, the edges of his black eye washed out in the liminal glow of the magenta floodlights overhead. "Out of the three of us, you're the professional."

A humorless laugh escapes my chapped lips. I haven't been a professional at anything in a while. In fact, I can't even get myself to change my bedsheets or fill a prescription now without feeling like the weight of the world is on my shoulders, so it's definitely no surprise that the slightly manic work ethic I embodied while *There's No Escape* was at the height of its popularity—chugging energy drinks until six AM, skipping shifts at Perfect Strike to churn out reviews three times a week, arranging for make-up homework with my teachers so I could fly from state to state and renegotiate sponsor compensation packages at thirty thousand feet—is long gone.

I dig my fingernails into my palms. My brain swells, flooding with stimuli: our collective body heat, the stifling air choked off by our dwindling oxygen supply, the stupid rubber rat underneath the industrial sink. "I think we're dealing with a psychopath," I whisper. "I think none of this is meant to give us a fair fight. I think the odds keep getting stacked against us. Just look at the newspaper clippings! Look at Charity's crushed skull, or my missing knife, or the *Wanderland* DVD! The photograph in the HVAC! Malachi's motionless body! The frozen LCD monitors, the rising heat, the hissing generator"—my voice rises—"Guinevere getting stabbed, Santo getting electrocuted…" I shake my head, desperation bubbling out of my mouth. "I think that none of this is normal, and I think the killer is one of us!"

When I'm finished, my chest is heaving and both Tobias and Guinevere are staring at me like I'm losing my mind. *There's No Escape Rule #2: Never turn on your fellow players.*

"Wow," Guinevere deadpans. "You're actually crazy."

"I'm not," I protest, which is not a great counterargument.

She scoffs, crossing her gore-splattered arms, and it hits me again, how every part of her is sleek and beautiful and prepared to strike. "I don't know how hard you hit your head last year, Stephanie, but there's no killer. It's been a year since the fire, so Malachi wanted to make us pay for the resulting lawsuit with his idea of a practical joke. Fine. BREAKOUT is a terrible franchise, so everything inside it is going wrong and people are dying. Fine. All that means is we need to escape this malfunctioning escape room before more of us wind up dead. We're not trapped here with a *murderer*."

"And what about the videos?" I ask Guinevere. "The photographs of our past games? The newspapers, the cut wires, and the missing knife? The electrified box? The fact that Charity's watch vanished?" I run a hand back through my hair. "Can you explain all of that away with just Malachi?"

"Yeah, Gee," Tobias adds, "you're experiencing a lot of cognitive dissonance right now, which is normal for traumatic situations. But when Santo suggested that Charity's death was an accident earlier, you fucking snapped at him, so you clearly also believe we're being intentionally targeted by someone who wants to kill us." He smiles, his freckled face all bruises and half shadow. "À la a killer."

Breathe. Get through this. Imagine you're talking to Dr. Quack.

"Listen," I start, because the more I think about it the more I realize it's true, "it makes sense. Collecting insider information, setting up this room, confirming the booking...Malachi had to have been in on this revenge plot, at least partially." I pause, letting the information settle. "But the rest of it needs someone on the inside. And since there are only three players remaining, it stands to reason that the killer is one of us."

Tobias raises his hand. "I think we should kill Guinevere," he offers, and the corners of my lips twitch upward against my will.

"You are not funny," Guinevere snarls. Her gaze turns to me. "But seriously, Stephanie, what are you suggesting?"

"Well, it would be good, right?" I say slowly. "To root out our true Game Master. But everyone's just going to claim their own innocence or pick a scapegoat"—here I glance at Tobias, who smirks knowingly—"and that's just going to divide us."

At this point, though, my suspicions regarding who set up this room for us lie with everyone equally: Malachi. The James-Mays. Sheriff Stallard. A deranged sociologist. Jacob Webber. Alyssa Hayes. Mr. Foxfield. Any other poor soul targeted by Cedar Creek Confessions. *Jigsaw. You.*

Tobias tugs at the fraying sleeve of his blood-stained chess sweatshirt. "I mean, we were all close to Matt in different ways, right? Gee dated him for four months. I played dozens of chess team tournaments with him. Steffi was his coworker and confidante. But we all had our issues with him, too." He holds up a hand at Guinevere's murderous expression. "So what we really need to ask is this: Which one of us would want revenge for what we did to Matt the most?"

"Enough to lure us here and kill us off?" I ask darkly, even though I'm still not sure what we fucking did last May. What I did. If I'm truly the monster I'm worried I might be.

Tobias's throat bobs. "Uh..." he says. "Yeah."

Guinevere glances between us. "Maybe we don't have to decide right now," she says. "If whoever wants us dead is trying to drive wedges between us, then maybe our best defense is to work together. If the murderer's been playing us—while playing alongside us—this entire time, then let's...I don't know, return the favor?"

"I'm good with that strategy," Tobias says, and I nod even though the lump in my throat is now the size of a bowling ball.

"I wish Santo were here," I tell Guinevere. "That's very *Survivor* of you."

She breathes out a laugh. "Christ, this is crazy," she whispers, the edge in her voice carrying a new note of uncertainty. "It's crazy." She rakes her trembling fingers back through her half-up caramel hair, removing a few more of her translucent, star-shaped claw clips. "And this plan...I mean, I know I proposed it, but what if *you're* our Game Master, Stephanie?"

"I'm not our Game Master." *Calm. Careful. Don't get angry, don't get mad.* "My best friend died in an escape room like this one. Do you think—" I cut myself off, unable to finish the sentence as my voice breaks. Return my focus to the girl who kissed me a year ago. "It's not me."

God, I hope it's not.

"Wow, what a coincidence, my boyfriend died in an escape room like this one, because it's the same fucking person, but okay. Say it's not you," Guinevere says. Sweat drips from her high cheekbones. "Say it's Tobias instead. Then we just...keep playing the game in front of him?"

I nod. "Because right now, we outnumber the killer."

And as long as that stays true, we have a chance.

"Think of it like the most important game of Mafia you'll ever play in your life," Tobias suggests, and I smile, but his expression is serious.

"Fine," Guinevere acquiesces, and it feels like a victory, this collective decision to stick together in a room filled with blood and death and deadly secrets. "How much time do we have before the gas leak kills us all?"

"Good question! Since carbon monoxide is a naturally occurring gas, usually formed as a byproduct of a variety of household appliances—generators, space heaters, gas stoves, and so on—it typically ventilates out in most spaces. But in high concentrations—say, approximately twenty-eight thousand parts per million—it can kill you within minutes." Tobias adjusts his tortoiseshell glasses. "In a space like this, though, the poisoning wouldn't be instantaneous…" He frowns. "But I'd posit that, depending on when the generator broke down, we may be dead by the end of this game."

"Lovely," Guinevere says. "So you're saying whoever organized this created an impenetrable escape room with no real way out, gave us clues to make us feel like we're progressing toward an end goal, and knew it wouldn't matter because we'd all asphyxiate anyway?"

"There's a way out," I insist, refusing to be demoralized. "We're working toward it. If we want it badly enough—if we prove ourselves—we *will* make it out alive. The clues are real. The keypad code is real. The photographs are real, and we're only missing *Raiders of the Lost Temple* and *Hijacked*. I bet the *Hijacked* photograph has the keypad code scrawled on the back, but we'll need to work together to find it, especially since the carbon monoxide leak isn't doing us any favors when it comes to our cognitive reasoning skills."

And then I pause. Because holy shit, there might be one last option.

Tobias says something in response, but I'm not listening to the group's razor-edged conversations anymore. Instead, I'm mentally mapping out BREAKOUT's floor plan. During our game last year, *Wanderland* had three interconnected areas: the Rabbit Hole, the Upside-Down Tea Party, and the Queen of Hearts's Rose Garden. So if the James-Mays used the *Wanderland* schematics for *Arsonist's Revenge*, then we still need to find one last room before we can fulfil our win objective: A warped, twisted, mirror version of the space where my best friend died last May.

"There's a third room," I murmur.

Guinevere blinks. "This is the second room, Leonard Shelby. Not the third."

"No," I insist, ignoring her *Memento* reference in favor of assessing every nook and cranny within the bathroom set's four walls. "Remember how in *Wanderland*, there were three different interconnected areas? Well, we've only found two here. If we find the third room, though, I'm positive we can get to the keypad code early." I tuck a flyaway behind my industrial-pierced ear; I don't need to see a mirror to know that my eyes are shining. "If a killer rigged the clues, we can avoid their setup by leapfrogging the game."

Tobias gives me a once-over. "Not bad," he admits with a begrudging note of respect in his voice. "Kind of amateurish, and also delayed, given your extensive history with this franchise, but it's something we can work with." He holds up a finger.

"Oh, except for one small hiccup: The game is cumulative, Steffi. Even if we assume there *is* a third room, which we currently have no evidence for, we won't be able to unlock it without a key. And I'd be willing to bet money we can only do that by progressing through the game. We're at our Game Master's mercy here." Tobias tips his chin to the mirror. "We've created a temporary alliance, but now our energy should probably go into deducing what *SECRETS ALWAYS LEAK* means." He frowns. "You know," he adds, "maybe it isn't about the generator at all. Every other clue we've found, even if it's been a threat, ultimately corresponded with another part of the room."

"So is there a dripping showerhead in the walk-in shower or something? A puddle of water by the bathtub?" As soon as Guinevere says the words, her gaze snags on the toilet. There's a fake water stain below it, on the concrete. "There."

Gee pries the piping out of the grout alcove while Tobias roots around in the space it left behind. Though it's hard to see in the glow of the bathroom's magenta floodlights, the item ahead of Tobias's outstretched fingers is unmistakable. I've played over two hundred escape rooms, which means I notice when items repeat. And this? It's a puzzle box. Six sides. Six faces. Six of us who left Matt to die.

A grin lights up Tobias's bruised face as he pulls out the grease-slicked puzzle box. "Hell yeah. We're in the endgame now," he says.

● ● ●

yelp.com | Recommended Reviews: BREAKOUT Escape Rooms Inc.

Located in Friendship Springs, TN | Have you been here?
Write a review!

Kind of boring ★★☆☆☆
Posted by Greg Beaufort at 2:07 PM
This escape room was okay. I wish there were more scary parts in the pirate room, though.

CHAPTER SIXTEEN

Wednesday, May 20, 2026, 11:47 PM

There's No Escape Rule #8: Avoid bottlenecks at all costs.

It's a good tip. But right now, we are at a bottleneck—the part in an escape room where players can't progress until they solve a specific puzzle—and there's nothing any of us can do about it. I glance up at the monitor: 12:32. Not ideal.

Tobias is sitting on the edge of the bathtub, his mouth screwed in concentration as his fingers dance over the puzzle box. On the other side of the room, across from him, Guinevere is hacking at the fridge door with our rubber ax, though her efforts are largely futile. I don't think any number of rage-fueled *thwack*s is going to succeed in moving steel alloy, but her effort is admirable. At least she's still trying, while I'm also breaking *There's No Escape*

Rule #21: Always work on a different puzzle from your teammates. Currently, there's nothing for me to contribute. If Tobias doesn't solve the puzzle box, and solve it soon, then the three of us are absolutely fucked.

So I'm here for moral support, I guess, or at least to make sure he isn't purposely screwing us over. I still haven't forgotten my theory about his mysterious illness or the *Cedar Creek Confessions* post Matt made about Tobias intentionally losing his chess matches to win money for his meds. All this to say, if Tobias *is* attempting to kill us for BREAKOUT's insurance payout, I'm going to haunt his hospital ward forever.

I bite the inside of my cheek as Tobias prods at another wooden piece and the next part of the puzzle box springs open. I need to micromanage less. To release control. To stop hovering. In every escape room I've done, I've never solved a puzzle box. But at the same time, I'm not going to ensure I survive BREAKOUT by twiddling my thumbs.

I scoot closer to him alongside the edge of the bathtub; the LED lights bathe my bloodied arms. "Hey," I whisper. I'm not sure if it would be rude to ask Tobias for more painkillers. "How's it coming?"

"Good," he answers, his voice clipped. When I keep staring at him, waiting for more, he sighs. "Why don't you go do something else, Steffi?"

"Tell me what you're doing first."

He sighs again, louder and longer, but the sound is strained. "Look, opening a puzzle box is a little like playing blitz chess.

You're operating under immense time pressure and you want to beat the clock. But if you're not careful, speed can be your worst enemy."

Tobias turns the puzzle box over. "Lucky for us, I'm great at blitz chess. My Elo on Chess.com is—" He coughs. Clears his throat. "Sorry. It's one thousand six hundred thirty in three-minute rapid mode."

If tonight's circumstances were normal, I might laugh. Instead, my chest pangs. I'm trying to make it through this hour by taking every puzzle, every lock, and every clue one second at a time. But with the dead bodies of my ex-friends, the constant adrenaline rush of near-death experiences, and the lethargy brought on by the ongoing gas leak, I'm running out of energy.

"I know you're busy," I tell Tobias, "but I'd love it if you finished what you were saying earlier." I press my hands against my tourniquet. "I told the group about Malachi—now it's your turn to return the favor to me with *Wanderland* and Matt."

Tobias coughs again. He tugs at another piece of the greased puzzle box, and Santo's electrocuted body flashes into my mind. I don't like this.

"Sure," he says with a sniffle. "So, my injuries." He turns another piece of the box, his freckled fingers twitching. "Santo gave them to me."

I suck in a breath that slides down my throat like smoke instead of air.

"It happened a couple of days ago," Tobias continues, his voice thick, "right when he came back from studying abroad. He asked to meet with me. Showed me this text message from, like, over a year ago. I didn't remember sending it, but it was after *Cedar Creek Confessions* exposed me for throwing my tournaments and splitting the reward money with my opponents, so I was definitely pissed. Apparently, before the state competition, I'd DMed Matt *I hope your bus blows up on the way to Cookeville and you asphyxiate from the fumes.* This was after he took my place on the team."

When I don't react, Tobias's hazel eyes flick up to mine. "It was a cruel text, okay? A coincidence. Bad timing, dramatic irony, whatever. I didn't mean it. I regret it, obviously." His gaze drops back to the puzzle box. "But can I go back and change it? No. So there's no use thinking about it." He scratches the back of his neck, turns another piece of the wooden box, and sniffles again. "Santo didn't agree, though. So there. Are you happy? You got what you wanted, right?"

I shake my head. "Of course not," I whisper.

Tobias clears his throat. "Yeah," he rasps. "Neither am I."

Another piece of the puzzle box springs open. I glance back at Tobias, and his mouth quirks humorlessly before I return my hard stare to the wood's intricate carvings. Santo isn't a violent person. There's no reason he would assault Tobias, even if Tobias had sent Matt an ominous message.

My temples throb. I can't make sense of this new information.

"Steffi," Tobias repeats. His voice is strangely hoarse. "Steffi—" He slumps, falling onto the tiled floor, and I snap my chin toward him so fast that I pull a muscle in my neck. Oh my God. Something's wrong.

Across the room, Guinevere's ax-thwacking stops. "What's happening?"

"I don't know," I choke, terror taking over as Tobias gasps for air. "He was fine a second ago. We were just talking—"

"Steffi," he wheezes, his bloodshot eyes bulging as hives begin to break out across his freckled skin, "get my... EpiPen."

"He's going into anaphylactic shock." Guinevere rushes over, but her prognosis can't change anything when Tobias's hypodermic epinephrine is in his medical bag, and that's currently locked away behind the fridge door. "There must have been something coating the puzzle box; one of his allergies must be triggered." She bends down to the slick box and sniffs it. "This isn't grease—it's peanut oil."

I swallow the residue of my acid reflux. "Jesus," I whisper, feeling small and stupid and helpless. But I'm not. I stood in BREAKOUT's lobby, I signed the fucking waiver, and I manipulated everyone into coming inside *Arsonist's Revenge*. And now, nothing I do is going to bring my friends back.

We can never go back to the way things were.

Warm bile lurches up my throat, and this time I can't force it down. I run to the toilet and vomit into the empty bowl. The LEDs. Tobias's purpling face. Guinevere's spilling tears. Santo's sizzling yellow-blond hair. Charity's empty wrists. Malachi's walkie-talkie panic.

When I close the lid and return, wiping the corners of my mouth, Tobias is still thrashing, and there's still nothing we can do for him. My heart drops. Another impending death on my hands, all because I wanted to know the unknowable.

Guinevere reaches for the puzzle box, her nails iridescent in the light, but I grab her wrist before she can touch the wood. "You can't."

It could be dangerous, I want to add, but the words get stuck in my acid-filled throat. Everything smells like mercaptan and white sage and the undernotes of her bougainvillea perfume.

The LEDs catch on Guinevere's sharp jaw; her eyes flash red. "Why not?" she asks, her voice rising a hysterical octave, and I immediately understand that whatever fragile peace was stretching between us is shattered now. "You constantly pilfer other people's shit: your dad's shirt. Matt's trench coat. Charity's watch, probably." She snatches the puzzle box from the floor before stalking to the other side of the bathroom set, back to her rubber ax. "You're a collector, Stephanie," she says as she sets the puzzle box on the floor. "You *collect*: plastic ducks, postpunk revival vinyls, people." She lines up the ax-head. "I wonder"—*THWACK*—"what it'll be"—*THWACK*—"from me." The puzzle box splits in two. "Which of my"—*THWACK*—"possessions"—*THWACK*—"are you eyeing?"

With a final *THWACK*, the puzzle box skitters toward my bloodied Converse. Guinevere keeps smashing. Wood chips explode everywhere.

By the process of elimination, she's the killer. I don't know if she's getting her practice swings in before coming for me, but I need to do something. Charity is dead. Malachi is dead. Santo is dead. Tobias is as good as dead. Guinevere almost died, we're both running out of air, and I'm sure the jig is up. At any moment now, she's going to turn on me.

But then again, if Guinevere is tonight's mastermind, then why is she bludgeoning the puzzle box instead of me?

My burning throat is paper-dry. "Enough," I rasp. Guinevere glances at me, and the cold fury in her face is enough to make my breath catch. "You opened it, Gee."

Between us, Tobias jerks as she levels the ax-head at me. "Stay right there," she demands, her voice wobbling, and for a second, I'm not sure if she's talking to him or me. Except Gee isn't looking at Tobias, and she doesn't break eye contact with me as she pulls apart the remaining peanut-oil-covered pieces of the puzzle box.

Inside it is another photograph. I don't need to see it to know it's from *Raiders of the Lost Temple*, the fifth escape room our friend group ever did. Guinevere flips the picture over, scanning the back, and I watch her, afraid to breathe. If she set up tonight's game—if she placed the *Raiders of the Lost Temple* photograph with our stabbed-out eyes inside the puzzle box meant to trigger Tobias's worst allergy—then why is she keeping up the act? She should be trying to kill me. My video should be cued on the LCD monitor. I should be dead.

"They're instructions," Guinevere murmurs, more to herself than to me. "The shower handle is a lever." She glares at me. "Fucking bitch."

Before I can respond, Guinevere raises the ax again, pointing it at me as she backs around the broken HVAC vent and toward the walk-in shower. "No sudden movements," she warns. She keeps one shaking arm up, still threatening me, while she reaches behind her to fiddle with the lever. I watch her spin it to the left, then the right, and then up. A protest rises in my throat, but then there's a terrible grinding as the half of the shower wall with the built-in mirror gives way. Guinevere pauses before letting the lever go; the one-way glass rolls back into place. I understand her hesitation. Because I was right: There's one more area inside *Arsonist's Revenge*.

And it follows the layout of the area that Matt suffocated inside last year.

Guinevere's chest heaves. She wipes her sweating forehead, still holding the ax, and I realize her crop top is wet with blood and gore and splattered tears. And it's only the two of us left now, and I don't know why I still care so much about her, but I do.

Except maybe it's because I hold on to friendships until my dug-in fingernails crack and bleed. And maybe it's because I always have.

"What do we have left?" Guinevere asks. I blink, startled. She's looking at me.

There's No Escape Rule #12: If you're stuck, consolidate.

"We haven't found the last photograph," I tell her, my shredded voice laced with bile. Tobias is still gasping for air. He needs his EpiPen, a doctor, an emergency room. Anaphylaxis can kill you in less than fifteen minutes—I learned that scouring WebMD in the wake of last year's fire—and the clock inside *Arsonist's Revenge* is at 10:18.

She nods. "This is the last room, then," she says, her storm-gray gaze fixed on my face. "You didn't think I'd be alive at this point, so whatever's in here... I'll either die exploring, or I'll discover your secret way out." The corners of her Cupid's-bow lips turn downward. "This is an enclosed space, though. And with the carbon monoxide…"

"Wait." I blink. "Do you think I set this up?"

"Shut up!" Guinevere screams, spittle flying from her mouth, and I flinch. "I don't need any of your mind games right now, Stephanie. Accept that you lost and just let me fucking *think*, Christ. It's almost over. I just…I just need to decide what to do."

Her attention flicks to the countdown. Together, we watch it turn from 10:00 to 9:59. Less than ten minutes left.

While Guinevere paces, my gaze drifts back to Tobias's arms, which are usually so full of nervous energy and now are oddly still on the washed-out, white-tiled floor. But then my vision snags on something poking out of his oversized CEDAR CREEK HIGH SCHOOL CHESS CLUB sweatshirt, so I crouch down and slip my hand against the soft maroon fabric. If it's a phone—if he was hiding a fucking phone and didn't mention it after three deaths, after a gas leak, after the argument where we could have called our parents or the fire department or, God forbid, Sheriff Stallard to come and break down this door—I'm going to actually lose my mind. But then my fingers meet cold steel, and my breath hitches as the object's silver cross glitters in the floodlights.

Oh my God.

It's my Swiss Army knife.

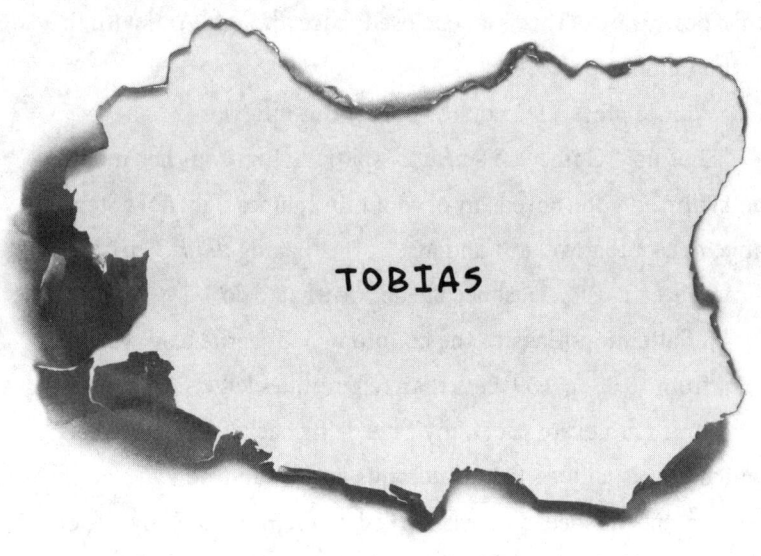

TOBIAS

13 Days Before the Accident

People say I'm a genius.

Allow me to revise: I *am* a genius.

"So, once again," I start as I turn toward Malachi with my voice lowered. "After spending all year attempting to hack into *Cedar Creek Confessions*, I finally hold access to the account." I spare Matt's brother a begrudging glance of acknowledgment for this simple fact before turning back to our Game Master. Honestly, Santo got lucky that his identical twin is stupid enough to not have Face ID disabled on his phone, but whatever. Not all of us can be Mensans. "This means we can unmask Matt as *Cedar Creek Confessions* to the entire student body. We'll be able to save Charity's election bid, discredit his post about Guinevere's jewelry business, get me back on the chess team, clear up the allegations against Steffi's blog, and reinstate your reputation as a..." I wave a hand, searching for the right word.

"Story influencer," Malachi supplies. "A creator of video narratives, providing entertainment to oft-underrepresented communities."

"Sure," I say, "whatever. All we need to do is create a post on the *Confessions* account while posing as Matt." I clear my throat, aware that it's suddenly itchy—probably because of all the dust and pollen gathering inside the towers of every geriatric computer in Mr. Foxfield's ancient media center—so I slide a bottle of Flonase from the pocket of my sweatpants and spritz it twice in each nostril before continuing. "For that, we'll need you"—I point at Charity—"to write it, and you"—I point at Santo—"to make sure it sounds authentic, and you"—I point at Steffi—"to keep Matt from his phone long enough for the post to spread without his knowledge." I smirk. "Ideally, the entire student body will take enough screenshots while Matt's out of commission for his digital footprint to be tied to *Cedar Creek Confessions* forever, and then our work will be done."

Steffi nods. "Since we only have a week left until the last day of school," she says, glancing at the rest of us, "any fallout from our master plan will happen over the summer. It'll make it harder for Matt to push back, which has the added benefit of destroying his leverage with the student body by the time we come back to school in August for our senior year."

To our left, a few stations over, Alyssa Hayes is nose-deep in a Google Docs essay. I can't see what she's writing, but it's probably an application to our local community college. Word on the street is, the last state college on her list just rescinded her acceptance after her criminal charges became official, which means she's out of luck for the rest of the year.

There's a visible trail of mascara tears smudged across her cheeks. Gross. I'll never understand how certain people can allow themselves to cry in public.

"So you're delegating," Malachi says, his eyes cutting to me, "and Charity is writing and Santo is proofreading and Steffi is distracting. But all this brings me back to my earlier question"—here, he throws me a dirty look—"which is: Where do I fit in with all of this?"

In response, Santo's dark gaze flicks from me, to Steffi, to the computer in front of us (which is quietly playing a video on the Riemann theorem in case Mr. Foxfield walks by and asks what we're supposed to be working on) before it finally settles back on Malachi. "Well," he says, "the post works better if we get Matt to confess he runs the account directly."

I narrow my eyes; I still don't like the fact that Santo is here, even if he did give us the password for his brother's gossip-driven Instagram. Out of all of us, he's the only one who hasn't been targeted by *Cedar Creek Confessions*. But since Malachi has, I guess that's enough for everyone to accept that Santo's playing turncoat.

I'm not sure if I quite buy it, though.

"Right," Charity says encouragingly, twisting the pearl necklace sitting at the base of her throat. "And we, like, were hoping to do that through a video? Because, you know, that's your area of expertise."

"Ah," Malachi says slowly. "You want @Mal.The.Reel.King to hook you up." His smile drops. "Y'all know that post was fake, though, right? I don't actually use the conversations I overhear while acting as Game Master to inspire my online content."

From the desk of the media center, Mr. Foxfield glances up at us. His gaze drops to our huddle, and he makes a cut-it-out motion with his hand to his neck.

"Sorry, Mr. Foxfield!" Charity chirps, already reaching out to adjust the volume. "We're getting extra help with AP Calculus, but we can turn it down."

Guinevere scoffs. "None of us are even in AP Calculus," she says. When I glance at her, she rolls her eyes. "Don't even try it, Tobias—I know you took it last year."

"Don't you take AP Calculus for two years?" Steffi asks.

Guinevere shakes her head. "Not if you're a fucking nerd and do both AB and BC in one."

Steffi blinks. "You can do that? As a sophomore?"

"*Anyway*," I tell Malachi, attempting to get the conversation back on track, "it's not like you're committing a HIPAA violation or anything. Regardless of the legality of the whole BREAKOUT surveillance situation, though, if we claim Matt is behind the account without proof—even with a well-written confession—he could just claim his account got hacked. No one will believe us."

"Right," Santo says, leaning across the keyboard's numpad to flutter his eyelashes at Malachi. "But with video evidence…"

"There may be a way to beat him," I finish. And I'm right.

Malachi doesn't smile at Santo. Instead, his gaze slides to mine, assessing. "What's in it for me?" he asks.

"How about restoring your reputation?" I say as I slip my Flonase back into my sweatpants. "Keeping your followers from canceling you? Helping out all your friends?"

Hell, how many times do I need to repeat myself before the plan sinks in? For all the snide comments my classmates make about my intelligence, sometimes I feel like my IQ is average and everyone around me is a complete idiot instead.

Steffi nods, her face grim. "We need to take him down, Mal. Matt's account is only spiraling more out of control every day. Say you're in."

"Please," Charity adds as Mr. Foxfield gives us another appraising look. Or maybe it's a warning glance.

Malachi chews his bottom lip, clearly mulling our proposal over, but I don't say anything as he does. If chess has taught me anything, it's that keeping a cool head can prevent you from losing, even if winning is impossible. But I don't think I'll need to force a draw here. I've noticed an uptick in hate comments on Malachi's Reels ever since the *Cedar Creek Confessions* post about his storytelling practices came out. And I'd bet he's all too willing to take revenge.

Finally, he sighs. "We just need to record him admitting that he runs the account?"

"Exactly," Santo says.

Now he's getting it.

"So...are you thinking what I'm thinking?" Steffi asks. A smile creeps across her face. Everyone else looks confused, but her dark brown eyes flick to mine, and I nod. She nods back.

"Pull up the BREAKOUT website," Steffi tells Malachi. "We need to book an escape room."

CHAPTER SEVENTEEN

Wednesday, May 20, 2026, 11:51 PM

Okay. Don't panic. Don't freak out. You're okay. It's okay. You'll both be okay.

Except I'm not and it's not and we won't be. I blink pooling tears from my eyes. Choke back salt water. Drop the cool metal blade. It skitters away, and when I reach for it again, my hands are trembling too fast for me to properly grip the handle. I mutter a string of obscenities and try again. *Fucking focus, Steffi. Tobias stole your knife. Pick it up. Move.*

Did he cut the wires of the emergency exit, too? Is he the reason we're stuck here? Did he lure us into BREAKOUT? Underneath my skin, the blood in my veins swirls with a deadly mixture of adrenaline, hysteria, painkillers, and carbon monoxide. It's not like I can ask him any of those questions now. I glance at his twitching body and force down the hot bile crawling up my throat. Instead of throwing up, I focus on the weight of the Swiss Army knife—my goddamn Swiss Army knife—against my sweating palm. My still-trembling fingers can't unveil the drop point blade, though, so I switch to my thumbnail until the metal flicks out into the oxidizing mercaptan-tainted air.

It's wet.

On the LCD monitor, the hot-pink smiley face reappears. *"Hey."* Not-Matt's voice razes through the room, echoing from everywhere, filling the roar of my blood-filled eardrums. I can't stop looking at the blade, the dark oil gummed to its sharp edge, the Rorschach inkblots curing on its hilt. *"Tobias. Because you have failed to escape in time, you have been eliminated, and your secret will now be revealed for you."* Not-Matt smiles. *"Now, this is disappointing, as I expected more of a fight from our premier chess player. But, oh well. Life moves on."*

There's a wet knife in my hand. Tobias used it. He used it here, on us.

Audio crinkles in through the speakers, crunchy and distorted, until there's no denying it: This is happening right now, whether we like it or not. Despite everything—Charity's motto, Malachi's unease, Santo's plan, Tobias's warnings, Guinevere's advice—I'm still drawn to the LCD monitor like a moth to a flame.

This time, I'm staring at the inside of the Cedar Creek gymnasium, watching the Sixth Annual Sevier County Chess Championship. This is old footage, streamed through YouTube for avid players and idle gamers to watch in real time; Tobias always used to invite us to watch through Discord links when he knew he was playing, but I always preferred to let the stream run in the background while I did AP Human Geography homework or brushed up on my online escape game skills—if I even clicked on it at all. The thought sours my stomach. For all my angst about my friends, I could've been a better one myself.

In my hands, the knife blade glints. On-screen, Tobias captures his opponent's rook. He lost this game, and afterward, *Cedar Creek Confessions* accused him of fixing his matches. The post—whether true or not—provided enough evidence for Tobias to get quietly pushed off the CCHS chess team.

And after that, Matt took his place as the star player.

Behind me, Guinevere's staccato breaths steady into an almost-rhythm. My throat thickens. I saw tonight playing out differently. I thought I'd have more control. I thought if we followed the rules from my blog, if we worked together, then we'd escape *Arsonist's Revenge* and I'd leave BREAKOUT at midnight with all of my newfound memories. With real answers. With the knowledge that I'm not a monster.

I was so wrong.

"*After I ratted you out to the chess team, you were dying to get me back. But humiliating me within BREAKOUT wasn't enough for you, so you proposed keeping me in the room overnight—and fought for the idea until everyone agreed.*" Not-Matt's voice pauses, and I lick my bloodied lips. "*Without your actions...*" the disembodied voice of my dead best friend continues, but I can't hear him, can't focus on the rest of his words when Tobias's purpling body is still sprouting new hives, can't understand anything except the knife I'm cradling awkwardly in my hands.

"Christ," Guinevere whispers. Her body is upside down and mirrored in the knife blade in front of me: muscled track-and-field legs, nicotine-patched olive-skinned arms, beautiful face all thunderstorm. She still looks indestructible. Divine. Phantasmal, even.

And now, she's the only ghost from my past still breathing.

"It's not what you think, Gee," I croak, turning to face her. I can hear my heartbeat in my ears. There's blood slimed in the spandex fabric of my knit I LOVE PRAGUE socks, and dirt caked under my battered nails, and a migraine behind my eyes that intensifies the longer I stare at the worn leather trench coat now hanging limply around Guinevere's sweating shoulders. I ruined the garment in the HVAC, and I ruined my friendships inside *Arsonist's Revenge*, and nothing I say is ever going to be enough for the girl reflected in the metal of the knife I'm holding.

I try anyway. "This is—I found it in—" I take a breath. "Tobias."

She needs to hear me. It wasn't me who did this, who set up the escape room, who sent the invitations. Even with my warped memories, I would have remembered. I would have.

But it's not Guinevere, either. If I can make her listen, make her understand, *show* her that Tobias Quinton Matthews has been torturing us all night—

Her eyes meet mine, and hope swells in my chest as I remember the birthday cards she sent me every year, or the way her collarbones glittered red and blue while we watched the Fourth of July fireworks at her grandparents' lake house, or the scent of her Marlboro smoke soaking my skin as we shared a cigarette up at the water tower on one of the last normal nights before the fire. I can almost feel the thick paper of her handmade cards and the messages in them, written year after year in her signature blocky script: *YOU LIVED ANOTHER YEAR, BITCH. I'M SO GLAD YOU'RE HERE. I LOVE YOU MORE THAN ANYTHING. I SWEAR TO GOD, DON'T READ THIS OUT LOUD OR I'LL KILL YOU. XOXO.*

But then Guinevere's hurricane gaze drops to the blade, and the wind-whipped rage in her expression as she flicks her eyes back to mine, seeing me see her, is enough to drown me.

Desperation floods my neurons like static as the two of us lunge to our feet: muted, buzzing, gray. She reaches me one millisecond before I realize I can't compete with her track-toned muscles or the heft of her rubber ax, so there's nothing to do but act on instinct: I turn the handle of my reclaimed Swiss Army knife, blade against my forearm, like Dad taught me, and hit the tiled floor right as she swings the ax toward my skull. *Whoosh.* A near miss.

Holy shit, holy shit, holy shit. She's trying to kill me.

I catch her arm with my knife and the blade tears the leather of Matt's jacket. Horror buzzes behind my temples at the fact that I'm fighting her, but I primed her for this. She believes it's her or me.

"Are you serious, Stephanie?" she screeches, readjusting her grip on the bludgeoning ax, and I prepare myself for another clash. "Are you going to kill me now, too?" Her nails are digging into the ax handle, and when she aims her next swing at my injured calf and I just barely roll out of the way I'm suddenly aware that it doesn't matter how much I've accomplished to make it out of *Arsonist's Revenge* alive, because Guinevere Mitchell-Moore can still pulverize me into nothing.

A sneer curls her mouth as she adopts a high falsetto. *"What a poor little blogger! She's the only survivor of the second BREAK-OUT fire! She has no idea what happened to her* FRIENDS!"

Another swing and a miss. I scramble backward, but Guinevere fills the space, tracking blood across the tile. "Maybe you've convinced the rest of Sevier County that you're innocent, but I know you. *I know you*, Stephanie. I watched your knees buckle from that beam. And you know what?" Her chest heaves; like this, with her bare shoulders bathed in magenta floodlights, she looks angelic. "It didn't hit you HARD ENOUGH!"

She swings again, but I duck, and this time her weapon shatters the mirror above the industrial sink. Guinevere hisses and jerks the ax free, her face contorted with anger, and I use the moment she's distracted to break for the walk-in shower. If I can just get to the third room—

I'm almost at the LCD monitor when the weapon sings through the air and embeds itself in the screen above me with a sharp *THWACK!* Broken glass rains on me, Gaga-style, and I immediately throw up my arms to shield my face from the damage. Jesus. She threw the fucking ax at my head.

Above me, the LCD monitor rainbows out. Not-Matt's fake face is splintered into a million fractals, his dark eyes immobile; as if to prove a point, the edges of the screen bleed hot pink and bright cyan. "You missed," I breathe, turning back to Gee, a stupid joke about her dad wasting his money by sending her to

Lenoir City Wild Hearts Equine Therapy & Outdoor Sports if she can't even throw an ax after an entire summer waiting at the tip of my tongue, but it dies as soon as I register the pain in Guinevere's expression. She can't kill me.

She overshot on purpose.

Gee wipes her bloodied mouth with the back of her hand. "Christ, Stephanie. When will you drop the act? You set this escape room up to kill us because you couldn't let the past go. Because it wasn't enough for you, after all this time, to stay blameless." She shakes her beautiful head. "When Matt destroyed our friendships, it happened because he publicized so many of our secrets on *Cedar Creek Confessions*: Charity's eating disorder. Malachi's master key misuse. Tobias's cheating. My hazardous resin-pouring practices." Her eyes spark, smolder, ash. "Don't you remember, Stephanie? Why you found out? What you did afterward? How much it cost us?"

"I didn't," I protest. Panic metastasizes through my chest. "I couldn't have."

"No?" Guinevere advances. "You're the one who swore we'd humiliate Matt as revenge. You're the one who used our secrets as leverage in your master plan."

I can't speak. I can't move. My tongue is locked to the roof of my mouth; my heart is slamming against my rib cage. Above me, the shattered LCD screen pulses, sputters, swells.

"One year ago," Guinevere starts. Her whole face is bathed in floodlights—her pointed chin, her canine teeth, her high cheekbones with their smattering of freckles. A waterfall of tangled hair tumbles down her torn crop top. "One year ago, you set up

Wanderland to fuck up Matt and roped us into it. Because of *Cedar Creek Confessions*. Because of what he wrote about your blog. Because you needed to keep him from posting it."

She stops close enough for her breath to ghost my face, and I fight the urge to reach out and steel my fingers against the familiar leather of Matt's trench coat—the trench coat she's wearing—to keep from screaming. She's staring directly at me. There's a cut on her forehead. The whites of her eyes are fluorescent; her Cupid's-bow lips look exactly like they did on that night in my beat-up Jeep after her boyfriend's funeral a year ago.

Let me give you a ride, Gee. You won't be able to drive yourself anywhere when you're crying too hard to see.

No, no, no.

"And now you're here," she whispers, "putting on this desperate amnesiac act as if you *need* to find out what happened to him or you'll just *die*, when you're the one who killed him, Stephanie." She swallows. "It was all because of you."

CHAPTER EIGHTEEN

Wednesday, May 20, 2026, 11:52 PM

"You're lying."

The rebuttal comes easily; right now, it's all that does. In front of me, Guinevere's hurricane gaze swirls with indignation. Her mascara—pristine just an hour ago—is now smudged across her eyelids; her caramel-brown hair is a whirlwind of blood, sweat, and drying snot.

"I'm not," she says. The dancing LEDs cast parts of her in shadow, and others in blinding relief: the gore-splattered mini claw clips snaggled in her hair, the crescent gouges on her arms, the blood-stained linen of her crop top. "You claim you're so desperate for the truth, Stephanie, so here I am, giving it to you."

I inhale, flicking my gaze from the ax-head embedded above

my head to Guinevere's burning face. "I'd never hurt Matt. I didn't *kill* him."

"How would you know?" Guinevere says quietly, and this stumps me, because it's exactly what the dark voice in the back of my mind says all the time. How would I know? How would I?

"Santo, Tobias, Charity, Malachi, and I all formed a pact after the fire last year," Guinevere continues. "*Tell no one.* That included you."

The others don't want to tell you—they think you can't handle the truth—but the truth doesn't matter if the only way we're leaving BREAKOUT is in body bags.

"Besides, you claimed you lost your memory," Guinevere continues, "and Matt was dead, so we promised one another we wouldn't tell you anything. But one year ago, you decided to get back at Matt for running *Cedar Creek Confessions.* You convinced Malachi to let us into BREAKOUT after hours, and you roped in the rest of us to help, because Matt planned to reveal your secret to the entire fucking school, so you planned out *Wanderland* to get revenge."

"What are you talking about? What post? What secret?"

"Your blog," Guinevere says, closing the space between us. "Your brand deals. Your sponsorships. You took bribes, Stephanie. You let companies buy your praise, and your dumb ass told Matt, and he decided to tank your credibility." She scoffs. "You didn't pull back from *There's No Escape* because of Matt's accident. You were forced to abandon the blog because you're a fraud."

I shake my head. This isn't real. This can't be happening. I don't remember any of this.

"And you're so fucking fragile that after Santo found the post in Matt's drafts," Guinevere adds, "you went into the garage and turned on your Jeep and just *sat* there. Your mom freaked. Called my dad, got you a hypnotherapist, had me take you out to *talk*." She snorts. "So you came out with me, and that's when you got the idea to hurt Matt before he could destroy you."

The speakers boom. The spiderwebbing monitor flickers— Not-Matt with another video, maybe?—before it flashes bright green and stays that way. Guess there are a few technical difficulties that not even our true Game Master can override.

For once, though, I'm not paying attention to the LCD screen. Instead, I'm staring at the girl in front of me. Even if what she's saying is true, then why did Matt write a post about it? He was my best friend. He wouldn't have intentionally damaged my reputation.

Right?

"Carbon monoxide is your MO, Stephanie, so tonight has to be you—your setup, your idea, your plan. It was the last time: We'd invite everyone to Cedar Creek's BREAKOUT: *Wanderland* escape room for the Cesari twins' birthdays, but halfway through the game we'd purposefully trap Matt inside the Queen of Hearts's Rose Garden, reveal that we knew he ran *Cedar Creek Confessions* through a series of pre-filmed videos we'd work with Malachi to show on the LCD monitors, and force him to publicly apologize to all of us—and to everyone he hurt through his posts—before leaving him inside the escape room overnight. In the morning, we'd snag the security footage from Malachi, post it on Matt's own *Cedar Creek Confessions* Instagram along with @Mal.The.Reel.King and *There's No Escape*, and publicly humiliate him for ruining the lives of so many members of our student body." Guinevere crosses her arms. "It was completely your idea—your drunk and stupid idea—and I was worried you were going to try and kill yourself again if I didn't go along with whatever you proposed, so I agreed to help you. I convinced everyone to pitch in, actually, but then it all went wrong." Her voice darkens. "As it turns out, everyone had their own agenda once we got inside *Wanderland* and the door locked behind us. Charity wanted to back out as soon as the game started; Tobias thought our plan didn't humiliate Matt enough. Malachi got cold feet about implicating his parents' business in a revenge plot. You almost blew everything by attempting to confront Santo about whether he told Matt about our plan, and the whole thing stressed me out so badly that I lit a cigarette to take the edge off and accidentally—and it really was an accident—started the fire." Guinevere is shaking now. "Matt died. He died, and while we were watching the whole plaza burn in the parking lot, you couldn't stop laughing, Stephanie. I told you to call 911, and you couldn't, because you couldn't stop *laughing*."

Her mouth twists; strands of caramel-brown hair fall in wisps around her contorted face. "So how dare you," she finally says. "How dare you come here tonight and pretend you can't remember anything. As if that's fucking fair."

"That's not...it's not true," I rasp, backing away, but there's not enough space—my back hits the tile of the walk-in shower. There's nowhere else to go.

"It is," Guinevere says. "And you know what, Stephanie?"

I reach beside me, fumbling for the lever of the walk-in shower, and then the door swings inward and I'm blasted by cold air. The change in temperature is a welcome balm after the sweltering interior of the other sets inside *Arsonist's Revenge*. My Converse sneakers crunch under a fine layer of white powder—fake snow, maybe?—but there's not enough time to examine it because Guinevere is still advancing, is still taking up space, is still pressing forward.

"I'm done," she says, following me into the third and final room. "I'm done watching you act like you did nothing wrong. I'm done trying to protect you from attempting again. And I'm done dancing around your fuckups when you're the one who lured us here for another insane revenge plot, except this time you're making sure there are no survivors."

"Shut up," I hiss, my throat tightening at the closeness of her: bougainvillea and white sage. The metallic tang of nicotine and sweat and want.

Guinevere takes one last step forward, and for a half second, I'm convinced she's going to kiss me and that I'm going to kiss her back, but then the walk-in shower door clicks closed and the moment disappears.

"Christ," Guinevere whispers, the fear in her tone finally unmistakable. And I think she's talking about the door, about the fact that we're definitely locked in here, but then her storm-gray eyes move above my head, the glassy panic swirling there now replaced by full-blown dread, and when I turn to follow her gaze, my own adrenaline spikes.

The two of us are trapped in an industrial meat locker.

And we're surrounded by six burlap-sacked bodies, hanging upside down by their wrapped-up ankles like slaughtered lambs.

• • •

"You were right," Guinevere whispers. The words come out in a puff of vapor. A filament in the fluorescents above us flashes, illuminating her blood-matted streaks of hair. She's pathetic, just like me. She's suffered, just like me. And as much as she hates me, as much as we've gone from being friends to enemies to almost-lovers to enemies again, right now we're on the same side. "This is just like where Matt…" Her beautiful face crumples. "You didn't do this."

I want to tell her that we'll get out of here, that we just need to stay calm, but my mouth refuses to form the words. Everything around us is awash in a soft UV glow, illuminating the gore splattered across our skin like the ceiling stars in the childhood bedroom I had before Dad left. Above us, the life-size twine-tied corpses—the ones I'm praying are made of Flex Foam—hang still and silent. They're clearly representative of us: Charity. Malachi. Guinevere. Santo. Tobias. And me.

ONE BY ONE.

Gee's hand lands on my shoulder. "Stephanie," she says, her fingers squeezing the hard bone of my shoulder blade, but I can't hear her. I'm floating away, outside myself, watching my body contract until I'm a pinprick of LED light, until I'm a glow-in-the-dark rubber duck, until I'm nothing at all. My chest is tight. The bloodstained knife edge cutting into my sweating palm is so sharp, and Guinevere and I are inside the sister room of the franchise that killed my best friend exactly one year ago, and I am going to die here, too.

Ringing. Humming, buzzing, grating. Louder and louder and louder. Guinevere whirls back and tries to lift the door handle. It doesn't budge. Now she's pounding on the smooth one-way mirror and calling for help despite there being no one left alive to help us. Now she's shaking my shoulders again. Now there's a light blinking at the edge of my vision like I'm already dying—

No. No, it's a working screen. There's an LCD monitor in this room, too, counting down from 7:02.

Jesus. We have seven minutes left to break out of BREAKOUT.

"Steffi, please," Guinevere says, her blood-splattered hands cupping my cheeks, and a dim part of me realizes that this is the first time she's actually called me by my nickname tonight. My eyes refocus, taking in her tear-streaked face. Two minutes ago, Guinevere was trying to kill me, and now she's acting as if she didn't just throw an ax at my head. "I need your help." She licks her lips, and there's a wildness to her expression as her eyes flit from the LCD monitor and then back to my face. "You want to redeem yourself for everything that happened last year? Then redeem yourself. Find a way to get us out."

I want to shake my head. Not with carbon monoxide filling up this liminal space. But then I refocus on the twine-tied bodies, and I realize I need to try my hardest to get through the rest of this escape room for everyone who will never be able to: Charity. Malachi. Santo. Tobias. Matt.

Pathetic or not, monster or not, fraud or not, I need to do this for all of us.

I glance back at the functioning monitor—6:39—and inhale. "Okay," I tell Guinevere.

She laughs, but her eyes are spilling over with tears. "There's the Steffi I know," she says.

A quick glance over our new surroundings reveals that we're trapped inside the long, narrow industrial meat locker with an assortment of cardboard boxes, a line of metallic racks filled with white-papered cylinders, a final blinking security camera next to another set of speakers, and a third LCD monitor. This is the smallest of the three rooms inside *Arsonist's Revenge*, which means it can't contain that many clues. And that's good for us.

"Start searching through those boxes," I instruct Guinevere. "I'll start sifting through all this fake snow, see if I can uncover something."

Almost as soon as I start sweeping through the synthetic snow with my Converse sneakers like my life depends on it, because it kind of does, my heartbeat stutters. Because right underneath the first burlap-sacked body, tucked away beneath a coat of shimmering polymer flakes, is another photograph.

I bend to pick it up. In this photo, taken at Pigeon Forge's BREAKOUT: *Hijacked*, the seven of us are perfectly frozen: Tobias with a knowing smirk, his black-and-white Magnus Carlsen T-shirt partially hidden by Matt flipping off the camera.

Charity with her long ash-blond hair down and her hand up to form half of a heart with Santo. Malachi next to him, cheesing at the fact that he didn't have to act as our Game Master for once. Me, with my head on Guinevere's shoulder, holding up half of the sign we're both supporting: WE (ALMOST) BROKE OUT! For once, nothing about the picture is out of the ordinary. It's just a normal photo.

A lump forms in my throat. This is from the last escape room all of us completed before the fire. And even though it shouldn't be such a gut punch, it is. For a second, I remember the moment we took it—*the artificial click of the camera, my bright smile, the laughter that followed*—and even if we did not, in fact, escape in time, we'd had so much fun.

Guinevere finishes upending the last cardboard box; about a dozen more white-papered cylinders tumble out of it. "Is that another photograph?" she asks. When I don't answer, she claps fake snow off her hands before she comes over to peer at it. "Man," she says. "Santo looks so different in this one, doesn't he?"

"Yeah," I agree. "Happier, I guess."

"Hmm," Guinevere says, as though that's not exactly what she had in mind, and then she reaches out to turn my wrist so that the photograph flips with it. There's a cipher on the back. Caesar, from the looks of it. Too easy. But our time limit makes it annoyingly dangerous.

"Oh, I know this!" Guinevere glances at me. "Remember the tape deck I was listening to earlier? It was in Morse code, but it said E equals twenty-one."

The date of last year's accident.

"Great. Help me decode it?" I ask Guinevere. She nods, and then the two of us attack the cipher from opposite ends, singing through the alphabet under our breath and swirling letters in the fake snow until our newest clue sits in plain text: *YOU NEED THIS TO LEAVE.*

"There," Guinevere says, breathless and a little disappointed. "It's a riddle."

Her expectant gaze flicks to me, the barest hint of a smile curving her full lips, and despite the frigid air of the meat locker, my cheeks warm. Jesus. I'm exhausted and hungry and tired, and I still don't understand how to fucking feel about her, this girl who acts like she wants nothing to do with me one second and then helps me solve a Caesar cipher the next. Part of me wishes we'd been working alongside each other like this the whole night, me and the version of Guinevere who's buried deep beneath the biting facade she's built up to manage her pain—I mean, fuck, part of me wishes we'd been spending every moment together in the months after Matt died. She wouldn't have had to say anything, even. It would have just been nice to have a friend.

But instead, both of us pulled apart after that one tear-streaked post-funeral Jeep kiss, and afterward the silence between us was so thick and strange that I didn't know what to do with my hands, whether it would be socially acceptable for me to wipe Guinevere's dark lipstick from my lips. And the whole time she had looked so terrified even though snot was dribbling from her nose, and then she'd just sniffled and hopped out of the passenger seat and it was like the kiss hadn't happened at all, like she hadn't leaned over and opened her warm mouth against mine while she was still crying and froze when I didn't kiss her back because she was scaring me and I couldn't tell if she actually wanted it; and so I just kept sitting there, wondering if I had imagined the whole scenario, stuck in fight-flight-freeze in her driveway until Judge Mitchell-Moore walked out and asked me what the hell I was doing in front of his house, only he didn't say that; he just said, *Maybe you should go home, Stephanie*, in that tired old voice of his, so I did.

I exhale sharply and refocus on our latest clue. The carbon monoxide is definitely getting to me, but I need to keep my eye on the prize, Peanut.

"Steffi?" Guinevere says quietly. "I don't know the answer to the riddle, but the packaged canisters are stamped with our birthdays, in case that means anything."

I glance at the discarded papers from what she's already unwrapped. One is melting by my Converses—the edges of the red-inked words BEST BY: 11/24/05 are seeping pink lines into the white powder. Jesus. From this vantage point, I spot at least eight containers with the Cesari twins' birthday: 5/20. There are a couple with Tobias's: 9/29. Charity's, 6/19. Mine is 2/15: a day after Valentine's Day. Guinevere's, 11/24, takes up an entire locker shelf.

"The accident," I murmur, staring at the overwhelming number of wrapped containers. "We need to find one with five-twenty-one. The fire started at midnight, so that's the day Matt died."

Guinevere moves off toward the end of the meat locker,

shoving aside burlapped body bags and tossing aside paper packaging. I reach forward and tilt the metal shelf until its wrapped containers spill out onto the fake snow. "Two piles," I call, picking up cylinders at random: 11/24, 9/29, 2/15. Beside me, Guinevere tosses rejects while I pile up my own by the still-locked mirror door.

"Anything?" she asks.

I rush to the next shelf. "No. You?"

"I don't... Hold on, yeah, actually. Look at this."

I'm over to her immediately. Guinevere tears away the butcher paper on the 5/21 package, and I scowl at the golden cryptex beneath the wrappings. It's just another puzzle to solve. With our luck, a vial of acid will sizzle away my skin the second I open it.

"Don't look so bitter—you're good at these." She hands the seven-ringed cylinder to me. "You'll figure it out."

I can't tell if it's a threat or a promise.

Carefully, I tug at the cryptex's endcap. It doesn't look like it's made of the sturdiest metal, and for a second, I wonder if I might be able to open it by loosening the screws with my Swiss Army knife. But whatever is inside may be dangerous: The only way to unlock it safely is to align the correct phrase—or keyword—into its spinning rings.

My shoulders give an involuntary shudder. For my sixteenth birthday, Tobias gave me a six-letter cryptex after I spent our entire winter break ranting about how much I loved *The Da Vinci Code*. I spent a full seventy-two hours puzzling out combinations before I landed on *SWITCH*, unlocking a digital download code for *Agent A: A Puzzle in Disguise*. Here, we have just over six minutes to figure out what seven-letter word opens *this* cryptex.

I twist the first spinnable ring just as a bang echoes through the meat locker. Guinevere's eyes meet mine in fear—*who the fuck is out there?*—and a crystallized moment of immaculate suspense stretches between us.

And then we shriek as the meat locker explodes.

● ● ●

Shards rain everywhere. Glass slices into my skin, ricochets off my raised arms, and tumbles innocently to the blood-speckled synthetic-polymer-powdered floor. I don't want to move, don't want to hear the telltale *crunch* beneath my sneakers, don't want to shake jagged slivers out of my curtain bangs. Not yet. Right now, I just want to stay crouched against the meat locker shelving, pretending there aren't dozens of gashes burning my skin like so much hot grief, static in a bubble where I can believe my life isn't marred by last year's fire, or this year's blackmail, or my ex-friends' deaths. Right now, it's still just me and the breath I'm holding. Just me and the girl I'm relying on to survive the night.

I can't look up. If I do, I know I'll come face-to-face with a ghost.

"Santo," Guinevere rasps, and my stomach sinks at the confirmation. Fresh cuts blossom across her olive-skinned arms. She hoists herself up and winces, doubling over, her split lip swollen under her perfect Cupid's bow. Burlap and metal and fluorescent lights. "You're...alive."

"Huh," his hoarse voice says. "I guess I am."

I imagine it: his curling smirk. The tilt of his jaw. The gleam in his expression. I picture staying crouched here forever, staring only at Gee's blanching face, lingering successfully in the past. Meat lockers and escape rooms and second chances.

But nothing can keep time from passing. And I'm done being a kind-of-pathetic person. As the past almost-hour inside BREAKOUT has proven, I've done it for far too long.

I meet his gaze through the shattered glass of the one-way mirror. When I blink, the afterimage of his body flying through the air lights up against the UV darkness. "We thought..." I say, and my raw voice splits with the word. "I thought I lost you, too."

Santo grins. Hefts the ax in one ring-adorned hand. "You know it would take more than that to get rid of me, Steff." His eyes aren't smiling.

Guinevere spits blood, and goose bumps erupt over my arms. "But we watched you die, Santo. You were electrocuted right in f-front of us."

"And yet, here I am," he replies. "Saving you." He rakes his burn-scarred fingers through his stringy yellow-blond hair. "If I were you, I'd be a little more...grateful."

My eyes gravitate to the bloodied cinder block lying in the middle of the industrial meat locker. "Grateful?" I repeat. "Your little maneuver almost killed us."

Santo blinks, and my throat bobs as I drop my gaze from his blank countenance to the ax he's still holding. "Ah. Which is your goal, I'm guessing." My voice cracks again. "I don't...I don't understand."

"Oh, but you do," he says. "Don't think I haven't seen you cutting glances at me for the past fifty-four minutes. Trying to figure out why I didn't quite match up to the lingering version of Santo Cesari in your head." He smirks. "So, Zamekova. You've had all night to ruminate on it. Why don't you enlighten us?"

His dark eyes flash, and here it is, *finally*, after 365 long and lonely days: my answer.

"It's you," I whisper, breathless.

Matteo Cesari tilts his head. "Hey, Steff," he coos. "Did you miss me?"

• • •

yelp.com | Recommended Reviews: BREAKOUT Escape Rooms Inc.

Located in Friendship Springs, TN | Have you been here?
Write a review!

An enjoyable (if pricey) experience ★★★★☆
Posted by Meredith Harrell at 7:09 PM

Escape room was good for what it was. Some neat details, but $40 per person means I won't go again unless it's for a special occasion. Some parts of our game had vague puzzles or clues in hard-to-reach locations, which meant it took us longer than we would've liked to escape. Overall, it's a good activity to pass the time...just too pricey for a Saturday afternoon.

Response from BREAKOUT ESCAPE ROOMS Inc. at 9:37 PM

We're sorry to hear that, Meredith! Thank you for stopping by—we're glad you enjoyed your game and we hope to see you again!
—**The James-Mays**

One Hour Before the Accident

"So, again, why are you dragging me to BREAKOUT at 10:56 PM on a Tuesday night?"

In the driver's seat, I slow down as we approach a yellow light and a drunken bachelorette party decked out in novelty headwear and matching sashes emerges from Ripley's Believe It or Not! and crosses the street in front of our car. "Deeper voice," I tell my brother. "Probably drop the PM—it's too specific."

"Accelerate into the yellow light," he says in response, pretending to brood as he stares out the window at the glitzy collection of businesses on either side of the street. We're in Cedar Creek tonight, and apparently so is everyone else. "Total embodiment means total embodiment, which includes my bad driving."

I roll my eyes as I signal into a parking garage with a twenty-five-dollar flat fee. "I still don't know why you needed me to be behind the wheel for this. I mean, don't get me wrong—I'm grateful to be driving, so that we're not in danger of fucking dying in a car crash for once—but it's not like they're going to see us."

Santo shrugs. "Part of the effect," he offers as I slide Momma's card into the reader. She might ask us about the charge later, but managing that new Pizza Plus seems to be doing a number on her lately, so maybe not. Besides, it is our birthday.

"Ta-da!" I say, doing the most pitiful jazz hands I can muster with one hand still on the steering wheel. "We're doing an escape room!"

This time, my brother scowls for real. "I don't sound like that," he says, except he totally does, and I've watched him pull this exact jazz-hand-driving maneuver on several occasions before. "Asshole."

A phone lights up in the cupholder, and I reach for it. "Malachi texted," I inform Santo as I finish parking, using Face ID to unlock his phone. "Said something about wanting a refund through Cash App for wasting his time. Cute."

"Give me that," Santo snaps, snatching the device back. The car jolts. "Don't read my texts with Mal unless you're prepared to be scarred for life." He gives me a skeptical once-over. "Which I doubt you are."

I press my lips together. The longer we sit here, the more unsure I am about this.

"Come on. It's going to be fine," my brother says, picking up on my vibes immediately. When I don't respond, he sighs. "Look.

Can we just focus on having fun tonight? Zamekova put this together, and she wants us to have a good time. She's been super overwhelmed with *Cedar Creek Confessions* drafting that post about her blog, you know? But she wanted to do this for you. Or, I guess, for me." He grins. "For *us*. A proper birthday party. And BREAKOUT isn't so bad, right?"

I glance down at the glinting rings on my fingers. I hate the weight they add to my hands, and I don't like the polish on my nails, either. "Do you actually want to do this?" I ask Santo.

He smiles. "It's an escape room. How hard can it be?"

But that's not what I'm talking about. And he knows it, too.

We get out of our car, the humid night air settling my nerves, and wind our way through the parking garage until we get to the neon-lit building: Cedar Creek's BREAKOUT. It's sandwiched between a million other glowing buildings, each promising their own form of unique entertainment... But none of those offerings matter, because this is the one we're going to, and all our friends are already here.

Tobias is furiously texting away, Guinevere is sucking down a cigarette, Charity is taking a swig from her water bottle, Malachi is fussing with the shoelaces of his ultra-bright sneakers, and Steff is already striding toward us with a wide smile.

"Matt!" she exclaims, pulling my brother into a hug. "Were you surprised?"

Santo grins in response. I step on the back of his shoe—*too cheery*—and he takes the note with ease, immediately relaxing into a soft smirk. "Yeah, definitely. You ready for this?"

Steff nods, and I sling an arm around her shoulders before she can assess my brother's face too closely in the harsh pink glare of BREAKOUT's flashing COME IN, WE'RE OPEN sign. The escape room will be dark. However Steff is planning to humiliate me inside *Wanderland* tonight, Santo has my back. Because even if it took a bit of convincing to regain my brother's trust after he confronted me about *Cedar Creek Confessions*, at the end of the day, our only constant in life is each other.

And because no matter how many shitty fucking lives I ruin through my exposés, I only started the accounts in the first place because I wanted to protect Santo. Because his ex-boyfriend in Ocean City, New Jersey, told everyone on his private Snapchat Story that my brother gave him gonorrhea after they broke up, and the rumors got so bad that we had to move; because the student athletes in Franklin, North Carolina, used to shoulder-check him into lockers for trying to revive the high school's Gay-Straight Alliance; because the bitchy cheerleaders in Hillwood, Louisiana, used to call him slurs in the hallways.

Through all of it, I always wanted to help save my brother from himself. I knew he was too trusting, too well-meaning, and too starry-eyed, but my attempts to talk with him about it always came off as awkward, especially because I'm straight and he's not. It wasn't until we moved to Portland and Santo started up a fling with this hipster who ran *his* school's most popular anonymous gossip account that all the pieces finally clicked into place. Because without any formal ties to an area, I hold no moral qualms about disrupting entire high school ecosystems through publicly revealing people's deepest, darkest secrets.

Oh, did Alyssa Hayes create a Close Friends story about how

she thought the queer-friendly Spring Fling dance wasn't godly? Guess who's writing a letter to the school board about her B&E and posting it on *Confessions*? Man, did Jacob Webber send in a post complaining about the entire GSA? Guess who's exposing him as the head of his scummy nude-sharing group chat? Spoiler alert: It's me. Because when everyone comes to you with their high school's most notorious gossip, you can head off the rumors related to your brother before they even have a chance to spread. And because after that first time, I realized it was so easy: to put on a mask, to wear the face, to hold all the power. Because I liked it. Because I knew we weren't going to stay long, anyway.

"How about you, Santo?" Steff asks, turning to me. She tilts her head, and for a second, I'm worried she's onto us—that she's one of the rare people who can instantly tell me and my brother apart. But an easy smile settles onto her lips, and I know she suspects nothing. "Are you ready, too?"

I smile. "You bet your ass I am," I tell her. And then my brother and I follow her inside BREAKOUT's double doors, because we're prepared, and because tonight, it's not just a game.

CHAPTER NINETEEN

Wednesday, May 20, 2026, 11:54 PM

The handle of the meat locker rattles violently, and it's only then that I realize just how fucked we are.

It was Matt, and not Santo, who didn't reply to my desperate brain-fog WhatsApp messages. It was Matt, and not Santo, who ignored my grief-ridden voicemails. It was Matt, and not Santo, who disappeared abroad and left me to mourn while I failed at picking up every jagged puzzle piece the Cesari twins left behind.

It was Matt, and not Santo, who's been inside BREAKOUT with me all night.

Guinevere laughs. "As if," she says. But Matt doesn't smile, so her own smile wavers, and then a look of horror passes over her face. "Oh my God. You're not kidding."

But Matt isn't looking at her. He moves closer to the shattered window, a muscle in his jaw twitching, and I realize that I can't pull away my gaze.

"Look at you," my best friend says softly. "Deer in headlights." The shadow of a smile threatens the corners of his lips. "I guess I owe you an explanation, huh?"

It was always him, I realize with stomach-sinking certainty. After the *Wanderland* game, after the fire, after the funeral. Matteo Luca Cesari is here, inside BREAKOUT, alive.

Which means that Santo Xavier Cesari, his twin brother, has been dead for an entire year.

I dig my nails into my palms as the UV-reactive walls of *Arsonist's Revenge* swim around me. I fill my lungs in a half breath, guilt and terror coursing through every one of my cells. I can't make a decision. I can't choose. I'm stuck in the parking lot again, unsure if I want to step inside BREAKOUT or punch the gas; I'm frozen in the Mitchell-Moores' driveway, unable to tell if I want to run after Guinevere or let her walk away from me forever.

God, I can't have an anxiety attack. Not here. Not now.

"The Facebook posts from your nonna," I breathe. "All your pictures. Your body language. You looked like your brother in every one. But you're identical twins. You've been avoiding me because you're grieving, and because you don't like me anymore." I blink, and tears splatter my T-shirt. "Not because you took your brother's place. Not because you've been lying to everyone since last May."

Matt shrugs. "Wild when our friends aren't who we think they are, huh? But hey, Steff, give yourself some credit. At least you solved a few clues, right?"

Guinevere glances at me, panic playing out across her face, as more memories flood my brain: the weird moments between Malachi and Santo at Matt's funeral, the Facebook posts I scrounged up while hate comments poured into my *There's No Escape* email, the times he called me *Steff* instead of *Zamekova* tonight. Every nagging feeling I've repressed for the past year.

This was all a game to him. Each premeditated death and clue and LCD screen video... they were all created so Matt could build up to this moment. Him standing in front of me. Me staring back at him. The ax in his hand, slowly twirling.

Before I blink, the weapon flashes through the broken shower mirror. Guinevere's eyes roll backward, lashes fluttering, as she slumps to the ground. Unconscious, hopefully.

Hopefully unconscious, and not dead.

"Hmm," my best friend says. More one-way glass tinkles to the ground as he pulls the rubber ax-head back through the window he's just created. "That was about sixteen minutes overdue."

I step backward, my mind spinning, and force myself to pocket the cryptex as nausea coats my throat. "How did you do it?" I whisper. "How did you take Santo's place?"

He shrugs. "We switched," he says simply. "For *Wanderland*, before we showed up. Santo knew we were going through a rough patch as a friend group, you know, after he found the post I wrote about you for *Cedar Creek Confessions*. And Tobias. And Charity. And Guinevere. And Malachi." His jaw clenches as nausea swoops through my stomach. "But I guess you know how that feels, don't you?"

"We're not the same, Matt. Just because the friend group ended up hating me doesn't mean that I'm like you. You hurt people."

"So did you," Matt counters. "The six of you *killed* me." He pauses. "Well, no. You wanted to kill me." This time, a menacing smile unfurls at the edges of his mouth. "I'm still here, though. And even if you had your suspicions about my identity, Steff"—he does another twirl with the ax—"you didn't *say anything*." His gaze flicks up, back to mine, and I shudder as he raises a mocking pierced eyebrow. "So what does that make you?"

"Not a murderer," I tell him softly, although I'm not sure if I believe it. "Not someone who killed my friends."

"YOU KILLED SANTO!" I step backward, startled, and Matt draws in a ragged breath. "You killed Santo," he repeats, attempting to steady his trembling hands. His scarred fingers aren't identical to his brother's, but I guess it hardly matters when your prints were burned off in a fire. When your DNA is the same.

Tears fill my eyes. "What happened to Santo was terrible. But it was an accident, Matt. I know the truth now—I've heard all our secrets. The six of us contributed to his death; we're all responsible for what happened. But none of it was premeditated. We didn't lie to the sheriff. We didn't mean to kill anyone."

"You're still holding the line?" Matt asks, and now I understand why I believed he was his brother: the pull of his mouth, the identical set of his yellow-blond brows, the sympathetic glint in his dark brown eyes. "No, Steff. Intent doesn't cancel out impact. Your actions—premeditated or not—killed someone. You and everyone else—Charity, Malachi, Tobias, and Guinevere—needed to pay, so I invited you here to even the score." Matt tilts his head. "Thankfully, Malachi was more than willing to help out his longtime crush. He thought Santo needed his help for one last prank—you know, giving you all one good scare the night before graduation—and was all too thrilled when I brought him some nachos as a thank-you gift." He smiles. "You'd be surprised at how easy it is in this state to get your hands on enough tractor supply horse tranquilizers to knock someone out cold." He sneers at the look of horror on my face. "No, he's not dead yet—you probably panicked while you were up in the HVAC. But once this entire place blows, he will be."

"*Blows?*" I repeat. "What the fuck, Matt? Malachi made one mistake. *One*, in all the time he stuck out his neck for us."

"And you think it was okay for his family to get off scot-free in the aftermath?" Matt demands, his burn-scarred nostrils flaring. "For them to claim Santo's death—*my death*—as inspiration for their latest attraction? For all of this"—he gestures around us with the ax—"for *Arsonist's Revenge*?" He scoffs in disgust, the UV lights of the industrial meat locker flickering across his purple-lit face. "No. People need to be held responsible for their actions, Steff. We've always agreed on that, at least. And BREAKOUT...BREAKOUT is unsafe. It was unsafe when the franchises didn't have fully functional sprinklers, when the Cedar Creek location got busted for wiring issues, when the lawsuit exposed the loopholes in the company's waivers, and it's unsafe now. I'm just proving that the James-Mays are cutting corners. Six deaths, exactly a year after the first one... They'll have no choice this time, will they? They'll have to shut it down."

Matt's eyes lock on mine, waiting, like he's only trying to get me to understand. But none of this is understandable. I finally have my answer, and after all this time, I don't want it anymore.

"And if I get revenge on the people who wanted to kill me—*who killed my brother*—in the process... Well, you know what they say about two birds, right?" Matt adds, lifting the ax.

Make a decision, Steffi. Choose. RUN.

I turn on my heel and scramble away from the door just as it bangs against the concrete wall. Glass and snow crunch behind me in tandem, but I don't turn to look. At the end of the industrial meat locker, the LCD monitor switches to the blinking hot-pink smiley face before it boots up another video—more grainy black-and-white footage—but I don't care. I need to escape. I have to get away from him.

Now, before he kills me.

"BECAUSE YOU HAVE FAILED TO ESCAPE IN TIME," Matt yells as the in-room speakers crackle to life, "YOU WILL BE ELIMINATED, AND YOUR SECRET WILL NOW BE REVEALED FOR YOU."

"*So, Miss Zamekova, tell me: Did you have a strained relationship with Matteo Cesari prior to his death?*"

I slip past a line of metal shelving just as a vibrant memory rears its head: fidgeting in an uncomfortable chair, sweeping my eyes over one-way glass, landing right back on Sheriff Travis Stallard's too-blue eyes. The version of myself on-screen, the one who's still freshly seventeen, shakes her head from side to side.

"No. Matt and I are best friends. He's had...issues with the friend group in the past. But we didn't hate him. Sure, he made all those heinous Instagram posts, but we eventually forgave him." On-screen, past me's throat bobs. *"Because that's what friends do."*

"Are you familiar with perjury, Steff?" Matt calls. "Because creating a plan to kill me makes what you originally told Sheriff Stallard look very disingenuous. And I would hate to see you caught in a LIE!"

I duck past the sixth burlap-sacked body. The flapping soles of my broken sneakers snag beneath me and I slip, crashing into metal. Iron fills my mouth. My shoulder smarts, but I manage to lurch upright just as Matt's laugh sounds behind me. "Are you trying to outrun me? You're sprinting toward a dead end, Steff. There's nothing beyond this room."

I slide behind a stack of cylinders and press my back against the wall, searching the props for a makeshift weapon, feeling impossibly cornered. At best, Matt is seconds away from killing me for what I planned to do to him and accidentally did to his brother instead. And honestly? Maybe I deserve it.

I can hear his shuffling footsteps. The dragging ax. I squeeze my eyes shut, suddenly hyperaware of my breath, my heartbeat, my blood as a rush of images flood my mind: the clothes that Illaria Cesari cleared out and donated. The paperwork, the cops, the burial. Guinevere's warm lips against mine, an old Radiohead song playing softly from my Jeep's speakers and mixing with her quiet sobs. The fucking GoFundMe. Congresswoman Adler's tearful speeches. Principal Buchanan urging us to honor Matt's memory when this whole time he's been hiding out in Italy, painting his nails, and catching up on over forty seasons of *Survivor*. Ignoring my messages. Listening to his brother's favorite Mongolian folk metal band. Forgetting to tone his yellow-blond head after he nuked it with bleach and 30 Volume Creme Developer, because he's a straight white man who had no idea how toner worked until I explained it to him tonight.

A silver-ringed hand parts the cylinders until I'm face-to-face with the signet ring Santo never took off when he was still alive: DON'T GIVE UP THE SHIP. "Found you."

"Matt. Wait," I gasp. He tilts his head, and I don't know where to go from here. I don't know what to do. This is the same person who wiped sticky arcade countertops and sprayed cleaner into bowling shoes with me for hours on end during our joint shifts at Perfect Strike. The one who made sure my hair was camera ready or checked whether I had something in my teeth at the beginning of every day before I ever hit RECORD in the newsroom for *Warrior Minutes*. The one I asked to proofread my blog posts. The one who helped me negotiate my first TERPECA-room-sponsored deal. The one who listened to my dad's old rock songs without complaint, who let me borrow his leather trench coat on the night Michal Zamek packed up and left me and my mom with a mountain of debt. Maybe that was why I started taking bribes in exchange for glowing reviews. With most of my blog money locked in the trust, selling out was probably the only method I had to escape our terrible financial situation. To help out Mom. To afford eggs.

"Before you kill me, I need to know... why did you make that post about me? All I ever did was try to help you adjust to living here. I thought of you as my best friend. So why did you want to expose my blog on *Cedar Creek Confessions*? You thought Mal was bad for Santo. Tobias fucked you over on the chess team. Guinevere didn't give you enough physical affection, and Charity never enjoyed your presence. But what did I do? Why did you sell me out?"

"You mean, other than for the usual moral reasons?" Matt's eyes flicker toward Guinevere's unconscious body, and I suddenly understand. He knew. This whole time, he knew that I liked her. That she didn't like him. That he had to make me pay for it.

"Oh," I whisper, realizing tonight's revenge game was personal on a lot of levels. Thinking about how Guinevere didn't die before her secret video played. How Matt couldn't kill her even now. "I'm sorry," I tell him, my voice hoarse. "I never meant to—"

"Yeah." His hot breath ghosts my forehead, and every hair on the back of my neck stands on end. "Well, you di—"

I flick out the blade of my Swiss Army knife and lunge forward, slashing at Matt as I break for the door. Startled, he swipes at me with the ax and succeeds in knocking the knife from my hand. It clatters to the floor, and I pause for a millisecond.

Leave it. Go.

I'm halfway to the shattered one-way-glass window when my arm wrenches backward and I cry out, slamming headfirst against the metal shelving. Stars explode at the edges of my vision as Matt grunts in my ear, but I elbow him and roll away. My head is killing me—I might be dealing with another TBI, I realize as I duck underneath the burlapped bodies, prepped for this cat-and-mouse game by my earlier confrontation with Guinevere, unable to believe I ever thought of her as my enemy—but I'm finally ready to leave all of this behind. I'm almost at the door when something warm and wet slides across my neck—*Zwinggg!*—and for the second time in the course of a year, my knees buckle out from under me.

My vision goes white, and then there's nothing but weightlessness and no breath. Absolutely no breath at all.

MATTEO

365 Days After the Accident

Growing up with an identical twin wasn't easy. Momma swears she accidentally switched us around at least once, so who knows if either of us actually ended as the twin we began. She used to paint our infant nails different colors so she'd remember who was who.

But becoming Santo Cesari was easy. Like slipping on a second skin.

Immediately after the fire, my face—my brother's face—was almost unrecognizable. So while stumbling out of BREAKOUT last May, choking on smoke and secrets and the crushing weight of Santo's death, I knew I had a choice to make. And I chose to let the good people of Cedar Creek, Tennessee, believe what they wanted.

I chose to let everyone think Matteo Luca Cesari—the reject, the weirdo, the charismatic yet antisocial loser—asphyxiated.

But he didn't.

He lived.

I lived, and I took on the life of my twin brother despite the fact that *Wanderland* killed him. My friends killed him. They wanted to kill me for revealing their secrets, and they killed my brother instead, and now we're playing one last escape room exactly a year later, and I am finally enacting my revenge.

So far, everything is going according to plan.

Below me, Steff stirs. It's clear that she's blinking between consciousness and a distant dreamworld. She's fighting me—fighting this—but she won't be for long.

Still, though, I want her to remember this. I want her last memory to be what it feels like to be betrayed.

"When you first contacted me after the fire," I tell her, dragging her out of the meat locker and into the gas-filled bathroom, my fingers twisted in her damp dyed hair, "you said you were checking in." The LED lights flood us. "All those texts. All those voicemails. All those letters. You wanted to know if I had nightmares, like you did."

Steff whimpers. I don't know if she can hear me.

"But after Santo died, my life became one long waking nightmare. Because my best friend—my *best friend*—was gone." I wipe my mouth with the back of my hand. "Every day, I woke up and put on Santo's clothes. Every night, I went to bed and listened to Momma sobbing for hours. I knew I needed to leave, so I went to Italy, but that didn't fix anything, so I started leaving myself voicemails. Texts from my own phone, just to try and make the loss feel less real, until I stopped being able to tell where Santo ended and I began." I pull out Charity's watch from my pocket and check the time: 11:55 PM. "Then my burns healed. I started seeing his face again, and I realized I couldn't do it anymore. But then I thought, why not go out with a bang?" A smile curves my lips. "And you know what? Right now, I'm feeling perfectly fine. Better than I've felt in a long time, actually." I swallow. "I've waited too long for this, you know?"

I readjust the sweat-slicked ax handle. No more games—it's time to finish what I started and avenge my brother. Because when I invited Charity Noelle Adler, Tobias Quinton Matthews, Guinevere Jade Mitchell-Moore, and Stephanie Marie Zamekova here tonight under the supervision of Malachi Ashton James-May, I meant every word: There's always a price to pay for your past mistakes.

And tonight? All six of us must die.

CHAPTER TWENTY

Wednesday, May 20, 2026, 11:56 PM

Stars. So many white stars exploding behind my eyelids. And then, with startling clarity: I remember.

I remember everything.

Our secretive texts in a separate group chat. The delineated roles: Guinevere to get the full group on board with my plan, Tobias to develop our in-room blocking like positions on a chess board, Santo to bring Matt to BREAKOUT, Charity to lure him inside the Queen of Hearts's Rose Garden, and me to goad him into confessing he ran Cedar Creek Confessions *while Malachi recorded everything. Arranging logistics with our Game Master in the media center over a notebook sketch of* Wanderland's *layout while the US National Debt Clock ran on our computer as a smoke screen for Mr. Foxfield. Using my* Warrior Minutes *expertise to decide the best shots to crumble Matt's reputation and expose him for his wrongdoing to everyone. The satisfaction of walking up to Cedar Creek's BREAKOUT and seeing my friends huddled outside, knowing we all shared the same goal: to bring Matt down together. To scare him, yes. To make him pay, yes.*

And to leave him alive.

I gasp. I didn't organize *Wanderland* to kill my best friend—I did it solely to expose him as the person behind *Cedar Creek Confessions* in front of BREAKOUT's cameras. I didn't mean to hurt him. During all our planning, injuring Matt in any way wasn't even a consideration.

I'm not the mastermind behind Matt Cesari's death. For Santo Cesari's death. For my own.

My lungs spike with rotten-egg air as my chin slams against hard tile. I'm here. I've made a decision. I'm done being pathetic. I can't blame myself, can't wallow in this grief, can't stagnate any longer. I thought I wanted to play tonight's game to know if I'm a monster, but over the course of the past hour, I've realized the morality of my past choices isn't so black-and-white. I'm not fully responsible, but I'm not blameless; I didn't mean for Santo's death to happen, but I can still take accountability for it. I had a part to play in last year's accident, and I'll live with that forever. But holding on to shame and guilt and rage? I know where that road leads, and it's in the grip of the misguided arbiter holding me down.

"We're the same, Steff," Matt says, readjusting the ax hilt.

Pennies flood my mouth. "You know what it feels like to be abandoned. You understand."

You're wrong, I want to tell him. *We're not the same. I thought I only knew how to drown in the past: grasp at ghosts. Leave claw marks in everything I love. And maybe my raging grief has only compounded: losing Dad. Losing my money to the trust he absconded with. Losing my fans and my best friend and the people who got me through so much of high school. But there's always a way out. I'm not dead yet. And I'm determined to escape this room alive.*

I run my tongue over the blood trickling from my gums, the iron pooling in my mouth. Matt's burn-scarred hand quivers; the tip of the ax he pulled from the shattered LCD screen teases its weight against the skin of my throat. It's dull, but the molded rubber is still hard enough to choke off my air supply.

"I forgive you," I rasp, warm tears sliding down my cheeks, copper and spit trickling from the corners of my lips. "I forgive you, Matt."

He stares at me; a muscle jumps in his burn-scarred cheek. For a moment, I almost think he's going to lower the weapon. But then he pushes it flush against my trachea, and his expression hardens. "You understand," he insists, and I'm not sure whether he's reassuring himself or me, but the world turns feverish, and the stars return. I am going to die here.

Gray blurs the edges of my periphery. I gasp, but my throat is burning and Matt's face is melting into fuzzy security footage static. I try to gag, to scream, to cry, but the stars only melt, fuse, become BREAKOUT's strobing neons. I choke, and the stars turn into bowling balls rolling toward center lane, ready to knock down the glowing green EXIT sign of the Cedar Creek BREAKOUT.

My vision whites out just as Matt's grip goes slack. He slumps on top of me, immobile; the ax clatters out of his hands.

I blink, dazed. The stars dissipate. Above me, the haloed face of a girl.

"Hey," Guinevere pants. She drops the blood-splattered cinder block and grimaces. Her hairline is soaked with sweat; her caramel-brown hair is storm-whipped and wild. But in this moment, she looks more beautiful than she ever did stalking the hallways of Cedar Creek High. "Turns out that adrenaline lets you lift basically anything."

She pulls me to my feet. I inhale as her bloodstained fingers gravitate toward my neck. "I'm okay," I tell her, even though I'm probably not. Except Guinevere nods, and the fact she's choosing to dance around it with me—around this shared, horrible, unspoken truth—nearly breaks me down. But I can allow myself to do that later. Right now, I only need to break us out.

I glance at Matt's crumpled body, and Guinevere follows my gaze. "Is he…"

"No," she rushes. "I mean…I don't think so. You can check his pulse, but he's breathing."

I silently trace my eyes over the angular lines of Matt Cesari: his hands, his chest, his burn-scarred throat. Guinevere's right—he's moving. Barely, but he's alive. We didn't kill him.

My ears buzz. My skull feels like it's splitting open, and my entire head throbs in one single, painful, recurring pulse. I finally know everything—the pact, my secret, my sin.

But I still don't know what will happen when the game's countdown hits zero.

Think. Matt put you here. Matt changed the clues. Matt wanted revenge. You know that, so use it. Find a way out.

Guinevere's mouth tugs into a frown as I pull out the cryptex. "It's over, Steffi. We gave it a good shot, but we're not getting out of here." She winces as she slides against the tiled wall, sinking to the blood-splattered bathroom floor, and I see it now, how every small movement saps her energy. All the research I did in the past year cascades through my already-flooded brain, rushing by in a blur of WebMD info boxes about asphyxiation and Wikipedia articles on carbon monoxide poisoning and Crash Course videos about hemoglobin. She's been stabbed. There's a gas leak. We're running out of time.

"It's okay," Guinevere says, her voice wavering, and I can't believe her, because it isn't. "I know you're going to keep trying to escape, because you never..." She closes her eyes, and my stomach knots. "You don't give up, Steffi. Even when the rest of us swore to never speak to you again, you kept fighting for the friend group. You kept fighting..." She leans her head back against the wall, her hair fanning out behind her, the singular remaining star-shaped mini claw clip glinting in the harsh glare of the overhead industrial light bulb. "For me."

I swallow. The industrial meat locker's LCD screen is at 1:43. How long has it been since Matt almost killed me? Seconds?

Minutes? I want to know, but I don't have time to calculate it—not with my mental math skills—so I just keep spinning the rings of the cryptex instead. I don't let myself think about what will happen if I don't find the seven-letter word to open it, because Guinevere is right: I'm not going to give up now.

I finish setting my newest word and pull on the endcap. For a moment, I almost delude myself into thinking it gives, but then: nothing.

"It's not *FRIENDS*," I tell Guinevere, my voice trembling. Talking makes me nervous, but not talking makes me want to tear off my skin. Whether she's given up or not, right now, she's filling in as my rubber duck. The person I can talk to in order to help my own thought process. The one who'll enable me to problem-solve more efficiently. "*ARSONIST* is too long. So is *BREAKOUT* and *PYROMANIAC*." One minute and thirty-seven seconds. *YOU NEED THIS TO ESCAPE.*

Calm down. You have time.

I'm lying. If I don't crack this, Matt wins. All of us die. He'll get his revenge for what we did to his brother a year ago, the *Tennessee Star* will get its next big story, and Sheriff Stallard will put the remaining pieces together for the biggest solve of his career. But giving up means my friends died for nothing. It means Matt gets away with everything. It means no one ever knows the truth—the truth I fought so hard to scrape together about the night Santo Cesari died. It means the cost is Charity. Malachi. Tobias. Guinevere. Me.

And I won't let that happen. I can't.

Across from me, Guinevere inhales raggedly. One minute, twenty-six seconds.

My eyes flick to the open fridge door, where the keypad of *Arsonist's Revenge* is once again visible. "Come on, we need to be ready to leave," I tell Guinevere, darting out of the room with the cryptex held loosely in my sweating hand.

I come face-to-face with the emergency escape button, the one hanging by a single wire. A fresh memory explodes in my mind: In *Wanderland*, as smoke swirled around us and everyone was coughing, I'd slammed my hand down on the mechanism to let us out.

And that mechanism had read ESCAPE HATCH. Not RELEASE.

I fumble with the cryptex. *YOU NEED THIS TO ESCAPE.* My hands shake as I line up the letter wheels from left to right—R-E-L-E-A-S-E—and tip the capsule to the side, blood-smeared and sweat-slicked and fucking ready for this to all be over with. The inner tube holds a small rectangular box, BREAKOUT-themed, with the hot-pink smiley face on it and everything.

From the bathroom set, Guinevere's eyelids flutter. "Seems like—" She breaks off, coughing, and when she looks back up at me, the sclera of her left eye is bloodshot. "Seems like you're not b-bad at this." Her lips quirk. "Maybe you should start a blog."

"It's a matchbook," I whisper, hoping I'm wrong even as I slide out the box. Inside lies a neat row of minimatches, their six heads perfectly arranged; one for each of us.

The LCD monitor is at 1:22 as I race toward the kitchenette and quickly consolidate all the eerie photographs. My fingers tremble as I arrange the printouts from left to right in the order that we found them: the first one from *Moonshine Cabin*. *Serial Killer's Hideout*, marred by blood. Our *Egyptian Tomb* game, with its eerie photoshopped faces. The dark, scrawled additions to *Deranged Clown Circus*. The greasy photo from *Raiders of the Lost Temple* with our stabbed-out eyes, still smelling of peanuts. *Hijacked*, frozen to my numbing fingers.

I think about our past escape rooms helping us in this one, Matt giving us a way out as long as we were clever enough to see it, to take it, to want it enough. Since the cryptex held a matchbook, I'll bet anything the photographs don't just have riddles on them—it has to be heat-resistant ink.

But if I'm right about the gas leak, and I strike the match...

No. There has to be another way.

Smoke. Fire. Horrible choking. Charity laughing in the middle of the cafeteria. The time we all got mono from hitting Malachi's vape during our Walmart-parking-lot Friendsgiving.

Breathe in for four seconds.

Matt slipping vodka into our punch cups at homecoming. Santo showing me how to throw a perfect spiral at midnight on the million-dollar Cedar Creek Astroturf football field. Late nights at the water tower and trips to the Gatlinburg SkyPark and blurry photos from whenever Guinevere brought a disposable camera to a function and we used up all the film with pictures of the two of us.

And as I hold my breath, I think about all the unknown memories still haunting me. The perpetual grief that engulfs this tourist-rich county like billowing smoke. The dark skeleton of the Cedar Creek BREAKOUT as the orange flames engulfing it writhed against the glowing moon. The firefighters trying in vain to salvage what we left standing. Matches and gasoline and the invisible thread of our secrets stitching us all together. The shared promise of the people who used to be my best fucking friends: *TELL NO ONE.*

And then I bend close to the photographs, and I exhale for eight.

CHAPTER TWENTY-ONE

Wednesday, May 20, 2026, 11:58 PM

With the heat from my breath, letters skip across the photograph paper. I pull away, my cheeks flushed with exertion, and just barely manage to catch the message spelled out across all six photographs before the letters disappear:

YOU LOSE.

No. No, no, no. There has to be some other way. This isn't the end—there's no world in which *Arsonist's Revenge* concludes with a gas leak from a broken generator, six hot-pink matches, and a line of photographs telling me there's no way to win. Accepting defeat now, after everything we've been through, is complete bullshit. We're so close. *I'm* so close.

One minute.

"MATT!" I scream, barreling through the fridge door, giving up the pretense of being a normal eighteen-year-old girl. "THE KEYPAD CODE! I NEED YOU TO TELL ME THE CODE, YOU GODDAMN ASSHOLE, DO YOU UNDERSTAND?"

Blood pounds in my temples, but I can't stop, so I grab his limp wrist and pray for the telltale *tha-thump*. For a second, I don't feel a pulse, and dread pools in my throat. But then Matt's eyelids flicker, and relief surges through me. Thank God. He's still alive.

"Manual...override," he says, the words hard and hacking. "In my...sh-shoes."

Guinevere's eyes snap open. She lunges forward, ripping Santo's shoes off Matt's bloodied body, revealing the seventh photograph blinking up at us from his left sole—*Wanderland*—and when she flips the glossy Kodak paper over, we both stare at a four-digit code scrawled in what I now know can only be Matteo Cesari's handwriting: S-N-T-O. Letters, not numbers.

But keypads don't just have numbers; they have letters, too.

S-N-T-O. 7-6-8-6.

I stumble to the door, the photograph clutched in my sweating hand, and mash the buttons into the greasy plastic. Dimly, I register Guinevere following. The keypad lights up green; the door clicks and swings outward. There. It's open. We're breaking out.

I half laugh, half sob, and step over the threshold. For Santo. For Charity. For Malachi and Tobias and Guinevere and me.

Behind us, Matt coughs. Guinevere freezes.

Don't look back. Don't you dare look back, Stephanie.

Desperation shoots up my throat, bright and hot like an

emergency flare as I turn, and for a moment, I can't breathe. I'm immobilized by fear, surrounded by flames in a room just like this one a year ago, unable to pick between saving a Cesari twin and saving myself.

Don't be pathetic. Don't get stuck. Make a decision. Choose.

"Steff," Matt gurgles, as if he can feel me staring at him, his fingers splayed out on oil-spill tile. A single tear rolls from his left eye; I watch it slowly trickle down his burn-scarred temple.

I ball my trembling fists. *You want to redeem yourself? Then redeem yourself.*

This time, I cannot afford to hesitate. This time, I am going to make the right choice.

"Shit," I hiss, stepping back across the threshold of *Arsonist's Revenge* as rotten-egg gas coats my teeth, slides down my throat, curls itself around my windpipe and squeezes. Matt is right where I left him. He's covered in blood and sweat and grime. He looks young.

A cough breaks out of me, hacking and corrosive, and I shudder. It feels like I'm throwing up pieces of my organs: liver, kidneys, lungs.

"You're going to have to work with us here," Guinevere tells him, materializing next to me. Thank Jesus.

I glance up at the countdown—thirty-one seconds. Thirty. Twenty-nine.

As Guinevere and I work together to lift Matt up, though, I realize that I don't know if I can leave BREAKOUT behind. It would be easier to give up. To succumb to the destruction around me. To burn with my friends.

Except I'm not alone. Even if I'm moving forward without them, those who died here will always be with me. I'll carry them in fragments: mementos, keepsakes, memories. Forever.

I drape one of Matt's arms around my shoulders; Guinevere does the same with the other, and together, the three of us stumble out of *Arsonist's Revenge*.

Alarms blare in the hallway as we stagger past the master scoreboard. Past the rooms housing *Alien Abduction* and *Haunted Mansion*. Past every birthday party, past every laughing moment, past every memory we shared before my friend group broke apart. Gas burning my throat. Imagined flames licking at the edges of my vision. Dragging the boy who tried to kill us down the hallway, because I'm not leaving him behind again.

We're almost to the lobby door when Guinevere stumbles, slamming a manicured hand against the wall for support. "Steffi, wait," she gasps. "We need to go back—Malachi's still alive."

My eyes widen with horror, shock, panic. "Gee, there's no time—"

Guinevere presses her full lips to mine. This time, she isn't crying. This time, I kiss her back.

When we pull apart, she is all wind-whipped rage and blazing fire. Hurricane. "I'll meet you outside," she says, and then she turns toward the control room, her track-star legs pumping as Matt's leather trench coat trails behind her.

My mental clock updates. Twenty seconds, probably. Less.

Matt and I burst into the lobby. The smell of gas is stronger here, pouring in from the overhead HVAC, and I fight back a sob at the stupid kitschy sign near the photo-op wall: WE (ALMOST)

BROKE OUT! No time. Nothing left to do but slam into the *Briefing Room*, drop Matt onto the plush loveseat, and fumble with the stupid locker until my shaking fingers curl around my phone. My brain throbs with phantom injury, with the rattling of the overhead HVAC, with every flicker of haywire LED light.

"Got it," I rasp, channeling all my adrenaline into shouldering Matt alone and stumbling out of the *Briefing Room*, the neon signs flanking the midnight-black walls flashing violently in the haze, my heart pulsing with every past version of myself.

The alarms blare louder, and I can feel the carbon monoxide now: in the oppressive smoke of my lungs, in the radiating heat of my skin, in the itching burn of my tongue. This BREAKOUT will burn exactly as the one a year ago, but right now it's me, staggering alongside the remembered versions of all the girls I've ever been—*Stephanie, Steff, Z, Steffi, Zamekova, Peanut*—in tandem toward the door.

• • •

yelp.com | Recommended Reviews: BREAKOUT Escape Rooms Inc.

Located in Cedar Creek, TN | Have you been here?

Write a review!

BREAKOUT knocks it out of the park once again!
★★★★★
Posted by Stephanie Zamekova at 3:30 PM

Out of all the high-quality escape room franchises we're lucky enough to have so close to home, BREAKOUT Escape Rooms Inc. is by far my favorite! Thank you, BREAKOUT, for inviting me to come tour this newest room with my friends. My full review is now posted: *There's No Escape* | BREAKOUT Escape Rooms's *Moonshine Cabin* Review

Response from BREAKOUT Escape Rooms Inc. at 11:00 AM

Thanks for coming, Z. We're so grateful for your continued support! **—The James-Mays**

CHAPTER TWENTY-TWO

Thursday, May 21, 2026, 12:00 AM

I burst through the frosted glass, Matt's dead weight on my stiff shoulders, just as the building explodes.

The blast throws us forward. I slam against concrete with the fury of a dozen *Cedar Creek Confessions* posts, two hundred escape rooms, and at least one wrongful death lawsuit while pieces of the building—steel, brick, wood—rain down around us. But I'm alive. I made it out. *Arsonist's Revenge* is burning, and the game is done. It's finished, and I'm still here.

I lie against the cool tar of the parking lot for a second. Two. Three. And for the first time since this nightmare began, time doesn't feel like it's against me.

I hiccup and clamber to my knees, the grit of the Sevier County Plaza parking lot embedded between the fraying, blood-crusted threads of my ripped jeans as I turn to look behind me. There's warm metal in my mouth, an ocean of blood roaring in my eardrums, and numb shock sizzling away in my veins. Somewhere in the near distance, my rusted Jeep sits in a sea of four cars that are missing their drivers.

But Suite 263 is burning.

As I watch, electricity sparks along exposed beams beyond the shattered frosted glass windows; dark blue smoke billows from the caved-in roof, and farther along the building's facade, plumes of brazen fire dance skyward.

A sob lodges in my throat. BREAKOUT is gone, destroyed from the inside out. The James-Mays won't be able to start over; this time, they'll have to let it go for good. The death toll is just too high: Santo. Charity. Tobias. Guinevere. Malachi.

Matt.

I glance at him then, his burn-scarred body flickering gold in the shimmering heat: Matteo Luca Cesari, my former best friend, who tried to kill me for the part I played in his twin brother's death after he stole his entire identity. He wanted to be martyred by his revenge plot, and it's a cruel irony that he's here, alive, when the rest of my friends aren't. When Charity and Tobias were killed playing the game, and Santo had died before tonight's countdown even started, and Gee sacrificed herself to try saving an unconscious Malachi. But this is how things are. And I need to believe that they'll get better this time, too.

Wetness splatters my cheeks, and at first, I think it's more of my unshed tears spilling over, but then I feel it on my arms, my shirt, my eyelashes. The gravity and weight. The pattern.

ᎠᏎᎴᏍ. Agasga. *Prší.*

The storm is here.

I tilt my face up to the Tennessee sky, to the air that felt so arid only sixty minutes earlier, and as the rain splashes against my skin and begins to wash away the gas and smoke and ash, it feels like a new beginning.

I did it. I now know the truth: Matt is Santo. Santo is Matt. I made a huge mistake in concocting a plan to expose him, but I didn't kill anyone. And while I almost let Matteo pay for it—the secrets, the lies, his own twisted version of what I tried to pull off a year ago—the vicious cycle ends here. This time, I saved a Cesari twin from BREAKOUT. And now my slate is clean.

Well. Almost.

I take out my phone and power it on with a trembling thumb. Rain splatters the glowing glass as the lock screen appears—a selfie of my friends and me, from a time when both twins were alive and my life was heart-wrenchingly easier—but instead of putting in my password, I hold down the side button and slide the familiar-looking sos circle to the right until it streaks red across the display. Then I clear my throat. Keep looking at the sky.

The call connects.

"Hello, 911?" I rasp, and this time I'm able to hold the hysterical laughter at bay, because I know what it's like to make lifelong friends who don't stick around. I know what it's like to spend your life thinking it may be better if you're not in it; I know what it's like to hold on to good memories so tightly that your fingers bleed. But my friends were right: I need to face it. No more secrets. No more lies. No more excuses. And no turning back, because there's no escape other than this one. The only one. The glowing EXIT sign I should've taken from the very beginning.

"I'd like to report..."

I pause. On the other end of the line, the operator asks if I'm still there. And I am, but I'm not, because there's a part of me that's burning inside BREAKOUT, too. The pathetic part. The indecisive part. Except maybe that's a good thing, because what's left is still me, and this time, I can make the right choice more than once.

I swallow the gasoline licking its way down my smoke-scorched larynx. The grief is still there, of course. It's never going away. But I'll make it through. One fucking hour at a time.

"A fire," I tell the operator, catching my breath for what feels like the first time all night. "I'd like to report a fire."

• • •

The Tennessee Star

MENU | NEWS | WEATHER | SPORTS | LOG IN | SEARCH
Four teens dead, two hospitalized following fire at local business one year after seventeen-year-old's tragic death

By Laurel Harkness | Sunday, May 24, 2026, 11:36 AM UTC−5

Fire crews in Friendship Springs, TN, responded to a fire in the Sevier County Plaza around midnight on Thursday morning.

CEDAR CREEK, TN (KSIB)—One year after flames first erupted at the BREAKOUT Escape Rooms Inc. of Cedar Creek, an incident long believed to have resulted in the death of Matteo Cesari, 17, another blaze buckled the local franchise. This time, four teenagers were killed in a fire at BREAKOUT's newly renovated location in Friendship Springs, TN.

"It's unbelievable," says Barbara Duncan, 48, of Sevier County. "We just went through this last year, and now it's happened again? With a higher death toll? Of course the community wants answers."

BREAKOUT Escape Rooms Inc. burned to the ground this Thursday, after a five-hour-long battle between the inferno and local firefighters. The East Tennessee company was originally created by Randall James and Taliyah May for the express purpose of delivering "a fun interactive escape experience in a competitive, edge-of-your-seat package." However, the pair's venture experienced its first hurdle after a teenage boy died from smoke inhalation in one of its escape rooms last year.

Although an investigation is still ongoing, the second BREAKOUT Escape Rooms Inc. fire seems to have originated from a spark that combined with a generator gas leak to produce an explosive blast, claims Friendship Springs Fire Department Chief Howard Egan. "We're trying to determine what exactly happened, but our working theory is that internal wiring issues exacerbated existing problems with the property's gas lines," Egan revealed in a press release earlier this morning. "Whether the gas leak was deliberate or accidental, however, we can't yet say."

This explanation closely mirrors the cited reason behind the Cedar Creek BREAKOUT fire, which was also believed to have been caused by wiring issues.

Out of the six teenagers who were inside the building when the fire occurred, only two survived. The remaining victims—all of whom were present at the first BREAKOUT fire last spring—included Guinevere Jade Mitchell-Moore, the daughter of federal circuit judge Edward H. Mitchell-Moore; Tobias Quinton Matthews, a state chess champion and the son of Neil and Blaire Matthews of Matthews Farms; Charity Noelle Adler, the daughter of Congresswoman Catelyn Adler; and Malachi Ashton

James-May, the only child of owners Randall James and Taliyah May.

While Matteo Luca Cesari is currently being treated at Cedar Creek General Hospital for third-degree burns, there is a <u>warrant out for his arrest</u>, leading others to question his involvement in the tragedy. Initially, the 18-year-old was believed to have died in the Cedar Creek BREAKOUT fire; sources have retroactively confirmed it was Matteo's twin brother, Santo Xavier Cesari, who died last May instead.

"The Cesari twin identification oversight is completely atypical for our department," said Sheriff Travis Stallard, 52, the official in charge of the investigation into both BREAKOUT fires. (The first BREAKOUT fire investigation, closed in late September of last year, has now been reopened.) "We were wrong when we claimed to have identified Matteo Cesari's remains; however, we're left with questions regarding why Matteo assumed the identity of his identical twin brother for the year following Santo's death, as well as concerns as to why no one from the Cesari family came forward to correct our initial error."

Amid this <u>scandal for the Sevier County Sheriff's Department, which is already making national headlines</u>, others are questioning the motivations behind the teenagers themselves. Cedar Creek locals are once again raising eyebrows at the involvement of the same young adults, who were dubbed the "Suspect Six" after the accident last year.

"It just seems suspicious," wrote resident Holly Eagleman in a Facebook post made following news of the accident. Eagleman, 53, like many Cedar Creek parents, is a member of the new Moms Invesigating [sic] Breakout Fire Facebook group. "You mean to tell me the same teens who were at the fire a year ago were also there when it happened again? 🙄 How much stupider can you get? Someone arrest these amateur arsonists ASAP!"

Many residents of Cedar Creek share Eagleman's sentiment.

"We're not at liberty to comment on a current investigation beyond what we've already disclosed to the public, although we are doing everything we can to deliver justice for this horrific tragedy," Sheriff Stallard stated in a phone interview. "However, we kindly ask the public to refrain from speculation while we continue our investigation into both BREAKOUT fires."

The second BREAKOUT fire survivor, Stephanie Zamekova, is "doing [her] best to let go of the past" after graduating from Cedar Creek High School on Saturday, she shared in an exclusive statement to the *Star*. When asked about her reaction to the accident, she had this to say: "Matt [Cesari] orchestrated the gamified deaths of my closest friends. I believe in our legal system, I believe in justice, and I believe he'll be held accountable for his condemnable actions."

The owners of BREAKOUT Escape Rooms Inc. declined to comment on the situation. Matteo Cesari is facing charges of especially aggravated kidnapping, felony murder, aggravated arson, vandalism, and aggravated reckless endangerment.

225 Days After the Second Accident

I'm going to prison.

"Your destination is on your right," the chirpy Australian man trapped in my phone informs me as I round the corner, the maneuver jostling the line of ducks on the dashboard of my Jeep. Ahead, the arch of the Northeast Correctional Complex looms like a waiting mouth.

My fingers tighten on the steering wheel as I roll past an impressive collection of highly unwelcoming signs. Luckily, I'm twenty minutes early and not planning on violating any major policies, so all that's left for me to do after I present my driver's license (along with the name of the person I'm visiting) is to park my Jeep and consent to a voluntary search of my vehicle.

I hope this is worth it.

None of the security officers from the NECX find anything amiss in my car, although Dr. Quack does get side-eyed, so then I'm frisked and escorted inside. I'm dressed according to the prison dress code, so it doesn't take me long to get to the next layer of official security: a blocky metal detector labeled with a CAUTION: X-RAY RADIATION warning. Another officer gestures for me to step through but stops when he notices I'm still carrying my tote bag.

"Can't go through here with that, ma'am," he says, pointing behind me. "You can rent a locker over there. Get rid of everything except your ID, then come back and see me again."

I nod and turn around. As I walk to the lockers, though, my mind wanders. It was a two-hour drive from Cedar Creek to get here, and I can't stop thinking about whether I'm going to be Matt's first visitor. I don't know if his mom or Italian nonna have come to see him since he landed in prison. If I were them, I don't think I would. His family already had to go through the ordeal of losing one son—I can't imagine how they must feel now. But today, I'm not here for them.

I open the locker and sling off my tote. I should have left it inside my Jeep, but since this is my first time visiting, I didn't manage to research every NECX policy. I'm slowly learning to forgive myself for my mistakes, though. For trying to hold on to people who brought out the worst in me. For letting every error I made in the past decide my future. For running from the truth for as long as I did.

I close the locker and turn back to the security officer. Once

I'm scanned and through, I'm led to a side room and frisked again. And then, at last, I'm taken to an empty room that reminds me of PanIQ's *Jailbreak*.

The visitation room.

"He should be here soon," my escorting officer says, and I give him a curt nod as I slide into a metal chair. Hopefully, Matt doesn't bail on me now. I had to write to him in order to get on his approved list of visitors, and I thought that would be a long shot. I mean, he'd already spent a year ignoring me when I thought he was Santo, so the chances of him responding as Matt seemed slim to none.

I'm still not sure why he approved me, exactly, but maybe he wants closure of his own.

Or, I think, as I survey the bleak white walls around me, the suffocating space devoid of all emotion, maybe he just got lonely.

The door opens.

"Hi, Matt," I say softly as he walks inside, escorted by another officer. He's directed to sit in the chair across from me—one of the only furnishings in this claustrophobic room—and he slumps into it. "I came to pay you a visit."

He doesn't look at me. Instead, he directs his attention to the long silver scratch in the metal table separating us. He isn't here because he confessed—he's here because of my witness testimony, and because Tobias was right: the James-Mays *do* use a cloud-based computing software to store their CCTV footage from each BREAKOUT location. Malachi's parents didn't turn the *Wanderland* videos over to the sheriff's department because it implicated their own son in the accident. But after the last fire, they surrendered the footage showing Matt-as-Santo coming in and out of *Arsonist's Revenge* with buckets of blood, with an armful of photographs, with a cinder block in a rolling cart. "*Make sure you delete this*," Matt tells Malachi at one point in the video, looking straight up at the living room set's camera. But Mal didn't. I wonder if our Game Master stopped trusting him, too, near the end.

Even without the direct eye contact, though, I can tell prison hasn't been kind to Matteo Luca Cesari. His hair is unruly and wild against the orange collar of his jumpsuit, and there are dark shadows under his eyes curving like half-moons.

He looks like he's falling apart. But he's here, and that's what matters.

"I wanted to talk to you," I continue, refusing to be deterred. "I thought it might be time, you know, since I'm heading to the Savannah College of Art and Design tomorrow."

After I escaped from BREAKOUT, I finally submitted my application to SCAD and got accepted for their winter quarter within the game development program. It's expensive, but it's my best bet for becoming more than just a washed-up blogger someday. And honestly? I can't wait to move. To start a new life somewhere far away from Cedar Creek and Friendship Springs. To pour my energy into creating fun, lighthearted games that bring people together instead of tear them apart.

First, though, I want to make sure I leave *everything* behind. Which means that I need Matt to answer me.

I don't fidget; I don't drum my chewed nails against the metal until I wear them down to the beds. Instead, I stare right at him. At my tormentor. At my ally. At my former best friend.

"It's weird, now that I'm finally getting ready to move away." I'm speaking quietly, but there's a razor edge to my voice, something dark and sharp lying underneath. "It's weirder that some of us will never get to."

Matt's throat bobs. It's almost laughable, how childish he's being about this, like I don't exist if he doesn't acknowledge me. But I don't need his attention. I beat the escape room. I made it out. And this time, I didn't come to fucking play.

My eyes glint as I lean forward. "You killed our friends," I whisper. "And you can tell yourself you did it to get justice, but I know that you did it because you hate yourself. Because you blame yourself for switching places with him."

Matt doesn't move. He just keeps staring at the lightning scratch in the table. I wonder if he's regretting approving me; I wonder if he's silently willing this space to open up and swallow me whole.

Either way, it doesn't matter anymore. I stand up, nod at the security officers standing back against the concrete walls, and hear the buzzer echo behind me as I'm ushered across a threshold that Matt can't cross. I got what I came for; I know exactly where he is. I know that he's locked in a room he can't break out of, and I know he won't be able to hurt anyone like he hurt me. Not ever again.

At the same time, I'm not stupid—I know this chapter of my life isn't over. I know that grief isn't something you can escape, even though I've been trying to outrun it for my entire life. It sits just underneath your lungs, where you can't get rid of it no matter how many times you breathe in a way that's supposed to relax you, or how much money you squirrel away in your bank account, or how many escape rooms you voluntarily lock yourself within to practice exerting control. All of this is going to stay with me; it doesn't end when this prison door closes.

But I'm not the monster. I know that now. And I don't intend to let myself forget it.

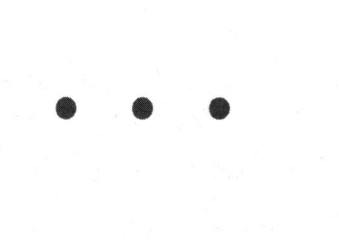

Acknowledgments

While writers are known for being hyperbolic, it is without a trace of exaggeration when I say that writing this book is the most challenging thing I've ever done. I weathered a lot while writing it—a campus shooting, my parents' divorce, the difficulties of a newly diagnosed autoimmune disorder—and as a result, there were times when I doubted that I'd ever complete a draft. So to everyone I'm about to thank: When I say this book would not exist without you, I mean it.

To the village who helped me turn this book from a jumbled six-POV tangle of unresolved plot threads into a focused yet twisty narrative: Jessica Errera, my stellar literary agent and forever champion; Alexandra Hightower, my fantastic editor and constant cheerleader; Crystal Castro, my wonderful assistant editor; Brandy Colbert, my genius copy editor; Dan Letchworth, my brilliant proofreader; Lindsay Walter-Greaney and

Rachael Herbert, my eagle-eyed production editors—thank you for your energy and insight. Special thanks to Gabrielle Chang and Sammy Yeun for creating a beautifully neon (pink!) cover, and also to the rest of the Little, Brown Books for Young Readers team: Janelle DeLuise, Andie Divelbiss, Amanda Gaglione, Stef Hoffman, Savannah Kennelly, Hannah Klein, Christie Michel, Martina Rethman, and Victoria Stapleton. Without you all, this idea would probably still be languishing in my Notes app.

Thank you also to Allison Hufford, Jack McIntyre, Madeleine McGrath, Julianne Tinari, Sonnie Dean, and the rest of the lovely people at Jane Rotrosen Agency. I am still indebted to you all. And to Becca Rodriguez at Subtext Literary for partnering with me (again!) to try bringing this book to the screen.

To Lois Duncan, for writing the novel that galvanized mine. To Leigh Whannell and James Wan, for creating a movie franchise that gave me the courage to write a locked-room thriller. To Takao Kato and SCRAP Entertainment Inc., for bringing the escape game concept to Kyoto in July 2007 and subsequently changing my life. To every escape room I've ever done, with a special shout-out to the Breakout Games location in Asheville, North Carolina. (Y'all rock and are nothing like the company in this book.) And to every early reader, for providing blurbs and hype of which I could only dream. Thank you for your time and appreciation. You all make this my dream job.

To the Big Five group chat—Ann Zhao, Sydney Langford, Layla Noor, and Famke Thy-Halma Webb—for offering me advice, compassion, and unconditional support at a time in my life when I needed it most. If we were ever trapped in a deadly escape room together, I have to believe we would all make it out alive. To CL Montblanc and Ann Zhao (again!), for being kind enough to read an early draft of this book and not telling me to give up on writing forever. And to all my ex-friends, for inspiring different pieces of this story at different points in my life. I hope you've been able to move on. It gets better once you do.

To my small but mighty tribe at the University of North Carolina at Chapel Hill, for believing in me even when I didn't believe in myself: Maddox Addy, Ash Chen, Sarah Grace Elliot, Madison Gagnon, Lizzie McLeod Herring, Luna Hou, Rio Janisch, Luisa Peñaflor, Susanna Skaggs, Maia Sheets, Hamsini Shivkumar, Zoe Wynns, and Audrey Zhou. Your support is so appreciated. And special thanks to Jaylen Roope, for patiently answering my never-ending questions about chess; to Riley and Peyton Wojcik, for kindly providing me with much-needed insight into what it's truly like to be an identical twin; to Blake Roller, for his East Tennessee expertise; and to Julianna Welch (who went to North Carolina State but deserves to be in this list regardless), for her time regarding her experience as an enrolled member of the Eastern Band of Cherokee Indians. And thank you also to Professor Ross White, Professor Adam Price, Professor Angela Velez, and Professor Daniel Wallace for nurturing my creative writing skills, always being willing to talk, and providing mentorship and camaraderie. The university is lucky to have you.

To my online writing groups, including WMC, and the people within them. If a mediocre white man can do it, why can't we?

To my family: Mom and Dad, thank you for your love and care. Natalia and Karolina, you two are still my favorite sisters. A děkuji zase také mé rodině v Čechách: Elišce, Valtrovi, Ivetě, Tomášovi, Ivetce, Nikolce, Heleně, Vladkovi, Radkovi, Dáši, Silvince, Tomovi, Danečkovi a Tomáškovi. Ja vás mám velmi ráda pořád.

To Amias: It wouldn't be a VW novel if you weren't thanked in the acknowledgments. From workshopping the plot with me in your camper until three AM to always making me feel seen creatively, I am so grateful for your continued love, friendship, and support.

To Elijah, always, for everything (but especially for taking me to my first escape room). Despite everything, it's still you.

And lastly, thank you for picking up this book. Whether this is your first time holding a thriller I've written or you're a returning reader, my gratitude runs so deep. I'm so glad you chose to stick it out with me for another novel. I hope you enjoyed the ride.

Photo Credit: Pavel Wlosok

VICTORIA WLOSOK

is the author of the young adult thrillers *How to Find a Missing Girl* and *Six Must Die*. A recent graduate of the University of North Carolina at Chapel Hill, where she majored in English and Business Administration, she now spends her time researching methods of murder for future books, attempting to break out of escape rooms, and teaching language arts in the mountains of the Czech Republic. She invites you to follow her on Instagram, TikTok, and X @xvictoriawrites, or visit her website at victoriawlosok.com.

CELEBRATING 100 YEARS OF PUBLISHING

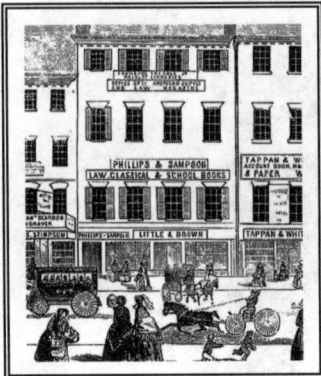

Dear Reader,

You may have noticed the words "Little, Brown and Company" on the title page of this book and wondered what they mean. Well, Charles C. Little and James Brown were the founders of this publishing house, and the "and Company" is all the editors, designers, marketers, publicists, salespeople, and more who help produce each book and bring it to readers like you. Little, Brown was founded in Boston, Massachusetts, in 1837, and some of its early publications included *The Writings of George Washington* and *The Works of Benjamin Franklin*. The catalog grew to feature works by Emily Dickinson and Louisa May Alcott, among many other notable authors. In 1926, recognizing that the literature we read when we are young has a deep and lasting influence and requires expert curation, the company appointed an editor to lead a dedicated children's department.

In 2026, Little, Brown Books for Young Readers celebrates one hundred years of excellence in publishing. Today, we are a division of Hachette Livre, the third-largest publisher in the world, and we are based in New York City. Our staff has grown from a team of two to more than one hundred people. And with the changes in technology, our books are read by more readers, in more ways, and in more countries than ever before. However, one thing has not changed: our commitment to providing a supportive home for all creators and superb stories for all readers. Thank you for being one of them.

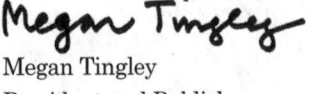

Megan Tingley
President and Publisher

LITTLE, BROWN AND COMPANY
BOOKS FOR YOUNG READERS

To learn more about Little, Brown's history,
authors, and books, please visit LBYR.com.